# THE
# WICCA
# HANDBOOK

# THE
# WICCA
# HANDBOOK

EILEEN HOLLAND

WEISER BOOKS
Boston, MA/York Beach, ME

First published in 2000 by
Red Wheel/Weiser, LLC
York Beach, ME
With offices at:
368 Congress Street
Boston, MA  02210
www.redwheelweiser.com

08  07  06  05  04  03
10  9  8  7

Library of Congress Cataloging-in-Publication Data

Holland, Eileen.
    The wicca handbook / Eileen Holland
        p.  cm.
    Includes bibliographical references and indexes.
    ISBN 1-57863-135-1 (pbk. : alk. paper)
        1. Witchcraft—Handbooks, manuals, etc.  2. Magic—Handbooks, manuals, etc.  I. Title.
    BF1566 .H645     2000
    133.4'3—dc21                     99-089151

Typeset in Garamond Book 11/13
Cover art copyright © 2000 Lori Baratta
Cover design by Ed Stevens

Printed in the United States of America

The paper used in this publication meets the minimum requirements of the American National Standard for Information Sciences—Permanence of Paper for Printed Library Materials Z39.48-1992(R1997).

"And Do What You Will be the challenge,
So be it in Love that harms none,
For this is the only commandment.
By Magic of old, be it done!"
                              —Doreen Valiente*


For all those who follow the right-hand path,
and with thanks to everyone who has been
part of Open, Sesame at
www.open-sesame.com and at
www.#open-sesame

* Doreen Valiente, *Witchcraft for Tomorrow* (Custer, WA: Phoenix, 1978), p. 173.

# CONTENTS

# INTRODUCTION

*The Wicca Handbook* is both a tutorial for new witches and a reference book for experienced practitioners:

- Part I covers getting started in Wicca, or witchcraft. It can also be used by seekers who explore pagan paths and spiritual alternatives.
- Part II is about what we do, and how and why we do it. (No devil worship, blood sacrifice, or broomstick flying.) New witches will learn from it, experienced practitioners will use it for reference.
- Part III is for everyone, from novice to adept. It contains useful information for writing spells, creating rituals, and making tools, charms, potions, and so forth.
- The Glossary defines words and terms used by witches.
- The Index of Spells lists all the spells from this book, ancient and modern.

Goddesses are listed before gods in the invocation lists (they have been separated in the shorter lists by a semicolon). Groups of god/desses and beings of dual or ambiguous gender are listed at the top of the lists. Don't be confused by the fact that there are different gods and goddesses with the same names. For example, Dön is the Celtic mother goddess as well as a Celtic pantheon god. Sin is the Irish fairy goddess as well as the Mesopotamian Moon god. Kwan-Yin is both the Chinese god and goddess of the Southern Sea. Recommended plants are denoted with a star (*). With the exception of the usual fruit, vegetables, and culinary herbs, they are meant as charms only and *not* to be eaten.

Note:
*The Spiral Dance,*[1] by Starhawk, was the first book I read about Wicca. It served as my guide when I started my Book of Shadows, so the tables of correspondences in this book are based on hers. *The Spiral Dance* is a wonderful book, one I recommend to all new witches who ask me what they should read.

---

[1] Starhawk, *The Spiral Dance: A Rebirth of the Ancient Religion of the Great Goddess* (San Francisco: HarperSanFrancisco, 1989), p. 142.

# PART I

# BECOMING A WITCH

# INTRODUCTION

Witch. What a powerful word it is. It attracts, it repels, it frightens, it fascinates. It offers hope to those who do not know where else to turn.

"How can I become a witch?"

I get thousands of letters from all over the planet asking this question. All Wiccans are witches, but not all witches are Wiccan. Wicca is a religion, a distinct spiritual path. There are many, many ways to be a witch. I am a Wiccan priestess, so this book is about the Wiccan way.

I'm a solitary—a witch who chooses not to belong to a coven or other working group of witches. I practice Wicca as seems right and natural to me; I do not follow any particular Wiccan tradition. I am an eclectic, which means I honor and work with gods and goddesses from different cultures and pantheons. Erzulie's flag, a pentacle wreath, and the Green Man all preside over my altar, which is cluttered with pyramids, obelisks, scarabs, and ankhs.

I don't think there is any one correct way to be a witch or to practice the Wiccan religion. I believe we each have the responsibility of determining a personal path within the faith, an individual path that is right for us. (The emphasis on personal responsibility is one of the things that drew me to this religion in the first place.)

If you ask ten witches the same question, you may get ten different answers. Some traditions prescribe that things be done in certain ways, but I say that you should trust yourself. If something feels right to you, it is right. If something works for you, that is the right way to do it.

# ABOUT WICCA

Modern Wicca began in England in 1939, when Gerald Gardner was initiated into a traditional British coven by Dorothy Clutterbuck (Old Dorothy). He later broke the coven's seal of secrecy and published books about the beliefs and practices of British Wiccans, because he feared the religion would die out. This began what continues to be a groundswell of people converting to Wicca.

Debate currently rages over whether Wicca is a new religion, or the oldest of all religions. Some say that Wicca has been practiced continuously in Europe at least since the Ice Age. They cite paleolithic carvings of female figures, such as the Venus of Willendorf, as evidence of Goddess worship having been the origin of all religions. No, say others, Wicca is a neo-pagan faith, a 20th century construct.

Wicca is actually both, I think, and see no point in debating the issue at all. Modern witches follow in the tradition of our earliest ancestors and are the shamans and healers of the 21st century. We are priests and priestesses of the Great Goddess; we practice the ancient art of sacred magic in the modern world. Certainly witchcraft has changed over the millennia, but we still have much in common with the neolithic practitioner crouched before a fire, crushing herbs for a healing brew. Methods and tools may be different, but the intent is the same: to help and to heal, to honor the Mother in all that we do.

Witchcraft has adapted when necessary—we are only just emerging from the siege mentality that the Burning Times imposed upon us. We are in the process of learning how to live openly as witches again. Witchcraft has also evolved—we no longer slay the sacred king each year to ensure the tribe survives and flourishes. There are no more burnt sacrifices in Wicca, no shedding of animal or human blood to make spells work.

Every Wiccan is a priest or priestess of the Goddess as well as a witch. We serve her in whatever ways we are able to serve, according to our talents, abilities, and personal circumstances. Each Wiccan determines his or her own code of personal conduct and behavior according to the Rede, so you will find Wiccans who are pacifists as well as Wiccans who are professional soldiers, some who are omnivorous and others who are vegans.

Wicca is an Earth religion—an accepting, open-minded faith that celebrates diversity and considers us all to be children of the same Mother. Gender, age, race, sexual orientation, physical status, family background, or ethnic heritage are not important in Wicca. We are male and female, old and young, gay and straight, healthy and disabled, and of all colors. There are no reliable statistics on this, but it seems to me that there are about the same number of male and female Wiccans.

We collect no dues, have no central organization, no governing body, no supreme leader, no great high priestess who speaks for the Goddess. Our temples are gardens and forests, libraries and beaches, mountains and bookstores. Wicca consists simply of its witches and their collective beliefs and practices. It is a voluntary association of individuals who share one faith, but practice it in myriad ways. No one is born Wiccan—not even our children, for we expect them to choose their own spiritual paths when they are old enough to make such choices. There is nothing like a dress code, but many witches wear a pentacle. We have no dietary restrictions, but many witches are vegetarians.

Wicca is an organic religion, one that is evolving and emerging as a worldwide faith. It is growing rapidly, although we neither seek converts or proselytize. This is not a faith that knocks on your door. It is one to which you make your own way. Wicca is a way of life, a belief system that reflects itself in the ways we interact with the world around us. Personal integrity and respect for Mother Nature are important parts of the Wiccan way.

The Wiccan faith has two pillars—the Great Goddess and a poem called "The Wiccan Rede." The first step in becoming a witch is to find your way to the Goddess. The second step is to establish an ethical system in which to use her gift of magic. I am often asked how someone can get involved in the occult without being seduced by its dark side. The answer is that you must have an ethical belief system, one with which you keep faith.

This book contains everything you need to know to begin to practice magic, but you won't be ready for magic until you have taken those first two crucial steps.

# THE GREAT GODDESS

Have you ever been jolted from a sound sleep by someone calling your name, then sat up and discovered you were all alone? What you heard was the call of the Goddess. She is always there, always with us, always calling, but only some of us can hear her. Those who can are witches, her priests and priestesses.

To be a witch, you have to find your way to the Goddess and establish a relationship with her. There are many ways to do this: studying mythology, spending time with the Moon or the sea, meditating, planting a garden, keeping bees, nurturing a child, taking long walks in the woods, and so forth. She is everywhere; all you have to do is look for her. When you find her, invite her into your life. Offer yourself to her service. Step back and watch the magic begin to flow through you and around you.

The Goddess is the universe itself, not something separate from or superior to it. Creation is the business of the universe, which destroys only to re-create. We personify this as the Great Mother. She is self-created and self-renewing. We share atoms with her, are one small part of the godhead, but we are just one product of her great creative nature. Her variety is infinite, as evinced by snowflakes and fingerprints. She is the yin and yang of being, composed of both female (goddess) and male (god) energy. We worship her by many names: Ishtar, Isis, Shakti, Asherah, Xochiquetzal, Brigit, Pelé, Copper Woman, Lupa, Luna. We also recognize old gods like Pan, Osiris, Tammuz, Jove, Quetzalcoatl, Cernunnos, Mithras, and worship them if we feel moved to do so.

Witches are pagans. We worship many gods and goddesses, but recognize all of them as aspects of the Great Goddess. Some witches worship both a lord and a lady, while others worship only the Goddess. For me, Thoth is the lord and Isis is the lady, but choosing what deities to serve, honor, or work with is something each witch decides for herself or himself.

This book is full of information about magic, how to cast spells and create them. Don't forget, however, that magic is only one part of Wicca. Witches use magic to improve their lives, but they also use it in service of the Goddess, as Part I of this book will explain.

# THE WICCAN REDE

All of Wicca's ethics and its moral code can be summed up in eight words. This is the Wiccan Rede, the law that we choose to live by:

*And it harm none, do what you will.*

This witches' saying is part of a poem, also commonly known as "The Wiccan Rede," which has long been handed from witch to witch, first in person and later through the Internet. Several slightly different versions of it have made the rounds, including one that modified the law to say, "Ever mind the Law of Three, lest in self-defense it be."

I always thought that the poem had been written by Doreen Valiente, working with material from Gerald Gardner's several Books of Shadows. Valiente, who was initiated by Gardner in 1953, wrote *The Charge of the Goddess*[1] our most important prayer, and a beautiful poem called *The Witch's Creed,*[2] but she did not write the Rede. The late Lady Gwen Thompson, high priestess of a Welsh tradition, wrote an article in *Green Egg* in 1975, saying this version of the Rede had been handed down to her by Adriana Porter, her grandmother, who was over 90 years old when she died in 1946.

### REDE OF THE WICCAE [3]

Being known as the counsel of the Wise Ones:

1. *Bide the Wiccan laws ye must*
   *in perfect love an' perfect trust.*

2. *Live an' let live—*
   *fairly take an' fairly give.*

3. *Cast the Circle thrice about*
   *to keep all evil spirits out.*

---

[1] Janet and Stewart Farrar, *A Witches' Bible* (Custer, WA: Phoenix Publishing, 1984), pp. 287-298.

[2] Doreen Valiente, *Witchcraft for Tomarrow* (Custer, WA: Phoenix Publishing, 1978), pp. 172-173.

[3] This version of the "Rede of the Wiccae" has been passed on by Lady Gwen, who received it from her grandmother, Adriana Porter. From "Wicca-Pagan Pot-Pourri" in *Green Egg,* Vol. VIII, no. 69, spring 1975, p. 10.

4. *To bind the spell every time,*
   *let the spell be spake in rhyme.*

5. *Soft of eye an' light of touch—*
   *speak little, listen much.*

6. *Deosil go by the waxing Moon—*
   *sing an' dance the Wiccan rune.*

7. *Widdershins go when the Moon doth wane,*
   *an' the Werewolf howls by the dread Wolfsbane.*

8. *When the Lady's Moon is new,*
   *kiss the hand to her times two.*

9. *When the Moon rides at her peak*
   *then your heart's desire seek.*

10. *Heed the Northwind's mighty gale—*
    *lock the door and drop the sail.*

11. *When the wind comes from the South,*
    *love will kiss thee on the mouth.*

12. *When the wind blows from the East,*
    *expect the new and set the feast.*

13. *When the West wind blows o'er thee,*
    *departed spirits restless be.*

14. *Nine woods in the Cauldron go—*
    *burn them quick an' burn them slow.*

15. *Elder be ye Lady's tree—*
    *burn it not or cursed ye'll be.*

16. *When the Wheel begins to turn—*
    *let the Beltane fires burn.*

17. *When the Wheel has turned a Yule,*
    *light the Log an' let Pan rule.*

18. *Heed ye flower, bush an' tree—*
    *by the Lady blessed be.*

19. *Where the rippling waters go*
    *cast a stone an' truth ye'll know.*

20. *When ye have need,*
    *hearken not to other's greed.*

21.  *With the fool no season spend
     or be counted as his friend.*

22.  *Merry meet an' merry part—
     bright the cheeks an' warm the heart.*

23.  *Mind the Threefold Law ye should—
     three times bad an' three times good.*

24.  *When misfortune is enow,
     wear the blue star on thy brow.*

25.  *True in love ever be
     unless thy lover's false to thee.*

26.  *Eight words the Wiccan Rede fulfill—
     an' it harm none, do what ye will.*

# WICCAN TRADITIONS

Wicca is a solitary religion for some of us, something we learned through books, lectures, or the Internet, or developed through personal experience and solitary practice. Some have studied Wicca in groves, study groups, or learning circles. Others grew up in Wiccan families, then chose Wicca for their own path. Many came to Wicca in the traditional way, through formal initiation into a coven that followed a specific tradition. Wiccan traditions include the following.

***Gardnerian Wicca:*** Gerald Gardner's traditional path, which honors Aradia as the lady and Cernunnos as the lord. This is a formal, hierarchal path with skyclad worship and degrees of initiation. It focuses on rituals and male/female polarity. Covens have no more than thirteen members and are led by a high priestess with a high priest. Gardnerians believe it takes a witch to make a witch, and tend to disapprove of the newer "do-it-yourself" Wiccans.

***Alexandrian Wicca:*** A formal, structured, neo-Gardnerian tradition founded by Alex and Maxine Sanders in England in the 1960s. Alexandrian and Gardnerian Wicca are sometimes referred to as Classical Wicca.

***British Trad Wicca:*** This is a formal, structured tradition that mixes Celtic deities and spirituality with Gardenarian-type Wicca.

*Celtic Wicca:* This tradition incorporates Celtic god/desses and spirituality with green witchcraft and faery magic.

*Dianic Wicca:* Named for the goddess Diana, this is a goddess-centered tradition that excludes gods and does not require initiations. Although Dianic Wicca is sometimes thought of as a feminist or lesbian path, there are also male Dianic witches.

*Faery Wicca:* This is an Irish tradition that centers on green witchcraft and faery magic.

*Teutonic Wicca:* A Nordic tradition witchcraft, this incorporates deities, symbolism, and practices from Norse and Germanic cultures.

*Family Traditions:* These are the practices and traditions, usually secret, of families who have been witches for generations.

Some witches hold that you must have been taught the craft by a living relative before you can be considered a hereditary witch, no matter how many witchy ancestors you dig up when you unearth your family roots. I think that, like blue eyes and diabetes, witchcraft can be inherited. I get some letters that start, "We found a handwritten book in the attic . . . ," others from witches who have discovered ancestors who were accused or admitted witches, and yet others from young witches who receive spirit messages from ancestors that contain guidance on following the witches' path.

The gift often seems to skip a generation, passing from grandparent to grandchild. Many witches were taught craft skills by their grandmothers, even if no one ever used the word *witchcraft*. Is there a connection between DNA and witchcraft? I think this would be an excellent subject for investigation by a scientific witch.

You may come across oxymoronic groups calling themselves Satanic Wiccans or Christian Wiccans. These are contradictions in terms. They are not Wiccan, no matter what they call themselves, regardless of whether they mean well by it or not.

# COMPARATIVE RELIGION

*Paganism* is an umbrella term that covers many faiths, including Wicca. I have heard from both Native Americans and Hindus who find similarities between their own religions and Wicca. There are many roads to enlightenment, and all religions are equally valid.

Wiccans respect other belief systems and value freedom of worship for all. Live and let live, as the Rede says.

Pagans are inclusive rather than exclusive. Karma, enlightenment, reincarnation, ch'i, Tantra, the Akashic Records—you are as likely to find witches discussing these things as adherents of the Eastern belief systems from which these words come. Ego, inner child, the unconscious, synchronicity, dream work—a group of witches is as likely to be using these terms as a group of psychiatrists might be.

Wiccans are polytheists who easily incorporate various god/desses and practices into their spells, prayers, and rituals. A witch who honors Sarasvati or Kwan Yin, however, will not do so in the same way as a Hindu or a Buddhist. Nor will a witch who has the raven for a spirit guide or the bear for a totem animal work with it in the same way that a Native American might.

Most witches believe in some form of reincarnation. We believe death is not an end, but a transition. We recognize the cycles of birth/death/rebirth just as we do the cycles of the seasons or the Moon. Some Wiccans believe we rest between incarnations in the Summerlands, a place where we are reunited with our loved ones before we are reborn in new bodies.

Wiccans do not believe in a hell or a devil. We do not refrain from negative acts because we fear we will be punished for them in an afterlife. We refrain from negativity because we choose to be positive. We certainly know what evil is, but we hold the individuals who perpetrate it responsible according to their actions (or inactions), not an entity called Satan.

For many witches, the lord is the Horned God, the Lord of Animals, the sylvan lord of the greenwood. He is usually depicted as a man with horns (Pan, Herne, Cernunnos), but he is a god of herds and fertility, not a demonic figure. Some witches believe in angels and some do not—just as some believe in fairies or dragons and some do not.

# INITIATION

No one should ever assume the title of witch lightly. To call yourself a witch is to set yourself apart from most humans, to appoint yourself a priest/ess of the Goddess. It is a binding contract to serve the life force.

Some traditions believe you are not really a witch unless you have been formally initiated by a high priestess and/or high priest. The rapid growth of Wicca currently makes this impractical, since there are not enough high priest/esses to train or initiate all the newcomers. Wicca is also establishing itself in new countries and cultures, places where there are no experienced witches to lead others.

I think that you are entitled to call yourself a witch from the day you feel entitled to do so. Some feel the need for a ceremony to mark this transition in their life, a ceremony that says, "Today I am a witch." Covens usually hold initiation ceremonies after the postulant has successfully completed a required course of study. This is often a period of a year and a day, at the end of which the postulant is expected to demonstrate thorough knowledge of Wicca or expertise in some area of the craft.

If you feel the need for a ceremony, have one. Those who have chosen to be solitaries or who are unable to find covens can hold self-initiation ceremonies of their own devising. If you feel lost and alone, are unable to clearly define what will make you a witch, set your self a task and a time period in which to complete it: read ten serious books about Wicca or mythology, learn how to make incense or candles or wands, or study herbalism or magical systems. Write yourself a detailed report about what you learned during this process and use it as the basis for your Book of Shadows. Decide that, if you are satisfied with your work, you are ready to consider yourself a witch. If you do not feel the need for an initiation ceremony, as I never have, just look yourself in the eye in a mirror and say it aloud: "Witch."

A natural witch is a born witch, someone who requires no initiation. This may be someone who is a hereditary witch raised in a family tradition, or someone who was a witch, priest/ess, or adept in a previous life.

Look for clues in your life, your family history, your birth chart, and your dreams to discover if you are a natural witch. Did you ever wish something and have it come true, to your horror or surprise? Did you suspect you caused this, intentionally or otherwise? Perhaps you did. Have you always known you were different from other people? Were you a pagan sort of child? Have you dreamt ancient dreams? Do you seem to have a natural affinity for magic? Have you got psychic gifts? Is there an ancient culture to which you are irresistibly drawn? Do inexplicable things happen to or around you? All of these are indications.

If you suspect you're a natural witch, you probably are. There are more people alive on the planet right now than have lived in all of human history, so it makes sense that many of us are Old Souls. Recycling is pleasing to the Goddess.

# WICCAN ETHICS

Once upon a time I assumed everyone was like me, considered magic sacred and would never use it in negative ways. Then I launched a Web site (www.open-sesame.com) and the e-mail came pouring in. Along with all the wonderful letters came some that horrified me, letters from people who use magic to hurt others intentionally. They sent death spells, revenge spells, cancer spells, car-crash spells, bankruptcy spells, and worse, on the assumption that I shared their enjoyment of such things. I heard from Satanists who kill animals in twisted rites, from lovesick people who wanted spells to kill rivals or break up marriages, from people who sought power over the lives or minds of others, from chaos magicians who derange functional systems just for the fun of it, and from very angry people looking for all sorts of spells with which to lash out.

It shocked me to discover how many advocates and practitioners there are of this kind of magic. I made it my policy to refuse to answer them. Finally, I put a notice on my Web site telling people who use black magic not to bother writing to me, and added this to my FAQ page:

> **Q:** Why won't you answer us if we're into black magic/ Satanism?
>
> **A:** You have chosen the left-hand path, which is contrary to our law. You are free to do so, as I am free to ignore you. Life is too short, too precious, to waste it on negativity. Consider that your urgent need to contact witches might be a message from the Universe: you're on the wrong road!

Biding the Rede is the only thing you *have* to do to be Wiccan. Do no harm. That is the essence of the Wiccan faith, our one law. No one imposes this on us. A Wiccan is a witch who chooses of his or her own free will to be bound by this law. We see life as magical and magic as sacred, so Wiccans are white witches who do not hex or harm.

To assume that white magic is less powerful than black magic would be to mistake kindness for weakness. Certainly we defend ourselves, but we generally do so by deflecting attacks rather than by attacking, as you will see in Part II (Protection).

# WHITE MAGIC

Magic itself is neutral, a tool. Like a hammer, it can be used to smash or to build. It is colored by your intent. *White magic* is a term used to describe that which is positive, constructive, or helpful. Black magic is that which is negative, destructive, or harmful. If you have a business and you work spells to make it prosper, that's white magic. Casting spells to destroy your competition would be black magic. These are not racial terms. The terms *good* and *evil*, or *dark* and *light*, are often used to express this same concept.

Why black and white, and not some other colors? To answer this question you have to go back into prehistory and imagine how terrifying the night was for humans before we learned to use fire. The black of night was full of unseen threats, a dangerous time that you might not survive. The white light of day brought illumination and safety, welcome relief.

White magic is the right-hand path, black magic the left. The symbolism of right and left is also very ancient. The right hand was used for eating, the left hand for bathroom functions. Imagine life without toilet paper and you'll understand why it's customary to shake hands with your right hand! This has nothing to do with being right- or left-handed. It does, however, explain why, in the past, left-handed people were often forced to learn to write with their right hands.

The term *green witchcraft* is sometimes used to describe Celtic magic, fairy magic, Earth magic, or any combination of these. There are several theories of "gray magic," but I think gray magic is what Hindus call *maya*—illusion.

One theory holds that since good and evil both exist, some people need to do black magic in order to balance white magic. I don't accept this. I agree with Scott Cunningham that

*Magic is love. All magic should be performed out of love. The moment anger or hatred tinges your magic you have crossed the border into a dangerous world, one that will ultimately consume you.*[4]

---

[4] Scott Cunningham, *Cunningham's Encyclopedia of Magical Herbs* (St. Paul, MN: Llewellyn, 1999), p. 8.

Do murderers balance nice people? Do child abusers balance loving parents? If they create balance, does this excuse their crimes? Try telling that to a judge! "Well your honor, I only stole that car to create balance in the universe."

There is another polarity theory, which states that if you do two hexes and two healings, they balance one another or cancel each other out. Although there may be some logic to this, it's still just a self-serving excuse, a way to delude yourself that you are a white witch when you practice black magic.

Some traditions hold that those spells you cast on yourself constitute white magic, while those you cast on others constitutes gray magic. The wordsmith in me quibbles with this on semantic grounds. I think a spell that harms you or anyone else is black magic; one that helps or heals anyone, including yourself, is white magic. Being of service to people in need or distress is one of the things witches do best. I therefore see nothing wrong in casting spells that help others—with their permission, of course.

Some witches argue that there are evils too great, situations too grave, to be handled with white magic. The end justifies the means, they say, making black magic necessary for the greater good. Although there is some merit to this argument, I have never encountered a situation I couldn't handle with white magic. Binding, banishing, and transformation are the powerful tools of a white witch.

There are excellent moral and ethical arguments against practicing black magic. If you are not convinced by those, however, here is a practical one:

*What goes around comes around.*

Everything we put forth is eventually returned to us. Moreover, Wicca recognizes the Law of Three, which states that this return is triple. Black magic may provide instant gratification, but it ultimately does you more harm than anyone else. Many white witches have learned this lesson the hard way.

Carefully examine any spell or magical working before you perform it to be sure that it is in accord with Wiccan law. Ask yourself if you are casting the spell *for* the person, or *on* the person. If you do harm inadvertently, try to right it. Many witches work a phrase into their spells that prevents accidental harm—something like, "And let no harm be done by this."

This knowledge I have taught
is more arcane than any mystery—
consider it completely,
then act as you choose.

Listen to my profound words,
the deepest mystery of all,
for you are precious to me
and I tell you for your good.[5]

# WICCAN RITES

Wicca's rituals are not obligatory. A Wiccan may hold a ceremony whenever he or she feels the need for one. The ritual may be private or public, celebrated alone or with other witches, or performed by a high priest/ess. The rite may be newly written for the occasion, one handed down in a particular tradition, or something from a book about Wicca. Our rituals include the following:

**Wiccaning:** A ceremony held to welcome a new baby and place her or him under the protection of the Goddess.

**Initiation:** Any ceremony held to mark the dedication of a new witch to the Goddess and the craft.

**Handfasting:** A Wiccan marriage ceremony, called a handfasting because the right wrists of the bride and groom are traditionally bound together, symbolizing their union. Jumping the broomstick, an ancient fertility rite, is often part of the ceremony. Some couples have only a handfasting, while others handfast before or after a civil marriage ceremony. The number of Wiccans taking legal orders entitling them to use the title Reverend make it increasingly possible for a handfasting to be a legally recognized marriage ceremony.

**The Great Rite:** The Great Rite is sacred sexuality, the union of lance and grail. The god is invoked into the male witch, the Goddess into the female. In classical Wicca, this is a formal ceremony that includes the Fivefold Kiss. The sex act is only symbolic when the Rite is performed before the whole coven; actual when celebrated in privacy.

---

[5] *The Bhagavad-Gita* (New York: Quality Paperback Book Club, 1998), p. 152.

In other traditions the Great Rite is any act of loving sexual intercourse performed within a magic circle as an offering to the Goddess. It is sex magic of the highest kind, using male/female polarity to raise and channel power. Gay couples have male and female energy as well, so I can see no reason why lesbians and homosexuals cannot also celebrate the Great Rite.

*Croning:* A ceremony that marks a female witch's change from mother to crone, the final stage of her life. (Menarche marks entry into the maiden phase, motherhood or mentoring into the mother phase.) The decision to crone may be based on the beginning or end of menopause, on an astrological milestone, on a personal life event like the last child leaving home, or simply because the witch feels the time is right.

*Death Rites:* Rituals held to mark the passing of witches. Wiccans see life and death as part of the same cycle. Death is merely a transformation of our energy into another form. A Wiccan requiem can thus be both a solemn occasion and a joyous celebration of the witch's life.

# THE WICCAN YEAR

Wiccans see the year as an ever turning wheel and celebrate its cycles: the waning and waxing of the Moon, the changing seasons, progression through the houses of the Zodiac, the agricultural year, and the solar year with its cycle of the Sun/Earth relationship. Eight Wiccan holidays mark the stages of the Wheel of the Year.

| Greater Sabbats Cross-Quarter Festivals | | Lesser Sabbats The Quarter Festivals | |
|---|---|---|---|
| FEBRUARY 2: | Imbolc | SPRING EQUINOX: | Eostre |
| MAY 1: | Beltane | SUMMER SOLSTICE: | Litha |
| AUGUST 1: | Lughnasadh | AUTUMN EQUINOX: | Mabon |
| OCTOBER 31: | Samhain | WINTER SOLSTICE: | Yule |

Following is a brief introduction to Wiccan festivals and some of the many ways to celebrate them. Look to the Internet and books like Janet and Stewart Farrar's excellent *A Witches' Bible* for more information about Wiccan holidays. Our feast days are based on those of the ancient Celts, so they make most sense in the northern temperate zones. Southern Hemisphere witches often celebrate them in reverse, reflecting their opposite seasons. Following the Celtic custom, we usually celebrate the holy days on their eves as well.

Please note that Solstice and Equinox dates are approximate, because they vary slightly in some years.

## December 21:
### WINTER SOLSTICE, also called Longest Night; this inaugurates the celebration of Yule, which ends at New Year

The Goddess gives birth to the god, the Child of Promise who is reborn with the returning Sun. Yule is a joyous celebration of family and friends, of peace and love and positive energy. Witches incorporate ancient pagan traditions into our festivities, traditions like yule logs, gift giving, wassail cups, mistletoe charms, and bringing evergreens into the home or decorating a tree.

## February 2:
### IMBOLC, also called Imbolg, Oimelc, Candlemas, Earrach, and Groundhog's Day

This is the quickening of the year. Winter buds appear on bare trees and green life stirs under the frozen earth. The infant Sun (the god) grows in size and strength. Imbolc is a fire festival, a festival of lights, sacred to the Irish goddess Brighid. Witches light candles to illuminate the winter darkness, and start spring cleaning.

## March 21:
### SPRING EQUINOX, also called Ostara or Eostre

The year is in perfect balance between light and darkness. The god is now a green youth and the Goddess is in her maiden aspect. Their courtship dance begins. Ostara is a solar festival of fire, light, and fertility sacred to the Saxon goddess of spring, Ostara/Eostre. Witches follow the old pagan custom of dyeing or painting hard-boiled eggs, then balancing the eggs on their ends to symbolize equilibrium. We work magic to balance any imbalances in our lives.

## May 1:
## BELTANE, also called May Eve, Samradh, Cetsamain, and Walpurgis Night

By May, the light has grown longer and everything is flowering. The virile young lord and the fertile maiden celebrate the evident consummation of their relationship. Beltane is sacred to Maia, Greco-Roman goddess of spring. It is a fire and fertility festival that celebrates the transformation from maiden to mother through the mystery of sexuality. Beltane Eve is a perfect time for the Great Rite. Witches gather dew on May morning, put flowers on their altars, leave offerings for fairies, and tend sacred places like groves and wells.

## June 22:
## LITHA, also called Summer Solstice, Midsummer, and St. John's Day

Earth is in full bloom. The Mother is pregnant and the god (the Sun) is King of Summer at the peak of his powers. Litha is the longest day, marking the division of the year. Witches celebrate abundance, fertility, virility, and the beauty and bounty of nature. This is a good time for handfastings and male rituals, for workings of empowerment, consummation, or culmination.

## August 1:
## LUGHNASADH, also called Lammas, Lunasa, and Hlafmass, the Festival of Loaves

The days start growing shorter and the fields are heavy with crops ready to be harvested. The corn king is sacrificed and mourning begins for the death of the god (the Sun). Lughnasadh is the first of the Wiccan harvest festivals, a festival of fire and light named for the Celtic god Lugh/Llew, Lord of Light. Witches bake bread, put grain on their altars, count their blessings and give thanks to the Goddess.

## September 21:
## MABON, also called Autumn Equinox

Crops are harvested; light and darkness are again in balance. The god sleeps in the womb of the Goddess, waiting to be reborn. Mabon is sacred to the Celtic god Mabon, a Son of Light, son of the mother goddess Modron. This second harvest festival is a time to enjoy the fruits of your labor and give thanks for abundance. Witches put the fruits of the season on their altars, bake bread and pies, work magic to balance imbalances.

---

**October 31:**
**SAMHAIN (pronounced sow-en), also called Halloween, Allantide, Shadowfest, and All Hallows Eve**

---

The harvest season closes, the days grow darker and winter is initiated. The Goddess enters her time of sleeping and dreaming. The god (the Sun) awaits rebirth. Samhain is witches' New Year, both solemn and joyous, the night when the veil between the worlds is thinnest. It can be celebrated in high revelry, with costume parties and witches' balls, or solemnly, as a night for honoring ancestors and contacting departed loved ones.

# CRAFT NAMES

Many witches elect to assume a craft name. This is optional, unless you join a tradition in which a new name is required. Your name, if you choose one, should say something about you. God/dess, plant, and animal names are popular, especially those that are variations on wolf, dragon, and raven imagery. Names that include the Moon, a color, or a stone are also common.

Some witches start with a single name, then add additional ones as they progress in the craft. In some traditions, each witch also has a secret name, one that is known only to family or fellow coveners. Witches sometimes change their magical names, choosing a new one when they want to change their luck or mark a new stage in life.

This is a free planet and you can call yourself anything you like, but young witches who assume titles like "Lord," "Lady," or "Sir" may find themselves criticized by older witches who think such titles should be earned, not assumed.

# STARTING IN MAGIC

This chapter explores useful preludes to working with magic. You would not be reading this if you were not already a seeker trying to find your way. Your search (and the inner work it involves) are what matter, not whether your path leads finally to Wicca. Walk in the light and you will never go astray.

The journey to magic starts with an inner voyage, the journey to self. It begins with the hand mirror of Venus: ♀ This symbol does not represent vanity, it means "Know Thyself"—the same lesson taught at Delphi.

You have been living with yourself all your life and probably assume that you do know yourself. Unless you are already an adept, however, you have not yet learned that there are two ways of knowing, two ways of experiencing the world. Magic will open your eyes, your mind, and your self to the other way of knowing. Reality is like an onion, composed of layers. Ordinary life takes place on its surface, or perhaps a little deeper for those with inborn psychic gifts. Magic will take you further and teach you how to penetrate the veils and layers of reality. Magic deals in ultimate truth.

This journey, should you decide to undertake it, is never-ending. We all have things we can still learn about ourselves and about magic, no matter how long we have studied.

Astrology, dream work and past-life work are all a part of this inner journey. Each of these are enormous subjects, however, that could easily take volumes to cover fully. It isn't within the scope of this book to do that. There are many excellent books on these topics that you can access for more information.

## ASTROLOGY

As above, so below—most witches believe in astrology. We know that the position of the planets at the time of our birth influences who we will be and what our lives will be like. This is not the sole determining factor, since forces like free will, genetics, chance, and synchronicity are also in play. The art and science of astrology is well worth study, however, for both witches and those who would be witches.

Your birth chart is a good starting point. Your natal chart is a chart cast specifically for you, based on the date, time, and place of your birth. It shows in which astrological house each planet was when you were born, and what the relationship of each planet was to the others. An astrologer is able to interpret this and tell you many things about yourself and your life.

Having your birth chart done by a professional astrologer can be costly. A less expensive alternative is to cast and interpret it yourself, with the aid of a book. A good astrology book can make you feel as if someone has been reading your diary or peering through the windows of your soul. You could also access the sites that do natal charts on the Internet.

Your birth chart can help you determine whether you have lived before. A lack of karma in your chart indicates that you may be a new soul joining us on the Wheel for the first time. A heavy accumulation of karma is a sign of an Old Soul. Different aspects can also give clues. The aspect of Saturn trine Neptune, for example, indicates you are a seeker far along the path. It means you probably practiced high magic in a past life and have the potential to be an adept in this lifetime. This aspect also shows an affinity for Earth magic.

# MYTHOLOGY

Time spent studying mythology is time well spent. Arthur Cotterell, in his preface to *The Encyclopedia of Mythology,* points out how mythology deals with fundamental human issues:

* The power of love; its attendant anxiety and jealousy;
* The conflict between the generations, between old and new;
* The violence of men;
* The mystery of death;
* The mischief of troublemakers;
* The sadness of illness and accidental injury;
* The possibility of an afterlife or reincarnation;
* The effect of enchantment on mind and body;
* The challenge of the unknown;
* The sadness of betrayal and treachery;
* The cycle of fertility in humans, plants, and animals;

- The horror of madness;
- Luck and fate;
- The nature of the universe;
- The creation of the world;
- The relationship between humans and the godhead.[6]

As you become familiar with the god/desses of the world, you will feel yourself drawn to particular deities or cultures. You may also find that you feel an affinity for a certain type of deity or archetype: sea goddesses, vegetation gods, Earth Mothers, Sky Fathers, or cultural hero/ines. This is another way to learn about yourself.

I am an American of Western European ancestry, to whom all myths are interesting. It is to Egyptian mythology, however, that I am most drawn. This tells me something about myself. It informs these pages and the way I practice witchcraft. It helps me to understand why all the roads of my life led to Egypt.

# MEDITATION

To meditate, you must get comfortable in a place where you will not be interrupted, then enter a state of deep relaxation, one step away from sleep. Clear your mind, then set it free to wander. Where it goes will teach you a lot about yourself. Regular meditation can support all the other inner work you do.

Meditation can also help you in other ways. To work magic, you must be centered, balanced, and very focused. Meditation is calming and teaches mental discipline. Most witches meditate. Some like to do it in natural places, lulled by birdsong or the splashing of water. Others do it at home or even on trains on their way to work. Turn off the phone to meditate at home, or do it in bed just before you sleep. Some find meditation devices helpful: incense, candles, recordings of chanting, drumming, quiet music, or nature sounds. By using the same device repeatedly, you can condition your mind to enter a meditative state.

# PAST-LIFE WORK

Old Souls are people who have lived before, often many times. Finding out if you are an Old Soul and who you were in past lives is fascinating. An attraction to witchcraft or magic in this lifetime

---

[6] Arthur Cotterell, *The Encyclopedia of Mythology* (New York: Smithmark Publishers, 1996), p. 6.

may mean that you were previously a priest/ess, mage, witch, or shaman.

There are psychologists who hypnotize people and regress them to reveal past lives. I have not tried this and so cannot express an opinion about it. I have met people who claim to be able to read your past lives in your aura. Again, I have no personal experience with this. I am not sure if either of these methods work, but, if they do, they would give instant gratification. What I am sure of is that there are a lot of charlatans out there who will happily separate you from your money by trying to convince you that you used to be Cleopatra or Merlin.

You must have a fearless soul to do past-life work, because what you learn may be disturbing. How you died, particularly if your death was violent, is often the first memory to surface. Happy memories are less likely to be recovered than traumatic ones. Remember that having been someone terrible in a previous life doesn't mean you are a bad person now. We're all here doing the same thing—working on our karma.

Learning about past lives is a process. It may be the work of a lifetime. Meditation, especially trance states, is a method that works for some witches. Carnelian is a useful stone to hold while you meditate. You can also try guided meditation, using tapes and books sold in New Age shops. Hanging out with other witches sometimes triggers past-life memories, especially if you have been doing some sort of psychic work together. Fire of Azrael, kindled of cedar, juniper, and sandalwood, is supposed to show you your past when you gaze into its flames.

Look for clues in your childhood, if you can. Interview people who had a lot of contact with you. Ask them if you ever said or did anything strange, something that did not make sense. My young son calls his Lego set Babylon, builds little cities with it. When he is upset, he tells me that he wants to go home, even though he is already at home. I grew up in New York City, but I tried to harvest grain when I was young. I collected grasses with seed heads and shut them away in metal boxes, tried to turn them into what I imagined raw wheat flour looked like by these magical means. It made no sense (and, of course, it didn't work), but it was a clue to my inner self, as was the strong urge to collect seeds that came on me every autumn. Can you imagine what a red wagon full of moldering chestnuts smells like after it has been shut in a garage all winter? My son and I both have birth charts that indicate we are Old Souls.

Eastern religions teach that enlightenment brings escape from the Wheel, freedom from the cycle of reincarnation. Wicca does not agree with that. Witches welcome this return because we find life joyful.

## DREAM WORK

A past-life dream is more like reality than a dream. If you have ever had one, you know exactly what I mean. In an ancient dream, you smell people's bodies, feel the heat of the torches, experience the fear or joy of the priestess. You wake up out of breath, with your heart pounding. You were actually there. You know your dream for what it was.

Dreams can reveal many things besides past lives—things such as directions, future events, and unresolved personal issues. The universe sometimes communicates with us through dreams.

Dream work is done by keeping a notebook near your bed, a book in which you write down your dreams as soon as you awaken. You can write down every dream, or just those that seem meaningful. Reviewing your dreams as they accumulate may reveal patterns and issues. It can also give validity to premonitions and predictions.

## CONFRONTING YOUR DARK SIDE

We all have a dark side we must confront before we can trust ourselves with magic. This requires absolute honesty with yourself. You must find a way to deal with your demons—negative impulses like aggression, jealousy, addiction, envy, depression, or compulsion. The solution is different for each of us. My own dark side is darker than most, but I work it out in my poetry.

Magic has its dark side as well—the black arts. They can be seductive, but you will ultimately destroy yourself if you choose the left-hand path. Protect yourself from this. Never participate in Satanism, black magic, demonology, blood sacrifice, or anything else that is negative. Avoid books by those who practice or advocate black magic. Develop your psychic radar so that alarm bells go off whenever evil comes near you.

## GETTING STARTED

It is said that, when you are ready, a teacher will come. You can study witchcraft on your own until then, through books and Web sites, or by attending lectures. You can also seek out a coven, study group, or another novice with whom to work. Some experienced witches accept students as a part of their service to the craft. The Internet and metaphysical bookshops are great places to make pagan contacts.

Remember that no one is going to spoon-feed you magic. You will have to work at learning it. You'll need to master a divinatory practice, erect an altar, start your Book of Shadows, learn how to make sacred space, and learn about the gods and goddesses. You'll have to be responsible for yourself, study witchcraft, and formulate your own code of ethics in which to practice it. These are the basics.

## DIVINATION

Every witch needs to learn some method of divination, be it runes, tarot, scrying, I Ching, or anything else. Divination is a way for the universe to speak to and through us. Spend some time in the New Age section of your local bookstore. You will likely find books and kits on several different divination systems. Investigate the one that calls to you.

## ALTAR

An altar is a place for worship and casting spells. Erect one if you can. It can be a formal altar with elaborate furnishings, or it can be simply a table, a bookshelf, a desktop, a slab of rock—any place you have available to you for this purpose. Typical altar furnishings include:

- Candles;
- Tools;
- Statues or other representations of deities;
- Incense;
- Crystals;
- Offerings, such as fruit and flowers.

As with all else, it's your altar and you can put whatever you like on it. Pay homage to a particular god, goddess, or pantheon. Decorate it for the seasons, the Sabbats, the Full Moon—whatever feels and looks right to you.

An altar is a wonderful thing to have—a convenient place for a witch to work and a spiritual center for the home. Don't worry if your circumstances prevent or forbid you from erecting one, however, because it is certainly possible to manage without one. Temporary altars can be put up for a ritual or spell, then taken down.

Before I was ready to come out as a witch I kept all my supplies in a witch's box in a closet. I'd get them out for a spell, put them away afterward. My witch's box was a wooden one I had made in carpentry class in high school, but yours can be any sort of box. When I lived in Egypt, where it can be dangerous to be known as a witch, I kept my supplies all over the house, in those places where each item would most likely be kept anyway, to prevent snoopy cleaning women from telling tales about me. I liked to use trays for spells then—big serving trays on which everything for a spell could be assembled ahead of time and then moved to the place (usually the kitchen) where I cast the spell.

# SACRED SPACE

Sacred space is space set apart for magic, rituals, meditation, work, or worship. Some witches are fortunate enough to have a permanent space, like a grove, a garden, or a room that isn't used for anything else, but most of us have to make sacred space when we need it. To do this, light some candles, burn incense, or play music you consider sacred, then mentally define the area you are thereby making sacred.

## MAGIC

Magic is real. It affects reality. It is serious business, something that should never be taken lightly or fooled with until you know what you are doing.

You must ask yourself, as T.S. Eliot did,

*Do I dare
Disturb the universe?*[7]

Magic is a tool, a double-edged sword. Magic disturbs the universe, so save it for the big stuff.

---

[7] T. S. Elliot, "The Love Song of J. Alfred Prufrock," *The Oxford Anthology of English Literature*, vol. II (New York: Oxford University Press, 1973), p. 1973.

Like anything else, you'll get as much from magic as you put into it. It takes a lot of time and study to become an adept. Be realistic in your expectations. Magic is not the answer to everything, so recognize situations that are better dealt with by law enforcement, doctors, or other professionals. Be reasonable. If someone is spouting blood, apply a tourniquet and call for help before you even think of doing a stop-bleeding spell.

Magic is natural, not supernatural. It's the manipulation of energy to achieve a desired result. Physicists have discovered that particles under study alter their movements, that you can change a thing merely by concentrating on it. That's how magic works. Learning to successfully cast spells is the least of it. Your ultimate goal should be to experience life itself as magical. The Buddha taught that all life is suffering. Witches beg to differ.

Magic is very powerful, but to look to it for power over others is to miss the point entirely. Magic isn't for compelling love or obedience, it isn't for destroying your enemies. Magic is about empowerment. This is why I teach people how to cast spells rather than doing spells for them. Magic is for transformation, healing, and betterment. It brings self-improvement and self-determination. Power over yourself and your own life is real power. Use magic to change your life. Battle your demons with it: fears, addictions, diseases, negative patterns.

Magic is limitless in its forms. Some types of magic include knot magic, kitchen magic, garden magic, weather magic, chaos magic, hand magic, candle magic, chant magic, Goddess magic, lunar magic, solar magic, crystal magic, dragon magic, sea spells, fire spells, and necromancy. There are as many kinds as there are witches.

Knowledge is power, so magical power accrues with study, experience, practice, and inner work. Never try to prove your powers to anyone else. Don't get bogged down in ridiculous "power contests" with other practitioners. The only one you have anything to prove to is yourself.

# BOOK OF SHADOWS

Most witches make a grimoire, or Book of Shadows. This is a blank book in which you write down any information you think is interesting or useful to you as a witch. You should begin yours as soon as possible. It can be any sort of book, but will need to be fairly large, because you will be writing a lot of things in it. Magical supply shops sell blank Books of Shadows. Booksellers and art supply stores often carry bound sketch books that serve well as grimoires.

I am not sure how these came to be called Books of Shadows. I prefer to call them grimoires, because they are, in fact, Books of Illumination. During the Dark Ages in Europe, witches kept a tiny flame of enlightenment burning, storing ancient knowledge in their books, and defending a bastion of literacy in the face of ignorance. To be caught with a grimoire during the Burning Times meant torture and death.

A Book of Shadows is a very powerful thing—the repository of magic. It grows more powerful with the passing years, as you expand it. It must be handwritten. You must always treat it with respect and never let anyone else handle it. A Book of Shadows usually includes:

- Spells;
- Rituals;
- Prayers;
- Magical correspondences;
- Information on magic itself.

It may also have:

- Incantations;
- Pictures or sketches;
- Charts (like Moon or tide tables);
- Symbols;
- God/dess pages;
- A coven section;
- Records of magical workings and experiences.

It's your book, so put whatever you like in it. Many of us keep more information in our computers than we do in our grimoires. This may make for easier retrieval and organization of information, but it is no substitute for the potency of a handwritten book. Do both, if you like.

You can hide your book away or keep it on your altar. Mine is usually on my altar these days, but I kept it under my desk for years. When you feel that your book has sufficient power, you may want to cast spells atop it.

## INVOCATIONS

Thoth, Lord of Books (the ibis-headed Egyptian god of writing, magic, and wisdom) is an excellent deity to oversee your Book of Shadows. Tao-chün, Lord of the Tao, guards magical writings. He can be invoked to protect your book.

## MY GRIMOIRE

My Book of Shadows was a big blank record book, the kind governments used before computers. My father gave it to me, thinking I might want to use it for my diary. I had that book for years. I knew it should be used for something special, but was unable to decide what that special purpose might be. I thought it could be a dream book and actually wrote one or two dreams in it. Then I decided that wasn't right and tore the dream pages out.

The book moved with me from apartment to apartment, back and forth across the United States, until I finally came to Wicca and knew for certain why I had been saving it. I drew a pentacle on its cover and began my Book of Shadows. I divided my Book of Shadows into three sections:

- Correspondences;
- Materia;
- Spells and Incantations.

Correspondences were important to me right from the start, because I knew I would need them to write my own spells. I organized them alphabetically (orderliness is a Taurus "thing"), with pages on topics that interested me:

**Correspondences:** Air, alchemy, angels, animals, the astral planes, Aquarius, Aries, autumn, birds, Cancer, candles, Capricorn, colors, creativity, Earth, East, fire, Gemini, god/desses, healing, incense, jewels, Jupiter, justice, Leo, Libra, love, magic, Mars, Mercury, money and business, the Moon, Neptune, North, numbers, Pluto, protection, psychic work, reincarnation, Sagittarius, Saturn, Scorpio, sex magic, South, the spirit world, spring, summer, the Sun, symbols, the tarot, Taurus, tools, Uranus, Venus, Virgo, water, West, the Wheel of the Year, winter, wisdom, yin/yang.

**Materia:** "By seed and root, by bud and stem, by leaf and flower and fruit."[8] This section became an herbal, with information on hundreds of plants in alphabetical order. When I collected specimens, such as leaves or seeds, I pressed them between the appropriate pages. I also drew or pasted pictures to help me in plant identification when I needed it.

**Spells and Incantations:** This section came to include prayers and rituals, especially ancient prayers, as well as spells and incantations. The first spells I put in it were those I copied from books. As I gained knowledge, however, I began to write my own spells.

---

[8] Janet and Stewart Farrar, *A Witches' Bible* (Custer, WA: Phoenix Publishing, 1996), p. 164.

# THE WITCH'S TOOLS

Tools are the implements we use to work magic. Some traditions make a great fetish of tools. This can be daunting for new witches, who sometimes think they cannot begin to cast spells until they have acquired everything on the list. Unlike many witches, I take a minimalist approach to tools. For years, I used a sword, an athame, and a pentacle. That's it. Occassionally I used a marble mortar that served as a chalice and for grinding herbs. A mortar is also a great place to burn things.

Start making or acquiring tools as you need them. Covens often give sets of tools to new members. I have found that, whenever I had need of a tool, I suddenly acquired it by one means or another. These are some of the (often-conflicting) superstitions about tools:

- They must be formally consecrated before use;
- Tools should only be used inside the circle;
- Using tools in the kitchen consecrates the food they are used to prepare;
- Tools must be made by yourself or received as gifts, not purchased;
- It is bad luck to haggle over the price of a tool;
- You should never allow anyone else to handle your tools;
- The finest tools are those you make yourself, from natural substances;
- Any sword, knife, or dagger that has ever drawn blood must be purified before consecration;
- Athames and swords should be symbolic, not actual weapons.

Accept or reject these beliefs as seems right to you. I have never consecrated my tools, because I have never felt the need to do so. Magical use seems self-consecrating to me. I dislike having the vibrations with which I imbue objects disturbed. I, therefore, never let someone touch my tools or my grimoire. I agree that actual weapons are unsuitable tools for a witch.

With the exception of the sword, my tools "hid in plain sight" while I lived in Egypt. I expect the notion of "kitchen witch" came from the fact that most of the things we use—like herbs, cauldrons, and candles—can be left about the kitchen without attracting attention. This probably helped some witches survive the Burning Times.

# CONSECRATION

Branch into wand, goblet into chalice, knife into athame, pot into cauldron. Consecration is a short ceremony that dedicates an object for sacred use. Lay your tools on the altar, cast a circle, and consecrate them. You can devise any sort of ceremony you like for this. Keep it simple, cast the circle, mix salt into water, and sprinkle the tool, saying something like: "Knife, you are brought within this circle of transformation to be forever after my athame." Handle the object with reverence, steeping it in your vibrations, then put it in its appointed place on the altar before closing the circle.

# ATHAME

An athame is a ceremonial knife that corresponds to the element of fire in some traditions, to air in others, and to the direction East. Like all the phallic tools, it has male energy and symbolizes animus. It a witch's weapon and most important tool. In some traditions, it must be black-handled (white-handled knives are used only as cutting tools). The hilt of your athame can be plain, or inscribed with magical markings. It can be a new knife acquired for this purpose, or it can be something you have had for a long time and now dedicate for ritual use. Antique stores and flea markets are good places to find daggers and interesting knives, but you must purify (with water, salt, sunlight, crystals, or any combination thereof) any object with unknown provenance in case it has black vibrations.

My athame is a bronze letter opener with an enameled handle that was given to me by a business mentor many years ago. The athame is used for:

- Mixing salt and water, or potions;
- Inscribing the circle;
- Charging, consecrating, or empowering amulets, talismans, or Poppets;

- Drawing lines;
- Discrimination and setting limits;
- Making choices and carrying them out.

# SWORD

"With this in my hands, I am the ruler of the circle."[9] A sword is used like an athame, but is more formal and authoritative. It corresponds to the planet Mars. Some traditions link it to the element of air, others to fire. It has male energy.

Your sword could be an actual weapon or a ceremonial object. I use a ceremonial sword that could not easily inflict damage on anyone. I bought it at Magickal Childe years ago, and chose it because I dislike the martial connotations of a real weapon. Use your sword for:

- Invoking the Lords of the Watchtowers;
- Ruling the circle;
- Making salutations.

A woman who straps on a sword becomes male in the context of a ritual. You can keep yours on your altar, mount it on the wall above your altar, or keep it hidden away. Swords are irresistible to small boys so are best kept out of sight if you have young children in your house.

# WAND

Anyone who's ever been to the movies knows what a wand is. Some traditions correspond wands to the element of fire, others to air. South is their direction; their energy is male.

Wands were traditionally cut from one-year-old trees, in a single stroke, at sunrise on a Wednesday. It is said that a wand's length should be the distance from your elbow to your fingertips. As with other tools, you can use any sort of wand you like, even a metal one. If you cut your wand from a tree, do ask the tree's permission first and leave it some small offering in return, like a feather or a stone. Some witches prefer to use a fallen branch or a piece of driftwood rather than cut a tree.

---

[9] Janet and Stewart Farrar, *The Witches' Bible,* p. 250.

Witches who make their own wands often carve magical symbols into them, or affix small crystals or gemstones to them. Wands are used for many things, including:

- Casting circles;
- Channeling energy;
- Inviting and controlling entities;
- Manifestation (changing spirit into matter, concept into form, idea into reality, etc.).

The Egyptian wand was called *ur hekau,* the mighty one of enchantments. It consisted of a sinuous piece of wood adorned by a ram's head wearing a uraeus at one end. Ur hekau was used in the Opening of the Mouth ceremony. Held before a mummy's entombment, this ritual allowed the deceased to speak and eat in the afterlife.

Aaron's rod, a biblical magic wand, was made from an almond tree. The Druid wand was made of ash, with a spiral decoration. Sometimes a curved yew branch hung with tinkling silver bells was used for lunar magic. Irish Druids made their wands of hazel, rowan, or yew. Gallic Druids used oak wands.

A wand with a pinecone on its tip is used to invoke Dionysus. Chinese wizards used peach branches for their wands. The Ainu people of Japan used long pieces of bamboo with leaves attached to make their sacred wands. They whittled the tops into spiral designs. Witch wands for divining metal are made of rowan wood.

# ✪ PENTACLE

A pentacle is a 5-pointed star, usually inside a circle (the circle symbolizes unity and infinity). It corresponds to the element of earth. North is a pentacle's direction; its energy is female. This is the star of the Goddess. It is pointed upward for protection, blessings, consecration, meditation, and positive energy; downward for banishing and binding. Some say you should never invert a pentacle, but rather draw it backward for banishing or binding. The five points (starting at the top) can represent any of the following sets of symbols:

- Birth, initiation, consummation, repose, death;
- Love, wisdom, knowledge, law, power.

In some traditions the points represent

* Spirit, Air, Water, Earth, Fire;

but in other traditions:

* Spirit, Water, Fire, Earth, Air.

A pentacle is also a tool used in magical workings. It is usually placed at the center of the altar and magic worked atop it. It can be simple or elaborate, handmade or purchased, fashioned of whatever you like. A pentacle that is drawn or written is called a pentagram.

I use glass—a round sheet of glass with smooth edges. I draw the pentacle on one side of it with a metallic magic marker. I like glass because of its availability, transparency, and clean vibrations. I often put something related to the spell—photograph, documents, whatever—under the glass while I work the spell. You are supposed to break your pentacle when you move to a new home, so glass has another advantage.

Pentacles are also meditation tools. They can be used to call spirits or invite entities. You make the sign of the pentacle by tracing the star in the air, or on some person or object. A silver pentacle offers the most protection.

Do pentacles really protect? I believe so. I kept bees at home for bee venom therapy. They escaped one day. More than fifty bees were loose in my bedroom. My little boy and I were home alone. I closed the bedroom door, trapping them in there, and opened the window. I managed to get out of the room without any of them escaping, shut the door tightly and sealed it with the sign of the pentacle. Then I remembered my son's diapers were in there, so I went back in and repeated the process. It is in the nature of bees to fly out of windows, but this was a cold, overcast day, so I wasn't sure that they would. By nightfall, the bees were gone, except for the ones who never left their box. No one got stung. I just had a lot of honey to clean up. Would the bees have left anyway, without the pentacle on the door? Probably. Did I worry a lot less because I had put it there? Definitely.

Satanists use a downward-pointing pentacle as a symbol of Satan or evil. Their perversion of our sacred symbol doesn't make our symbol evil any more than their inversion of the cross makes that Christian symbol evil.

# CHALICE

The chalice is the vessel of the Goddess, the Holy Grail. Water is its element; its energy is female. Made of glass, metal, or wood, it is used for:

- Mixing salt and water;
- Mixing potions;
- Invoking the power to be human, to be real, to be whole;
- Conjuring emotions;
- Nurturing;
- Presenting offerings and pouring out libations;
- Drinking ritual wine (in traditions that use wine).

I usually use my athame to pour a quantity of salt into a chalice of water, stir it with the athame, then proceed with the spell. I always use tap water, but you can use spring or distilled water if you like.

The chalice I use now is just a glass goblet from a set in my kitchen. It sits on my altar, always full to remind me of all my blessings. It usually just contains water, but I use rosewater when I am giving special thanks to Isis. Water evaporates, so I wash and refill it periodically.

# CAULDRON

This is the womb of the Goddess, the cauldron of inspiration, a place of resurrection. Its element is water, its direction is center, and its energy is female. Cauldrons are sacred to the Welsh goddess Cerridwen, Keeper of the Cauldron of Inspiration. They are traditionally made of cast iron and have three legs. I don't have one because I'm a city witch, but I'd get one if I lived in a house with a hearth or a place where I could make fires in the yard. I'd make pumpkin soup in my cauldron for Halloween, if I did have one. The cauldron is used for:

- Brewing herbs and potions;
- Renewing (rebirth, regeneration, and transformation);
- Reflecting the Moon (for lunar magic);
- Jumping over (for fertility);
- Safely burning things.

The Metropolitan Museum of Art in New York City has a wonderful ancient cauldron in their Islamic Art collection. It's huge and oddly shaped, has a fancy rim, and it's made of black iron and has three legs. I always wonder if it was used for cooking or magic.

# CENSER

A censer is a vessel, usually brass, in which incense can be burned. It corresponds to the elements of air and fire, for obvious reasons. Its directions are East and South. A censer may be simple or elaborate, and is usually kept on the altar. Middle Eastern shops and Catholic religious stores sell covered censers that come with chains so they can be swung back and forth. These are dramatic when used in rituals.

Put some sand or salt in the bottom of the censer. Heat lumps of charcoal until they are red hot, then use tongs to drop a few of them into the censer. Sprinkle solid incense—dried herbs, gum resins, or seeds—on them. Seeds tend to pop, so covered censers are safest. The bottom of the censer may get very hot, even with the sand or salt, so place it on a surface that is not likely to burn.

Censers are also good for burning incense cones. Joss sticks can be safely burned stuck into the earth of a planter, or in ceramic, metal, or wooden holders made for this purpose. Incense is used for:

• Fumigating and smudging;
• Purifying;
• Raising power;
• Achieving trance states;
• Banishing evil spirits;
• Encouraging and welcoming good spirits.

# BROOMSTICK

The witch's besom is a decorative broom used for:

• Symbolic cleansing;
• Sweeping away evil, negative influences, or bad vibes;
• Expelling evil spirits;
• Aspurging and purification (with water).

A broom symbolizes the union of male and female, the joining of phallic stick to feminine brush. Because of this, brooms have long been used in fertility rites such as jumping over at handfastings or "riding" through crops for the fertility of the land. A mistletoe besom is the broom of the thunder god.

# BOWLS

Since water and salt are almost always used in casting spells, you may want to have two special bowls for this purpose. My grandmother's china set came with small footed bowls, so I just use some of these from the kitchen. Witches also often have a special bowl for making offerings to god/desses.

# BELL

A bell or gong can be kept on the altar and rung to banish spirits, entities, negativity, or anything else. It can also be used ceremonially, to indicate that a ritual is beginning or ending. Whatever use you make of your bell, remember the old saying that you cannot "unring" a bell.

# NECKLACE

Priestesses sometimes wear a special necklace inside the circle. This necklace is the circle of rebirth, a sign of the Goddess. It is traditionally made of alternating jet and amber beads, but you can select any sort of necklace that has meaning for you. I wear a gold ankh from Egypt that I never remove, and I have a string of blue and yellow Sumerian beads that are about 5000 years old. I don't see why priests can't also have special necklaces.

# CORDS

Solitary witches don't need these unless they're for cord magic or knot magic. Usually made of silk and 9 feet in length, cords are used by some traditions in coven work for:

- Binding;
- Initiations;
- Control;
- Taking someone's measure.

There are initiation ceremonies in which novices are literally bound, sometimes naked, to the altar. This is supposed to be a solemn, symbolic, religious act and no doubt has ancient origins. It seems darkly sexual to me, however, and I see much potential for abuse in it. I think it's safest to follow the same rules for sex and Wicca: never, ever, allow anyone to tie you up.

## SCOURGE

Solitary witches don't need this either. A scourge is a many-tailed whip that is used by covens in some traditions. Like the flail of the pharaohs, it is an emblem of authority. (Having lived in Egypt, however, I suspect the pharaohs actually used them as fly whisks.) Scourges are used for:

- Severity;
- Enlightenment;
- Astral projection;
- Gaining the Sight;
- Domination/power over others;
- Initiation ceremonies.

They can even be used for punishment in hierarchal traditions in which coven members are under the authority of a high priestess. Forty (gentle) lashes is traditional. This seems more like "S & M" than Wicca to me, but to each his own. Fasting is another way to achieve the first four objectives on this list.

## CELTIC TOOLS

The Celtic torc, a metal circlet worn around the neck, symbolizes power and divinity. The four Tools of Power in ancient Ireland were:

- The sword/arrow of Nuadha;
- The spear/rod of Lugh;
- The cauldron/cup of the Dagda;
- Stone/shield/mirror of Fal.

# THE ELEMENTS

You may have been wondering why I have given elemental correspondences for the tools, or even what the elements are. Earth, air, fire, and water are the four elements of magic. They are sacred to the Hindu goddess Shakti, who embodies the concept of energy. There is something that represents each element in the circle when a spell is cast. This is usually:

- Salt—earth;
- Incense—air;
- Candles—fire;
- Water—water.

Most of us feel an affinity for certain elements over others, and this influences our style of practicing magic. Many things determine this affinity, including astrology, life events, and geography.

Examine your life to determine your own elements. I am a double Taurus who collects rocks and studies herbalism. I keep crystals and other stones on my altar, burn incense on most days, and almost always use plants in my spells. Earth is clearly my element, reflecting both my Sun and Moon signs. Yet most of my spells are fire spells. Why? Perhaps because I almost died in a fire as a young woman, when a building's gas lines blew up.

I have practiced solar magic in Cairo and Los Angeles, but don't use it in New York. If I lived at the beach, I expect I'd be into sea spells and lunar magic. Everything is connected. Everything influences everything else.

Do you go scuba diving, bungee jumping, or mountain climbing? Has your house got a fireplace, fish tank, or wind chimes? Do you garden, fly kites, make pottery, or walk in the rain? What do you collect? What do you fear? Examine your preferences and activities to determine your elements.

Remember that a Wiccan who works weather magic does so *with* Mother Nature, not against her.

# EARTH
## For: Money Spells, Rock Magic, Fertility

PLANET: Earth, Saturn, Venus
TIME: midnight
SEASON: winter
QUALITY: emotional, melancholic, feminine
DIRECTION: North
JEWEL: salt, rock crystal, agate, bloodstone, smoky quartz, carnelian, tiger's eye, emerald
TOOL: pentacle
ZODIAC: Taurus (Fixed Earth), Virgo (Mutable Earth), Capricorn (Cardinal Earth)
COLOR: black, brown, green, white
NUMBER: 4, even numbers
INCENSE: benzoin, fumitory (earth smoke), storax
SYMBOL: grain, globe, orb, stones, acorns, cornucopia, soil, pottery, sand
PLANT: adonis, amaranth, barley, comfrey, grain, hops, ivy, maize (corn), licorice, millet, oak, oats, rice, root vegetables, rye, wheat
ANIMAL: cattle, bison, stag, earth-dwelling snakes, mole, dragon (earth energy), sphinx
RULES: life, birth, growth, nature, money, food, prosperity, silence, wisdom, agriculture, creativity, canyons, caverns, chasms, rocks, caves, metals, agriculture, crystals, matter, stability, strength, trees, bones, mountains, the body, physical reality, standing stones, the sense of touch, the first astral plane, the ability of life to sustain itself
INVOCATIONS: gnomes, grain and mountain god/desses, the sidh, sphinxes
Goddesses:
Anath, Artemis, Bona Dea, Ceres, Cybele Magna Mater, Danu, Demeter (Queen of the Fruitful Earth), dryads, Durga, Ertha, Eve, Fauna, Flora, Gaia (Mother of Life), the Great Goddess, the Great Mother, Hamadryads, Inanna, Isis, Kore, Maia, Mother Earth, Mother Nature, Nokomis, Parvati (the Lady of the Mountain), Persephone, Pomona, Prosperine, Rhea, Rhiannon, Sheela Na Gig, Tellus, Terra, Themis
Sit to invoke Earth Goddesses, with your palms on the ground.

GODS:

Achilles, Adonis, Arawn, Ariel, Atlas, Attis, Baal (Lord of Earth), Bacchus, Cernunnos, Chango Dagon, the Dagda, Dionysus, Enki (Lord of the Goddess Earth), Enlil, the Green Man, Green Zeus, Hades, Marduk, Osiris, Pan, Robin Hood, Uriel, vegetation gods, Vertumnus, Yahweh, Zeus Chronius

---

# AIR
## For: Psychic Work

---

PLANET: Mercury, Jupiter

TIME: dawn

SEASON: spring

QUALITY: contemplative, sanguine, masculine

DIRECTION: East

JEWEL: topaz

TOOL: athame, sword, censer

ZODIAC: Gemini (Mutable Air), Libra (Cardinal Air), Aquarius (Fixed Air)

COLOR: pastels, white, clear, pale blue, bright yellow

INCENSE: frankincense, fumitory, galibanum, myrrh

SYMBOL: incense, feathers, balloons, bubbles, kites, windmills, sails, fans

PLANT: anemone (windflower), aspen, bodh tree, epiphytic plants (such as bird's nest fern), plants and trees that provide incense, pansy, poplar, primrose, vervain, violet, wall fern (polypody), yarrow

ANIMAL: bird, insect, eagle, hawk, sphinx

RULES: thoughts, ideas, flight, knowledge, wind, intellect, breath, learning, intuition, towers, aeries, high and windy places, the mind, the abstract, the mental plane, the sense of smell

INVOCATIONS: fairies, the lilitu (wind spirits), sylphs, sprites, undines, wind god/desses

Goddesses:

Aditi (the Unfettered), Aerope, Aphrodite, Aradia, Arianrhod, Cardea (Queen of Winds), Cybele, Hathor, Hera, Iris, Lilith, Maman Brigette, Mary, Nut, Oya, Semiramis, Urania (Queen of Winds)

Gods:

Aether, Anu, Ariel, Baal (Rider of the Clouds), Boreas, Enlil (Lord Wind), Favonius, Gabriel, Haddad, Horus, Hurakan, Indra, Jupiter, Khepera-Marduk, Mercury, Michael, Mithras,

Njoerd (Lord of Fair Winds), Orion, Quetzalcoatl, Thoth, Typhon (Lord of Destructive Winds), Uranus, Yahweh, Zephyrus, Zeus

WIND SPELLS: Important in the ancient world, when ships depended on their sails for power. To raise a wind, people whistled three times in honor of the White Goddess. White clay whistles were used to summon winds in Majorca, Spain.

## FIRE
**For: Purification, Sex Magic, Healing (to Destroy Disease), Candle Magic, Hearth Magic**

*O for a muse of fire, that would ascend*
*The brightest heaven of invention[10]:*

PLANET: Sun, Mars, Jupiter
TIME: noon
SEASON: summer
QUALITY: destructive, choleric, masculine, phallic
DIRECTION: South
JEWEL: fire opal, pyrite/firestone, amethyst, fire garnet
TOOL: censer, wand
ZODIAC: Aries (Cardinal Fire), Leo (Fixed Fire), Sagittarius (Mutable Fire)
COLOR: red, gold, crimson, orange, white
INCENSE: copal, frankincense, olibanum, rose
SYMBOL: swastika (fire wheel), candle, crucible, matches
PLANT: alder, almond tree in bloom, dittany (burning bush), fire thorn, flame tree, garlic, hibiscus, mustard, nettles, onion, hot peppers, red poppy, rose
ANIMAL: salamander, lion, snake, fire-breathing dragon, horse (when their hooves strike sparks), serpent
RULES: energy, activity, motivation, sight, quickening, blood, sap, spirit, purification, heat, flames, bonfires, lust, life, enthusiasm, passion, the hearth, inspiration, transformation, vitality, sexuality, leadership, combustion, healing, volcanos, destruction, authority, metalwork, incandescence, deserts, eruptions, explosions, anger, the masculine, the power of will, inspiration

---

[10] *The Complete Works of William Shakespeare* (New York: Dorset Press, 1983), p. 459.

INVOCATIONS: djinn, hearth and smith god/desses, the Manes, Salamander

Goddesses:

Astarte, Ashtoreth, Bastet, Berecyntia, Brighid (Lady of the Hearth), Hestia, Ishtar, Kali, Minerva Belisima, Oynyena Maria (Fiery Mary), Pelé, Pyrrha (the Red One), Sekhmet, sylphs, Vesta (the Shining One)

Invoke fire goddesses by throwing salt into flames.

Gods:

Agni (the Purifier, the All-Possessor, the Resplendent, the Divine Fire), Ariel, Baal, Bel, Belenus, Chango, Govannon, Hephaestus, Horus (the Mighty One of Transformations), Michael, Mulciber, Ogun, Prometheus (who stole fire), Raphael, seraphs, Shiva, Surya, Uriel (Flame of God), Velchanus, Vishnu, Vulcan

FIRE SPELLS: To Hindus, fire is the light of life, the brilliance of intelligence, the ardor of strength, the glow of health, the energy of passion, anger and lust, the spark of divine desire.

Fire of Azrael, used to see into the past and learn about past lives, is kindled of cedar, juniper, and sandalwood.

The ancient fire festivals were Sun charms. A burning fire wheel represents the course of the Sun through the sky. Midsummer fire was considered the fire of heaven. In Ireland, coals from the bonfires of the fire festivals were carried into the grain fields as a charm against blight.

Bale fire, or baelfire, is a fire kindled for rituals such as a Sabbat festival. Some credit baelfire with the power to consume negativity or erase misdeeds.

---

## WATER
**For: Healing, Love Spells, Purification, Psychic Work, Fertility, Weather Magic**

---

PLANET: Moon, Neptune, Saturn, Venus
TIME: twilight
SEASON: autumn
QUALITY: emotional, phlegmatic, feminine
DIRECTION: West
JEWEL: crystal, coral, sea salt, jade, pearl, mother-of-pearl
TOOL: chalice, cauldron
ZODIAC: Cancer (Cardinal Water), Scorpio (Fixed Water), Pisces (Mutable Water)

**COLOR:** blue, black, green, clear

**INCENSE:** lotus, myrrh, aromatic rush roots

**SYMBOL:** pitcher, wave, tear, raindrop, snowflake

**PLANT:** aquatic plants, ferns, fungi, lotus, moss, reeds, rushes, seaweed, soma, squill, watercress, water lily, willow

**ANIMAL:** sea mammals, marine life, crocodile, salamander, serpent, sea bird, water-dwelling snake

**RULES:** emotions, fertility, sensuality, intuition, change, sorrow, compassion, receptivity, feelings, tides, love, ecstasy, courage, mystery, daring, oceans, rivers and streams, springs, wells and lakes, waterfalls and pools, marine life, psychic ability, the feminine, the sense of taste, the unconscious, the subconscious, the womb

**INVOCATIONS:** merfolk, Kelpie, Kludde, undines, Wadj Wer, water sprites

Goddesses:

Amphitrite (Goddess of Salt Waters), Anahita (the Great Goddess of Waters), Aphrodite Anadyomene, Artemis, Asherah of the Sea, Astarte, Atargatis, Carmenta, Cerridwen, Erzulie, Eurynome, Gwenhwyfar (the Mermaid), Ishtar, Isis, Kupala, Luonnotar (the Water Mother), Marina, Minerva (navigation), the Naiads, the Nereids, the Oceanids, Ondines, Oshun, Sarasvati (Flowing Water), sirens, the Telchines (the Sea Children), Tethys, Thetis, Tiamat, Yemaya

Gods:

Haddad, Aegir, Apsu (the Deep), Ariel, Baal, Cephissus, Dylan (Son of the Wave), Ea (God of Sweet Waters, Lord of the House of Water), Enlil, Enki, Gabriel, Ganymede, Glaucus, Hapi, Llyr, Manannán Mac Lir, Michael, Neptune, Nereus (the Old Man of the Sea), Njoerd, Oceanus, Osiris of the Mysteries (who springs from the returning waters), Poseidon, Proteus, Raphael, Triton, Typhon

WATER SPELLS: In spell casting, pooled water represents the occult realm. These are three types of water used in spells:

*Holy Water:* usually rainwater, but some witches use water from sacred springs or holy wells, or have their own recipes. I like rosewater.

*Shape-Changing Water:* melted snow, for changes and transformation.

*Virgin Water:* water that has never flowed through pipes: sea water, well water, spring water, and so on.

Rain was often made by sympathetic magic in the ancient world. Making sounds to imitate thunder was a common shamanic technique. The Danaids, priestesses of Demeter at Argos, made rain by pouring water through a vessel with holes in it. Native Americans used rain dances.

PLANTS for rain spells: cotton, ferns, rice, toadstools
INVOCATIONS for rain spells:
Goddesses for rain spells:
Ashnan, Gauri, the Hyades (Rain Makers), Inanna, Ino, Io, Juturna (to end drought), Libya (Dripping Rain), Mujaji (the Rain Queen), Sadwes, Tallay (Daughter of Showers), Sao-Ching, Tefnut, Yemaya
Gods for rain spells:
Abu Ruhm, Chac, the Chiccan, Cocijo, Frey (God of Rain), Hahana Ku, Ilat, Indra, Itzam Na, Kura-Okami-No-Kami (Great Producer of Rain on the Heights for rain or snow), Lung-Wang (the Dragon Kings), Menzabac, the Nommo, Nyame (Giver of Rain), Ryujin, Sudrem, Tlaloc, Tonenili (Lord of the Celestial Waters)

Rain baths were once in vogue for healing chronic rheumatism and nervous disorders. A rain bath consisted of standing naked in the rain, followed by a brisk massage. This was said to heal because of the minerals in rainwater.

Unlike rain spells, sea rituals invoked the ocean deities and used plants like ash and sea kelp. Frankincense is a good incense for sea rituals.

---

## OTHER ELEMENT SYSTEMS
### For: Transformation, Transcendence, Astral Work, Workings That Relate to Time Itself

---

Some traditions count spirit, sometimes called ether or akasha, as a fifth element.

COLOR: clear
INCENSE: mastic
PLANT: almond tree in bloom, mistletoe
ANIMAL: sphinx
INVOCATIONS:
Goddesses: Isis, Shekinah
Gods: Akasha, IAO, Jehovah, Shiva (Lord of Yoga)

Four elements unified by spirit were the basis of Celtic magic. The Druidic universe contained four elements unified by balance.

The Chinese work with five elements, each with its own correspondences:

<u>Water:</u> can give rise to wood; conquers fire:

| | |
|---|---|
| Direction—North | Quality—Salty |
| Season—Winter | Emotion—Fear |
| Numbers—1 and 6 | Rules—Ears, Bones, Bladder, |
| Virtue—Good Faith | Kidneys |
| Nature—Soak and | Color—Black |
| Descend | God—Hsÿan Ming |

<u>Fire:</u> can give rise to earth; vanquishes metal:

| | |
|---|---|
| Direction—South | Quality—Bitter |
| Season—Summer | Emotion—Joy |
| Numbers—2 and 7 | Rules—Tongue, Blood Vessels, |
| Virtue—Propriety | Heart, Small Intestine |
| Nature—Blaze and | Color—Red |
| Ascend | God—Chu Jung |

<u>Wood:</u> can give rise to fire; conquers earth:

| | |
|---|---|
| Direction—East | Quality—Sour |
| Season—Spring | Emotion—Anger |
| Numbers—3 and 8 | Rules—Eyes, Sinews, |
| Virtue—Goodness | Gallbladder, Liver |
| Nature—Be Crooked | Color—Green |
| and Straight | God—Kou mang |

<u>Metal:</u> can give rise to water; destroys wood:

| | |
|---|---|
| Direction—West | Quality—Sour/Sharp |
| Season—Autumn | Emotion—Sadness |
| Numbers—4 and 9 | Rules—Nose, Body Hairs, Lungs, |
| Virtue—Justice | Large Intestine |
| Nature—Yield and | Color—White |
| Change | God—Ju Shou |

<u>Earth:</u> can give rise to metal; overcomes water:

| | |
|---|---|
| Direction—Center | Quality—Sweet |
| Season—All | Emotion—Worry |
| Numbers—5 and 10 | Rules—Mouth, Muscles, |
| Virtue—Wisdom | Stomach, Pancreas |
| Nature—Seed growing | Color—Yellow |
| and Harvest | God—Hou T'u |

Egyptians assigned the following cardinal points to the elements:
North—Earth
South—Water
East—Fire
West—Air

There are five elements in India, each corresponding to a sense:
Ether/Space—Hearing
Air/Wind—Touch
Fire—Sight
Water—Taste
Earth—Smell

# ELEMENTALS

There is more in this world than meets the eye, and elementals fall into that category. Have you ever been transfixed as you watched a building or a forest burn? Have you ever stood on a high balcony, on the deck of a ship, or at the edge of a precipice and felt a sudden, unaccountable urge to throw yourself from it? If so, you have experienced something of the power of elementals.

Elementals, also called devas or djinn, are said to live in the deva kingdom or fairy realm. Envocation is one way to contact them. You find them wherever they may be: by fireplaces, in fields, wells, and windy places, during storms, earthquakes, and brushfires, at the shore—wherever an element makes itself known.

Some people have a natural affinity for a particular element, and a natural ability to make contacts there. This can relate to your astrological sign. Dion Fortune speaks about contacting elementals in *Psychic Self-Defense:*

> *Any elemental contact is stimulating to us, because elemental beings pour forth in abundance the vitality of their own particular sphere, and this vitalizes the corresponding element in ourselves. But if a four-element creature is drawn into the sphere of a single element he is poisoned by an overdose of the one element in which he finds himself, and starved of the other three. It is for this reason that mortals in the fairy kingdom are always said to be enchanted or asleep.*[11]

---

[11]  Dion Fortune, *Psychic Self-Defense* (York Beach, ME: Samuel Weiser, 1992), p. 82.

Elementals, except these of earth, are dangerous to work with. They are very powerful, unpredictable, and usually destructive. Like spirits, they are easier to summon than to banish. Fascination, mental unbalance, and obsession are all hazards of working with them. It is a good idea to have fire insurance before working with fire elementals, and I wouldn't fly if I had been working with air elementals. Dion Fortune says:

> *Elementals have got a one-way intelligence, and it is not well that they should be senior partners in any alliance with human beings.*[12]

For all these reasons, I work with deities rather than elementals. They are not as powerful, but are much safer. Gods and goddesses get the job done. Work with elementals at your own risk.

---

[12] Dion Fortune, *Psychic Self-Defense*, p. 83.

# CASTING SPELLS

If you ask ten witches how to cast spells, you will definitely get ten different answers, because each of us has our own way of working. Magic is a very individual thing. Some witches prefer candle spells, others like image magic or cauldron spells. There is no right or wrong in this—just what is right for you, what works and what doesn't.

I will tell you how I cast spells, but that doesn't mean this is the best way for you to work. You have to practice and experiment until you find your own style. Creativity is of great importance in spellcraft. (While working with this material, please refer to Part III.)

## MAGIC CIRCLES

Imagine a circle inside a square. This is where magic happens, in a circle cast inside the square of the cardinal points. A magic circle is a sacred space that is prepared for rituals or magic. A sexual act is just a sexual act unless it takes place inside a magic circle. Then it becomes the Great Rite, a ritual of the Goddess. Quantum mechanics may someday explain the physics of it, but witches know that the laws of physics operate just a little differently inside a magic circle. Fire burns differently for one thing, and things that do not usually explode are liable to do so.

Witches make magic circles and invoke the Lords of the Watchtowers because it works, because this is an effective way to make magic. Other practitioners make circles to protect themselves from the forces that magic can unleash, but witches do so because circles contain and amplify the power that we raise.

You can make a magic circle by facing each of the cardinal points in turn and invoking a god or goddess of that direction. There is no right or wrong way to do this, just whatever feels proper to you. I usually place a candle or a crystal to mark each of the quarters. I start with North, because that is where the power is. I go N-E-S-W if my spell is one of invitation or increase, N-W-S-E if it is one of decrease or banishment. I describe a circle in the air with my sword, then salute each of the quarters with it.

Each witch has his or her own way of casting a circle. Most witches actually walk or dance in a circle, usually three times. I'm far too crippled for ring dancing, so I use a method that works within my physical limitations. You will have to experiment with different methods until you find the one that works best for you.

A magic circle can exist in your mind, or it can have a physical reality. It can be an actual circle of earth, candles, sand, shells, stones, bones, glitter, chalk marks, or anything else that appeals to you. It can also, like mine, be a circle described in the air with incense, a sword, or a wand. You create the circle with your mind, using the power you channel to construct it. We call them circles, but they are actually spheres that encapsulate the sacred space where the witch is working.

Circular clearings in forests or groves are excellent places to practice magic. If I lived in the country, I would have a circle of trees planted and a slab of rock added for an altar. A circle of standing stones, like a miniature Stonehenge, would also be ideal. Your circle is your own, so make it any way you like.

You can create your own circle ritual or use one found in a book or on the Internet. The invocations should be made aloud. These can be very simple:

> **Hail to the Lord/Lady of the Watchtower**
> **of the _____.**

They can also be quite elaborate, naming the deity and the powers he or she represents:

> **Hail Isis, Queen of the South, gentle Lady**
> **whose strength is love. Let your spirit inform**
> **this circle, add your will to mine.**

You can write your own prayer or invocation with the information given in Part III. Prayers from *The Book of the Dead* included for each direction can serve as circle invocations.

Have everything you need for the spell or ritual ready in the place where you will make the circle. No one should enter or leave a circle, once it is cast, until the spell is finished and the power has been grounded. Again, there are many ways to return the power you have channeled for the spell. I usually open my palms face down, and imagine it flowing from me back into the earth. I say:

> **Circle open/but unbroken,**
> **Power down/to the ground.**

Never forget this step, because omitting it can leave the door open, allowing entities or spirits to slip in and cause strange things to happen.

# MAGIC, MAJOR AND MINOR

I think of magic as being of two types, major and minor. Major magic is more formal. It includes casting a circle, the use of tools, and invocations. It is the most effective type. Practical magic is worked without a circle, often uses commonplace items, and may not require tools at all. It can also be very effective, provided your will is strong enough and properly focused.

Any place that has good energy, that is quiet, private, and without interruptions, will do for casting a spell. I usually work spells in the kitchen, because most of what I need is already there. It's also the safest place in my house in which to burn things. If you have a special place like a grove or garden available to you, use it. If not, don't let that stop you.

Spells are usually performed according to the lunar cycle:

- *Waxing Moon* for spells of invitation, growth, or increase. Example: money and fertility spells.
- *Waning Moon* for discovering inner secrets and spells of banishing, binding, or decrease. Example: spells to end loneliness or financial problems.
- *Full Moon* for maximum power, coven work, sex magic, love spells, and workings of culmination.

There is great wisdom in this. I must admit, however, that, as an urban witch who can't see the Moon from her apartment windows, I pay no attention to the Moon whatsoever. I did follow the Moon, though, whenever I lived in a place where I could see it each night.

Spells can also be performed in accord with the Zodiac. The Sun or Moon in each astrological sign generates the following correspondences.

Aries: battle, beginnings
Taurus: money spells, sex magic
Gemini: communication
Cancer: psychic work, lunar magic
Leo: leadership, solar power

Virgo: purification
Libra: balance, work in law or for justice
Scorpio: power
Sagittarius: honesty, expansion
Capricorn: overcoming obstacles
Aquarius: healing
Pisces: psychic work, endings

## SPELLS AND CORRESPONDENCES

Think of correspondences as lists of ingredients. What exactly do you do with them? Let's take friendship as an example. The correspondences for friendship are:

PLANET: Sun, Venus
ZODIAC: Aquarius
NUMBER: 3
INVOKE: Gilgamesh and Enkidu, Mitra (for intimate friendship)
PLANT: lemon, rosemary, passionflower
JEWEL: rose quartz, alabaster, turquoise, emerald (to strengthen friendship)

Suppose you want to make new friends. First, write or find an appropriate spell for this. Then using these correspondences, you could:

- Cast the spell at noon, when the Moon is in Aquarius;
- Place three lemons in an alabaster bowl on the altar;
- Fill your chalice with passionfruit juice, make a potion of it by charging it with the spell, then drink it down before you close the circle. You could also refrigerate the potion or make a syrup of it and drink some each time you will be meeting new people.
- Wear a turquoise ring until you make a new friend.

## DIRECTING SPELLS

For a spell to work in the intended way, it must be properly directed. You can do this with words, naming your intent aloud. You can also use images, putting representations of the person or thing you want the spell to affect on the altar while you cast it. Old spells sometimes call for hair or fingernail clippings, but I've never used anything arcane like that. We have cameras now.

A person need not be present for you to work magic on, for, or against them. Anything associated with the person can be used to direct the spell—documents, personal items, letters, gifts, pictures—whatever you have. You can also write the person's name on a piece of paper or a candle and use that.

## SPELLS AND POPPETS

A poppet is a humanoid figure. It can be a root, a "voodoo doll," a chess piece, a Barbie doll, a puppet, a paper doll, a piece of twisted wire, or whatever you have at hand. To empower it, say,

**Poppet, I name you _____.**

For magical purposes the figure then becomes that person. If you have a photograph of the person, their face can be affixed to the doll. Poppets should be safeguarded or destroyed once a spell has done its work.

## TIME AND SPELLS

Sometimes, the effect of a spell will be astonishingly immediate. Sometimes, you will have to wait awhile. Be patient and believe in your spell. Repeat your spell if you see no effect after two weeks, making the second spell stronger. If you still see no effect, you can assume the spell was not in accord with the universe and move on to something else. If it's something that's too important for you to drop, try approaching the problem from another direction.

## DISTANCE AND SPELL WORK

Geography is not a barrier. Spells can be worked over great distances. I have often cast spells that worked from one continent to another. A personal connection to the people or situation involved is helpful with this.

## MATERIALS

Don't torment yourself trying to acquire exotic items, use whatever is available to you. Be creative. Learn correspondences, so that you can find good substitutes when a spell calls for something you don't have.

## HERBS

When spells call for herbs, you can plant them, pick them, burn them, eat them, brew them, strew them, make floor washes or decorate the altar with them, put them in a mojo bag—whatever seems appropriate to the spell. Don't ingest any herbs that are not meant to be eaten.

Vegetable markets, florist shops, supermarkets, and health food stores (for essential oils and herbal teas) are good places to start. Dried herbs sold in jars as spices usually work just fine, but fresh herbs are better. You have sources all around you. Identify the trees that grow near your home. Find out if there is a farmer's market or botanical garden near you. Plant an herb garden. Study herbalism.

## CANDLES

Any type of candles can be used. You can get them from a hardware store, a supermarket, or a card shop. Tapers or votives work well. Unscented candles are best, unless you can identify the scent appropriate to your spell. Vanilla candles, for instance, are good for love spells. The colors of the candles should also be appropriate. A stock of candles in various colors is useful to a witch.

An all-purpose unscented white candle can be used for any spell, no matter what color candle is called for. A white candle burned upside down represents a black one. It's always a good idea to charge a candle before you light it. Do this by holding it in your hands as you concentrate on your purpose. You can also rub the candle with oil as you do this, but let it dry before lighting it.

## INCENSE

Joss sticks, smudge sticks, little cones—the form isn't important, but the scent should suit the spell. Some resins, barks, seeds, and dried herbs can be burned directly as incense, over charcoal, but be sure to practice fire safety when doing so. Sandalwood incense is like a white candle. It can be used in any spell or ritual.

Look for incense at card shops, New Age and health food stores, ethnic markets, metaphysical bookstores, on the Internet, and through other religions. Learn to make your own incense if need be. Witches always have incense on hand, for use in spells or as offerings.

## STATUES/ICONS/PICTURES/POSTERS

Try museum gift shops, magical supply shops, bookstores, botanicas, and the Web.

## PAPER

There's no telling from what ordinary paper is made, so I like to use papyrus or linen bond. Papyrus and flax (for linen) are plants that can be made into paper. Papyrus comes from Egypt and may be difficult to obtain, but linen bond is available from stationers and office supply stores.

# FORMAL MAGIC

There are five steps central to formal magic. Each plays a different role in guaranteeing the success of your magical working.

## INTENTION

Your intention focuses your spell and channels your absolute will to succeed. I try to never do a spell unless I feel it well up inside of me beforehand. Spells don't work unless you are able to focus your will. Your intent must be clear, or your spell may have unintended results.

## PREPARATION

The spell actually begins as you assemble your tools and materials, because your will starts to focus itself as you gather the herbs, select the candles, choose the incense, decorate the altar, and lay out your tools. Knowledge of correspondences is essential here, so that you select materials appropriate to the spell.

Incense, candles, music and ceremonial dress, and makeup or masks can all be used to make your space sacred and set the mood for a spell. You should have something to represent each element—earth, air, fire, water—on the altar or other working surface.

## CAST THE CIRCLE, RAISE POWER

- Call corners (also called calling quarters): Magic relates to both time and space. Ancient peoples divided space into the four quarters: North, South, East, and West. Sometimes, they further subdivided it, but the four basic directions are the crucial ones.
- Cast the circle, invoking the Lords of the Watchtowers: The ancients also assigned deities to guard each of the quarters, deities to whom the power of each quarter accrued. The Lords of the Watchtower can be male or female. By invoking them, we call upon their spatial powers to guard and inform our magic circles.
- Raise power: You should feel it between your hands, like the force of two magnets that repel each other, as you invoke the lords or ladies and cast the circle. The power, as the good witch told Dorothy, is in you. Or, to be more precise, the ability to *use* the power is in you. We are conduits for the natural power in the universe. We channel it through our bodies when we do magical work. You effect magic with your will. Spells, incantations, candles, herbs, and crystals are just props that help you channel it in the desired direction.

There are eight ways to raise power:

1. Meditation or concentration;
2. Chants, spells, poetry or invocations;
3. Trance, or projection of the astral body;
4. Incense, drugs, or alcohol;
5. Rhythm (dancing or drumming);
6. Binding, to control the flow of blood;
7. Flagellation, light scourging (traditionally fourty lashes);
8. The Great Rite (ecstatic sexual union).

I usually use incense and psychic concentration, drawing power from wherever I can feel it: the jet stream, an approaching storm, trees, rain, the city, my love, my anger, my desire, the Sun or Moon, even the universe itself. You have to experiment with different methods in order to find the best way for you to raise power. With practice, you will come to recognize the state of psychic readiness that tells you when you are prepared to make magic.

We all experience the sensation of magical power rising in different ways. For some, it is a tingling or warmth, while others may feel it vibrating or hear it whooshing around them. You'll know it when you feel it, whatever form the sensation takes for you. You will also come to know when someone with whom you have a strong connection is casting a spell, even if they are hundreds of miles away.

You can boost your power by invoking the Mighty Ones (the Old Gods), by working with spirits or elementals, by working with other witches, by practicing regular meditation, and by going barefoot, to draw on earth energy.

Power is connected to the Moon. It increases as the Moon waxes, decreases as it wanes. Witches are most powerful at the Full Moon. Many witches wear their hair long because cutting your hair can diminish your power. This is probably why Joan of Arc had her hair shorn before she was burned at the stake.

## CAST THE SPELL

Perform the spell, reciting its words and carrying out whatever actions it requires. The words of a spell should be said aloud, in a commanding voice. This is the word that "goes forth and comes into being, so mote it be." This manifestation of word into deed or of thought into reality is the essence of magic.

## CLOSE THE CIRCLE

Close the circle and ground the power you have raised. Clean up. Carry out any after-spell actions required.

If you have a headache or feel dizzy after casting a spell, you have probably not grounded the power properly. Remove your shoes and socks, if you are still wearing them, and try it again. Go outdoors, if necessary, and actually place your palms on the earth while you do this. If you still feel odd, drink some water and eat something containing sugar or carbohydrates. If you crave salt, have something salty or drink a sports drink designed to replace electrolytes.

# PRACTICAL MAGIC

Practical magic uses intention and preparation, as outlined above, then gets right down to the spell. Visual aids and other props can be used, or you can work the spell with your mind and will alone. The possibilities for this kind of magic are limitless. Inventiveness is the key here.

My usual method is to assemble things on a tray: candles, incense, herbs, the elements, stones or crystals, and things that represent what I am trying to manifest. As with any spell, I make careful choices in selecting the materials. I leave the tray like that for several days or a week, until I feel it has done its work. I may light the candles or burn the incense if I feel like it, or talk to the tray in passing, stating my purpose aloud. If I see no results, I recast the spell formally, with a circle.

Spell bottles can also be used in this way. Everything needed for the spell is assembled in a bottle, which can then be buried.

Balloons can be used for spells. Blow one up, write a name or draw a face on it saying,

**Balloon, I name you _____.**

You can then pop it to deflate someone's overblown ego, let a little air out of it every day to decrease someone's influence, or set it adrift (on air or water) to release someone else, or yourself.

Meditate on ordinary items like keys, ice, pockets, bird cages, mirrors, and photo albums. Use the witch's way of thinking, and I am sure you will invent more spells than I ever could.

# MAKING INVOCATIONS

An invocation is a formal calling upon a god or goddess. Witches work with both the goddess (female) and god (male) energy of the universe, the yin and yang of being. The balance or tension between the two kinds of energy, their polarity, is the source of magic. The names of goddesses and gods are *hekau*, words of power that are chanted to strike a desired vibration in the universe. They are keys that open the correct doors and channel energy in intended directions.

Ancient deities (except for the Great Goddess, who *is* the universe) are thought forms. They are human creations in which particular powers have been invested over hundreds or thousands of years. For example, Aphrodite rules love and sexuality, Neptune rules the oceans, Jehovah/Allah rules power over others, Isis rules help and protection, and Brighid rules healing.

Invocations can be simple:

O, _____!
>  Example: O, Mithras!

Hail, _____!
>  Example: Hail, Marduk!

I invoke _____ . . .
>  Example: I invoke Damkina . . .

I invoke _____ for . . .
>  Example: I invoke Hecate for lunar power.

I call upon _____ . . .
>  Example: I call upon Janus . . .

By _____ I command . . .
>  Example: By Ishtar I command . . .

By the power of _____, I command . . .
>  Example: By the power of Anu, I command . . .

Help me, _____!
>  Example: Help me, Kali!

Or they can be complex:

> **O thou that was before the earth was formed—**
> **Ea, Binah, Ge,**
> **O tideless, soundless, boundless bitter sea,**
> **I am thy priestess, answer unto me.**
> **O arching sky above and earth beneath,**
> **Giver of life and bringer-in of death,**
> **Persephone, Astarte, Ashtoreth,**
> **I am thy priestess, answer unto me.**
> **O Golden Aphrodite, come unto me.**[13]

Invocations can praise:

> **I call upon thee, the ruler of the gods, high-thundering**
> **Zeus, Zeus, king, Adonai, lord, Iaoouêe.**[14]

> **Glory be to Osiris Un-nefer, the great god within**
> **Abydos, king of eternity, lord of the everlasting, who**
> **passeth through millions of years in his existence.**
> **Eldest son of the womb of Nut, engendered by Seb**
> **the Erpat, lord of the crowns of the North and South,**
> **lord of the lofty white crown. As Prince of gods and**
> **of men he hath received the crook and the flail and**
> **the dignity of his divine fathers.**[15]

Or they can invite:

> **Coventina, Mother of Covens, we welcome you to this**
> **circle . . .**
> **Auspicious Sita, come thou near.**

Ancient prayers can be used to form new invocations. This last invocation could be used to invite any deity:

> **_____ (adjective) _____ (name of deity),**
> **come thou near.**
> **Mighty Thor, come thou near.**
> **Golden Aphrodite, draw thou near.**
> **Goat Pan, I call thou to me.**

---

[13] Dion Fortune, *The Sea Priestess* (York Beach, ME: Samuel Weiser, 1991), pp. 218–219.
[14] E. A. Wallis Budge, *Egyptian Magic* (New York: Dover, 1971), p. 177.
[15] E. A. Wallis Budge, *The Egyptian Book of the Dead: The Papyrus of Ani* (New York: Dover, 1967), p. 253.

Adding a deity's title(s) to an invocation increases its power.

| | |
|---|---|
| Ares, Throng of War | Lugh, Lord of Light |
| Yemaya, Queen of Witches | Scylla, She Who Rends |
| Nergal, the Unsparing | Mot, Prince Dissolution |
| Fortuna, Lady Luck | Ushas, Mistress of Time |
| Marduk, King of Kings | Mary, Queen of Sorrows |
| Nut, Mighty One of Valor | Carmenta, Revealer of Wisdom |

God/desses can also be invoked in special places, at certain times of the day or year, or in particular lunar or solar cycles, and with images, herbs, numbers, and colors.

Knowledge of mythology is helpful with this. Don't worry about it if you are not sure how to pronounce a deity's name. It is my experience that invocations have just as much power if you say the name incorrectly. Intent is what matters.

Deities often have more than one name, or different spellings of their names:

| | |
|---|---|
| Amon/Amun/Amen/Ammon | Chango/Shango/Xango |
| Hela/Hel | Uranus/Ouranos |
| Ra/Re | Bast/Bastet/Ubastet |

For some reason, Ammon, Hela, Ra, Chango, Uranus, and Bastet seem more powerful to me than the other variations of their names. There is no logic in this, but I follow it in my spells. You can do the same, using those names and titles of any deity that evoke the strongest response from you.

# EGYPTIAN INVOCATIONS

I often use Arabic to invoke Egyptian god/desses:

| | |
|---|---|
| Ya, Thoth | Ya, Hathor |
| Ya, Isis | Ya, Ma'at |

The Arabic greeting "ya" functions as "yo" does in Brooklyn (think of Rocky yelling, "Yo, Adrian!"). The *a* is pronounced like the *a* in apple. No expert has the faintest idea how the vowels of the hieroglyphic language were pronounced, so feel free to say Egyptian names any way that sounds right to you. I sometimes use modern Arabic (Egyptian dialect) pronunciations for Egyptian god/desses ("th" pronounced as "t," long vowels, rolled "r's," and so on). The following invocations are adapted from *The Egyptian Book of the Dead*.[16]

For a fire goddess:

> **Mistress of Flames, Lady of Strength, Dispenser of Light**

> **Blazing Fire, Lady of Unquenchable Flames, she with tongues of flame which reach afar, the Slaughtering One, irresistible, through which we may not pass . . .**

For a battle goddess:

> **Lady of Terrors, the Sovereign Lady, Mistress of Destruction, who uttereth the words which drive back the destroyers, she who delivereth from destruction . . .**

For astral or Uranus goddesses:

> **Lady of Heaven, Mistress of the World, Lady of Mortals, greater than all men!**

For any goddess who is honored in your home:

> **Lady of the Altar, the Mighty Lady to whom offerings are made . . .**

For a Sun goddess:

> **Lady of Light, the Mighty One to whom we cry aloud . . .**

For a goddess in her dark aspect:

> **I know thee and I know thy name, Goddess with the back-turned face, keeper of secret things, the overthrower, "Sword that smiteth when its name is uttered" is thy name.**

---

[16] E. A. Wallis Budge, *The Egyptian Book of the Dead: The Papyrus of Ani,* pp. 295–298.

For death goddesses:

> Lady of the loud voice, the Terrible One who causes
> those who entreat her to cry, the Fearful One who
> feareth not . . .
>
> Terrible One, Lady of the Rainstorm, who planteth
> ruin in human souls, devourer of our dead bodies,
> the orderer and creator of slaughters who cometh
> forth to judge.

# WRITING SPELLS

The cadence of rhyming words carries great power in magic. The *Wiccan Rede* tells us:

> *To bind the spell every time—*
> *Let the spell be spake in rhyme.*[17]

Rhymes have more power than blank verse because rhythm can be used to make magic. A rhyming dictionary can be very helpful with this. Begin by writing short spells. Need inspiration? Just look around you.

> **Air surround**
> **Plants abound**
> **What was lost**
> **I make found.**
>
> **Candle glows**
> **Water flows**
> **Goddess knows**
> **Our love grows.**
>
> **By the Sun and by the sea**
> **Let good fortune come to me.**
>
> **By the corners of the Moon**
> **I witch good things to happen soon.**
>
> **By the stars that shine above**
> **Let me soon find true love.**
>
> **By the grass, sparkling with dew,**
> **I make my heart's wish to come true.**

Little spells like this are charms, easy to create. You'll be able to create them on the spur of the moment once you have some experience. Then you can progress to writing real spells.

---

[17] Lady Gwen Thompson, "The Rede of the Wiccae," *Green Egg*, vol. VIII, no. 69, Spring, 1975, p. 10.

# CORRESPONDENCES

The first step in writing a spell is to research the correspondences that relate to the subject of your spell. These include the gods or goddesses you want to invoke, the colors and plants you want to use, the planet under which the spell falls, and anything else that will strengthen your spell. This book is full of such information.

If your topic has numerous correspondences, select those that seem most meaningful or powerful to you. A spell can be simple or complex, but it must be specific. You cannot achieve your intended result unless you clearly build it into the spell.

> **I entreat you, Holy Mother,**
> **Send it to me and to no other.**

If the spell has a time factor, include that as well.

> **This spell shall lose its force**
> **When the Moon has run its course.**

# CREATING SPELLS

The easiest way to teach you how to write a spell is by example. Study the correspondences in Part II (Love), then consider these example spells:

**SPELL FOR BRINGING LOVE INTO YOUR LIFE**

Aphrodite is an appropriate deity to whom both men and women may appeal:

> **I in She and She in me**
> **Aphrodite of the Sea**
> **O mighty Aphrodite,**
> **Let love find me!**

The strongest spells employ props and actions as well as words. In this case, you can complete the spell by getting five pink or orange balloons (heart-shaped ones if you like), writing your name on slips of red paper with silver ink, and putting one in each balloon before it is filled with helium. Do this on a Thursday. Attach peacock feathers to each balloon and tie them to your altar overnight. Scatter herbs of love on the altar. Then burn five pink candles and rose, patchouli, or some other appropriate incense (away from the balloons!). Using the list of god/desses from Part II (Love), invoke those deities who grant the type of love you hope to find. Pray. Take the balloons outside on Friday and separate them. Release them one by one, as close as possible to the place where you live. As you release each balloon say:

> **I in She and She in me**
> **Aphrodite of the Sea**
> **O mighty Aphrodite,**
> **Let love find me!**

A similar spell could be created with a net, if you live near the ocean or a mighty river. Use symbolism of casting a net upon the waters and invoke Aphrodite in her Fish Goddess aspect.

If you wish to attract a lover rather than love, perform the spell over a bowl of fruit: figs to attract a female lover, bananas to attract a male, both if you're hoping for an orgy. Charge the bowl with the spell, then eat the fruit. Wear something orange for several days thereafter.

### SPELL TO FIND A HUSBAND

The Egyptian goddess Hathor grants husbands to those whom she loves. Gold and turquoise can be used to invoke her, so this spell uses a necklace made of them.

Cast this spell at midnight on a Friday, when the Moon is waxing or full. Decorate the altar for a love spell, using roses and the color red. Include an image of Hathor if you can get one. Place the card of the Emperor from a tarot deck at the center of the altar, atop the pentacle. Cast a circle. Swing the necklace like a pendulum, back and forth over the card, as you say:

> **Send me the Emperor, the good king of my life,**
> **The man who will love me as both witch and wife.**
> **Make him kind and never cruel,**
> **Let him treasure me as a jewel.**
> **Give me a home and give me a hearth,**
> **A safe space for worship and freedom from want.**
> **Send me the Emperor, the good king of my life**
> **The man who will love me as both witch and wife.**

Repeat this seven times, swinging the necklace over the card. Close the circle. Wear the necklace until a husband appears. (Men can craft a spell that invokes Ah Kin, who brings wives to bachelors.)

## SPELL TO ATTRACT THE
## ATTENTION OF THE ONE YOU DESIRE

Get essential oil or extract of marjoram. This is often sold in health food stores and vitamin shops. If you cannot locate it, get dried marjoram from a gourmet shop or supermarket and put it in a glass jar or bottle with just enough olive or sunflower oil to cover it. Seal it tightly and leave it in the Sun for a week, then strain off the oil and use that for the spell.

Take a big orange candle and set it in a dish of glue on your altar. A picture of the person or a slip of paper with their name written on it can be put in the glue. Cast a circle. Light the candle and perform the following spell, charging the oil with it.

> **By the four posts of my bed**
> **I turn your head,**
> **I turn your head.**
> **By my loins and by my thighs**
> **I draw your eyes,**
> **I draw your eyes.**
>
> **With marjoram and a bowl of glue**
> **I make you think of me as I think of you.**
> **I cause you to look at me,**
> **I cause you to look at me**
> **I make you enchanted by what you see.**

Keep the candle on the altar until it burns out and the glue sets completely. Don't worry if melted wax mixes with the glue, just leave it alone until everything hardens.

Wear the oil as perfume until the spell works. Make a surreptitious trail of it from that person to yourself. Do this on a map if the person lives far away. Put several drops of the oil on your doorstep.

Note that, if the spell does not include the last two lines, you may attract the person's attention without attracting his or her affection.

# CLOSING SPELLS

The usual closing for a spell is, "So mote it be." I have no idea where that phrase originated. It may be nothing but pseudo-arcana, so I prefer to end spells in this way:

**I make this the Word**
**That goes forth and comes into being.**

This manifestation closing, derived from ancient Egyptian sources, can be altered in any way you like, for example,

**I send this Word forth**
**And bring it into being.**

# LANGUAGES

Spells can be written in any language you understand, ancient or modern, as long as they make sense. Your communication with the universe is actually psychic. Mystical-sounding nonsense words will not work unless you have a firm idea of what they mean to you.

# INSPIRATION

It may be difficult for you to get started in this if you are not accustomed to creative writing, but there are things you can do to unblock yourself. Use moonlight and white candles for inspiration. Pray to Isis, Lady of Spells (an Egyptian goddess), Ogma, for words of bespelling (a Celtic god), Kamrusepas, Goddess of Spells (a Hittite/Hurrian goddess), or Thoth (the Egyptian god of creativity, writing, and magic).

# SOURCES

Use a thesaurus to expand your vocabulary and find more creative ways of expressing yourself. The holy books of other religions (the Rig Veda, the Bible, the Book of the Dead) can be sources of inspiration. These lines, for example, are from the Koran, and can be used to cast a wind spell:

> By the emissary winds
> Sent one after another
> By the raging hurricanes
> Which scatter clouds to their destined places
> Then separate them one from another[18]

These, also from the Koran, could be used for casting a spell that relates to time:

> By the stars that run their courses
> And hide themselves
> And the night when it departs
> And the morning when it brightens.[19]

It isn't all that difficult to write a spell. Try it and see what happens. Don't worry if your early spells aren't very effective, you'll get better at it with practice.

---

[18] M. H. Shakir (trans.), *Holy Qur'an* (Elmhurst, NY: Tahrike Tarsile Qur'an, 1985), p. 399.

[19] M. H. Shakir, *Holy Qur'an*, p. 405.

# PART II
# THE CRAFT

# INTRODUCTION

Disengagement from the world is the highest spiritual path of Hinduism; not so in Wicca. Active, positive engagement with the world around us is the way of the witch. Witchcraft usually begins on a personal level, with spells for love, money, or wishes. As witches mature in the craft, however, they become adept at raising power and using it. Bearing witness to the transformational power of magic, magic starts to turn outward and be used for the good of others.

Participation in life does not mean we should be magical busybodies, casting spells every time we see things in people's lives that we think need fixing. Magical ability is not a license to impose or intrude, especially not on people whose belief systems forbid magic. Some witches say that, if you use magic on someone's behalf without their permission, the positive energy you put forth will be returned to you negatively—threefold. People generally ask for help when they need it, especially from witches.

We use our sensitivity and intuition to hear cries for help in whatever form they may take. A cry for help can be subtle, so we must pay attention to what people are not saying as well as to what they are saying. We use our experience and common sense to decide whom we should help, and to determine how and when we should help them. We definitely *do* impose our will on people who are doing great harm—people like serial killers, rapists, and tyrants. But we also recognize those situations wherein people must help themselves. We do the best we can, but know that we cannot help everyone or fix everything. We know that witchcraft is about what we can give, not what we can get. We also know that, in accordance with the Law of Three, the more we give, the more we will get. We put forth positive energy and accept the blessings that flow to us in return.

Community renewal, healing, helping a couple to have a child, binding criminals, protecting sacred places, averting storms, helping a spirit move into the light, resolving conflicts, finding lost children—these are all examples of the work of a witch in the world.

This section explores several areas in which the craft may be used. Goddesses are listed before gods in the invocation lists (they have been separated in the shorter lists by a semicolon). Groups of god/desses and beings of dual or ambiguous gender are listed at the top of the lists. Don't be confused by the fact that there are different gods and goddesses with the same names. For example, Dön is the Celtic mother goddess as well as a Celtic pantheon god. Sin is the Irish fairy goddess as well as the Mesopotamian Moon god. Kwan-Yin is both the Chinese god and goddess of the Southern Sea. Recommended plants are denoted with a star (*). With the exception of the usual fruit, vegetables, and culinary herbs, they are meant as charms only and *not* to be eaten.

# CREATIVITY

There are old superstitions about ways to distract witches, but if you want to distract a whole room full of us, all you have to do is start talking about food. Most witches are great cooks. No surprise there, since cooking utilizes some of the same talents used in spellcasting: creativity, knowledge of herbs, an eye for design, and the ability to apply oneself seriously to the task at hand. A pinch of this, a dash of that, add fire, and *voilá*. Cooking and magic both provide tangible results.

Witches are creative people, as the number of personal witchcraft sites on the Web demonstrates. Many witches are professional craftspeople. This is a direct result of our religion. To make anything is to participate in the great creative nature of the Goddess. Whether it be through poetry, gardening, woodworking, fabric arts, smithcraft, pottery, or sculpture, creation is holy, a sacred task. Many witches have found their path through their craft.

*So far as I know, the Bronze Age and early Iron Age smiths who, like the poets and physicians, came under the direct patronage of the Muse, never embellished their work with meaningless decoration. Every object they made—sword, spear-head, shield, dagger, scabbard, brooch, jug, harness-ring, tankard, bucket, mirror, or what-not—had magical properties to which the shape and number of its various decorations testified.[1]*

## CORRESPONDENCES FOR CREATIVITY

**PLANET**: Earth, Mercury (for communication), Moon (for inspiration), Sun
**ELEMENT**: All

---

[1] Robert Graves, *The White Goddess* (New York: Farrar, Strauss and Giroux, 1966), p. 292.

**BEST TIMES**: Monday, Wednesday, Sunday, waxing Moon for beginning a work, nearly Full Moon for inspiration, Full Moon for completing a work, waning Moon for self-criticism and reworking

**ZODIAC**: air signs for words and mental work, earth signs for crafts and handiwork, fire signs for creative energy, water signs for emotional expression

**NUMBER**: 1, 3, 4, 6, 9

**COLOR**: violet, yellow, gold, silver, white

**PLANT**: cinnamon, ginseng, laurel, lavender, myrtle, nutmeg, skullcap, *valerian, fennel, hazel

**ANIMAL**: turtle, spider, parrot, scarab beetle

**INCENSE**: *cinnamon, ginseng, nutmeg, storax

**JEWEL**: aventurine, green tourmaline

**CANDLE**: white for fallow periods

**INVOCATIONS**:

Goddesses:

Brighid, Carmenta, the Triple Muse, Cerridwen, Mnemosyne, Moon goddesses, the Muses:

Calliope, for music and epic poetry

Clio, for history

Erato, for love poems, lyric and erotic poetry, songs and mime

Euterpe, for lyric poetry and flute music

Melpomene, for tragedy

Polyhymnia, for sacred poetry, sacred songs and mime

Terpsichore, for song, dance, lyric poetry, and choral dancing

Thalia, for comedy and pastorale poetry

Urania, for astronomy

Rhiannon, Rigantona, Shakti, the Triple Muse

Gods:

Brahma, Dionysus, Ea, Enki (god of shaping), Genius, Goibniu, Khnum (Who Fashions Forms), Lugh (Lord of Skills, Master of all Arts), Marduk, Mimir, Nudimmud (Image Fashioner), Prometheus, Ptah the Artificer, Thoth, Weng Shiang

FOR:

Acting:

Invoke: Polyhymnia (mime), Thalia (comedy), Melpomene (tragedy); Kao Kuo-Jiu

Architecture:
   Invoke: Athena; Mushdamma
Art (see also sculpture):
   Invoke: Chibirias (painting), Tx Hun Tah Dz'ib (Lady Unique,
   Owner of the Paintbrush); Ganesha
The Arts:
   Invoke: Tezcatlipoca
Astronomy:
   Invoke: Urania; Aktab Kutbay, Mercury, Thoth
Boat Building:
   Invoke: Kan, Tanemahuta
Brewing:
   Invoke: Govannon
Communication:
   Invoke: Vac (oral communication); Al Lisan (the Tongue), Al
   Shafi, Hermes, Mercury, Ogma Cermait (the Honey-
   Mouthed), Thoth (Lord of Divine Words), Vagisvara (Lord
   of Speech), Ve (speech)
Eloquence:
   Invoke: Oya, Sarasvati Vagdevi, Vagdevi; Arawn, Bragi, Ogma
Construction:
   Invoke: Ea, Mushdamma (Great Builder of Enlil)
Crafts:
   Invoke: Ishi-Kori-Dome (stone cutting and mirror making),
   Minerva (the useful and ornamental arts), Xochiquetzal;
   Credne, Ea, Goibniu, Hephaestus, Kabta, Kothar-and-Hasis,
   Luchtaine (Wheelwright), Mummu, Ptah (the Artificer),
   Vulcan, Wayland Smith
Creative Vision:
   Invoke: Turan (visionary imagination), Vac
Dance:
   Invoke: Hathor (erotic dance), Hulda, Terpsichore, Xochi-
   quetzal; Shiva Nataraja (Lord of the Dance)
Entertaining:
   Invoke: Aryaman (formal hospitality)
Fabric Arts (see also Weaving):
   Invoke: Arachne, Athena, Klotho (spinning), Minerva (spin-
   ning, weaving, embroidery, needlework), Penelopeia
   (tapestry work), Perchta (spinning), Tonantzin (spin-
   ning)
Fashion:
   Invoke: Inanna, Uttu

Hairstyling:
 Invoke: Lu Tong Pin, Ninkarnunna
History:
 Jewel: amber
 Invoke: Clio
Inspiration:
 Planet: Moon
 Element: Fire
 Number: 1, 5, 9, 11
 Jewel: opal, selenite, blue topaz, amethyst, blue onyx (higher inspiration), blue celestite (divine inspiration)
 Invoke: Artemis Caryatis, Athena (who inspires architecture), Brighid (Lady of Bright Inspiration), Cardea, Cerridwen (Keeper of the Cauldron of Inspiration), Coventina, Gwenddydd wen adlam Cerrddeu, Sarasvati (poetic inspiration), Sulis, the White Goddess; Dionysus, Mimir
 Plant: the sound of wind in the willows for poetic inspiration
Interior Design:
 Invoke: Lu Pan
Jewelry Making:
 Invoke: Chantico (precious stones), Sokar (goldsmithing), Tama-No-Ya, Xipe Totec (precious metals)
Literature (see also Poetry and Writing):
 Invoke: Nissaba, Parna-Savari; Anantamukhi, Cermait, Kuei Shing, Ruda, Shong-Kui, Weng-Shiang
Martial Arts:
 Invoke: Scathach, Ursel
Masonry:
 Invoke: Kulla
Mathematics:
 Invoke: Sheshata
Metalwork:
 Invoke: Brigid (smithcraft, metalwork); Credne, Gibil, Govannon (smithcraft), Hasameli, Itztapal Totec (precious metals), Kinyras, Ninegal (Strong-armed Lord, smithcraft), Qaynan, Sokar (goldsmithing), Volundr (smithcraft), Vulcan, Wayland Smith, Xipe Totec (precious metals)
Music:
 Invoke: Calliope, Echo (sad songs), Erato (songs), Euterpe (flute music), Harmonia, Hathor (erotic music), the Hesperides (singing), Hulda, Morgen, the Naiads, Polyhymnia (sacred

songs), Sarasvati (the Flowing One), the Sirens (song), Terpsichore (song), Vina, Xochiquetzal; Apollo, Apollo Citharoe-
dus (lyre music), Bes, Chango, Ihy, Kai Yam (Singing Lord),
Kinnar (Divine Lyre), Mabon, Orpheus, Pan (piping), Thoth

Poetry:
Invoke: Banfile, Boand, Brighid, Calliope (epic poetry), Erato
(love poems, lyric and erotic poetry), Euterpe (lyric poet-
ry), the Graiae (poetic mysteries), Marina, the Naiades,
Polyhymnia (sacred poetry), Sarasvati (poetic inspiration),
Terpsichore (lyric poetry), Thalia (pastorale); Ah Kin Xoc,
Apollo, Bragi, Ogma
Plant: for poetic inspiration, the sound of wind in the willows

Pottery:
Invoke: Athena, Kumbhamata (Mother of Pots), Nin-bahar
(Lady Potter)

Scholarship:
Invoke: Acchupta, Cakresvari, Kulisankusa, Mahakala (Great
Kali), Mahamanasika, Manavi, Naradatta

Science:
Invoke: Mahakala, Thoth

Sculpture:
Invoke: Athena, Nin-dim (Lady Fashoner); Enki (god of shap-
ing), Khnum (Who Fashions Forms), Nudimmud (Image
Fashioner), Ptah the Artificer

Tattooing:
Invoke: Acat

Weaving:
Invoke: Chibirias, Ix Chel, Ix Zacal Nok (Lady Cloth Weaver),
Minerva, Penelopeia, Tonantzin

Web Work:
Invoke: Arachne, Ariadne, Spider Woman, Anansi

Writing (see also poetry and literature):
Invoke: Kubjika, Ratnolka, Sarasvati, Sefkhet-Abwy, Seshata
(Lady of the House of Books); Aktab Kutbay (the Greatest
Scribe), Arsu, Ea, Enoch, Ganesha, Hermes, Idris, Nebo,
Ogma, Thoth (Lord of Books)

Woodworking:
Invoke: Hiko-Sashiri, Luchtar, Lu Pan, Nin-ildu, Yvastar (Divine
Builder)

# FERTILITY

Fertility has become an issue in the West, as we delay having children into our thirties, our forties, and beyond. The fertility of Earth and all her creatures is also of concern to witches, who try to live in harmony with nature. The myth that witches fly on broomsticks came from the practice of "riding" broomsticks through fields to ensure good crops. A broomstick isn't necessary, however. You can simply walk through a field or around a garden, channeling the life force, to achieve the same result.

If you are trying to have a child and medical science has failed you, magic is definitely the way to go.

- Get in touch with the Goddess, the universe, god, the Big Energy—call it by whatever name you will. Communing with the Moon, which rules semen, menstruation, and the womb, is a good way to do this. When you can feel the creative energy of the universe, the urge toward life, draw it into yourself. Don't be discouraged if it takes you some time to learn to do this. Practice it on a regular basis, especially when the Moon is full.
- Children choose their parents, not the other way around. Make a place in your heart, your home, and your life for the baby. Take a concrete step: buy a teddy bear, stop smoking, get out your childhood toys, write a poem, set up a room— whatever feels right to you. Trust yourself.
- Practice the magic and rituals that feel appropriate to you, your partner, and your situation.
- When you are ready, address the universe. Speak to the pool of souls awaiting rebirth. Inform them that you are ready to host a soul, and that you promise to be the best possible parent/s for the child that chooses you. Fill yourself with love for the yet-to-be-conceived child, because love overcomes all physical obstacles.
- Wait patiently, remain committed to your goal. A soul may have already chosen you, but is waiting for the planets to line up so that it can come through at the right karmic time. Keep following whatever medical regimine you have been following, if that feels right to you.

- Be open to the idea that biology isn't everything. Consider adoption or fostering a child. The soul that chooses you may be born to someone else, but may nevertheless become your child. Egyptian mythology gives us the example of Isis adopting her nephew, Anubis, the jackal-headed god who had been abandoned as an infant. She reared him and he became her devoted ally. Adoption is pleasing to the Goddess.

This method worked for me. I made a deal with the Goddess. I told her that, if she had the soul of a witch waiting to be reborn, I would be willing to host that soul, to love and cherish and raise it to the best of my ability. I got pregnant almost immediately, without medical assistance, when doctors in two countries had declared me completely infertile. A red-haired mojo boy of mixed Celtic, Saxon, and Egyptian blood came through—the Goddess's own child, born in love and magic, at midnight on a Friday.

Opening to the Goddess also worked for my sister, a Christian who had her first child with the aid of fertility drugs and a novena to St. Anthony. Desperate for a second child, she finally got pregnant with an extreme fertility treatment that almost killed her and caused the baby to miscarry. She spent weeks in the hospital and then in a wheelchair. The physical recovery was nothing, however, compared to her emotional trauma. The healing took time, as all healing does. When she was ready to try something new, she stopped seeing her fertility doctor, got in touch with the universe, and had a healthy second child.

## FERTILITY CHARM

In India, three types of soil are considered to have the power of fertility: earth dug up by the horns of a wild boar, earth dug up by the horns of a bull, and earth from a prostitute's doorway. These were all offered to Durga during the festival of Durga Puja.

## HATHOR SPELL TO GET PREGNANT

Offer leafy green vegetables to Hathor with this prayer:

**Mother of Children, be kind to me.**[2]

---

[2] Jonathan Cott, *The Search for Om Sety: A Story of Eternal Love* (New York: Doubleday, 1987).

Remember that, with this spell, you are leaving it up to the goddess. It may be that, for some reason, you should not get pregnant.

## CORRESPONDENCES FOR FERTILITY

PLANET: Moon, Full Moon
ELEMENT: earth, water
DIRECTION: South, in Ireland
SYMBOL: yoni
NUMBER: 7, 8
COLOR: dark blue, green, emerald green, red
JEWEL: amethyst
INCENSE: patchouli, pine, violet
ANIMAL: cattle, horse, pig, fish, serpent, snake, dove, parrot
PLANT: banana, bistort, bodh tree, carrot, chickweed, cuckoo flower, cucumber, cyclamen, dock, fig, fly agaric, gentian, grape, juniper, *lettuce, mandrake, *mistletoe, olive, peach, pine, *pomegranate, poppy, *pussy willow, *rice, sage, *St. John's Wort (gathered naked on Midsummer Eve), sunflower, violet, *wheat
INVOCATIONS: Anjea, tree spirits, Wadj Wer (the Mighty Green One)
Goddesses:
Abundantia, Aditi, Althaea (She Who Makes Grow), Amaterasu, Anahita, Anath, Aphrodite, Aradia, Arianrhod (the High Fruitful Mother), Artemis, Asherah, Ashtoreth, Astarte, Atargatis, birth goddesses, Bona Dea, Brighid, Ceres, Cerridwen, cobra goddesses, Cybele, Demeter (Mother of Abundance and Fertility), Diana, Durga, Earth goddesses, Freya, Frigg, Ganga, Goda, Habondia, Inanna Ishtar, Isis (the Green One), Ix Chel, Kadesh, Kore, Lailah, Lakshmi, Latona, Maeve, Mardoll, Mater Matuta, Myrrha, Nemain, Nerthus, Oya, Parvati, Renenutet, Rhiannon, Rosmerta, Sita, Smyrna, Sri Lakshmi, Syria Dea
Gods:
Haddad, Adonis, Amun, Attis, Bel, Chango, the Dagda, Dionysus, Ea, El, Enki, Eros, Freyr, Haddad Hapi, Hermes, Indra, Jaguar, Khonsu, Kronos, Liber, Min, Mithras, Father Nanna, Pluto, Priapus, satyrs, Shiva, Tammuz, Zeus Chronius

FOR:
Children:
Invoke: Anahita, Astarte (Conceiving Womb), Hathor (Mother of Children), Heket (to get pregnant), Kishimojin (to get

pregnant), Kwan-Yin (Hearer of Cries, for childless women), Lucina, Sarasvati (procreation), Sasthi, Sung-Tzu Niang-Niang (the Lady Who Bestows Children), Yemaya (to cure infertility); Enki (male infertility), Mutinus, Obatala (who makes barren women fertile), Wamala, Wepwawet (who opens the way to the womb)

A Fruitful Marriage:

Invoke: Xochiquetzal

A Son:

Invoke: Sarasvati (the Bountiful, invoked by men who want sons); Chang Hsien

Fertility of Animals:

Invoke: Artemis (Lady of all Wild Things), Epona (domestic animals), Hatmehyt (fish), Perchta (sheep and cattle); Damuzi, Enten

Fertility of Crops:

Invoke: Al 'Uzza, Ashnan (grain), Durga; An (Father Who Makes the Seed Sprout), Damuzi (grain)

Fertility of the Earth:

Invoke: Damkina, Spandaramet, Tellus; Pan

Fertility of the Land:

Invoke: the Vanir; Baal, Serapis

Fertility of the Natural World:

Invoke: Inanna

Fertility of Plants:

Invoke: Al-Khidr (the Green One), Damuzi, Enlil

Fertility for Trees and Vines:

Invoke: Ningishzida (Lord of the Good Tree)

Plant: vervain root

# HEALTH AND HEALING

It is incumbent upon us, as witches, to use the craft in positive ways. Healing—whether of people, animals, nature, or situations—is a wonderful use of our skills. This is the thing for which people most often seek our help.

Doctors swear the Hippocratic Oath before they begin to practice medicine. They swear by Apollo the Physician to do no harm, an oath very like our witch's law. Basic knowledge of herbalism, psychology, and astrology can help a witch to help others. Common sense is also important, however. Magic isn't the answer to every problem, so we must not hesitate to refer people to doctors, 12-Step Programs, or counseling. We should practice complementary medicine, using magic to augment medical or psychological care.

I know a lot about healing because I have multiple sclerosis. I think of the disease as a dragon that sleeps curled around my spine, a kind of reverse kundalini energy. Sometimes the dragon sleeps. At other times, it awakens, stretches, and breathes fire. There is a renewed need for healing with each attack. I battle this dragon with witchcraft. I seldom go to doctors or take medication. Instead, I have sustained myself with herbs, bee venom, magic, and positive thinking. It works. I am supposed to be blind and in a wheelchair by now, according to the doctors, but I am not. I will never again be as I once was, but I am doing much better than expected. Healing is something that witches do well.

I have tried to see MS as a gift rather than an affliction. It has destroyed my former life, taking from me everything that I once had. But it has given me other things. Because of it, I have had time to read, to study, to write, to find my way to the Goddess, and to grow spiritually. It has made me a better human being. It gave me my marriage and my son. It took me to Egypt. It allowed me to discover the witch within me. I have, at times, been blind or bedridden, but it has not been all bad.

Illness can be instructive, and MS has taught me a lot. I have learned that we are not our bodies. This simple truth is one that took me a long time to learn. My body is sick, not I. I'm just fine, inside my malfunctioning shell. In our normal preoccupation with diet, fashion, beauty, and fitness, it is easy to lose sight of the fact that our bodies are only containers for our real selves. Call it ch'i, prana, or bioenergy, we are actually something infinite and immortal, creatures of light, of energy and spirit. Our bodies sicken and die, but we go on. We come back. The Goddess recycles.

Let me share some of the things that I have learned about healing.

# HEALING YOURSELF

*Quiet Heals:* There were posters all over the maternity ward of the hospital where I had my son that read, "Quiet Heals." This struck a chord with me. Healing takes place in stillness, in peace and quiet. Getting yourself to such a place, internally and externally, is essential to healing. I had a C-section at midnight, refused pain medication, was up and about at 6 A.M. The doctors expected I would be paralyzed—even assigned me to a room with a paralyzed woman—but I checked myself out a day early.

Our bodies contain a healing force that we need to contact in order to get well, or to keep from getting worse. It is in stillness that we can reach this force. I often use visualization for healing, so I do this late at night, when everyone else is asleep and the house and the neighborhood are quiet. Still the noise and you will begin to heal.

*Bend Instead of Breaking:* Trees are wise. There were tall, narrow evergreens in the yard of the house where I grew up. Weighted by snow after a heavy storm, they bent almost in half, until they were laid across the back roof. They bent instead of breaking, waiting for spring. This is what we need to do when our bodies are assaulted by injury or illness: acknowledge the weight of the burden, then flow with it instead of resisting it. Being in rhythm with nature can accelerate healing.

*Have Patience:* Healing takes time. Time itself is a healing thing. The clichés are true: there are no quick fixes and the only way out is through. Allow at least a year for any major physical healing that you have to do. Psychological problems like addiction and trauma can take even longer. Impatience, anger, and frustration only retard healing. Wait for your cure. Wait for healing. Wait for spring.

***Accentuate the Positive, Eliminate the Negative:*** You must be absolutely ruthless in cutting negative people, habits, and situations out of your life. Your very survival may depend on this. Anyone who really cares about you will understand that you need a positive attitude and environment in order to get well.

***Take Control:*** Be in charge. It's your body, your life, your disease, condition, or problem, not your doctor's. You cannot simply hand it to another and expect that person to deal with it for you. Be a partner, not a patient. Knowedge is power, so empower yourself by learning all you can about what ails you. Taking control will make you feel better. Be open to alternative medicine and therapies, but don't get taken in by charlatans. Seek spiritual help if you need it.

***Major, Chronic, and Terminal Illnesses:*** Diagnosis can be a great shock, one from which some people never recover. Dr. Elisabeth Kübler-Ross, who has done great work on the subjects of death and dying, outlines the stages of reaction to diagnosis as follows:

> denial (not me!)
> anger (why me?)
> bargaining
> depression
> acceptance

I was never angry about having MS, but I did experience these other stages. I can tell you that you should work toward acceptance rather than getting stuck at another stage. Acceptance brings peace, the inner peace required for healing.

We will all die one of these days, no matter how gifted we are at healing or magic. I feared death as obliteration—the Big Sleep—until I found peace in the Goddess, who brings reunion with those who have gone before. If you are facing death with fear or dread, study reincarnation.

***Use Magic:*** Use magic to augment medical care. Spells work for some kinds of healing, but not for others. I have found that a magical attitude is better for dealing with chronic illness.

# HEALING OTHERS

Sick and distressed people are naturally drawn to witches. The quality of our energy attracts them, I suspect. We are not physicians, but we are metaphysicians. We can treat the psychic body. It is our sacred duty to the Goddess to offer whatever help and comfort we can when people come to us for it.

***Tea and Sympathy:*** I always tell people that, if a witch offers you a cup of tea when you aren't feeling well, accept it! This is the simplest thing that we can do for people: boil water, infuse the herbs or tea bag, add lemon, sugar, honey, a shot of rum, or whatever we have on hand that will make someone feel better. A cup of tea prepared by a witch can be a magic potion. Long before I knew I was a witch, I noticed that people felt better when they drank the tea I made for them, if I made it with the intention of helping them.

Listening to people, really listening to what bothers them, is important. Draw them out by giving them your complete attention, without judgment or comment. Let them vent. This alone can make someone feel better. It can also help you diagnose the actual problem. A person may be nauseous because they literally cannot stomach something in his or her life, or may have eye problems because of a refusal to see something. When people complain about a chronic malady or situation, always ask them, "What do you think you should do about this?" You will find that people often already know their solution or remedy, but just have not accessed that information. Never underestimate the power of tea and sympathy.

***Laying-On of Hands:*** Touch can be a healing thing, especially for the elderly, or others who do not have enough physical contact. You can summon power and channel it as healing energy into a person by hugging them. Almost everyone responds to massage. Holding someone while they have a good cry is another healing gesture. When something prevents you from touching a person, summon the power, steeple your fingers, and direct it to them in that way. The last time I did this, the patient, who had been overmedicated, suddenly began vomiting and immediately felt better.

***Healing Circles:*** Covens and other groups of witches can do good work in healing circles, uniting to channel energy to a specific person, group, or situation.

***Remote Healing:*** You don't have to have physical contact, or even be near a person, to help him or her heal. All you have to do is raise power, concentrate on the person and the ailment, then channel energy with the intent of destroying the tumor, easing the pain, or helping the heart to pump. This is advanced work, work that may take some time and practice to master. This is what witches usually do for each other when one is ill or under great stress. They send energy.

# SPELLS FOR HEALING

### FIRE SPELL

Make an image that represents the disease, injury, condition, or problem. This can be a poppet, or something ugly labeled with the disease. It can also be a piece of paper with alcoholism, HIV, asthma, or drug abuse written on it. Make the image something that represents the problem, something that will burn.

Burn this image with healing herbs inside a circle of white candles, invoking any healing gods or goddesses who appeal to you. If you are making this spell on behalf of someone else, place their photograph or something that evokes them inside the circle. Say:

> By _____ I destroy you.
> By _____ I am/you are healed.

Be forewarned, however, I have not found magic to be effective in treating addictions of any kind unless the person is out of denial and asking for help. Great selfishness often underlies addiction, so many people never reach the stage at which you can help them. Move on.

### THE BEAUTY WAY

In her book *Motherpeace: A Way to the Goddess Through Myth, Art and Tarot*, Vicki Noble suggests the Navajo Beauty Way ritual for treating rape victims. Try this prayer:

> The world before me is restored in beauty.
> The world behind me is restored in beauty.

The world below me is restored in beauty.
The world above me is restored in beauty.
All things around me are restored in beauty.
My voice is restored in beauty.
It is finished in beauty.
It is finished in beauty.[3]

I think this is a great idea. The Beauty Way ritual can also be used to treat people who are working out issues of incest or child abuse, emerging from domestic abuse, war, or any other violent situation. The Beauty Way is about survival, about healing and wholeness. The full Navajo ceremony takes several days to complete, including a sand painting made by the shaman who performs it. This prayer, which is part of a much longer one, can be used with purification rites to form a Wiccan healing ritual.


## COLD FIRE

A doctor discovered that I could bring fevers down. It takes a little practice, but I'll bet that most natural witches can do it. Use the Cornish invocation to St. Brigit:

Three ladies came from the East
One with fire and two with frost
Out with thee, fire, and in with thee, frost.[4]

This can be used in conjunction with a laying-on of hands. To remove fever from someone, summon an energy like cold fire from your body. I usually do this by invoking the Snow Queen, who was always a goddess to me.

Direct the energy into your hands, then lay them on the person's neck or forehead. Make the cold fire flow into the person until you feel it confront the fever. When you feel the fever, set up a second channel to draw it into your own body. It may be easiest for you to use your receptive hand to draw the fever, the other to deliver the cold fire. Do this until you feel the cold fire has overcome the fever. If the person is shivering with fever, direct the heat out of the body and onto the skin while you fight the fever. It may help to wrap your arms around the subject.

---

[3] Vicki Noble, *Motherpeace: A Way to the Goddess Through Myth, Art and Tarot* (San Francisco: HarperSanFrancisco, 1994), pp. 123–124.
[4] Robert Graves, *The White Goddess*, p. 394.

This technique is not a substitute for aspirin or other fever-reducers. It is something you can do while waiting for the medicine to kick in. It can also be used in emergencies, when there is no medication. You may feel a bit flushed for a while afterward, but you will not actually take on the fever. Fevers are cyclical, so you may need to repeat the spell whenever the fever spikes.

# CORRESPONDENCES FOR HEALING

PLANET: Sun, Earth, Full Moon, waxing Moon for increased health and the power of healing, waning Moon to banish or diminish disease

ELEMENT: all, fire (to destroy disease)

ZODIAC: Scorpio, Aquarius (for the healing force of the universe)

NUMBER: 1, 3, 7, 9

JEWEL: amber, bloodstone, jade, ruby, green agate, sapphire, turquoise, jasper, jet, aventurine, hematite, garnet, coral, diamond, emerald, beryl, carnelian, peridot, amber and amethyst (for psychological healing), for other kinds of healing:

- Amethyst for addiction and compulsive behavior;
- Aquamarine to soothe the heart;
- Moonstone to balance hormones;
- Opal, onyx, moonstone for emotional balance;
- Pearl for emotional clarity;
- Peridot for mind/body balance;
- Pyrite for vitality;
- Ruby to heal a relationship with a father;
- Sodalite for physical healing.

Bedouins wear gemstone necklaces for healing

COLOR: white, blue, green, gold, orange, magenta (for spiritual healing)

CANDLES: white, red (for organic healing)

INCENSE: cedar, cinnamon, eucalyptus, frankincense, ginseng, pine, rosemary, sandalwood, violet

PLANT (for charms, not as medication!): adder's tongue, amaranth, anemone, *angelica, apple, *balm, *balm of Gilead, barley, bramble (blackberry), burdock, calamus (sweet sedge), cannabis, carnation, cedar, horse chestnut, cinnamon, citron, coriander, cotton, cowslip, cucumber, cypress, dock, elder, *eucalyptus, fennel, flax, gardenia, garlic, geranium, *ginseng, hazel, laurel, lime, mandrake, milkweed, *mistletoe, mugwort, pine, plum, potato, rose, *rosemary, rowan, rue, saffron, sandalwood, wood sorrel, *thyme, vervain, violet, willow, wintergreen

ANIMAL: dog, serpent, two entwined snakes

INVOCATIONS: angels, Alauwaimis (a "demon" who drives away sickness), Nanan Bouclou

Goddesses:

Artemis of the Thousand Breasts, Athena, Brighid (who heals by poetic incantations at sacred wells), Carmenta, Earth goddesses, Gaia, Hygeia, Inanna, Ishtar, Isis, Kadesh, Kupala, Meditrina, Moon goddesses, Panacea, Sarasvati, Sekhmet (Lady of Life), Spes (for the healing power of drug-induced sleep), Sulis Minerva, Tara (Queen of Physicians)

Gods:

Adonis, Asclepius the Healer, Apollo the Physician, Baal Marqod, Babalu-Aye, Belenus, Chiron the Centaur (the Wounded Healer), Dian Cecht (who makes whole again), Govannon, Hercules the Healer, Hermes, Khonsu, Marduk (Great Healer), Mars Ocelus, Mercury, Paeon (Healer of All Ills), Raphael, Shakaburu, Thoth, Vishnu

FOR:

Bleeding:

Invoke: Mud-kesda (Blood Stauncher)

Childbirth:

Invoke: Alemona (health of an unborn child), Aruru, 'Aveta (the Midwife), Brighid (safe delivery), Candelifera (who brings newborns into the light), Carmenta, Eileithya (She Who Aids Women in Labor), Freya (easy childbirth), Hannahhannas Hecate (final stage of labor), Heket, Lucina (She Who Brings to Light), Ninhursag (Lady Mother), Toci

Children (see also Newborns):

Invoke: Edusa (who nourishes children)

Plant (as charms only!): pomegranate blossoms for stomach ailments in children, daffodil for teething pain

Cough:

Plant: black hellebore root

Depression:

Charms and spells may ease the blues, but serious depression requires medical intervention.

**Planet:** Mercury
**Plant:** lemon balm, rosemary, sage, St. John's Wort, wild thyme, valerian, lemon verbena, blue vervain, yerba maté
**Candle:** pink, yellow
**Metal:** gold
**Jewel:** carnelian, coral, garnet, fire garnet, carbuncle, lapis lazuli, sardonyx, sapphire, sodalite, tiger's eye.

Disease:
Invoke: Gula-Bau (Great Physician), Sha'taqat; Hatdastsisi, Hayenezgani (diseases caused by witchcraft)
Plant: hemlock, mugwort, woody nightshade, rue

Epilepsy:
Plant: anise, peony root, vervain

Eye Problems:
Invoke: Yen Kuang Niang-Niang (who cures ophthalmia); Bugid Y Aiba (who restores failed eyesight)
Plant: polygonum root

Fatigue:
Plant: mugwort, southernwood

Giddiness:
Plant: combs made of rosemary wood

To Heal Sick Cattle:
Plant: St. John's flower

To Heal the Heart:
Plant: cuckoo flower

To Heal a Broken Heart:
Invoke: Branwen (who cures passion), Oenone (who heals jealousy and remorse), Tara (Queen of Physicians, who heals sorrows)
Plant: balm of Gilead (poplar buds, carried as close to the heart as possible)

Health:
Color: red, green
Number: 7
Jewel: agate, aquamarine, carnelian, peridot, jet, pearl, ruby
Animal: serpent
Plant: anemone, ash, caraway, carob, camphor, coriander, ferns, figwort, rue, St. John's Wort, wood sorrel, sunflower, tansy, thyme, walnut
Invoke: Ganga, Hygeia, Paraskeva-Platnitsa (health with marriage); Babalu-Aye, Lubanga, Salus, Teharon

Hemorrhoids:
    Plant: lesser celandine
Herbalism:
    Invoke: Greine, Morgen (herbal cures); Acamede (who knows
        all the drugs that grow on Earth)
Hysteria:
    Plant: pennyroyal
Impotence:
    Invoke: Uliliyassis
    Plant: yohimbine
Infection:
    Plant: southernwood
Leprosy:
    Invoke: Oreithyia
    Plant: white poplar leaves
The Limbs:
    Invoke: Khnum (who knitteth together and strengtheneth the
        limbs)
Long Life:
    Invoke: Hsi Wang Mu, Takotsi (Our Grandmother Growth),
        Ushas; Fukurokuju, Junrojin, Shou-hsing, Shou-lao
    Plant: angelica, cypress, lemon, peach, sage, tansy
Mental Disorientation:
    Plant: pennyroyal
Newborns:
    Invoke: Juno (for a healthy baby), Juno Lucina, Lucina (eyesight
        of newborns); Mayin (who breathes life into newborns),
        Weri Kumbaba (speedy recovery after circumcision)
Pain:
    Jewel: aquamarine, jasper
    Invoke: Achelois (She Who Drives Away Pain), Kwan-Yin (who
        frees from pain); Achelous (He Who Drives Away Pain)
Pestilence:
    Plant: angelica
Preventive Medicine:
    Invoke: Hygeia
Poison:
    Invoke: Janguli (Knowledge of Poisons)
    Plant: black hellebore root, figs and rue, heliotrope, mistletoe
Rheumatic Cramps:
    Plant: willow leaves and bark

<u>Seasickness:</u>
   Plant: feverfew
<u>Skin Eruptions:</u>
   Plant: henbane, lesser celandine
<u>Snake Bite:</u>
   Invoke: Janguli (Knowledge of Poisons); Aker
<u>Vertigo:</u>
   Plant: woody nightshade
<u>Warts:</u>
   Plant: beans

# LAW AND JUSTICE

As we mature in the craft, there comes a desire to reach out and do some good in the world. Work in law and justice is an excellent outlet for this. There is much good that a witch or a coven can do. Crime prevention, justice spells, binding criminals, influencing sentencing, preventing passage of laws that limit freedom, and helping authorities solve unsolved crimes are all good ways to be of service.

There have been recent cases in the United States of children forbidden to wear pentacles to school, schools banning Wicca, even witches threatened with losing their jobs or children because of their religion. Witches in legal professions are the ones best able to protect all of us from bigotry, ignorance, and religious intolerance, but there are ways we can all help.

Freedom of religion is of paramount importance to witches— freedom of religion for all. When Congress considered passing a law forcing public schools to post the Judeo-Christian Ten Commandments, American witches were outraged by this proposed infringement of the constitutional guarantee of separation of church and state. We wrote thousands of letters to schools and lawmakers. Our letters did not insist that the Wiccan Rede be posted alongside the Ten Commandments. On the contrary, they insisted that, if the Ten Commandments were posted, the sacred codes of *all* religions should be posted along with them.

Witches need to be vigilant lest the witch hunts begin again. Wicca seeks no converts, engages in no proselytyzing, yet our numbers swell each year. Even though we live and let live, state religions and quasi-state religions may begin to feel threatened as our numbers grow. I doubt it will be long before some witch somewhere sues to have a Yule pentacle erected beside the Hanukkah menorah and Christmas nativity scene. Our best defense is a proactive approach. Vigilance requires that we work to protect everyone's right to worship as they choose, that we protect it by writing letters, signing petitions, and doing whatever else we can.

There are historians who claim that nine million witches and accused witches were put to death during the Burning Times. That number sounds high to me, but who can say for sure? I would like to see the Catholic Church legally challenged in the World Court (or the international court of public opinion) to release all records from the Inquisition. I'd also like them to apologize for their historical atrocities against us and other Pagan peoples.

What goes around, comes around. The universe eventually rights all wrongs. Remember that if the legal system fails you or your spell doesn't seem to work.

## BLUE JUSTICE SPELL

This is a spell for affecting outcomes. It uses the color blue—particularly cobalt blue, ultramarine, royal blue, electric blue, or any vibrant shade of dark blue. This is not a judgment spell; it does not attempt to find facts, determine justice, affix blame or penalties. This is a justice spell that invites the universe to step in and right a wrong, to restore balance where imbalance exists.

The final outcome is left to the Goddess, whose notion of justice may differ from ours, whose sense of time is eternal, who applies the Law of Three without pity. Justice may result immediately, or it may take karmic form. In the end, however, justice will prevail.

This spell has two parts and can be used for any matter at law: civil proceedings, criminal cases, trials, or administrative hearings. Binding and banishing spells can be used to augment it. As always, you can modify the spell in any way you like to suit your circumstances.

Justice has been much on my mind as I write this book. They say every family has one (a problem child), and in mine it is a brother—a brother long ago disowned, disavowed, and disinherited for "crimes" like keeping himself supplied with beer and cigarettes while his children went without. We always knew he'd wind up in jail but thought it would be for drugs or fraud.

Instead, my brother beat his girlfriend to death. "Damn shame," he said. I cast the following spell. He was denied bail and kept in jail for over two years awaiting trial. I cast some form of this spell each time his trial was supposed to begin, and each time it was postponed. Finally, he plead guilty to manslaughter and accepted a deal that will keep him in prison for several years. I was very satisfied with that outcome, since it saved my family the trauma of a trial. I hope my brother will learn what he should from this hard lesson, emerge from prison a productive human being, and never again harm anyone (including himself).

For this spell you'll need:

- A tall blue candle (I used a big votive, the sort of glass-encased candle that you see left on doorsteps and beside roads after tragedies);
- Frankincense (it usually comes in a blend with myrrh, which is fine; cedar or sandalwood could be substituted);
- A blindfolded female poppet (I used a black female candle, with a strip of white Egyptian cotton for the blindfold);
- Dark-blue glitter, several vials;
- Sea salt (substitute ordinary salt if necessary);
- A bowl of water;
- A tray or other surface on which to work the spell (I use a cobalt blue tray with a Sun/Moon/stars pattern on it, a cheap tin thing on which I often cast spells, but you can use anything you like).

OPTIONAL:

- A scale, the old-fashioned kind with two balances; this is a symbol of justice that can be placed on the altar while you are working the spell;
- An ostrich feather, if you can get one, to decorate the altar (I don't have a scale or ostrich plume, so I use a set of three black stone pyramids from Egypt. They are inscribed with heiroglyphs including the only one I know how to read, the feather of Ma'at.);
- If you have one, wear a diamond from the time you begin the spell until the case is concluded.

Some witches say you should never mix deities from different cultures in a spell or ritual, but I work mainly with god/desses and find it can be very effective to do so. The caveat here is that the deities must correspond in some way to each other or to the spell. This spell invokes several justice god/desses from the Greco-Roman, Celtic, and Egyptian pantheons.

Ma'at is the Egyptian goddess of truth, justice, and social order. The ostrich plume, her symbol, became a heiroglyph that represented her name as well as those concepts. It is this feather against which Osiris weighs your heart on the scale in the Hall of Justice to determine your eligibility for eternal life.

Mabon is the Welsh god of youth, son of the mother goddess Modron. As a son of light, he intercedes with the Matrix on behalf of humans. Mabon, who was stolen as a baby and wrongfully imprisoned, also rules justice.

## BLUE JUSTICE SPELL: PART ONE

Arrange the altar or working surface in your usual way, then add everything you will need for this spell.

- Inscribe the candle with the feather of Ma'at, then write her name on it. (I used a metallic marking pen, writing on the glass.)
- Stand the blindfolded poppet in the bowl of water and place that on the tray with the candle and incense.
- Add anything you have that relates to the crime or dispute on the altar: photographs, newspaper clippings, legal documents, letters, evidence, etc.
- Call quarters and cast a circle.
- Light the incense and the candle.
- Pour the sea salt and blue glitter into the tray as you say:

> **By Justicia I rock the scales**
> **By Libra I bring them back into balance**
> **I call down justice**
> > **By Nemesis, by Tisiphone**
> > **By Dike and Athena**
> **I call down Blue Justice**
> **By Justicia the scales are rocked**
> **By Libra they are brought back into balance**
> **Let it it rain Blue Justice**
> > **By Nemesis, by Tisiphone**
> > **By Dike and Athena**
> **Let it rain Blue Justice on _____**
> **Let it rain Blue Justice for _____**

Repeat this as many times as feels necessary to you. Use your athame to stir the glitter and salt together. Close your eyes, open your palms, and pray to Ma'at. Tell her what result you would like the spell to have, but acknowledge her right to effect justice as she sees fit.

- Close the circle and ground power.
- Pour the melted wax over the poppet. Leave the altar set up that way.
- Each day, for several days, burn the candle and more incense. Pour the wax over the poppet each time, praying to Ma'at.
- Mix the ash from the incense into the glitter and salt.

This part of the spell can be cast at any time: before a proceeding begins, or while it is underway.

## BLUE JUSTICE SPELL: PART TWO

This next part should be done at a signifigant point—for instance, at the start of a trial, the beginning of jury selection, or when deliberations begin.

- Dress in blue clothes.
- Remove the blue justice powder from the tray. Clean up, throwing the poppet and candle away. The poppet can also be buried or destroyed. If you like, and if it is possible, it can be left outside the person's home in a place where they will be sure to see it, mailed to them, or buried on their property or near the courthouse. For urban magic, consider throwing it away in a trash receptacle at the court.
- Take the powder to the courthouse. (This is best done late at night or on a holiday or weekend, when you are least likely to be noticed or interrupted.)
- Stand before the courthouse and recite these words over the powder (change or omit the first part of the spell if you are not of Celtic descent):

> **Hail Mabon, Son of Modron**
> **My Celtic blood calls out to thee,**
> **It cries for Celtic justice**
> **It requires victory.**
> **Hail Mabon, Son of Modron!**
> **I commend your Celtic justice,**
> **I call you to this place**
> **To command your Celtic justice.**

> By your power, I transform this building into a Palace
>    of Justice,
> By your power, this building is transformed.
> I make of it a place where right is known from wrong,
> A place where Truth is known from lies,
> A place with judges fair and honest.
> By Mabon's power I enchant this powder,
> With Mabon's power I enchant this powder.
> By the power of Mabon
> I command Justice be done here.

Sprinkle the powder everywhere that the judge, jury, defendant, or plaintiff are likely to walk: on the steps, outside the courtroom, at entrances and elevators, wherever you have access. Make an invoking circle around the entire courthouse if possible (by sprinkling the powder as you walk clockwise). Say or think "Blue Justice!" as you sprinkle the powder. When you have finished, return to the front of the courthouse and pray again to Ma'at. Thank her and Mabon for considering the case, and for their anticipated intercession.

Keep the phrase "Blue Justice" in your mind until the legal proceedings are concluded. Get everyone else who wants the same outcome to keep thinking about blue justice as well. If the attorney or prosecutor who represents your interest is open to such a thing, tell her or him to think "Blue Justice" every time the case seems to be going against them.

Dress in blue if you attend the trial.

# CORRESPONDENCES FOR LEGAL SPELLS

SYMBOL: a blind or blindfolded woman, left hand with spread fingers, scales
NUMBER: 4, 8
ZODIAC: Libra
PLANT: cypress, garlic, *justicia*, nettles (to bind the spells)
INCENSE: frankincense, cedar, sandalwood
BEST TIMES: Sunday for freedom, Tuesday for strength in conflict, Thursday for justice and success, Saturday for prosecution, to bring someone to justice, to bind a criminal, to limit freedom
INVOCATIONS:
  Goddesses:
  Adrastea, Aedos, Akonadi, Alecto, Ananke (Neccessity), Aradia, Astraea, Elektra, Eunomia, the Fates, Fortuna, the Harpies, Irene,

Justicia, Kadi, Kwan Yin, Libra, Ma'at, Maman Brigette, Megaera, the Morrigan, Nanshe, Neith, Nina, the Norns (Urdur, Verdabdi, and Skuld), Oya, Themis, Tyche, Victoria, White Tara, Yansa
Gods:
Baal, the Dagda, Dharma, Dian Cecht, Forseti (Divine Giver of Good Laws), Hendursaga, Horagalles, Minos, Nabu, Father Nanna, Osiris, Perun, Rama, Rhadamanthys, Shakaburu, Shamash, Thor, Tiw, Ull, Yeloje

FOR:
Arbitration:
Invoke: Forseti (the Great Arbiter, to arbitrate disputes)
Binding Spells for Work in Law and Justice:
Plant: nettles, vine
Constitutional Government:
Invoke: Concordia (democracy), Lady Liberty, Libertas
Contracts:
Invoke: Vör (marriage contracts); Arom, Berith (contracts and agreements), Mithras
Defense:
Invoke: Adrastea (who defends the rightous), Alphito-Baitule Lusia (Deliveress from Guilt)
Divine Judgment:
Invoke: Themis (Divine Justice); Mandanu
Forgiveness after Penitence:
Invoke: Apollo
Good Faith:
Invoke: Fides
Guarantee That Judgment is Executed:
Invoke: Enki
Judgment:
Color: white (unbiased judgment)
Jewel: jade (diviner of judgments)
Invoke: Danaë (She Who Judges), Neith; Istanu, Kuan Ti (the Great Judge), Michael (Angel of the Last Judgment), Rashnu (the Just Judge), Thoth (the Judge of Right and Truth)
Justice:
Planet: Jupiter, Sun
Color: dark, vibrant shades of blue
Plant: frankincense
Jewel: diamond, rose quartz
Invoke: Alidice (Mighty Justice), Athena of the Just Deserts, Biadice (Justice by Force), Calladice (Fair Justice), Chango,

Dike (Human Justice), Eurydice (Wide Justice), Itone of
the Just Deserts, Justicia (the Scales), Laodice (Justice of
the People), Ma Kiela (for women who die of knife
wounds), Nekmet Awai, Nemesis (justice against offend-
ers), Themis (Divine Justice); Anbay, Lugalsisa (the king
who rights wrongs), Mabon, Rashnu, Utu

Justification:
    Invoke: Renenutet (Lady of Justification)
Law:
    Planet: Jupiter
    Jewel: chalcedony, to be fortunate at law
    Invoke: Astynome (Lawgiver of the City), Ceres (Lawgiver),
    Demeter Thesmophoros (Bringer of Law), Dike (Natural
    Law), Laonome (Law of the People), Thesomophoros
    (Lawgiver), Torah; the Dharmapala (Guardians of the
    Law), the Manu (Lawgivers), Quetzalcoatl (the Lawgiver)
Law (its implementation):
    Invoke: Uttu; Vidyraja
Law and Order:
    Invoke: Euonomia, Ma'at; Igalima (High Constable), Marduk
    (Guardian of Law and Order), Tiwaz
Legal Matters:
    Plant: buckthorn, cascarda sagrada, celandine
Mediation:
    Invoke: Freya; Orunmila, Thoth
Mercy:
    Invoke: Athena, Kwan-Yin, Mary (Our Lady of Pity), Tara;
    Juichimen, Latipan
Morality:
    Invoke: Jakomba, Vishnu
Oaths:
    Invoke: Fides, Mamitu, Vör; Hazzi, Helios, Horkos, Jove, Jupi-
    ter, Mithras, Ullr, Zeus (who enforces oaths)
Order:
    Invoke: Themis (social order), Vishnu
Punishment:
    Invoke: Ushas (enemies); Chango (thieves, liars), Katavul
    (who punishes and rewards), Lei Kung (criminals whose
    crimes have gone undetected), Mithras (who punishes
    wrong), Pu'gu (the evil, the violent)
Resolving Conflicts and Disputes:
    Invoke: Mercury

Retribution:

 Color: black

 Invoke: the Erinnyes (vengeance), the Furies (Tisiphone, Alecto, and Megaera, vengeance), Hecate (vengeance), Hera the Throttler, Itone of the Just Deserts, Nemesis, Sekhmet (divine vengeance), Tisiphone (to avenge murder); Ra

Secure Operation of World Systems:

 Invoke: Varuna (god of cosmic law and order)

Success in Court:

 Plant: jalup root (High John), laurel, *mustard seeds, St. John's Wort, vervain

 Jewel: rose quartz, brown chalcedony

Success in Court if You Are Being Persecuted by an Enemy:

 tobacco

Treaties:

 Invoke: Mamitu

Truth:

 Symbol: ostrich feather

 Color: white, blue

 Number: 7 (ultimate truth)

 Jewel: sapphire

 Animal: owl

 Invoke: Asase Yaa, Rhiannon; Ahura Mazda, Mabon, Mithras, Ra (the Lord of Truth), Thoth, Varuna (Lord of Truth)

Victory:

 Invoke: Nike, Victoria, Vahagn

# LOVE

"The law of the Goddess is love," Starhawk tells us in *The Spiral Dance*, "passionate sexual love, the warm affection of friends, the fierce protective love of mother for child, the deep comradeship of the coven. There is nothing amorphous or superficial about love in Goddess religion," she goes on to say. "It is always specific, directed toward real individuals, not vague concepts of humanity. It includes ourselves and all our fallible human qualities."[5]

I get lots of mail asking for love spells, and almost as many letters from people who have created problems for themselves with love spells. Love spells are tricky for several reasons.

***Ethics:*** The most effective love spells are those that compel someone to love or want you. You cast them *on* the object of your desire, imposing your will upon that person. These spells work. You get what you wanted (or thought you wanted), but you violate the law. What you put forth gets returned to you threefold. Things that can go wrong include:

• Having the person you won with the spell taken away by another;
• Having a love spell cast on you;
• Losing interest in the person but being unable to be rid of them.

These hazards can be avoided if you

• Invite attraction rather than compelling it;
• Put the matter into the hands of the Goddess. Cast a love spell or use a love charm, but make it contingent on Her approval. Add:

**If you will it, make _____ mine.**

---

[5] Starhawk, *The Spiral Dance: A Rebirth of the Ancient Religion of the Great Goddess* (San Francisco: HarperSanFrancisco, 1989), p. 97.

- Remember that learning to love yourself is the best way to bring love into your life.

*Their Very Nature:* Love spells are serious. They can backfire on you and shouldn't be taken lightly. In trying to bind someone to you, you are also binding yourself to that person. This can complicate things when it is time to move on. It can cause you a lot of pain if your spell doesn't bring the person to you. Another danger is that you can overdo the intent or intensity of the spell and have things go badly wrong. Love spells can be difficult to reverse, so be sure about your feelings before you cast one.

*The Goddess of Love:* Love spells fall under the provenance of the Love Goddess, whether you call her Venus, Aphrodite, Hathor, Freya, Inanna, or by another of her many names. To understand love spells, you have to understand the nature of the Love Goddess. She is beautiful . . . and cruel. You may get more than you bargained for—obsession rather than passion, or a stalker instead of a lover. She is capricious. Your spell may work—but on the wrong person. The mating of humans is delightful to her. When you cast a love spell, you invite her management of your affairs. But beware— she may have a different notion of who is a suitable partner for you. Aphrodite laughs. Be careful.

Love and sexuality are "paths," just as asceticism and celibacy are. The path of love brings both ecstacy and suffering, with spiritual lessons to be learned from each. All of that said, here are some love spells. Use them at your own risk. More love spells can be found in Part I (Writing Spells).

# LOVE SPELLS

## CANDLE SPELL

To encourage someone to fall in love with you. This spell is adapted from an ancient one reported by the poet Theocritus. It is best performed while the Moon is waxing. You'll need:

- A dozen roses (the roses are an offering to the Love Goddess, so don't be cheap and use fewer than twelve);
- A large candle, the kind that will drip wax, with the name of the person written or carved on it (a human-shaped candle in the correct gender is great, if you can find one);

- A photograph of the person, or a piece of paper with their name written on it;
- A tray.

Clear your altar or working surface. Set the photograph in the middle of the tray and place the candle on top of it. Arrange the roses around it. Take the candle in your hands and say:

> **Candle, I name you _____ (the name of the person).**

You must believe this as you say it, because it is your belief that makes it so. Place the candle back atop the photograph and light it. Keep repeating the spell as the candle burns, concentrating on your wish and being careful not to start a fire.

> **I melt your heart as I melt this wax**
> **Even as this wax flows,**
> **So your love glows for me**
> **I melt your heart as I melt this wax**
> **Even as this wax flows,**
> **So your love flows to me**
> **I melt your heart as I melt this wax**
> **Even as this wax flows,**
> **So your love grows for me**
> **I melt your heart as I melt this wax**
> **And by its molten flow**
> **Your love for me will show.**

Allow the candle to burn down completely. Gather the roses, tie them together, and hang them upside down to dry. Pick up the wax-encrusted photograph once the wax has cooled. Safeguard these things in a secret place until the spell has worked. If you see no change by the next Full Moon, cast the spell again while the Moon is full—but this time, cast it formally, within a circle.

## SPELL FOR THE JOINING OF SOULS

This spell is definitely not ethical, but it is very effective. Remember that magic is a two-way street and that you will be equally bound—even at the karmic level. I know of no way to reverse this spell, so be very, very sure before you use it. This is a spell for a married or otherwise seriously committed couple, not a boyfriend/girlfriend situation. You'll need:

- Dried white roses (buy fresh ones and hang them upside down for a week or two until they are very dry, then cut the flowers from their stems);
- Almond oil (try health food stores and gourmet shops, or substitute almond extract, which is usually found in the baking section of a supermarket);
- A piece of paper with both of your names written on it.

Arrange things as you usually do for a spell. Put the roses and the paper in a container where it will be safe to burn them. Raise power and cast a circle. Sprinkle the roses with the almond oil. Set them ablaze and cast the spell while they burn.

> **By all that lives on land and sea**
> **By the incoming and the outgoing**
> **By the odd numbers and the even**
> **By the power of three times three**
> **Thy waking thoughts shall be of me**
> **From now throughout eternity**
> **No peace or increase shall you find**
> **Until your hand is joined in mine**
> **I bind thee heart and soul and mind to me**
> **I bind thee eyes and thoughts and loins to me**
> **I bind thee to me forever**
> **With cords of velvet longing**
> **By the white rose and the rosemary**
> **By the caverns and the groves**
> **By the silence of the mountains**
> **By the chasms and the standing stones**
> **I bind thee forever to me**
> **With cords of silken danger**
> > **Isis, Astarte, Ishtar**
> > **Aphrodite, Venus**
> > **I bind thee to me forever**
> > **So mote it be.**

Close the circle and earth the power you raised. Clean up. Bury the ashes, preferably beneath a tree or under a rosebush. For urban magic, you can use a potted plant.

## THE BLESSING OF UNION

There are two kinds of union. One is temporary, for this lifetime or for part of this lifetime. The other is the eternal marriage, which brings reunion across time through reincarnation. The eternal marriage is an experience to be shared with a soul mate. It should not be undertaken lightly. Making it with the wrong person can adversely affect your karma, as can making it without reciprocation. Making it with more than one person can make for a tumultuous love life in future incarnations. Be careful. For this spell you will need:

- A piece of papyrus or other good-quality paper with both your names written on it;
- Red thread;
- Dried herbs of love or Venus (see the correspondence lists below and in Part III);
- A safe container in which to burn these things.

Scroll the paper and use the red thread to bind it tightly. Make ready a place to burn the paper and the herbs. This spell is best performed by burning everything over hot coals, but you can also set fire to the paper and use it to ignite the herbs.

Ready your altar or working surface in your usual way. Raise power and cast a circle. Get the paper and the herbs burning, then cast the spell.

> Aphrodite,
> Goddess of Degraded Love
> And the sanctity of marriage,
> Make our cup to runneth over
> And bless us with your Love.
>
> Aphrodite rising
> From the wine-dark sea,
> Grant us health and fertility,
> Fidelity and trust,
> Grant us wealth and virility,
> Honesty and lust.
>
> Aphrodite bless this union,
> Make our two hearts
> Beat as one.
> Make the flames of passion

Burn without burning us,
Hot without hurting us,
Blaze without blinding us,
Fire without end.

Aphrodite,
Force of nature,
Let us love each other
So long as we shall live.
Let us give each other
All we have to give.
Let us be together
In this life and the next.

Aphrodite,
Queen of Beauty,
We do you honor
Each time we make love.
Make our bond to last forever,
Grant us eternal Love.

Aphrodite,
Goddess of the windblown foam,
Give us healthy children
And a happy home.

Aphrodite,
Bless this union,
And smile upon our Love.

Close the circle and ground power. Clean up. Bury the ashes beneath a tree, or scatter them near the pyramids in Egypt. This spell is eternal, unless you alter it. If you are able to obtain some, Sands of Time (sand taken from between the paws of the Great Sphinx at Giza) can be used as a base for the coals, then mixed with the ashes before you bury them.

# CORRESPONDENCES FOR LOVE SPELLS

PLANET: Venus, Moon, Full Moon, Mercury
ELEMENT: Earth, Water, Fire
DIRECTION: South
DAY: Friday
BEST TIMES: Friday or Monday

New to Full Moon in: Taurus for earthy, sensual love
  Cancer for home and family, maternal, or paternal love
  Libra for idealistic love
  Scorpio for sexual love
NUMBER: 3, 5, 6, 7, 9 (impersonal love)
LETTER: O
METAL: copper, silver
JEWEL: ruby, amber, pearl, coral, diamond, lapis lazuli, emerald, sapphire, turquoise, garnet, malachite, green agate, pink or blue tourmaline, rose quartz, pairs of lodestones, amazonite (send love), rhodonite (activate love)
SYMBOL: heart, mermaids (for the bittersweetness of love)
COLOR: red, green, white, deep pink, rose, orange (attraction), violet (gay love)
ANIMAL: lynx, deer, horse, dove, swallow, partridge, peacock feathers, wryneck, pairs of birds
CANDLE: red (to find love, to keep love), purple (any shade, for gay love)
INCENSE: benzoin, cinnamon, civet, copal, gingseng, jasmine, lavender, musk, myrrh, patchouli, rose, rosemary, spikenard, vanilla, violet
PLANT: *acacia flowers, *almond oil, aloe, *apple, apricot, avens, balm of Gilead, barley, basil, beans, beet, betony, birch, *cannabis, cardamom, carnation, cassia, catnip, cornflower, cherry, chestnut, chickweed, chili pepper, cinnamon, clove, clover, coltsfoot, columbine, coriander, autumn crocus, cupid's dart, *cyclamen, daffodil, damiana, devil's bit scabious, dodder, dragon's blood, elder berries, elecampane, elm, feverfew, fig, gardenia, gentian, ginger, ginseng, hollyhock, maidenhair fern, male fern, *jasmine, lavender, lemon, lime, love grass, madonna lily, maidenhair fern, male fern, mandrake, marjoram, marsh mallow, meadowsweet, mimosa, mint, mistletoe, myrtle, opium poppy, orange, pansy, peach, pear, peas, pennyroyal, periwinkle, poppy, primrose, purslane, quince, raspberry, *rose, rosemary, rye, sarsparilla, sea holly, skullcap, sorrel, southernwood, strawberry, *sweet william, tamarind, tansy, thyme, *tuberose, valerian, Venus flytrap, verbena, vervain, violet, willow, wormwood, yerba maté
INVOCATIONS:
  Goddesses:
  Aegea, Anahita, Anath, Aphrodite, Artemis, Asherah, Ashtoreth, Astarte, Atargatis, Benzaiten, Blathnat, Branwen, Cytherea, Diana, Erzulie, Freya, Frigg, Gaia, Galatea, Goda,

Guinevere, Hathor, Hera, Hulda, Inanna, Io, Ishtar, Isis, Juno, Kadesh, Kwan-Yin, Lakshmi, Maia, Myrrha, Neith, Olwen, Oshun, Ostara, Rauni, Rhea, Rosamund, Sarah, Semiramis, Shakti, Shekinah, Syria Dea, Turan, Uma, Venus, Yemaya

Gods:

Adonis, Amor, Angus, Anteros, Attis, Cernunnos, Cupid, Damuzi, Dulha Deo, Eros, Evander, Faunus, Haddad, Hymen, Kama, Krishna (the Adorable One, Lord of Love), Mithras, Angus (Lord of Love and Death), Pan, Phanes, Pothos, Robin Hood, Soma Shakarabru, Tammuz, Vishnu, Yarillo (the Uncontrolled)

FOR:

Advice:
Invoke: Freya, Neith

Affection:
Color: pink (to draw affection)
Invoke: Rati

Attracting the Opposite Sex:
Plant: lovage, orris oil

Attracting Love from Females:
Plant: henbane

Attracting the Attention of the One You Want:
Plant: marjoram

Domestic Harmony:
Invoke: Concordia, Uma

Fatal Attraction:
Invoke: Angus

Fidelity:
Invoke: Fides, Hera
Animal: turtledove
Plant: chili pepper, clover, rye, skullcap, yerba maté
Jewel: garnet

Fidelity in Marriage:
Invoke: Hera, Pattinidevi

Gaining the Favor of the One You Love:
Invoke: Benzaiten

Harmonious Relationship:
Invoke: Concordia; Lu Pan

Intimate Friendship:
Invoke: Mithras

Living Together:
Invoke: the Gandharvas

Loving-Kindness:
   Invoke: Kwan-Yin
Love (divine):
   Jewel: amethyst
Love (emotional):
   Invoke: Radha
Love (homosexual):
   Invoke: Eros
   Color: any shade of purple, especially lavender
   Incense: lavender, violet
   Candle: a purple citronella candle, if you can find one
   Plant: oil grasses (vetiver, citronella grass, camel grass, lemon
      grass, ginger grass)
Love (married):
   Invoke: Gaia, Hera, Juno, Selket
   Jewel: green beryl
   Plant: periwinkle, pomegranate, rosemary
   Animal: turtledove
Love (maternal):
   Invoke: Eileithyia, Isis
   Jewel: mother-of-pearl
Love (mutual):
   Invoke: Anteros
Love (profane):
   Invoke: Venus
Love (romantic):
   Invoke: Erzulie; Kama
Love (spiritual):
   Invoke: Charité
Love (potions):
   Plant: periwinkle, *rose, stinkhorn, vervain, violet
   Jewel: lodestone

Potions can be used as adjuncts to spells. I've never used a
love potion, because it seems dishonest to me—akin to spik-
ing someone's drink. The only potions I have ever made are
those I drank myself. There is also the difficulty of getting the
correct person, and only that person, to drink the potion. But
if you really want to make one, try this:

- Get rosewater, which is sold in gourmet shops and Middle
  Eastern grocery stores. Fill your chalice with it and add five

drops of red food coloring. Cast a circle, perform a love spell, and use your wand or athame to charge the potion with the spell.

- Rosewater is used in baking and confectionary so the potion could be added to baked goods or candy, which might be easier to administer. I'd suggest a rosewater-scented angelfood cake, frosted with pink vanilla icing and decorated with candied violets (unless the object of your affection is diabetic or dieting, of course).
- You could also mix the potion with vodka, cut a plug in a watermelon, pour it in, and allow it to steep overnight in the refrigerator. The same potion and vodka mixture could also be used to marinate a bowl of fruit salad made with apples, pears, figs, apricots, raspberries, peaches, orange slices, and strawberries.

Marriage:
    Animal: duck
    Jewel: beryl (especially green beryl)
    Invoke: Benzaiten, Hera, Hulda, Juno; Dulha Deo, Hymen (god of wedding feasts)
A Wedding: Hera
Marriage (preparations):
    Invoke: Unxia
Marriage (finding a wife):
    Invoke: Ah Kin (who brings wives to bachelors)
Marriage (finding a husband):
    Invoke: Hathor (who gives husbands to those whom she loves), Soma, who provides husbands for spinsters
Marriage (happiness):
    Invoke: Freya
Marriage (a woman's good fortune):
    Invoke: Bhaga
Marriage (ending quarrels):
    Invoke: Juno
Passion:
    Invoke: Oreithyia (She Who Rages Upon the Mountains, passionate love); Dionysus (insane passion)
    Plant: myrtle
    Animal: turtledove
Protection Against Acts of Passion:
    Plant: white heather

Reconciliation:
  Jewel: moonstone, lodestone (reconciliation in marriage)
  Plant: beans
Success in Love Affairs:
  Invoke: Urvasi
  Jewel: emerald
Union:
  Invoke: Branwen


TO:
Accept Love:
  Jewel: freshwater pearl
Attract Love:
  Color: pink or orange (attract new love)
  Jewel: topaz, lodestone, blue tourmeline
  Color: orange
Avenge Slighted Love:
  Invoke: Anteros
Break Love Spells:
Letting someone know that you cast a love spell on them will often break the enchantment.
  Plant: nuts (especially pistachio)
Get a Lover:
  Plant: cuckoo flower
Heal a Broken Heart:
  Plant: balm of Gilead, feverfew, myrtle, white rose petals
Heal Passions and Griefs of the Heart:
  Plant: cinquefoil
Influence the Heart:
  Plant: cinnamon
  Jewel: ruby (to open hearts)
Keep Someone from Leaving:
  Plant: caraway
Know Whom you will Marry:
  Invoke: Ch'i ku-niang (the Seventh Lady)
Learn to Love Yourself:
  Jewel: freshwater pearl, rose quartz
Protect Young Couples:
  Invoke: Ya'halan
Punish a Heartless Lover:
  Invoke: Nemesis

# MAGIC

This chapter provides correspondences for magic itself, as well as a variety of magical workings. I told you earlier in this book that you will get as much out of magic as you put into it. That still applies even after you have completed your studies or training and become a working witch. The craft should always be approached with respect. On a practical level, this means keeping your altar or other sacred space clean and tidy, your tools polished, your offerings fresh, and so on. At a sacred level, this means honoring the gods before you call upon them, and always remembering to thank them after a spell or ritual. I also give thanks when I discover that a spell has worked.

Honoring and thanking the gods/desses can be very simple or a long, involved ceremony—whatever feels right to you. You may want to develop a personal ritual or ritual phrase you use for this, one specific to the lord or lady with whom you work.

Respecting the craft also means not abusing it by using it for trivial things or in mean-spirited ways. Be realistic in your expectations of magic. It affects reality but usually in subtle ways. Sometimes you will get immediate results that astound you, other times it will take awhile for proof that a spell has worked. Be very specific in your spells or you may get what you asked for, but not in the way you wanted it.

Remember that mouthing phrases and going through the motions isn't enough, not even if you follow a spell's instructions to the letter. You have to believe in yourself and your ability to make something happen in order for a spell to work. You have to raise power and apply it correctly. No matter what the words of a spell say, it is your intent that actually directs the power. That is why it's a bad idea to use magic if you have any doubts or conflicts about the working.

Correspondences for many kinds of spells are given here but you don't always need a spell. Simply turning your magical attention to a problem or situation can often affect it positively.

# CORRESPONDENCES FOR MAGIC ITSELF

PLANET: Mercury
DIRECTION: North
INVOCATIONS: Vilmeth and Vidolf
Goddesses:
Aradia, Arianrhod, Baba-Yaga, Circe (Divine Sorceress), Diana (Queen of the Witches), Durga Mahamaya (the Great Sorceress), Freya, Frigg, Hecate (Goddesses of Witches, She Who Has Power Far Off), Isis (Lady of Spells, Mistress of Magic), Jezi-Baba, Kali Mahamaya (the Great Sorceress), Medea, Medusa, Morgan le Fay, the Morrigan, Nemain, Nimuë, Pasiphaë, Pelé, Renenutet, Sarasvati, Selene
Gods:
Chango Ea, Enki (Lord of the Sacred Eye), Fintan, Gwydion, Hercules the Dactyl, Hermes Trismegistus, Horus, Loki, Lugh, Mait' Carrefour, Marduk (Great Sorcerer), Mapp ap Mathonwy, Mercury, Merlin, Mithras (Mystery of Sorcerers), Nudimmud, Odin, Tezcatlipoca (Smoking Mirror), Thoth

FOR:
Alchemy: (see also Part III, Metals):
Invoke: Lao-Tsze
Plant: lady's mantle
Jewel: cinnabar
Metal: quicksilver
Beauty:
You are already beautiful, a precious child of the Mother.
Planet: Venus
Candle: green, pink, light blue
Plant: catnip, flax, ginseng, lily, maidenhair fern
Jewel: amber, jasper, topaz, opal (inner beauty)
Day: April 23, the Vinalia
Invoke: Aphrodite, Chalchihuitlcue, Deirdre, Erzulie, Hathor (the Beautiful Face in the Boat of Millions of Years), Hebe, Helene, Oshun, Sarah, Semiramis, Venus, Zaria
Bespelling:
Invoke: Ogma (for words of bespelling)
Bewitching:
Plant: sorrel leaves
Jewel: opal
Binding:
Planet: Saturn

Invoke: Isis, Linda (the Binder with Linen Thread), Ninurta; Oghma (for words of binding), Varuna

Color: black

Metal: lead

Jewel: obsidian

Plant: bindweed, linen thread (flax), periwinkle vines

Black Magic:

Invoke: Carman, Hecate, Kali

Black Magic (blasting):

Invoke: Hecate; Apollo

Plant: *blackthorn (sloe)

Black Magic (hexing):

Plant: mugwort

Blessing:

Color: blue (new home)

Plant: mistletoe

Invoke: Hecate; Apollo

To Bless:

Jewel: lodestone, pearl (worn when asking blessings of Isis)

Plant: jalap root (High John the Conqueror, for spiritual blessings)

Invoke: Deae Matres (the Divine Mothers), Pandora

Calling Spirits:

Remember that spirits are easy to summon but difficult to banish. I respect the dead by allowing them to rest in peace. Shamanic traditions have a long history of spirit work, but many Wiccans think it is wrong for witches to disturb any spirits but their own ancestors.

Plant: dandelion, *wormwood

Cat Magic:

Invoke: Bastet

Plant: *catnip

Jewel: tiger's eye

Charms:

Invoke: Artemis (for magical charms); Ogmios

Charms Against Spells:

Plant: angelica, bamboo, black hellebore, chili pepper, horehound, thorn apple (datura), toadflax, wintergreen

Charm Against the Jealousy of the Moon Goddess:

Plant: willow

Charms Against Lunar Magic:

Plant: garlic, moly, squill

Cleansing Bad Vibes:
  Plant: gingerroot, onion bulb
  Jewel: crystals, salt
Comfort:
  Metal: gold
  Number: 6
  Plant: cypress
  Jewel: emerald
  Zodiac: Taurus
  Invoke: Yemaya (to comfort children in crisis)
Courage:
  Element: water
  Direction: West (courage to face deepest feelings)
  Zodiac: Leo
  Invoke: Vahagn, Wachabe (Black Bear)
  Number: 1
  Color: green, red
  Plant: *borage, columbine, thyme, yarrow
  Jewel: amber, turquoise, diamond, carnelian, turquoise, jas-
    per, topaz, amethyst, carnelian, red tourmeline, red and
    black agates
  Animal: cougar, lion, boar
Coven Work:
  Invoke: Coventina (Mother of Covens)
Cursing:
  Invoke: Carman, Hecate, Ninhursag, Sulis (who empowers
    curses)
Destiny/Fate:
  Invoke: Alphito, Ananke, Fata, the Fates, the Graiae, Gula-Bau,
    Karta, Manawat, Shait, the Telchines; Orula, Zurvan
  Jewel: diamond (impassivity of fate)
  Animal: pig
  Plant: cannabis, flax, strings of palm nuts
Destruction:
  Planet: Uranus (destruction of the old to make way for the
    new)
  Element: fire
  Zodiac: Scorpio
  Invoke: Inanna (destroying the indestructible); Shiva
  Animal: locust
Development of Human Potential:
  Invoke: Brighid

Disorders of Magical Powers:
    Plant: tamarisk

Enchantment:
    Planet: Moon
    Invoke: Moon goddesses, Nimuë, Rhiannon, the Telchines (the Enchanters)
    Plant: willow, vervain
    Letter: S (female enchantment)
    Number: 7 (female enchantment)
    Jewel: sapphire (freedom from enchantment), diamond (to turn an enchantment back upon its maker)

Escape:
    Plant: celandine

Exorcism:
    Color: black, red
    Incense: frankincense, fumitory, sandalwood
    Plant: angelica, asafetida, avens, basil, beans, blackthorn, buckthorn, clove, clover, devil's bit scabious, dragon's blood, elder, ferns, garlic, logwood, mandrake, peach, peony, pepper, pine, rosemary, rue, *Solomon's seal, tamarisk, yarrow
    Invoke: Hastsebaad; Asalluha

Fame:
Be careful, or you might wind up with infamy instead.
    Invoke: Ushas
    Jewel: heliotrope, green beryl
    Plant: a crown of amaranth flowers

Fame Spell (adapted from *The Egyptian Book of the Dead*[6]):

- Get 9 small bowls, cups or glasses and line them up on the altar or working surface. Prepare the altar otherwise as you usually do.
- Write the name of each of the god/desses on a slip of paper: Temu, Shu, Tefnut, Seb, Nut, Osiris, Horus, Ra, Uatchet. Papyrus works well if you can get it. These papers will represent the gods, so put some effort into doing this nicely. If you can get a picture or small figure of each god/dess, that is even better.

---

[6] E. A. Wallis Budge, *Egyptian Magic* (New York: Dover Publications, 1971), pp. 159–160.

- Put the papers into the bowls or cups, in the order given above. You will make an offering to each of the gods as you name them in the spell. You could use nine sticks of incense, lighting each one from your candles as you say the god/dess's name, or an offering of bread and ale made by pouring some ale into the bowl and then adding a bit of bread. Wine and flowers are also suitable offerings.
- Raise power and cast a circle when you have everything ready. Recite the spell, making the offerings as you get to each god/dess.

> O Great Company of the Gods, grant that _____
> may flourish, even as the name of Temu, the
> Chief of the Nine Gods, doth flourish.
> If the name of Shu, the Lord of the Upper Shrine,
> flourisheth, then _____ shall flourish!
> If the name of Tefnut, the Lady of the Lower Shrine,
> flourisheth, the name of _____ shall be
> established to all eternity!
> If the name of Seb flourisheth, then the name of
> _____ shall flourish unto all eternity!
> If the name of Nut flourisheth,
> the name of _____ shall flourish unto all
> eternity!
> If the name of Osiris flourisheth in the nome of
> Abydos, then the name of _____ shall
> flourish unto all eternity!
> If the name of Horus flourisheth, then the name of
> _____ shall flourish unto all eternity!
> If the name of Ra flourisheth in the horizon,
> then the name of _____ shall flourish unto all
> eternity!
> If the name of Uatchet flourisheth, then the name of
> _____ shall flourish,
> and his/her work shall flourish,
> and what s/he builds shall flourish unto all
> eternity!

Remain at the altar as the candles and incense burn down, concentrating on what sort of fame you desire. Be very, very specific. Close the circle, ground the power, and leave the offerings there for several days.

Fighting Werewolves:
    Plant: wolfbane (aconite)
Finding Stolen Goods:
    Invoke: Punarvasu (who restores stolen property)
    Plant: marigold
Finding Treasures:
    Plant: cowslip, fern seeds
Finger Magic:
    Invoke: the Dactyls
    Plant: finger grass
Flower Magic:
    Invoke: Aphrodite Antheia (Aphrodite of the Flowers), Blath-
        nat, Blodeuwedd (the Flower Woman), Clytie, Flora, Sus-
        annah, Xochiquetzal, Hyacinthus, Narcissus
    Plant: all flowers
Friendship:
    Planet: Sun, Venus
    Zodiac: Aquarius
    Number: 3
    Color: pink
    Plant: lemon, rosemary, passionflower
    Jewel: rose quartz, alabaster, turquoise, emerald (strengthen
        friendship), beryl (eternal friendship)
    Invoke: Gilgamesh and Enkidu, Mithras (for intimate friendship)
Garden Magic:
    Plant: apple, grape
    Jewel: green agate, jade
    Invoke: Aphrodite of the Gardens, Pomona, Venus; Vertumnus
Guarding Magical Writings:
    Invoke: Tao-chün (Lord of the Tao)
Happiness:
    Color: yellow, pink
    Plant: catnip, celandine, cyclamen, marigold, marjoram,
        purslane, quince, saffron, St. John's Wort, savory
    Animal: bat
    Jewel: turquoise, moss agate, amethyst, ruby
    Invoke: Ganga, Ekajata, Fu-hsing, Sasthi (happiness of children)
Herbal Magic:
    Invoke: Morgen, Tellus (by whose power plants potent for en-
        chantment are produced), Vedma
Hope:
    Planet: Sun

Zodiac: Aquarius

Tarot: the Star

Plant: fir tree, flowering almond, Norway spruce (hope in adversity)

Metal: tin (secret hope)

Jewel: opal

Animal: goat stag (the hope of immortality)

Invoke: Astraea, Branwen, Spes

## Image Magic:

Color: blue (for healing image spells)

Plant (roots): bryony, ginger, ginseng, mandrake, potato

Invoke: Ogma

## Immortality:

There is no physical immortality. The best an immortality spell can do is give your name, your line, or your work great longevity.

Symbol: unicorn horn, narwhal horn, spiral

Plant: amaranth flowers, apple, coriander, *everlasting, frangipani, laurel, *lotus, peach, sage, sorb apple, tansy, vervain

Jewel: cinnabar, jade

Animal: pig, crane, dragonfly, serpent, birds (immortality of the soul), goat stag (the hope of immortality)

Invoke: Alys, the Hesperides, Hsi-Wang-Mu, Mu Gong

## Incantations:

Plant: hemlock

Invoke: Brighid (poetic incantations); the Dactyls (magical incantations), Dian Cecht (healing incantations), Ea (Lord of Incantations), Ogma

## Invincibility:

Invoke: Abraxas, Goibniu

Plant: chicory, jalap root (High John) and St. John's Wort, decoction of any plant found growing as a parasite on a tamarind tree

Animal: brown hare, lion, porpoise, hoopoe

## Invisibility:

Actual physical invisibility is impossible. An invisibility spell can render you less likely to be noticed, that's all. But that can amount to the same thing.

Jewel: moonstone, bloodstone, diamond, opal

Plant: amaranth, fern seed, oil of heliotrope, black hellebore, poppy, wolfbane

## Making Children Happy and Apt to Learn:

Plant: *vervain

Making the Imperishable Perish:
  Invoke: Inanna
Making Venomous Things Harmless:
Try adding this to a salad for someone with a vicious tongue whose words cause harm.
  Plant: rue (only a *very* tiny amount!) and walnuts
Manifestation:
  Number: 4, 12 (complete cycle of manifestation)
  Zodiac: Capricorn
  Invoke: Sussistanako (Thinking Woman); Anu, Ea, Ellil, Enlil
  Jewel: turquoise
Opening What is Shut:
  Invoke: Cardea
Overcoming Obstacles:
  Zodiac: Capricorn
  Invoke: Aditi (who clears obstacles and frees from problems), Ekajata (to remove personal obstacles); Ganesha (to overcome difficulties or remove obstacles), Ogun
  Plant: chicory
Peace:
  Planet: Saturn
  Color: blue, light blue
  Jewel: amethyst, carnelian, aquamarine, blue tourmeline, yellow hyacinth, red agate, sapphire (to make peaceful)
  Number: 7, 42
  Animal: dove, golden eagle
  Invoke: Ertha, Irene, Mary (Queen of Peace), Nerthus, Pax, Shekinah, Turan; Belobog, Belun, Freyr, Frodi, Jesus (Prince of Peace), Manannán Mac Lir, Obatala (King of Peace), the Vanir
  Plant: gardenia, *olive branch, passionflower, sea holly, skullcap, vervain, violet, branches of winter bark
Power:
  Planet: Jupiter, Mercury (occult power), Moon (psychic power, healing power), Full Moon (maximum power), Neptune (spiritual power), Sun (natural power), Venus (the power of love)
  Direction: North
  Element: fire (power of will)
  Zodiac: Scorpio
  Symbol: torc, unicorn horn
  Number: 3 (power of unity), 8, 12 (established power)

Color: black, yellow, red (female power)

Jewel: lodestone, pearl (sea power), sapphire (to maintain male power)

Metal: gold, bronze (matriarchal power), mercury (the power of becoming fluid), alloys (magical power)

Plant: cinnamon, elder (magical power), gentian, ginseng, rowan, St. John's Wort, fern seed (magical power)

Animal: bear, serpent, horse, elk, cougar, lion, elephant, scarab beetle (creative power), pair of birds (the power of love), buffalo (power to cure), otter (female power), pig (power of transformation), eagle (power in battle), snake (magical power), raven (shamanic powers)

Invoke: Amaunet (hidden power), Bia, Dynë, Hecate, Oya, Pelé (magical power), Amun (hidden power), Gonaqade't Mariamne is a name of triple power

Charm: boars' bristles

Spell: Words of Power (adapted from *The Egyptian Book of the Dead*[7])

- Recite this as a trigger to help you raise power or to calm and center yourself before a magical working.
- You can also memorize it and recite it mentally whenever you are in a situation where you could use some power or protection.

**Now as concerning the words of power and all the words which may be spoken against me, may the gods resist them, and may each and every one of the company of the gods withstand them. Behold, I gather together the Word of Power from wherever it is, swifter than greyhounds and quicker than light. I live by reason of the words of power which I have with me. Heaven hath power over its seasons, and the words of power have dominion over that which they possess; my mouth therefore shall have power over the words of power which are therein. I am wholly provided with thy magical words, O Ra, those which are in the heaven above me and the earth beneath me.**

---

[7] E. A. Wallis Budge, *Egyptian Magic,* pp. 126-127.

Purification:
Witches use salt, water, sunlight, incense, smoke, and crystals to purify objects. The item can be put into a bowl and covered with sea salt or surrounded by crystals, then left on a sunny windowsill. It can be placed in a bowl of salt or left overnight with crystals, then washed in the morning—or washed in running water then left in the sun to dry, and so forth.

Element: fire, water
Zodiac: Virgo
Color: white
Jewel: salt, quartz, sea salt, peridot, amethyst, garnet, crystals
Incense: benzoin, cedar, copal, rosemary, lavender
Invoke: Nisŝaba, Sarasvati; Agni (the Purifier), Apollo (purification rituals)
Plant: alkanet, asafetida, avens, betony, birch, bloodroot, broom, cedar, centaury, fennel, ferns, hyssop, lemon, mugwort, rosemary, holy thistle, thyme, turmeric, vervain, yucca

Purifying Evil and Negativity:
Witches use eggs, onions, and crystals to clear bad vibrations out of places. We do this by leaving them in the space overnight to absorb the negativity, then purifying the crystals or throwing the eggs and/or onions away. Hyssop water and sea water can also be used to purify places.

Jewel: quartz
Plant: acacia, eggs and onions

Raising the Dead:
Lazarus aside, you cannot physically raise a dead person or animal. You can, however, raise a dead issue, relationship, plan, and the like.

Plant: yew

Raising Magic Mists:
Invoke: the Telchines
Plant: willow

Rebirth/Resurrection:
Planet: Pluto, Sun, Moon, Waning Moon
Symbol: the shed skin of a snake
Color: black
Animal: frog, butterfly, chicken, stag, goat, cock, scarab beetle
Invoke: Isis; Attis, Itzam Na, Jesus, Osiris, Poseidon
Plant: alder, ash, cypress, white poplar

Render Witches Powerless:
Plant: elder

Rituals:
  Jewel: sea salt (merfolk rituals)
  Invoke: Kamrusepas (magical rituals), Vac (spoken and chanted
    rituals)
Sacred Space:
  Color: white
Seasonal Magic:
  Invoke: Themis
Secrecy:
  Zodiac: Scorpio
  Invoke: Angerona; Horus
  Plant: rose
Shape-shifting/Skin-walking:
Despite all those werewolf films, it is not possible to actually physically transform into an animal. Shape-shifting is a psychic experience, in which you perceive reality from an animal's viewpoint. It is used for escape and to gain knowledge or advantage. Many cultures have used drugs to achieve this state, but I don't recommend that. Try drumming and dancing with magical intent.
  Animal: raven
  Metal: quicksilver
  Invoke: Annis, Badb, Goda, Lilith, Morgen, Otter Woman,
    Pelé, Scylla, Tatsuta-Hima, Thetis, Vila, White Buffalo
    Woman; Atabyrius, Cuchulainnn, Cu Roi, Damuzi, Dionysus, Eshu, Llew Llaw, Loki, Merlin, Odin, Periclymenus, Quikinn A'Qu (Big Raven), Zagreus
Shutting What is Open:
  Invoke: Cardea
Sleeping Spells:
  Season: winter
  Jewel: amber, amethyst, lodestone, peridot, blue tourmeline
  Color: blue
  Number: 5
  Plant: passionflower, *poppy, pillows stuffed with linden and
    lavender
  Invoke: Ea, Hypnos, Somnus
Sorcery:
  Jewel: jet
  Invoke: Circe, Greine, Pelé, Sheng-Mu; O-Kuni-Nushi, Veles
  Plant: nightshade
Speed:
  Animal: cougar, cheetah

Use this ancient Egyptian phrase in spells to make something work fast or happen quickly:

**Swifter than greyhounds and fleeter than light.**[8]

Spells:
Color: black (indrinking spells)
Jewel: sea salt (sea spells), aquamarine (sea spells)
Plant: pistachio (to break love spells), wintergreen (charm against spells)
Invoke: Freya (casting spells), Hecate, Isis (Lady of Spells), Kamrusepas (Goddess of Spells), Marduk

Spirituality:
Meditation is a great way to increase your spirituality.
Color: violet, white, blue, light blue
Jewel: amethyst, amber
Number: 5
Plant: cinnamon, gardenia, sandalwood
Animal: birds
Invoke: Kwan-Yin; Obatala

Strength:
Planet: Mars, Saturn (strength through persistence and endurance)
Element: earth, fire (the ardor of strength)
Direction: West
Color: orange, red, white (spiritual strength)
Jewel: amber, diamond, crystals, chalcedonyx, chalcedony (physical strength), red jasper (inner strength), garnet (strengthen magical workings), pyrite (strengthens the will)
Tarot: Strength
Animal: lion, elephant, ox, elk, horse, bear (gentle strength), boar (warrior strength)
Invoke: Isis (strength in adversity), Romë, Savasi, Ushas; Hercules, Horus, Kratos, Ra, Wachabe (Black Bear)
Plant: carnation, garlic, mugwort, saffron, St. John's Wort, thistle
Charm: boars' bristles

Supernatural Abilities:
Plant: *crown of amaranth flowers, soma

---

[8] E. A. Wallis Budge, *The Egyptian Book of the Dead: The Papyrus of Ani* (New York: Dover Publications), p. 307.

Trance Magic:
  Invoke: Freya
Transformation:
  Planet: Moon, Full Moon, Pluto
  Zodiac: Scorpio
  Invoke: Annapurna, Cerridwen; Horus (the Mighty One of Transformations), Poseidon
  Metal: quicksilver
  Jewel: sodalite, amethyst, obsidian (very powerful), black onyx (personal transformation), coral (personal transformation)
  Animal: frog, butterfly, snake
  Charm: shape-changing water, the shed skin of a snake
Unbinding:
  Invoke: Aditi the Unfettered (freedom from bounds), Kali; Teshub, Varuna
Unblocking:
  Jewel: opal, peridot, gray moonstone
Victory:
  Planet: Jupiter (political victory)
  Jewel: alabaster, amethyst (victory over enemies), opal (victory against adversaries), diamond (victory in court or at war, if your cause is just)
  Plant: laurel, fennel, palm tree
  Animal: conch shell (victory in battle)
  Invoke: Aparajita (the Unconquered), Nike, Korravai, Victoria; Vahagn
Wind Spells (see also Part I,  The Elements, Air):
Wind spells were important when ships had to rely on sail power. If you aren't a sailor, ask yourself if you have a purpose for raising winds before you trouble Mother Nature. Part of respecting magic is only using it with good reason.
  Invoke: Air deities, Cardea, Oya; Aquilo, Astraeus, Boreas, Ellil, Enlil, Eurus, Favonius, Notus, Quetzalcoatl, Volturnus, Zephyrus
  Plant: broom, saffron, sea kelp
Wishes:
The basic mechanism of a wish spell is any method of broadcasting your wish to the universe in order to manifest it. For example, you could write the wish down then:

• Burn the paper, sending the wish skyward;
• Seal the paper in a bottle and give it to the sea;

- Make a paper airplane of it and give it to the wind;
- Make a votive boat by folding it into a little boat and adding a small candle, lighting the candle, and setting the boat afloat on a river or stream;
- Inserting it into a balloon, filling the balloon with helium, then releasing it.

Whatever method you use, it is the magical intensity of your wish that empowers it. Herbs, stones, or things directly related to your wish can be added to the spell to make it stronger. For example, you can add herbs of love, healing, or creativity to the boat, balloon, or bottle if your wish concerns those things. If you are wishing for a house, you can make make the votive boat out of a page from the real estate section of the paper; the employment section, if your wish is for a new job; the Personals if it is for a new relationship, and so on.

Remember to be careful what you wish, because you just may get it. Sometimes the wanting is better than the having.

    Invoke: Tara

    Plant: bamboo, beech, buckthorn, dandelion, ginseng, peach, pomegranate, sage, sunflower, violet, walnut

Work for Small Children:

    Invoke: Artemis

    Plant: *clover

    Color: white

Youth:

    Invoke: Chalchihuitlcue, Hebe, Juventas; Horus, Mabon

    Color: green, pink, rose

    Plant: cowslip, rosemary, vervain

    The light blue or green Egyptian Amulet of the Papyrus Scepter was used for vigor, the renewal of youth, and Isis-power:

*It is in sound state and I am in sound state;*
*it is not injured, and I am not injured;*
*it is not worn away and I am not worn away.*[9]

Youth (eternal):

(Be careful with this one, because an early death can be a kind of eternal youth)

    Plant: ferns

    Invoke: Iduna

---

[9] E. A. Wallis Budge, *Egyptian Magic*, p. 50.

# MONEY AND BUSINESS

Let's face facts: if money spells really worked as we would like them to, every lottery or sweepstakes winner would be a witch. None of us would have day jobs, bills to pay, school loans, or mortgages. Temples of the Goddess, white marble inlaid with gold and lapis lazuli, each with its replica of the Ishtar Gate, would rise all over the planet.

Be realistic. Magic is more likely to give you what you need than what you want. A greedy witch is usually a frustrated witch. Spells can be made for things like a better job, debt collection, increased business, a successful project, or protection from unfair competition. The only way I know to make money is to work hard and earn it, so I haven't got any grand money spells for you.

What I do have is a simple way to manifest prosperity in your life: always keep the chalice on your altar full. Each time you wash and refill it say: My cup is empty, I make it full. Focus on the financial well-being of yourself or your family as you do this, not on riches or schemes. Replace it on the altar with your right hand. Believe in the efficacy of this simple act and be patient as it gradually manifests itself. Don't forget to give thanks for blessings when they come.

Magic is not for sale. Being a witch is a calling, not a job. Magic is sacred and no ethical witch will accept money for casting a spell. If you're interested in witchcraft because you think it will give you an easy life or make you rich, you're in it for the wrong reason.

Fairly take, and fairly give. It is ethical for Wiccans with crafts to sell the things they make: wands, windchimes, potions, candles, besoms, or books. Shopkeeping witches have the right to make a profit. Witches adept at psychic readings, casting horoscopes, reading cards, palms, or runes may charge for their professional services. Witches with Web sites, or those who organize festivals and fairs, may do so as a business, or as a service to the pagan community. If someone asks you for money in return for removing a curse from you, you are dealing with a crook.

# CORRESPONDENCES FOR FINANCIAL SPELLS

**PLANET:** Jupiter, Mercury, Sun, Pluto
**ELEMENT:** air, earth
**NUMBER:** 1, 4, 7, 8
**COLOR:** green, gold, silver
**CANDLE:** green (money spells), orange (success)
**BEST TIMES:** Wednesday, Thursday, Sunday
**MOON:** Waxing to Full Moon (increase), Full Moon in earth sign (material gain), Full Moon in air sign (plans and ideas), Full Moon in fire sign (growth or energy)
**SUN IN:** Virgo (for detail-oriented work), Leo (solar power), Sagittarius (expansion, business trips), Aries (for beginning a new enterprise), Capricorn (overcoming obstacles)
**INVOCATIONS:** the Alad Udug Lama, the Shichi Fukujin

Goddesses:
Aditi, Agathe Tyche, Bona Eventus, Demeter, Earth goddesses, Hecate, Hera, Inanna Juno, Lakshmi (She of the Hundred Thousands), Minerva, Olwen, Ops, Sarasvati, Sri-Laksmi, Tyche, Ushas

Gods:
Agathodaemon, Chango Macho, Cernunnos, Dionysus Plutodotes, Dis, Earth gods, Hades (the Rich), Hercules, Kubera, Mammon, Pluto, Volos, Zeus

FOR:
Abundance:
Invoke: Astarte, Gauri, Habondia (She of Abundance), Inanna, Lakshmi (She of the Hundred Thousands), Oshun; the Dagda, Ellil
Affluence:
Invoke: Ch'eng-huang
Business:
Planet: Mercury (business transactions)
Jewel: bloodstone (increasing business), blue tourmaline (business success), amethyst (makes expert in business)
Invoke: Ek Chua (god of merchants), Heracles Melkart (merchants and bargains), Hermes (patron of all important financial transactions), Kuan Kung (restaurants, pawnshops, curio dealers and secret societies), Lugh (commerce), Manannán Mac Lir (Patron of Merchants), Mercury (god of merchants), Sukuna-Hikona (trade), Xaman Ek (the Guide of Merchants)

New Business:
: Invoke: Ganesha (invoked before moving, traveling, or opening a new business), Janus (the god of good beginnings)

Business Travel:
: Invoke: Fortuna (successful journey and a safe return); Yacate-cuhtli (who guides business travelers)

Charm and Elegance When Asking a Favor of Authority:
: Plant: cinquefoil

Contracts:
: Invoke: Arom

Fair Dealing:
: Invoke: Inanna; Aequitas

Favor:
: Jewel: lodestone (favors), sapphire or topaz (to procure favor with princes)
: Plant: crown of amaranth flowers, chicory
: Invoke: Concordia, Hecate, Siddh

Gambling:
: Plant: jalup root (High John), lucky hand
: Jewel: topaz, lodestone (attract luck)
: Invoke: the Apsaras (who protect gamblers), Fata (for chance)

Good Fortune:
: Planet: Jupiter, Waning Moon (reversal of fortune)
: Jewel: chrysophase, carnelian, turquoise, moonstone, jasper
: Number: 1, 2, 3, 4, 5, 7, 9
: Animal: pair of cranes
: Plant: laurel (bay leaf)
: Invoke: the Pa-hsien (the Eight Immortals); Felicitas, Habondia, Nortia, Saubhagya-Bhuvanesvari (Buddha of good fortune), Sheng-Mu, Shri-Devi (Good Fortune); Gonaqade't, Li T'ieh-Kuai

Good Luck:
: Planet: Jupiter
: Color: green
: Jewel: jade, opal, aventurine, lodestone, garnet, amber, tiger's eye, pearl, sapphire, topaz, chrysoprase, emerald (worn on Friday)
: Plant: aloe, bamboo, banyan tree, cabbage, calamus, caper, cotton, daisy, dill, ferns, white heather, kava kava, maize, male fern, mistletoe, orange, pomegranate, poppy, purslane, rose, St. John's flower, star anise, vervain root, violet

Good Luck for Females:
: Plant: ivy

Good Luck for Males:
  Plant: holly
  Invoke: the Apsaras (for gamblers), Benten, Felicitas, Kishijo-
  ten, Lakshmi; Belobog, Bishamon, Daikoku, Fu-hsing
  (Lucky Star), Jorojin, Koto-Shiro-Nushi, Sors
Good Omen:
  Plant: holly
Good Will:
  Invoke: Concordia
Increase:
  Color: brown (material increase)
  Number: 2, 16
  Invoke: Al Yazid
Losses:
  Invoke: Punarvasu (who restores lost or stolen property)
Material Benefit:
  Invoke: Maia
Money Spells:
  Color: green, gold, silver, copper
  Jewel: jacinth, moss agate, bloodstone, peridot, emerald, fire
  opal, pearl, brown agate, aventurine, sapphire, topaz, green
  tourmeline
  Metal: gold, silver, copper
  Incense: cedar, cinnamon, fumitory, lavender, nutmeg,
  patchouli, pine, storax
  Plant: almond, balm, borage, bramble (blackberry), bryony, cala-
  mus, cascarda sagrada, cedar, chamomile, horse chestnut,
  cinquefoil, clove, clover, comfrey, dill, dock, fenugreek,
  flax, ginger, goldenrod, gorse (furze), grape, jalap root (High
  John), laurel, lavender, mace, mandrake, *moneywort, *oak
  leaves, oats, orange, peas, periwinkle, pine, poplar, poppy,
  rice, *saffron, sage, St. John's Wort, sarsparilla, sea kelp, ses-
  ame, sunflower seeds, valerian, vervain, wintergreen
Opportunity:
  Invoke: Sesheta (Whose Opportunity Escapeth Her Not)
Personal Advancement:
  Invoke: Santoshi Mata
Plenty:
  Animal: buffalo
  Invoke: Ana (Goddess of Plenty), Habondia; Ganaskadi
Power:
  Invoke: Amauntet (hidden power), Bia, Dynë, Oya; Amun
  (hidden power), Gonaqade't

Productivity:
 Invoke: Kubera
 Animal: ant, beaver, bee
Profit:
 Invoke: Habondia; Ebisu, Ts'ai-Shen (profit from commercial
  transactions)
Prosperity:
 Planet: Earth
 Animal: dove, eagle, dragon, pair of fish
 Incense: benzoin
 Color: green
 Jewel: sapphire
 Plant: alkanet, almond, ash, banana, elder
 Invoke: Inari (the Vanir); Felicitas (agricultural propserity),
  Freya, Sasthi, Sri-Devi; Cernunnos, Ih P'en, Majas Gars
  (prosperity of the family home), Teharon, Ubertas
  business prosperity: sage, St. John's Wort
Riches:
 Planet: Jupiter
 Jewel: emerald, jacinth
 Plant: ferns
 Invoke: Al 'Uzza, Dyaus
Status:
 Invoke: Inanna; Lÿ-hsing (Star of Status)
Success:
 Planet: Jupiter, Sun
 Number: 7
 Animal: wolf, eagle
 Color: purple, green, orange
 Jewel: rose quartz, turquoise, lodestone, malachite, black ag-
  ate, green tourmeline (business success), jasper (financial
  success)
 Metal: gold
 Plant: balm, cinnamon, clover, ginger, rowan, winter bark
 Invoke: Siddh; Al Yazid (worldly success), Al Yusif, Ganesha
Wealth:
 Planet: Jupiter, Mercury, Pluto
 Animal: bear
 Metal: gold
 Jewel: ruby, topaz
 Plant: basil, pomegranate

Invoke: Califia (mineral wealth), Dhisani, Ganga, Hecate, Lupa (material wealth), Prithivi, Purandhi, Rosmerta, Sri-Devi, Ushas; Cernunnos, Ih P'en, Kubera, Njoerd (Giver of Wealth), Olokun

TO:

Attract Money:
Plant: borage, lavender
Jewel: lodestone
Get a Job:
Color: green
Jewel: lodestone
Plant: jalap root (High John), laurel, lavender

# PROTECTION

Hexing is not ethical in Wicca, but protecting yourself, your home, your work, your possessions, or your loved ones certainly is. We do this by establishing general or specific protection around ourselves. Protection is a force field that bounces the harmful intentions of others back onto them. They may self-destruct, but they are the agents of their own destruction—not you.

Banishing and binding are other methods of protection. Banishing removes someone from your life, but leaves them free to become someone else's problem. Binding is more difficult. It prevents a person from harming themself or others. You have to break all connection between yourself and someone you bind, so you may also want to do a banishing.

Everything we do comes back to us. Be creative when facing threats, avert them instead of attacking whenever possible. Those who have studied martial arts know how effective simply reversing the energy of an oncoming thrust can be. Finding ethical ways to deal with threats is the best way to protect yourself.

## PROTECTING YOUR HOME

Making a safe place for yourself and your family is one of the most important things a witch can do. Experience teaches us that no one is ever really safe anywhere, but a little magic certainly can't hurt. Here are some ways to protect your house:

- Put a picture of Anubis (the jackal-headed Egyptian god) over the door.
- Get a familiar, an animal with whom you establish a special psychic/magical relationship.
- Modern Egyptians dip their right hands in paint and make palm prints on the outside walls of their houses to ward off the evil eye. Bright blue paint is best for this.
- In the East, the names of deities who protect doors, gates, and arches are written on them (see entrances and exits on the list below). This is said to work even if you write the names and then paint over them.

# PROTECTING YOURSELF

- Wear a silver pentacle.
- Empower a piece of jewelry with protection and wear it as an amulet.
- Make a mojo bag to wear, fill it with protective herbs, stones, and charms.

# PSYCHIC PROTECTION

You can drive yourself crazy by believing your are under attack from elementals, spirits, demons, black magicians, or ex-lovers. Protecting yourself from your own imagination or paranoia is as important as being aware of actual threats. The following things provide psychic protection:

> salt and water
> garlic
> pentacles
> familiars

Dion Fortune, a spiritualist writer much respected by witches, recommended the following in her book *Psychic Self-Defense.*

| | |
|---|---|
| sunlight | a hot water bottle on the solar plexus |
| laughter | moving your bed |
| a full stomach | repairing your aura |
| hot baths | breaking contact |
| open bowels | crossing running water |
| a change in diet | burning incense of protection |
| a positive environment | (consult the list below) |

Fortune also advised the following protective measures:

- *Against someone whose influence disturbs you:* Visualize a plate of glass (or force field) between you.
- *Against domination* (try this one at work): Stare at a point between the person's eyebrows.
- *Against someone who drains your energy:* Close the circuit of your body by touching your feet together, pressing your elbows to your sides, and placing your folded hands, with interlaced fingers, across your solar plexus.

She also says that while under psychic attack you should avoid drugs, alcohol, sleeping pills, fasting, solitude, occult practices, and objects with black vibrations.

# SPELLS FOR PROTECTION

### HOUSE-BLESSING SPELL

This spell places protection around you and yours. Salt and water are two basic elements of magic. Mix them together in sacred space, reciting:

> **O Great Mother**
> **In your name we purify**
> **With water and with salt**
> **Cleanse this place of evil**
> **And fill it with your Love**
> **O Great Mother**
> **Make this cave a safe space**
> **A warm and dry place**
> **And shelter us from harm**
> **O Great Mother**
> **Make this house our home.**

Use garlic salt and add powdered rosemary if you need to clear out ghosts or spirits.

Begin at the main entrance of the house or apartment. Sprinkle some of the salt water by dipping your fingers in it and making the sign of the pentacle. Say:

> **Evil shall leave but not enter.**

Use a firm voice. Make it a command, with all of your power behind it. Proceed counterclockwise through the house, repeating the procedure in every corner of each room, at all the windows, doors, and mirrors. Don't forget telephones, computer modems, fax machines, intercoms, and televisions that are connected to the Internet. It doesn't hurt to do the mailbox and the car as well.

Make the downward pentacle with your left hand if this feels right to you, or the upward pentacle with your right hand. Either will work. Repeat the spell annually, or whenever you feel in need of it. It is important to perform a spell like this on a new home before you move into it.

## BANISHMENT SPELL

This is a fire spell for love gone wrong, for ending a personal, family, or business relationship that you no longer wish to continue. I wrote it years ago as an anti-stalking spell and have not been troubled by or even laid eyes on the spell's subject since then. To work the spell, you will need:

• Herbs of protection (consult the list on page 146);
• An image of the person (photograph, poppet, etc.); something written in their own hand, a lock of hair, a piece of clothing, or a personal object will also do.

Arrange your altar or working surface in your usual way. Raise power and cast a circle. Put everything into a fireproof container —iron cauldron or marble mortar, for instance—and set fire to it as you perform the spell. Add the photograph or a piece of paper with the person's name on it if you have trouble getting the fire going. It should make a very satisfactory blaze that reduces to ashes. If you have a lot of items from this person to get rid of, you can use a bonfire for the spell and feed them all to it.

> By the crimson and the gold
> By basilisk and bloodstone
> By the garlic in the fields
> By the poppies and what they yield
> Invisibly I make my shield
> To detect thee and deflect thee
> And keep thy harm from me.
> By dragon's blood and salamanders
> By horses when their hooves strike sparks
> By the dragon breathing flames
> From the Book of Life I erase thy names
> I cut the cords and unlock the chains
> I sever all the ties by which we were bound
> And with impenetrable walls myself I surround
> Against thy power and its source
> Against thy evil and its force
> > Vesta, Pelé, Lilith
> > Kali Kali Kali
> I banish thee forever from me
> And any harm from thee to me
> Doubles back and tables turned

Thou shalt by thyself be burned
Lilith, Vesta, Pelé
Kali Ma Kali Ma
By the power of three times three
I banish thee, I banish thee, I banish thee
I am set free
So mote it be!

The ashes can be buried or washed down a drain. Flush them down a toilet if you are very angry. Dispose of all the objects that connect you to the person: gifts, letters, photographs, and the like. It is especially important to get rid of jewelry. Move if you have to.

Be careful with this spell. It's permanent, so don't use it unless you really mean forever. It's also powerful. The person I used it against had a pregnant wife, and I learned later their child had heart problems. The last I heard of him, he was having a quadruple bypass operation.

## BINDING

Get a large white candle, the kind that drips wax, and set it up on a tray. Affix to it a photograph or other image of the person you wish to bind. Make a ring of sea salt around it. Make a second ring with protective herbs. Fill the rest of the tray with images that represent what you are binding the person from: pictures of your family, keys to your house, legal documents, whatever. If the problem is too complex for images, write what the person is bound from on slips of paper and place them around the candle. Papyrus or paper made from cotton or linen work best for this. Use red ink if you are angry, purple ink if you are sad.

Wrap the candle and the image with black thread (linen, if possible). Invoke Isis and Linda, the Binder with Linen Thread. Do this with strong intent, saying aloud what you are binding the person from. Light the candle and let it burn until the wax begins to drip over the thread and image. Burn it every day for a week, until the image is thick with wax. Use this as a meditation device to direct your will to binding the person.

## ODIN'S BINDING (Binding and Transformations)

This is a major spell, one that should be reserved for the most serious problems. Imposing your will on another is not something you should normally do. It is a kind of psychic rape, so be sure the circumstances justify using magic this way—for instance to bind a rapist, a child abuser, or an active practitioner of black magic.

This spell is not meant to punish the person it binds. It is meant to help them. You should cast it out of necessity and compassion, not in anger. It is designed to stop people dead in their tracks, freeze them from doing harm to themselves or others, and give them pause, a clear space in which positive transformation can occur. You will need:

* A poppet—any sort of poppet is fine, in the correct gender if possible. Personalize it in some way to represent the person you will bind. Embroider a name on it or affix a picture to the poppet's face. I like to use a human-shaped candle with the person's name written on it or carved into the wax.
* Two candles, black ones if possible.
* Black thread (cotton is good, linen is better).
* Incense (copal, fumitory, sandalwood, and frankincense are good, but use whatever you can get).
* An image of or something connected to the person. If you don't have anything, write a name on a piece of paper.
* A healthy, living tree.

Gather everything (except the tree) where you will cast the spell. Raise power. Light one candle and the incense, cast a circle in your usual way. Bind the poppet with the thread, wrapping it around and around, making knots whenever you feel they are necessary. Speak to the person as you do this, telling them specifically why you are binding them and what you are binding them from.

Leave a long piece of thread hanging from the poppet. Tie nine knots in this. Drip molten wax on the bindings to seal them. Use wax to seal any body parts you are binding, such as the hands of someone who beats his wife or kids, the crotch of a sexual predator, or the mouth of someone who is verbally abusive. Close the circle and ground power.

Leave the poppet on the altar, touching what you are using to connect the person to the spell, until the candle and incense have burned out. Take the poppet and use the thread to tie it upside-down to a tree—an indoor tree will work as well as an outdoor one, but it must be a healthy, living tree. Make the five-fold bond, joining hands, neck, and feet if it is possible to do this with the type of poppet and bindings you are using. You can copy the position of the Hanged Man on the classic tarot card instead, if you like. Say:

**I ween that I hung on a windy tree,**
**Hung there for nights full nine;**
**With the spear I was wounded, and offered I was**
**To Odin, myself to myself,**
**On the tree that none may ever know**
**What root beneath it runs.**

This is the transformation part of the spell, the Norse god Odin's words about his experience of hanging himself as a sacrifice to gain wisdom. Leave the poppet on the tree for nine days and nights. Recite the poem to the poppet at least once each day, sending the person strong thoughts about the changes you want to manifest. Send compassion, send enlightenment. Hold a mirror up to the poppet while you recite the poem if you want the person to "see" a certain situation. Yell at the poppet if you have anger you need to release. This spell can be therapeutic for you as well.

Take the poppet down after nine days and nights, leaving it bound. Light the second black candle and drip its wax all over the poppet. Speak to the person while you do this, saying whatever you think he or she needs to hear. As soon as the wax sets, get the poppet out of your house and into the trash. Seal it in something if the person was a great threat. Do *not* bury it.

If the tree shows signs of growth afterward, that is a good sign that the transformation part of the spell is working. If it's spring and the tree was going to bloom anyway, more than the usual number of blossoms is a good sign.

### VEXATION BOX

This spell is for dealing with someone who is more of an annoyance than a threat, someone who really gets on your nerves or stresses you out by intruding in your life or violating your space. It is for someone you have already asked to stop, but who persists in bothering you. It is not a spell to use on those whose actions within their own life or space trouble you. You will need:

- A box;
- Two heads of garlic (or more, if you are using a big box or dealing with a group of people);
- Herbs of protection (see the list on page 146);

- A photograph of the person, or the person's name written on a piece of paper.

Put everything in the box. Cover the box and give it a good hard shake, mentally yelling at the person to modify the behavior that annoys you. Put the box away, in a drawer or up on a shelf. Take it out and give it a hard shake and yelling, every time the person annoys you. After the first week or so, you should seldom need to shake the box. Throw the box away in a few months, when the garlic begins to spoil.

## WARNING SPELL

This one is a good substitute for a hex when your fear or anger tempts you in that direction. It sounds dire, but this spell works more on you than it does the other person. It allows you to take charge of the situation, to vent, to calm yourself so you can think clearly and decide what to do about the problem. It prevents you from actually cursing or hexing anyone.

> **Blood turn black and flesh turn blue**
> **I will curse you if you force me to**
> **By the left hand and the unclean food**
> **I'll curse your eyes, I'll curse your lies**
> **I'll call down a plague of flies**
> **Blood go black and flesh go blue**
> **Evil from me and back to you**
> **My soul clean and yours on fire**
> **You mess with a witch you get burned, liar!**

# CORRESPONDENCES FOR PROTECTION

PLANET: Neptune
BEST TIMES: Waning Moon to banish evil or negativity, waxing to Full Moon to establish protection
METAL: silver
COLOR: white, bright blue, silver, red
ANIMAL: lion, tiger, scarab beetle
JEWEL: carnelian, onyx, chalcedony, quartz, lodestone, ruby, amethyst, emerald, garnet, ruby, topaz, jade, aquamarine, diamond, mother-of-pearl, tourmaline (black, pink, or green), red jasper, peridot (to feel protected)

CANDLE: black (to bind), white or bright blue (for protection), yellow (to make a safe space)

INCENSE: cedar, cinnamon, frankincense, ginseng, patchouli, pine, rose, sandalwood

INVOCATIONS: Your best bet in an emergency is:

## Isis help me!

angels, Apacita, the Balam, cherubim, gargoyles, the Manes, seraphim

Goddesses:

Aditi, Alcyone (the Queen Who Wards Off Storms), Amphitrite (who calms stormy seas), Anahita, Anna Perenna, Athena (who protects those in need of defense), Cardea, the Devi, Frigg, Hera, Hygeia (who protects from danger), Isis (who enfolds us in her wings), Kwan-Yin (Hearer of Cries, invoked for help in times of need and when danger threatens), Mary, Moon goddesses, Neith, Nut (the Great Protectress), Sarasvati, Securitas, Tanith

Gods:

Cuchulainnn, the Dagda, Elegua, Ganesha, Jupiter, Kutkhu, Morning Star, Neptune, Ochosi, Terminus (Guardian of Boundaries), Thor, Varuna (Coverer), Vidar (for strength and support in times of danger), Vishnu

PLANT: acacia, agrimony, aloe, amaranth, anemone, *angelica, *asafoetida, ash, balm of Gilead, bamboo, barley, basil, beans, betony, birch, bloodroot, blueberry, bodh tree, bramble, broom, bryony, buckthorn, burdock, cactus, calamus, caraway, carnation, carob, cascarda sagrada, cedar, celandine, chrysanthemum, cinnamon, cinquefoil, clove, clover, cotton, cyclamen, cypress, devil's bit scabious, dill, dogwood, *dragon's blood, elder, elecampane, eucalyptus, *Eye of Satan, fennel, ferns, figwort, flax, foxglove, *garlic, gentian, ginseng, gorse (furze), hollyhock, hyssop, jalup root, kava kava, laurel, lime, logwood, maize (corn), *mandrake roots, marsh mallow, mimosa, motherwort, mugwort, nettles, papyrus, peony, pepper, periwinkle, pine, primrose, purslane, quince, rice, rose, *rosemary, rowan, sage, *St. John's Wort, sea kelp, snapdragon, Solomon's seal, southernwood, squill, star of the earth, tamarisk, thistles, thorn apple (datura), toadflax, unicorn root, vervain, willow, wintergreen, witchgrass, witch hazel, *wolfbane, wormwood, yucca

TO PROTECT:

Agriculture:
  Invoke: Aphrodite of the Gardens, Ashnan (Protectress of the Grain), Pomona (gardens and orchards), Venus (gardens); Aristaios (herds and beekeepers), Bhumiya (fields), Saturn (the sower and the seed), Svantevit (crops), Tanu'ta (plants), Vertumnus (orchards and gardens)

Animals:
  Invoke: Caipora (forest animals), Diana Tabiti, Pales (sheep and cattle); Ah Cancum, Ah Tabai, the Brown Man of the Muirs (wild animals), Tanu'ta, Wai (forest animals)
  bears: Artio of Muri
  cattle: Disani, Lamaria (cows), Sekhet-Hor; Geus Urvan

Beauty:
  Jewel: jasper

Caravans:
  Invoke: Sai' Al Qaum, Tayon al-Kutbay

Children:
  Jewel: coral
  Invoke: Artemis, Athirat, Bastet, Boldogasszony, Decima (who guards gestation), Deverra (newborns), Gefion (unwed girls), Hecate, Intercidona (newborns), Juno (newborns), Kishimojin, Laima (newborns), Potina (who lets infants drink safely), Sasthi (happiness and welfare of children), Volumna (infants and the nursery), Yashoda; Bes, Chang Hsien (Protector of Children), Pilumnus (newborns), Vagitanus (the first cry of newborns), Zeus (orphans)

The City:
  Invoke: Athene Polias (Protector of the City), Baalath, Pallas Athene (Goddess of the City), Salus (public safety and welfare), Tanith, Tyche; Ch'eng-huang, Zeus Polieus

The Downward Direction:
  Invoke: Sambharaja

The Earth:
  Invoke: Heimdall (Earth Watcher)

Entrances and Exits:
  Invoke: Patadharini (curtains and doorways); Bhairava (doorways), Janus (Guardian of Doors), Ksetrapala (doorways), Kushi-Iwa-Mado-No-Mikoto (entrance gates), the Men-shen (gods of gates and doorways), Portunus (entrances, gates, doors), Weng Shiang (the back door)

The Family:
  Invoke: Cardea, Disani; Kuladevata (the family god), Lar, Nang Lha, Tsao-chün (Lord of the Hearth)
Forests:
  Invoke: Durga (forest fires), Fauna (woods and plants); Faunus (woods and plants), Sucellos
Freedom:
  Invoke: Zeus Eluetherious
Fugitives:
  Invoke: Zeus (Preserver of Fugitives)
Gamblers:
  Invoke: the Apsaras
Gardeners:
  Invoke: Pomona
Grasslands:
  Invoke: Ve'ai (Grass Woman, the shamanka who protects grasslands)
Harbors:
  Invoke: Portunus
Hospitals:
  Invoke: Dhanvantari, Kantatman (Guardian of Hospitals)
The Household:
  Invoke: Astarte, Bastet, Hestia, Nephthys (Lady of the House), Vesta; Anubis, Asuha-No-Kami (houses and courtyards), Kunado-No-Kami (the way to the house), Lar, Zeus Herkeios
Hunters:
  Invoke: Hastseyalti
Intestines:
  Invoke: Selket
The Land:
  Invoke: Bran, Merlin
Love:
  Invoke: Hathor
Marriage:
  Invoke: Vara
Men:
  Invoke: the Oceanids (young men until they are fully grown)
Mines:
  Invoke: Min
Mountains:
  Invoke: Tork (mountains and those who live on them)

Nature:
 Invoke: the Horai (the order of Nature)
Oceans:
 Invoke: the Nereids
Places Where Goodness is Taught:
 Invoke: the Celestial Kings
Poets:
 Invoke: Brighid
The Poor:
 Invoke: Aradia; Shamash, Zeus
Property:
 Invoke: Zeus Ktesios
Prostitutes:
 Invoke: Inanna, Sheng-Mu (the Holy Mother)
Rivers:
 Invoke: Aha
Seafarers:
 Invoke: Amphitrite (who calms stormy seas), Aphrodite, Hat-mehyt (fishermen), Kwan-Yin (Hearer of Cries), Leucothea (who saves sailors from shipwreck), Ma-Tzu (boats and fishermen), Miao-shan, Nehalennia; Castor and Pollux (the Dioscuri, who protect sailors and who rescue people in distress or danger, especially at sea), Faivarongo (Grand-sire of the Ocean), Hung Sheng (fishing vessels), Kwan-Yin of the Southern Sea (who helps those menaced by water and rescues shipwrecked people), the Munakata-No-Kami, Sirsir
Sexual Organs:
 Invoke: Diana (female reproductive organs), Prajapati
Soldiers:
 Jewel: amethyst
 Invoke: Meness (military expeditions)
Spiritual Development:
 Invoke: the Dharmapatat
The State:
 Invoke: Emperor Kuan (guardian of the state and its officials, who protects against external enemies and internal strife)
Storehouses:
 Invoke: Inanna; Mi-Kura-Tana-No-Kami
Strangers:
 Invoke: Zeus Xenios

Suppliants:
    Invoke: Zeus Hikesios
Tents:
    Invoke: Mahakala
Traders:
    Invoke: Hermes
Travelers:
    Invoke: Apollo, Chung-kuei, Hasameli, Hermes, Ilmarinen, the
        Kumado-No-Kami (roads, crossroads, boundaries), the Lares
        (crossroads), Meness, Pusan (journeys and pathways), Sha-
        mash, Tayon al-Kutbay (patron of travelers), Zeus
    Plant: comfrey, sea holly
Treasure:
    Invoke: Andvari (Guardian of Treasure), Fafnir
The Universe:
    Invoke: the Lokapala (world protectors)
    Animal: dragon
The Upward Direction:
    Invoke: Usnisa
Virginity:
    Invoke: Diana
Warriors:
    Invoke: Reshep (who protects in battle)
Wild and Weak Things:
    Invoke: Artemis
Women:
    Invoke: Akonadi, Bastet, Boldogasszony, Hathor (pregnant
        women), Hera (married women), Hesat (pregnant wom-
        en and nursing mothers), Hulda (maidens), Inanna (pros-
        titutes), Juno (who protects women all their lives and
        saves from domestic abuse), Kwan-Yin (mothers), Laima
        (women in labor), Lupa (courtesans), Mama Quilla (mar-
        ried women), Sheng-Mu (mothers), Taweret (pregnant
        women); Bes (women in labor)
The Wronged:
    Invoke: Shamash

FOR:
Protection Away from Home:
    Jewel: moonstone

Safe Passage:
  Invoke: Adeona (for children), Diana of the Crossways, Ella-
  man (Lady of the Boundary), Suleviae; the Michi-No-Kami,
  Wepwawet (Opener of the Way)
Safety at Night:
  Invoke: Ratri
Safety and Rescue:
  Invoke: Baalith

TO PROTECT AGAINST:
Accidents:
  Jewel: jade, turquoise, coral (violent accidents)
  Plant: feverfew
Animals and Insects:
  Plant: centaury (snakes), avens (venemous beasts)
  Jewel: sard (snakebite), serpentary (venemous creatures)
  Invoke: Buk (crocodile attack), Durga (wild animals), Janguli
    (snakebite), Manasa (snakebite); Geb (scorpions), Harpa-
    khered (dangerous creatures), Nehebu-Kau (snakes and
    scorpions), Ningirama (snakes), Sukuna-Hikona
Bad Dreams:
  Jewel: yellow chrysolite set in gold
  Plant: anise, heavenly bamboo, betony, *chamomile tea (drunk
    at bedtime), peony seeds, rosemary
Bad Luck:
  Plant: coca leaves
Bad Weather:
  Charm: charred embers from the Midsummer bonfire
Blight of Crops:
  Jewel: coral
  Charm: coals from fire-festival bonfires
The Dangers of the Forest:
  Invoke: Revanta
Darkness and Ignorance:
  Invoke: Virudhaka
Demons:
  Jewel: coral
  Plant: St. John's Wort
  Invoke: Gramadevata (forest demons); Bi-har-Fu-mo ta-ti (the
    Great Ruler Who Banishes Demons), Kwan-Yin, Shong-Kui

Devils:
  Plant: St. John's Wort, avens and vervain (the devil)
Disease:
  Invoke: Ix Chel, the Mares (the Mothers), Pattinidevi, Raksha-Kali (the Protectress, epidemics), Sekhmet
  cholera: Hardaul
  plague: Ayiyanayaka
Earthquakes:
  Invoke: Raksha-Kali (the Protectress); Poseidon Asphalios
Evil:
  Invoke: Alcyone (the Princess Who Averts Evil), T'ao Hua Hsi-ennui (Peach Blossom Girl); Ah Kin (evil that comes in darkness)
  Plant: angelica, basil, *birch, daffodil, elder, garlic, hemlock, laurel, wild olive, *pomegranate tree, rosemary, St. John's Wort, vervain
Evil Eye:
  Color: bright blue, red
  Jewel: amethyst
  Plant: *Eye of Satan, *garlic
  Charm: blue beads, the Hamsa hand, the Hand of Fatmah, porcupine quills, a quill filled with mercury, sealed at both ends and bound to the body
Evil Intentions of Others:
  Plant: cedar oil
Evil Psychic Forces:
  Plant: rowan
Evil Spirits:
  Jewel: jacinth, emerald
  Plant: Aaron's rod (great mullein), angelica, avens, balm, dill, black hellebore, laurel, mistletoe, mugwort, wild olive, peony root, periwinkle, rosemary, St. John's Wort
  Invoke: Bes
Evil Thoughts:
  Jewel: amethyst, zircon, ruby
Execution:
  Invoke: Durga
Famine:
  Invoke: the Mares (the Mothers), Raksha-Kali (the Protectress)
Fascination:
  Jewel: carnelian, coral

Plant: hyssop, lily, madwort (hung up in the house), kernel of the fruit of a palm tree

In Children:

Charm: sweep the face gently with a pine bough

Fatal Envy:

Plant: *garlic

Fear:

Planet: Mercury

Number: 7

Jewel: sapphire, coral, chalcedony (to banish), amazonite (to banish), ruby (to overcome fear), emerald (treats fear), jasper (treats fear), onyx with white veins (to provoke fear), banded red agate (strike enemies with fear)

Animal: eagle (for fearlessness)

Plant: daffodil root (carried at night), nettles and yarrow

Invoke: Tara

Fire:

Invoke: Brighid, Durga (forest fires), Kwan-Yin (who helps those menaced by fire), Kakaku

Plant: *houseleek

Ghosts:

Plant: *rosemary, garlic, and sea salt, St. John's Wort

Goblins:

Plant: rue

Guests:

Invoke: Zeus

Imprisonment:

Invoke: Durga

Imps:

Plant: St. John's Wort

Incubi:

Plant: peony seeds

Injury:

Charm: charred embers from the Midsummer bonfire

Injury by Others:

Plant: daffodil root (carried at night)

Lightning:

Jewel: spinel ruby

Plant: holly branches, a broom of mistletoe, houseleek, laurel, rowan, St. John's Wort (thunderbolts)

Invoke: Brighid

Magic:
    Jewel: coral (incantations)
    Plant: rue
Natural Disasters:
    Invoke: Avalokiteshvara (Merciful Lord)
Negative Energy:
    Jewel: selenite
Psychic Vampirism:
    Plant: *garlic (kept near the bed)

Psychic vampirism occurs when someone directs a need toward you while you sleep, sucking the life force out of you. It can be intentional or involuntary. Addicts of any kind are dangerous to live with because they do this naturally, selfishly, unknowingly.

I know that garlic is effective against psychic vampirism because of an experience I had when I first moved to Egypt. I lived in a remote place, untouched by tourism, in which I was the only foreigner. It was natural, in such a sexually repressed culture, for me to become the object of erotic speculation and yearnings. I began having strange dreams and trouble sleeping. Figuring that I was the object of psychic vampirism, I put bulbs of garlic on and under my bed and the problem was solved.

Sorcery:
    Jewel: agate, amber, sapphire
    Plant: asphodel, moly
The State:
    Invoke: Amun (Protector of Commoners)
Strangers:
    Invoke: Zeus
Theft:
    Jewel: coral
    Plant: garlic
    Invoke: Durga
Violence and Chaos:
    Invoke: Agayu
War:
    Invoke: Kuan Ti (who averts conflict and protects in war),
        Kwan-Yin (who helps those menaced by sword)
Water:
    Jewel: coral (tempests)
    Plant: ash (drowning)

Invoke: Kwan-Yin (who helps those menaced by water), Raksha-Kali (the Protectress, droughts and floods), Sao Ching Niang Niang (flood)

Witches:

Plant: angelica, betony, broom, cinquefoil, gorse, laurel, mistletoe, rue, St. John's Wort

Witchcraft:

Plant: dill (hung over the door), flax flowers, black hellebore, holly, marjoram, mistletoe, woody nightshade, snapdragon

Witchcraft of Strangers:

Plant: rue

Witches' Charms:

Plant: rowan

# PSYCHIC WORK

The phone rings, and you somehow know who is calling. You're thinking of someone, and they stop by to see you. You talk about a film you haven't seen in years, and suddenly it's on television. You dream something, and it comes true. All humans are psychic. It's just that some of us bang on pianos while others play Chopin at Carnegie Hall. This is a matter of natural talent, training, and practice, practice, practice. Were I to spend the rest of my life trying to mentally move a pen across a table, I am sure I would never be able to do it. I am equally sure that I would never waste my time in such a meaningless pursuit.

I am not especially psychic, but here is something that has often happened to me. Someone tells me in conversation about a health problem they are having. They recite their aches, pains, and symptoms and I blurt out, "Ah, you have _____." When I do this, I have no idea where I get that information. It just comes out of my mouth before I can even think about what I am saying. My diagnosis may seem unlikely at the time, but medical tests later prove me right. Sometimes they are arduous medical tests and it is a long time later. When people come or call to tell me that my diagnosis was confirmed, they usually add, "What are you, a witch?"

We are witches, the Wise Ones. We often know things without knowing how we know them. We have the ability to access information we could not possibly have acquired by normal means. Does it come from the astral plane? Past lives? The collective unconscious? The gods? I have no idea. I just know what I know. I am no more psychic than any other human. I just have an occassional gift for medical divination. Many witches have had similar experiences with whatever their gift happens to be, but most psychics are not witches. Psychic gifts mean you are psychic, not necessarily a witch. The difference between magic and psychic work is sometimes misunderstood. You don't cast a spell to learn the truth, find out if someone loves you, or if it's safe to fly on a certain day. You use divination.

Psychic gifts intrigue some people, frighten others. The more powerful the gift, the more difficult it can be to live with or control. A gift for premonition can be a very difficult one, constantly presenting you with the dilemma of whether or not to tell people what you see ahead for them. Remember that, if you dream something terrible and it comes true, you did not cause it to happen. You only sensed it coming. You are not responsible for it happening. People often refuse to heed warnings, and there are some bad things that no one can prevent.

Psychic gifts often strongly manifest themselves in childhood, then fade as we grow up, lessen as our open minds become cluttered and preoccupied. To develop psychic abilities:

- Meditate.
- Pay attention to your dreams. Keep a dream notebook to help you remember them.
- Hang out with witches.
- Respect your hunches. Trust your feelings and inner promptings—listen to your little voice.
- Study or practice some form of divination, preferably on a daily basis.
- Work with crystals.
- Find a legitimate psychic to guide you.

If you have trouble reaching a psychic state, try something like this. Wait until a quiet time of night when you can be alone and uninterrupted. Turn off the phone and anything else that might distract you. Wear loose, comfortable clothing. Light a candle, or several candles, and turn off all the lights. Burn enough incense to make the room smoky. Get comfortable, breathe rhythmically, and relax. Allow at least an hour for this, since deep relaxation can take time to achieve. Let your mind go wherever it will, or concentrate on a particular goal or problem.

# ASTRAL PROJECTION

When witches speak of flying, they mean astral projection, a journey of the mind. "Astral journeys," Dion Fortune tells us, "are really lucid dreams."[10] Far-sensing, far-seeing, shape-shifting, and travel on the astral planes all involve projection of your etheric body. Adepts can actually be seen in other countries when they are in fact home in bed.

---

[10] Dion Fortune, *Psychic Self-Defense* (York Beach, ME: Samuel Weiser, 1992), p. 157.

There are many techniques for achieving astral projection. Deep relaxation and reaching a trance state are good first steps. Applying drug plants to the skin in the form of flying ointments was a traditional method for witches, but this is not advisable without expert knowledge of herbs. Drumming, dancing, and gentle flagellation or other rhythmic physical stimuli can also be used. (Slow, rhythmic massage works for me.)

Imagination is a big part of it, so each person's journey is unique. AP (astral projection) comes naturally to some, is very difficult for others. Earth is my element, so out-of-body experiences hold little interest for me in and of themselves. I need a good reason in order to do anything. I find myself stubbornly resistant to astral projection unless I have an urgent, specific goal that requires it. I have had two excellent guides in AP, my friend Ororo and an Egyptian sheikh who has taught me many things.

I use the jet streams for far-sensing and remote viewing. This kind of Earth-orbit work is the easiest. You get very relaxed and allow your mind to float above you. You see this planet in your mind, picture where you are and where you want to go. You "feel" for a wind moving in the direction you want to go and allow your mind to flow with it. Winds, or even breezes, will do for local work, but you need the jet streams to reach other continents.

The experience of working with jet streams is similar to flying overseas in an airplane at night—you are in cold blackness, in or above the clouds. You can see the stars if you are above the clouds, but this isn't up to you, it depends on the winds. You use your inner sense of direction, your psychic navigation skills, to direct yourself. If you are able to see the land below you as you fly over it, you can use rivers to orient yourself and find your way. When you cannot see the land, feel for cities. They have more energy than the countryside and small towns. Be drawn to the energy and direct yourself from there. It is easiest to find your way to places where you have been before, or to find someone with whom you have a strong connection. Sometimes you will actually see the place you visit, see the people and what they are doing. At other times, you may only get a feeling for the place or people, a sense of things being well or ill.

The return trip is an instant one. You think of home or your body, especially your feet, and there you are, back in bed, inside your own body. I usually fall right into a sound sleep.

When I first tried to go beyond Earth-orbit work, I could reach the second plane, which to me looked like a room cut from rock.

Sometimes there were robed men there. It had torches on the walls and a leopard-skin divan, but I always lost interest and left.

The news was full of stories about Iraq in late 1998, with televized footage of sick and starving babies that moved me to tears. I grew more and more upset with Saddam Hussein, upset that he could build palaces while his people suffered. Having all the power means having full responsibility. I knew Western propaganda was working overtime, but you can't fake pictures of emaciated babies or the expressions on the faces of their desperate, heartbroken mothers. It seemed to me that, even with the embargo, Saddam, who didn't look like he'd been missing any meals, could feed the children and provide them with medical care if he would just reallocate his resources.

I decided to see if I could do anything about that. I am in the mother phase of my life as a woman and I feel a responsibility toward all children, everywhere. This seemed a serious enough situation to warrant breaking the rule against interfering and imposing. I decided to see if I could dream-magic him into turning one of his many palaces into a hospital for children. I was willing to accept whatever came back to me because of this working.

I have an unusual rock from Iraq that was given to me by a brother-in-law who had worked there as a geologist in better times. It looks like a slice of layer cake, with white rock icing atop and between layers of brown stone. I have never been to Iraq, so I used this rock to help me forge a connection with that country. Saddam and I are both Tauruses, so I used that to try to connect with him.

It was ridiculously easy to find him the first time I went. He was asleep on his side, alone in an underground room. I got into bed with him and held him as you would a child, talked to him about the sick babies and his responsibility to his people. I went into his mind, which seemed concerned only with primal instincts such as self-preservation. I showed him images of a palace changed into a hospital, of sick babies getting well and their grateful parents singing his praises. His mind was greedy, hungry, needful, and unsatisfied. It was hard to get him to pay attention.

America began bombing Baghdad a day or two later. I went back many times that winter, worked on Saddam whenever I could find him alone. I felt as if he welcomed my visits. I tried to teach him compassion, tried to get him to feel his people's pain. I recited ancient poems about the black-haired people, showered him with love and understanding, but it seemed useless. There were no news reports of palaces turned into hospitals.

I could feel others working on him as well, but I found it hard to believe that I was doing anything more than imagining the whole experience. I looked for reality checks, noted where he was when I found him and what he was wearing, uniform or suit, coat or robe. I had it right the few times there was news footage of him, so I kept going. Sometimes I went astray on the astral plane and wound up in Babylonia instead of Baghdad. When that happened, I found us standing side by side on a stone roof, looking out at the view. "I" would be hovering over the body that was me so I could never really see myself to know if I was male or female, old or young. He, however, always had a long, curled black beard.

I gave up hope that he could be taught compassion, began sending him thoughts of a way out, of resignation and a luxuriously happy exile. One day I found him outdoors before a crowd of people. It was cold and he wore a heavy coat. I floated up to him, took his face in my hands and looked straight into his eyes. I felt his astonishment when I did that, as if he recognized me, and things changed afterward. It was as if psychic shields went up and I could no longer get next to him, no longer find him while he slept.

The last time I went, it was daylight in Iraq and winter was just ending. I found myself in a bed in one of his palaces, somewhere outside Baghdad. I got up and started looking around, opened a door, and found a bathroom. It was bare and impersonal, a soldier's bathroom with nothing in the medicine cabinet but shaving gear and shampoo, linament and bandages all with Arabic labels. I opened another door and found a hallway bustling with palace staff. I could see and hear them, but they could not see me. The atmosphere was busy, almost festive. No one seemed fearful. I explored further and was surprised to see a few rugged westerners, fighting men. I had the idea they were mercenaries, Australians or maybe South Africans, employed to protect Saddam from his own forces should they turn on him.

Did Saddam have mercenaries? Or magical help? Did I dream or imagine all of this? Possibly. Did my astral work do any harm? I think not. Did it do any good? Probably not. America stopped bombing, the Western media got distracted by other stories and ceased covering Iraq. Life went on as usual there, I expect. It's hard to be sure about lucid dreaming, hard to know where reality ends and imagination begins. I do hope that life got better for the children, however.

I came out of this experience with compassion for Saddam Hussein, for his inner wounds and his emptiness. He wasn't parented properly, did not have his needs met, cannot understand normal human emotions. The source of his pain and violence lies in his never having gotten enough love. This does not excuse him in any way, but it does allow me to feel sorry for him. He is needy, rather than greedy, a deep well of longing that nothing will ever fill, ever satisfy.

You must mean well if you do this sort of work. You must have a legitimate reason for intruding on someone's mind and be willing to accept whatever is returned to you because of it. Remember that, if something has you concerned enough to get magically involved, it has doubtless affected others the same way. We are seldom alone when we do global work, and so must be careful that we are not working at cross-purposes.

# CORRESPONDENCES FOR ASTRAL PROJECTION

COLOR: purple, yellow
JEWEL: opal
PLANT: belladonna, cinquefoil, hemlock, henbane, mandrake, mugwort, poplar leaves, opium poppy, wolfbane
NOTE: Most of these are highly toxic and none of them should be ingested.
ASTRAL PLANES: the Fourth Dimension
   Symbol: ankh
   Color: violet
   Jewel: celestite
   Tarot: Judgment
   Animal: owl

Planes 1 through 4 involve the personality, which lasts for a single incarnation. You always take on a new personality when you are reincarnated, but one of these seven levels tends to predominate.

   First Plane: Physical
      dense matter, the material body
      Planet: Earth
   Etheric Plane:
      the tenuous energy web of near-matter, links the physical with the subtler planes
      Planet: Moon
   Second Plane: Lower Astral
      instincts, passions, the desire to attract or to possess
      Planet: Mars

Third Plane: Upper Astral
    abstract emotions, attraction, the desire for union
    Planet: Venus
Fourth Plane: Lower Mental
    form, definiteness, concrete mind, memory
    Planet: Saturn

Planes 5 through 7 involve individuality, an immortal characteristic that remains throughout all incarnations.

Fifth Plane: Upper Mental
    abstract mind
    Planet: Mercury
Sixth Plane: Lower Spiritual
    concrete spirit
    Planet: Jupiter
Seventh Plane: Spiritual
    pure spirit, abstract spirit, the divine spark, sustenance
    and energy, straight from the source
    Planet: Sun[11]

# CORRESPONDENCES FOR PSYCHIC WORK

PLANET: Moon, Sun
ELEMENT: all
BEST TIMES: Sunday, Monday, just before sleep
COLOR: silver, white, blue
NUMBER: 3, 4, 5, 8, 9
JEWEL: moonstone, quartz (amplifies psychic energy)
METAL: silver
SYMBOL: pentacle
INCENSE: patchouli
PLANT: *mugwort
INVOCATIONS: marine dieties
    Goddesses:
    Carmenta, Cassandra, the Camenae, Cybele, Fortuna, Freya,
    Gaia, Hecate, Moon goddesses, Nephthys, Python
    Gods:
    Ahura Mazda Glaucus, Gwydion, Helenus, Ifa, Math, Merlin,
    Nereus, Neptune, Phorcys, Poseidon, Proteus, Shamash,
    Thoth, Tiresias

---

[11] Janet and Stewart Farrar, *A Witches' Bible* (Custer, WA: Phoenix Publishing, 1984), p. 117.

FOR:

<u>Augury</u> (the interpretation of omens):
Invoke: Athene; Car
<u>Clairvoyance:</u>
Color: white
Plant: cannabis, mugwort
Invoke: Amphiaraus
<u>Discipline:</u>
Planet: Saturn
Jewel: hematite, onyx (self-control)
Animal: ant (self-discipline)
Number: 7
Invoke: Athena, Disciplina, the Vasita (willpower)
<u>Disrupting Psychic Shields:</u>
Plant: eyebright
<u>Divination:</u>
Planet: Moon, waning Moon
Color: purple, black, yellow
Jewel: jet, topaz
Plant: broom, alder, ash, catsfoot, cherry, camphor, dandelion, dodder, dogwood, fig, ginseng, goldenrod, maize, mandrake, morning glory, nutmeg, orange, polygonum, pomegranate, rose, rowan, St. John's Wort, vervain, willow, *yarrow
Invoke: Brighid, Dione (divination from the sound of rustling leaves), Freya, Oya, Teteoinnan (medical divination); Aktab Kutbay, Apollo, Arawn, Chiron, Hermes (who foretells the future, divination by pebbles), Ifa, Mercury (divination by dice), Neptune, Ogma, Poseidon, Shamash
<u>Female Leadership:</u>
Invoke: Oya
<u>Forethought:</u>
Invoke: Providentia
<u>Intuition:</u>
Planet: Moon, waning Moon
Element: air, water
Number: 2, 11
Color: violet, green
Jewel: blue topaz, azurite
Invoke: Prajnaparamita (transcendent intuition)
<u>Logical Analysis:</u>
Invoke: Prattisamvit

Meditation:
  Number: 7
  Color: white, light blue, black (to reach the deepest levels)
  Jewel: aventurine, amethyst, sapphire
  Plant: bodh tree, cannabis
Omens:
  Animal: falcon, pairs of fish (good omen)
  Invoke: Carmenta, Danaë; Phorcis, Zeus
Oracles:
  Invoke: Akonadi, Inanna (oracles of war and battle), Nina,
    Sibyl, Sul; Apollo, Baal Karmelos, Endouellicus, Glaucus,
    Nereus, Orula, Phorcys, Proteus, Ryangombe, Ta'lab, Tir,
    Wamala
Perception:
  Invoke: Sia
Prophecy:
  Planet: waxing Moon
  Candle: purple
  Jewel: emerald
  Animal: raven
  Invoke: Albunea, Brighid, Cardea, Carmenta, Cassandra, Cer-
    ridwen, Coventina, Danaë, Delphine, Goda, Gullveig, He-
    cate, Hera, Oenone, Rahab, Rhea, Sarah, sirens, Sulis,
    Tamar, Themis, Tzu-Ku-Shen, Völva; Ahura Mazda (pro-
    phetic revelation), Apollo, Arawn, Baal Zephon, Orunmila,
    Phorcys, Tatevali
Psychic Dreams:
  Planet: Moon
  Color: blue
  Jewel: amethyst, celestite (lucid dreaming)
  Animal: crab, lizard
  Plant: ash leaves, chamomile, *chamomile, skullcap and mug-
    wort, cinquefoil, laurel, lavender and linden, mimosa, mis-
    tletoe, mugwort, saffron, southernwood, tarragon, wild
    lettuce, wormwood
  Invoke: Pasiphaë (dream oracles); Asclepius (dream oracles re-
    lated to healing), Faunus (prophetic dreams), Hypnos, Kal-
    isia (dream messages), Morpheus, Somnus
  Interpretation of Dreams:
    Invoke: Geshtinanna, Gula-Bau, Nanshe
Psychic Power:
  Invoke: Amaunet (hidden power), Bia

Plant: acacia, bistort, borage, celery, cinnamon, citron, elecampane, eyebright, flax, hollyhock, marsh mallow, rose, rowan, saffron, sea kelp, star anise, thyme, wormwood, yarrow

Mental Power:
Plant: caraway, celery, eyebright, grape, periwinkle, rosemary, rue, summer savory, walnut

Inner Power:
Plant: *dragon's blood, elder flowers, holly leaves or berries, jalup root, laurel, mistletoe, oak leaves, rosemary, vervain

Psychic Work:
Planet: full Moon (maximum power)
Color: purple, silver
Jewel: aquamarine, lapis, sapphire
Incense: cinnamon, patchouli, saffron, wormwood
Plant: *mugwort

Energy in Psychic Work:
Plant: yerba maté

Energy and Visualization:
Plant: *ginseng

Memory and Concentration:
Plant: balm, eyebright, marjoram, nutmeg, parsley, pettigrain oil, *rosemary, sage

Mental Steadiness:
Plant: chamomile, celery and rosemary

Relaxation in Psychic Work:
Plant: anise, catnip, chamomile, dandelion, clover, hops, lavender, linden, mint, nutmeg oil, parsley, sage, savory, tarragon, wild thyme, valerian, vervain

Trance Work:
Invoke: Freya
Plant: ginseng, *laurel, wild lettuce, nutmeg, polygonum, saffron

Visions:
Jewel: green beryl (magical visions), jasper (magical visions), onyx (ugly visions)
Plant: angelica, autumn crocus, cannabis, coltsfoot, damiana, kava kava
Charm against visions: nettles and yarrow, rosemary

Visualization:
Plant: skullcap

TO:

## Get the Sight:
Incense: cinnamon, juniper, mastic, myrrh, patchouli, aromatic rush roots, sandalwood

## Refresh Psychic Power:
Plant: lovage water

## Strengthen Psychic Power:
Jewel: moonstone, azurite

## Understand Animals:
Invoke: Melampus

# SEX MAGIC

*Note: This chapter is not meant for teen witches,*
*it's strictly for adults.*

Desire is the force that holds the very atoms of being in place. To celebrate your lust, therefore, is to participate in the creative nature of the universe—". . . for behold, all acts of love and pleasure are my rituals."[12]

Witches, ever in tune with nature, do not deny their sexuality. They embrace it, enhance it, and celebrate it with joy. Any act of pleasure that takes place with mutual desire between consenting adults is lawful.

Shame and guilt with respect to sexuality are patriarchal concepts, only valid in abstemious faiths that espouse denial of the truth of our bodies. The sex act is a sacrament in Wicca. Wiccans make no apology for their sexuality, but they also never have sex with someone against his or her will, never use their powers to compel a person to do something he or she would not otherwise do. They abhor rape, child abuse, bestiality, and any sexual act that takes advantage of those they should be protecting.

Some witches say that sex is only sacred when performed in love, while others insist that lust is just as sacred. I think we all agree that the union of love and lust is the most desirable circumstance, the most satisfying experience. There is no higher form of worship than the Great Rite performed in such a union.

The god is invoked into the male witch, the Goddess into the female (or into same-gender partners enacting those roles). They make love, worshiping at the altars of each other's bodies. Power rises above them as the sacred marriage is enacted. Blessings flow from their union. In ancient times, this ritual was the annual duty of the king and high priestess. They celebrated the sacred marriage of Ishtar and Tammuz, Inanna and Damuzi, of Venus/Aphrodite and Adonis, thereby ensuring the well-being of their people for the year. Their rite was believed to activate the fruitfulness of the land, the fertility of humans and animals.

Lust, satisfied or unsatisfied, is a potent force that can be used to raise power for magic. Sexual union is magical in and of itself—

---

[12] Janet and Stewart Farrar, *The Witches' Bible,* p. 298.

the tension of polarity, the attraction and merging of opposites, the crescendo of power-raising, and the bliss of release. Combine the intensity of sex with the power of love, in a couple united in magical purpose, and you really get the mojo working.

Those witches who have partners who are not witches can still practice sex magic. One way to do this is to invoke the god or Goddess into yourself and then make passionate love with your partner inside a magic circle. Some say that doing so without your partner's knowledge and consent is abusive, but I disagree with that. I think you'll likely find your partner praising or thanking you for a more than usually intense and satisfying experience.

One method of sex magic is to focus on your objective in the moments just before orgasm, then use the psychic power of the orgasm to picture your objective as already accomplished, thereby manifesting it. It can be easier to use your partner's orgasm for this than your own, but this technique will also work with masturbation.

We're only talking about safe sex between consenting adults here, of course.

## SEXUAL HEALING

Sacred promiscuity and sacred prostitution were part of the worship of Dea Syria, the Syrian goddess known by many names: Ishtar, Inanna, Cybele, Astarte, Ashtoreth, and so on. Her temple priestesses were sacred prostitutes, the Goddess incarnate for those men who came in need and made the correct offering. The sexual nature of their service may be shocking to some, but we must remember that theirs was a sacred task. I suspect that sexual healing was their higher function.

Sexual healing is one of the greatest gifts a witch can give or receive. To heal someone sexually is to hold them passionately when they feel all alone, to convince them that they are beautiful when they think they are ugly, desirable when they feel unwanted. It is to replace their feelings of impotence with potency and leave them reborn as man or woman, recharged with all the power of their gender. Sexual healing renews the person who receives it, restore their self-esteem and self-confidence. People who are just emerging from toxic or abusive relationships are especially in need of this healing in its most tender forms.

Sexual healing can be performed by a priest or a priestess, performed out of deep romantic love, or as simple compassion. It can happen in single encounters as well as serious relationships, can include any sexual acts the healer is willing to provide. It isn't unusual for someone to cry when you heal them sexually, because the experience is much more emotional than it is physical, usually releasing tensions and anxieties that have been in place for years. A good sexual healing irons out all the wrinkles in somone's soul. It also isn't unusual for the person to fall at least a little bit in love with you. If this is just a case of loving and leaving on your part, you have to disengage gently but firmly so as not to damage the sense of self-worth you just restored.

Sexual healing is something a witch never does without desire on his or her own part. It isn't something that anyone can impose on you. It is a gift you give of your own free will. This is advanced work, offering your body as an altar. It is done with absolute attention, with the whole self. It can be difficult or dangerous, depending on the nature of the healing required. A man suffering pain and rage may need to discharge his pent-up violence in a sexual way, for example, to prevent him from acting it out in life and actually hurting someone. Sexual healing should never be undertaken lightly, or without consideration of all its dangers and possible consequences.

(We're still only talking about safe sex between mutually consenting adults.)

# APHRODISIACS

I set little store by aphrodisiacs. I think that you're either in the mood or you're not in the mood, you either desire someone, or you don't. The following, however, are those plants with reputed aphrodesiacal qualities. Those starred are the ones that might actually work. It is against our law to administer an aphrodisiac to someone without their full knowledge and consent, but you can use the plants in spells. An erotic massage will probably work better, however.

PLANT: aloe-wood oil, ambrosia oil or perfume, cardamom, oil of cardamom as perfume, carline thistle, coriander, cow parsnip, garden cress, ginseng, licorice, lovage, mandrake stems, mistletoe berries, myrrh, nasturtium, nut grass, orris oil, periwinkle, purslane, *Rhodymenia palmata* seaweed, savory, saw palmetto, Solomon's seal, vervain, watercress, white beth root, wormwood

Female Aphrodisiac: damiana, *damiana with saw palmetto
Male Aphrodisiac: celery, lettuce, wild lettuce, *yohimbe
Anaphrodisiac: rue

# CORRESPONDENCES FOR SEX MAGIC

**PLANET:** Venus, Mars
**ELEMENT:** fire
**BEST TIMES:** Friday, Full Moon
**ZODIAC:** Taurus, Leo, Scorpio
**CANDLE:** red, violet (gay sex magic)
**ANIMAL:** goat, dove, sparrow, sphinx
**JEWEL:** pair of lodestones
**INCENSE:** cinnamon, ginseng, patchouli, violet
**PLANT:** bishop's weed, caper, caraway, carrot, celery, cinnamon, cyclamen, damiana, devil's bit scabious, dill, garlic, ginseng, licorice, mandrake, pear, periwinkle, radish, saffron, sea holly, southernwood, violet, yerba maté, yohimbe
**WHEEL OF THE YEAR:** Beltane Eve and Samhain, when the Goddess descends into women, are the best nights for female sex magic.
**INVOCATIONS:** the Apsaras
Goddesses:
Aisha Qandisha, Anath, Aphrodite, Asherah, Astarte, Ashtoreth, Bastet, Cytherea, Desire, Erzulie, Freya, Frigg (her name is still used as a synonym for the more common English obscenity), Gypsy May, Harsa (desire), Hathor, Inanna, Ishtar, Ix Chel, Lilith (goddess of wet dreams), Mary Gypsy, Medb, the Morrigan, Oshun, Qadesh, Shakti, Sheela-na-Gig, Sphinx (who devours men), Venus (Queen of Pleasure), Voluptas
Gods:
Anael (Angel of the Star of Love), Azazel, Bacchus, Cernunnos (the Horned God), Chango Macho, Coyote, Cupid, Dionysus, Eros, Hercules, Hermes, Kama, Krishna (Lord of Love), Linga, Lupercus, Mars, Min, Neptune, Pan, Poseidon (Mare-tamer), Priapus, satyrs, Seth, Shiva (Lord of the Dance)
**AMULET:** the Egyptian amulet of the Sam, made of lapis lazuli, was used for union and carnal pleasure. It was wrapped in a mummy's bandages to ensure these delights in the afterlife. The Menat amulet, which contained the united power of male and female genitals, was used for joy, health, strength, and nutrition.

FOR:
Desire:
Planet: Venus
Invoke: Desire, Harsa, Kilili-Mushritsu (to satisfy desire), Venus;  Himeros (god of longing), Pothos (Desire)

To Attract Desire:
    Plant: *rose hips
    Rose Charm (to attract desire): This charm uses the concentrated power of rose hips to get you noticed in a sexual way. I know it works on males, but am not sure if it will also attract females.

- Get essence or extract of rose hips. This is a small bottle of red liquid with a stopper in it, available from health food stores, vitamin shops, homeopathic pharmacies, and places like that. Try the Web if you can't find it locally.
- Just before you go out put two drops of the rose hips on one wrist, then rub your wrists briskly together. It has a medicinal smell so you may want to also wear perfume—anywhere but on your wrists.
- People will flirt with you when you wear it but it only works at close range. Take the bottle with you to refresh it, if you need to keep it working for hours.

Ecstasy:
    Color: white (white hot)
    Jewel: diamond (spiritual ecstasy)
    Invoke: Od
Erotic Dreams:
    Invoke: Lilith, succubi; incubi
Frigidity:
    Plant: chicory, savory
    Spell: An ancient Egyptian papyrus says that if a man gets a whip and ties several knots in it, then places it under a woman's bed, this induces her to grant him uninhibited carnal pleasures. A thin whip placed between mattress and bed springs is what I suggest. I think of this as the Princess and the Pea Spell. I have had no reason to try it, so I cannot say how well it works.
Inventiveness in Love-Making:
    Invoke: P'an-chin-Lien
Lust:
    Planet: Venus
    Metal: tin
    Jewel: ruby (restrains lust)
    Animal: goat, serpent

Male Potency:
Introduction of the drug Viagra has surely decreased the need for impotence spells!

> Invoke: Babi (virility in the afterlife), Cernunnos, Ganymedes (Who Rejoices in Virility), Kama, Min, Te Tuna (Phallus), Uliliyassis (who removes impotence)
>
> Plant: banana, beans, caper, dragon's blood, oak, savory
>
> Restore Lost Virility: artemisia oil, yohimbine
>
>> Charm: Romans and Greeks wore iron thumb rings, the thumb being a phallic symbol and sacred to Venus, to maintain virility.

Orgasms:

> Invoke: earthquake deities, Thalli-Yjolta

Passion:

> Planet: Mars (emotional passion), Venus (physical passion)
>
> Element: fire
>
> Direction: East
>
> Color: red
>
> Number: 5 (passion as an end in itself), 7
>
> Animal: turtledove
>
> Plant: myrtle
>
> Jewel: moonstone, amethyst (to subdue passion), spinel ruby (to restrain passion), topaz (to treat lunatic passion)
>
> Invoke: Oreithyia (She Who Rages Upon the Mountains)

Animal Passion:

> Invoke: Bastet

Sensual Passion:

> Letter: U
>
> Invoke: Semiramis
>
> Incense: rosa ava

Angry Passion:

> Letter: Z
>
> Invoke: Ares, Mars

Sacred Prostitution:

> Invoke: Kilili-Mushritsu, Mary Gypsy

Sex in the Morning:

> Invoke: dawn goddesses, Eos


TO:
Awaken Sexual Energy:

> Incense: patchouli

Enhance Sexuality:

> Plant: *cannabis, mint and savory

# WISDOM

This quote from Blake has been with me for many years, through all my wanderings. It has hung over my desk, whenever I have had a desk. It is meaningful to me because I recognize its truth.

*The road of experience leads to the palace of wisdom.*[13]

Every experience teaches us something, especially the difficult and painful ones. This is a short chapter, because wisdom isn't something you can get from a spell or a potion, or even a book. It comes through life.

The meaning of life is to live, so embrace life passionately, with no hesitation. See, feel, hear, taste, and touch. Make mistakes and learn from them. Never be afraid to move on. Never be afraid to stick with something. Test your mettle and learn who you really are. Be not afraid—period. Blessed Be, as you live a magical life.

Here are some things you can do to accrue wisdom:

- *Meditate;*
- *Fall in love;*
- *Raise a child;*
- *Read:* Read everything that interests you, with an open mind.
- *Spend time with trees:* Blake also said that "A fool sees not the same tree that a wise man sees."[14]
- *Reflect on your life:* Consider keeping a journal, diary, scrapbook, or other record to help you keep track of where and who you have been. Remembering what you have done (and not done) can help you figure out what it all means.
- *Listen to children:* Children often have wisdom surpassing that of adults. As I write this I am thinking of the many women who have told me they finally found the strength to leave an abusive relationship because of something their children said to them about it.

---

[13] William Blake, "Proverbs of Hell," *The Marriage of Heaven and Hell* (New York: Dover Publications, 1994), p. 31.
[14] William Blake, *The Marriage of Heaven and Hell*, p. 31.

- *Travel:* Travel fearlessly, travel passionately. Travel alone. Eat strange foods and meet all kinds of people. Try new things. Learn another language. Be a little reckless. Visit the pyramids. Be a foreigner. Stay long enough in another country to learn how people live and think there.

Use the correspondences provided here for your inner work, your meditation and contemplation, even your spells, but don't let this be a substitute for life experience.

# CORRESPONDENCES FOR WISDOM

PLANET: Jupiter, Moon (the inner eye of wisdom), waning Moon, Mercury (the wisdom of rebirth)

ELEMENT: earth

DIRECTION: East

SYMBOL: pyramid

NUMBER: 7, 9 (lunar wisdom)

JEWEL: jade, carnelian, coral, jacinth, lapis lazuli (higher wisdom), zircon

METAL: gold

INCENSE: lotus

CANDLE: purple

ANIMAL: crane, elephant, griffin, owl

PLANT: almond, bodh tree, hazel, lotus, nut trees, sage, sunflower

INVOCATIONS:

Goddesses:

Asherah, Athena, Brighid, Car, Carmenta (Revealer of Wisdom), Cerridwen, Crone, Cunneware (Female Wisdom), Danu, Eve, Greine, Gwenhwyfar, Hannahhannas (wisdom beyond wisdom), Hecate, Kundalini (enlightenment), Mens, Metis, Minerva, Pandora, Reason, Sarasvati, Shekinah, Sophia (the Holy Wisdom), Sulis, Tara, Vajravarahi (wisdom through experience)

Gods:

Ahura Mazda (Wise Lord), Apollo, Dagda (Mighty One of Knowledge), Ea (Lord of Wisdom), Enki (Lord of Wisdom), Ganesha, Hermes, Manannan Mac Lir, Mithras, Nabu (Wise God of Wednesday), Quetzalcoatl, Shaka (the Silent Sage), Thoth, Tir

# PART III
# CORRESPONDENCES

# INTRODUCTION

Correspondences are relationships that can be used for magical workings. "The primary principle of magic is connection," Starhawk writes.[1] They make use of the connectedness of things. Think of correspondences as lists of possible ingredients from which you can make selections. There will be correspondences that relate to your spells: planets, herbs, colors, god/desses, and so on. Select those that are available to you or that call to you and use them to craft your spell, ritual, potion, or charm. Magus Francis Barrett, in *Occult Philosophy*, described the use of correspondences of stones and incense for making talismans:

> *The manner of making these [Talismanic] rings is this:—when any star ascends in the horoscope (fortunately), with a fortunate aspect or conjunction of the moon, we proceed to take a* Stone, *and herb, that is under that star, and likewise make a ring of the metal that is corresponding to the star; and in the ring, under the stone, put the herb or root, not forgetting to inscribe the* effect, image, name, *and* character, *as also the proper suffume [a decoction of root, herb, flower, seed, etc., the smoke of which is conveyed into the body from a close-stool].*[2]

Are these all the possible correspondences for a given subject? No. There are many more. These are just some I came across while doing research for my Book of Shadows. I'll be using my own copy of this book as a grimoire, and expect to be scribbling plenty of notes in the margins as I come across new correspondences for things.

---

[1] Starhawk, *The Spiral Dance: A Rebirth of the Ancient Religion of the Great Goddess* (San Francisco: HarperSanFrancisco, 1989), p. 142.
[2] Francis Barrett, *The Magus* (London: Lackington, Allen, and Co., 1801), p. 95. Reissued by Samuel Weiser, 2000.

# THE CARDINAL POINTS

This is where magic takes place, within a circle cast inside the square of the cardinal points. Some traditions add a fifth direction, called the zenith or center. An obelisk represents dominion over the four quarters, plus the zenith.

The Egyptian Amulet of the Tet was also called the Backbone of Osiris. The four crossbars at the top of the tet represent the cardinal points. A symbol of great religious importance, the Tet Amulet enabled reconstitution of the body in the afterlife. A tet made of gold was steeped in flower water, empowered with these words, then worn as a necklace:

> **Rise up thou, O Osiris! Thou hast thy backbone, O Still-Heart! Place thou thyself upon thy base, I put water beneath thee, and I bring unto thee a Tet of gold that thou mayest rejoice therein.**[3]

## NORTH

North is the most powerful direction, the location of magic, and the source of Otherworld powers.

ELEMENT: earth, air

SEASON: winter

TIME: midnight

TOOL: pentacle

COLOR: brown, black, green

ANIMAL: white buffalo

RULES: lungs, the body, rudeness, mystery, silence, secrets, purity, clarity, renewal, vision, the unseen, the power to listen and know what not to say

INVOCATIONS:

> **Hail, thou beautiful Power, thou beautiful rudder of the northern heaven.**[4]

---

[3] E. A. Wallis Budge, *Egyptian Magic* (New York: Dover Publications, 1971), pp. 44-47.

[4] E. A. Wallis Budge, *The Egyptian Book of the Dead: The Papyrus of Ani* (New York: Dover Publications, 1967), p. 367.

Goddesses:
Athena, Baaltis Zapuna, Belili, Earth goddesses, Meretseger
(Friend of Silence), Nebhet, Neith, Nephthys, Nerthus, Uatchet
Gods:
Baal Zebul (Lord of the Mansions of the North), Baal Zephon
(Lord of the North), Bel, Hapi (Lord of the Watchtower of the
North), Jupiter, Osiris, Seth (Lord of the Northern Sky), Soma,
Uriel, Zeus

## NORTH WIND

The Silver Castle, the Corona Borealis, is at the back of the north
wind.
INVOCATIONS: Aquilo, Atemu (for cool breezes from the North),
 Boreas, Cardea (Queen of Winds), Erichthonius, Ophion

### *Northwest:*
INVOCATIONS: Mahabala, Tiksnosnisa, Vayu

### *Northeast:*
INVOCATIONS: Isa, Soma, Ulu'tuyar, Uru'n Ajy Toyo'n

# SOUTH

ELEMENT: fire, water
SEASON: summer
TIME: noon
TOOL: wand
COLOR: red, orange
ANIMAL: lion, coyote
RULES: liver, energy, spirit, will, love, gentleness, trust, innocence,
 warmth, hospitality, rapid growth
INVOCATIONS:

> **Hail, thou who dwellest in the temple of the bright-
> faced ones, thou beautiful rudder of the southern
> heaven.**[5]

Goddesses:
fire goddesses, Isis (Queen of the South), Mahamantranusarini,
Mahapratisara, Meretseger, Nirrti, Satet, Satis, Satjit, Tin Hau,
Vajrapasi

---

[5] E. A. Wallis Budge, *The Egyptian Book of the Dead: The Papyrus of Ani,* p. 367.

Gods:
Ea, Imset (Lord of the Watchtower of the South), Michael, Ninib, Prajnantaka, Ra, Sachiel, Saturn, South Star, Yama, Zocho

**SOUTH WIND**

INVOCATIONS: Auster, Cardea, Ninurta, Notus, the Breath of Set (Lord of the Chambers of the South)

*Southeast:*
INVOCATIONS: Agni, Takkiraja, Tejosnisa

*Southwest:*
INVOCATIONS: Niladanda, Nirrti, Surya
SOUTHWEST WIND: Auster, Notus

# EAST:
# THE WORLD DIRECTION OF THE NEW DAY

ELEMENT: air, fire
SEASON: spring
TIME: dawn
TOOL: athame/sword
COLOR: white, violet, pastels, green
ANIMAL: eagle, high-flying birds
RULES: stomach, spirit, mind, illumination, passion, wisdom, beginnings, the power to know
INVOCATIONS: all dawn god/desses

> **Hail, thou shining one, who livest in the temple wherein are the gods in visible forms, thou beautiful rudder of the eastern heaven.**[6]

Goddesses:
Aja, Aurora, Eos, Hesionë (Lady of Asia), Mahamantranusarini, Neith, Nephthys, Salmaone, Zorya
Gods:
Chac (Lord of the East), Duamutef (Lord of the Watchtower of the East), Horus (Lord of the East), Indra, Mars, Morning Star, Raphael, Shar, Sopedu (Lord of the East)

---

[6] E. A. Wallis Budge, *The Egyptian Book of the Dead: The Papyrus of Ani*, p. 367.

**EAST WIND**

INVOCATIONS: Cardea, Eurus, Volturnus

# WEST

ELEMENT: water, earth
SEASON: autumn
TIME: twilight
TOOL: chalice/cauldron
COLOR: sea green, blue, gray, purple, white
ANIMAL: fish, dolphin, sea serpents
RULES: intestines, emotions, guts, introspection, undercurrents, vitality, daring, strength, endings, the courage to face deepest feelings
INVOCATIONS: all sunset god/desses

> **Hail, thou who goest round about heaven, thou pilot of the world, thou beautiful rudder of the western heaven.[7]**

Goddesses:
Amenti, the Hesperides (Daughters of the West), Hsi Wang Mu Gong (Royal Mother of the Western Paradise), Isis, Meretseger, Sekhmet (Lady of the West), Selkis
Gods:
Cteryon (King of the West), Ehecatl-Quetzalcoatl, Favonius, Itzam Na, Gabriel, Hastehogan, Khenty-amentiu (Foremost of the Westerners), Sachiel, Salim, Thoth, Qebehsenuf (Lord of the Watchtower of the West), Ra, Varuna

**WEST WIND**

INVOCATIONS: Cardea, Favonius, Zephyrus

# BELIEF SYSTEMS

Mayans assigned these correspondences to the cardinal points:
NORTH:
   *color:* red
   *jewel:* bloodstone
SOUTH:
   *color:* white
   *jewel:* pearls, shells

---

[7] E. A. Wallis Budge, *The Egyptian Book of the Dead: The Papyrus of Ani*, p. 367.

**East:**
   *color:* yellow
   *metal:* gold
**West:**
   *color:* black, blue
   *jewel:* jade, turquoise

The Celts had a fourfold cycle:
**East:** life, beginning
   *element:* air
   *season:* spring
   *time:* dawn
   *tool:* the sword of Nuadha
**South:** light, increasing
   *element:* fire
   *season:* summer
   *time:* noon
   *tool:* the spear of Lugh
**West:** love, maturing
   *element*: water
   *season*: autumn
   *time*: evening
   *tool*: the cauldron of the Daghda

**North:** law, destroying
   *element:* earth
   *season:* winter
   *time:* night
   *tool:* the stone of Fal

The ancient Irish divided their land into five directions, each with its own correspondences:
**East** (Leinster):
   benefit, farmers/householders, prosperity and hospitality
**South** (Munster):
   music, poets/minstrels, knowledge and fertility
**West** (Connaught):
   learning, Druids, judgment, chronicles and storytelling
**North** (Ulster):
   battle, warriors, conflict, struggle and pride
**Center** (Meath):
   kingship, king/stewards, stability, bounty and renown

# THE LORDS OF THE WATCHTOWERS

$M$any cultures are represented in the invocation lists: from Asia to Europe, from Africa to the Americas. This illustrates the universality of the division of space into the cardinal points. You can invoke any gods or goddesses who appeal to you, but these are examples of mythologically consistent invocations:

## ANGELS

North: Uriel
South: Michael
East: Raphael
West: Gabriel

## AZTEC

North: Mictlantecuhtli
South: Huitzilopochtli
East: Tlahuizcalpantecuhtli
West: Ehecatl-Quetzalcoatl

## BUDDHIST

North: Vajraghanta
South: Vajrapasi
East: Vajrosnisa
West: Vajrasphota

Buddhists count five directions, assigning each to a member of the Buddha family:

NORTH:
*color:* green
*negative quality:* envy and jealousy
*positive quality:* all-accomplishing wisdom
*sacred to:* Amoghasiddhi

**SOUTH:**

*color:* yellow
*negative quality:* pride
*positive quality:* wisdom of equanimity
*sacred to:* Ratnasambhava

**EAST:**

*color:* blue
*negative quality:* aggression
*positive quality:* mirrorlike wisdom
*sacred to:* Akshobhya

**WEST:**

*color:* red
*negative quality:* passion and longing
*positive quality:* wisdom of discriminating awareness
*sacred to:* Amitabha

**CENTER:**

*color:* white
*negative quality:* ignorance that causes the cycle of
    reincarnation
*positive quality:* wisdom of ultimate reality
*sacred to:* Mahapratisara, Vairochana

## EGYPTIAN

North: Hapi,* Neith, Osiris
South: Imset,* Isis, Ra
East: Duamutef,* Nephthys, Horus
West: Qebehsenuf,* Sekhmet, Thoth
(*These are the four sons of Horus, who appear on canopic jars.)

## HINDU

North: Soma
South: Yama
East: Indra
West: Varuna

The eight Lokapala, Hindu Lords of the Watchtowers, are each assisted by an elephant:

| | |
|---|---|
| East: Airavana | West: Anjana |
| Southeast: Pundari-Ka | Northwest: Pushpadanta |
| South: Vamana | North: Sarvabhauma |
| Southwest: Kumuda | Northeast: Supratika |

Each direction corresponds to a color in India:

| | |
|---|---|
| North: green | East: white |
| South: blue | West: red |

# THE HEAVENLY BODIES

There is more lore associated with the Sun, Moon, and inner planets, because the outer planets were not discovered until modern times. The planets are sacred to: Al Uzzah (the Arabian goddess who regulates the course of heavenly bodies), Grahapati (King of Planets), the archangel Michael, the Hindu creator god Narayana, Shani (god of the planets) and Surya (the Hindu god of infinite knowledge).

## EARTH

See Part I (Elements).

## JUPITER

The Inuit consider the planet Jupiter dangerous to magicians.

**ACTION:** leads, expands, succeeds
**DAY:** Thursday
**TIME:** day
**ELEMENT:** air, fire, wood (China)
**DIRECTION:** East (China)
**ZODIAC:** Sagittarius (masculine aspect), Pisces (feminine aspect)
**NUMBER:** 3, 4, 5, 34
**LETTER:** D, Th
**ASTRAL PLANE:** lower spiritual
**METAL:** tin
**JEWEL:** amethyst, chrysolite
**COLOR:** blue, dark blue, royal blue, purple
**SYMBOL:** thunderbolt, arrow, baton
**INCENSE:** cedar
**PLANT:** agrimony, anise, ash, avens, balm, white beet, betony, bloodroot, blueberry, borage, chervil, chestnut, chicory, cinquefoil, clover, costmary, couch grass, dandelion, dock, fig, hart's tongue, henbane, houseleek, hyssop, juniper berries, linden, lungwort, maple tree, marsh woundwort, mint, mistletoe, nutmeg, oak tree, olive tree, red rose, sage, samphire, scurvy grass, terebinth, milk thistle, unicorn root, walnut

**ANIMAL:** eagle, unicorn

**RULES:** pride, power, law, justice, benevolence, abundance, generosity, optimism, responsibility, honor, politics, royalty, leadership, apparel, expansion, wisdom, business, wealth, success, luck, riches, things desired, public acclaim, political victory, the higher mind

**BODY:** aids digestion and nutrition, governs liver, lungs, blood, ribs, midriff, gristle, sperm, pleurisy, major headaches, heartburn, cramps, apoplexy, glandular diseases, lung infections, blood diseases.

**INVOCATIONS:** thunder god/desses

Goddesses:

Danu, Devi, Hathor, Hera, Isis (Queen of the Universe), Juno (Queen of Heaven), Nut, Optima Maxima, Oya, Shakti, Themis, Unial, Victoria

Gods:

Haddad, Allah, Amun, Anu, Baal, Bel, Chango the Dagda, Dis, Dyaus (Sky Father), El, Indra, Jehovah, Jupiter, Jove, Marduk, Odin, Perun, Sky Father, Taranis, Telamon, Teshub, Thor, Yahweh, Zeus (Thunderer)

**Table 1.**
MAGIC SQUARE OF JUPITER[8] (adds up to 34 in every direction).

| 4 | 14 | 15 | 1 |
|---|----|----|---|
| 9 | 7 | 6 | 12 |
| 5 | 11 | 10 | 8 |
| 16 | 2 | 3 | 13 |

# MARS

**ACTION:** begins, acts, grows
**DAY:** Tuesday
**TIME:** night
**ELEMENT:** fire

---

[8] Janet and Stewart Farrar, *The Witches' Bible* (Custer, WA: Phoenix Publishing, 1996), p. 88.

DIRECTION: South (China)
ZODIAC: Aries (masculine aspect), Scorpio (feminine aspect)
NUMBER: 2, 3, 4, 5, 16, 65
LETTER: T
ASTRAL: 2nd plane, lower astral
METAL: iron, steel
JEWEL: bloodstone, garnet, ruby, pyrite, tiger's eye
COLOR: red
SYMBOL: sword, helmet, battle-axe
INCENSE: pine, dragon's blood
ANIMAL: ram, woodpecker
RULES: birth, anger, action, wrath, work, growth, energy, aggression, warfare, enmity, conflict, strength, matrimony, prison, sexual drive, emotional passion, physical skills, positive (outgoing energy), the yang (the masculine)
BODY: governs kidneys, gallbladder, testicles, left ear, migraine, ringworm, premature birth, broken veins, choleric diseases, chronic fever
PLANT: aloe, all-heal, anemone, asafoetida, asarabacca, barberry, basil, betony, broom, broomrape, bryony, butcher's broom, caper, chili pepper, chives, coriander, cow parsnip, cuckoo-pint, dragon's blood, garlic, gentian, ginger, gorse, hawthorn, holly, holly oak, hops, horseradish, madder root, masterwort, mustard, nettles, onion, pepper, radish, restharrow, sarsaparilla, savin, star thistle, tobacco, tarragon, thistles, toadflax, valerian, wormwood
INVOCATIONS:
Goddesses:
Anahita, Anath, Aparajita (the Unconquered, victory in war), Ashtoreth (Lady of Horses and Chariots), Astarte, Athena, Badb (the Fury), Bellona, Durga, Eris, Fea (the Hateful), Inanna, Ishtar (Lady of Battle, Queen of Attack and Hand-to-Hand Fighting), Macha, Maeve, Medb, Minerva, the Morrigan, Nana, Neith (Mistress of the Bow and Ruler of the Arrows), Sekhmet (The Powerful One), the Valkyries
Gods:
Ares, Ashur, Belatucadros, Chango Hercules Melkarth, Indra, Jehovah Melkarth, Lugal-Irra, Lugh Lamhfhada (Lugh of the Long Arm), Mars, Melicertes, Melkarth, Mithras, Nergal, Ninurta, Nodens, Nuadha, Odin, Ogun, Ogun, Quirinius, Reshep, Seth (the Red God), Teutates, Thor, Tiwaz, Tyr, Vahagn

**Table 2.**
MAGIC SQUARE OF MARS[9] (adds up to 65 in every direction).

| 11 | 24 | 7  | 20 | 3  |
|----|----|----|----|----|
| 4  | 12 | 25 | 8  | 16 |
| 17 | 5  | 13 | 21 | 9  |
| 10 | 18 | 1  | 14 | 22 |
| 23 | 6  | 19 | 2  | 15 |

# MERCURY

**ACTION:** communicates
**DAY:** Wednesday
**Element:** air, water (China)
**DIRECTION:** North (China)
**ZODIAC:** Gemini (masculine aspect), Virgo (feminine aspect)
**NUMBER:** 1, 4, 6, 8, 260
**LETTER:** C, W
**ASTRAL:** 5th plane, upper mental
**METAL:** quicksilver/mercury, alloys
**JEWEL:** agate, amber, emerald, opal, peridot, smoky quartz, tiger's
   eye, topaz
**COLOR:** violet, orange, mixtures of colors
**SYMBOL:** caduceus, hermaphrodite, twins
**INCENSE:** nutmeg, storax
**ANIMAL:** coyote, fox, jackal, birds, bluejay, ibis, twin serpents
**RULES:** writing, communication, correspondence, eloquence, com-
   merce, debt, intelligence, cleverness, fear, magic, falsehood,
   interpretation, love, wealth, wisdom, travel, vagabondage,
   trickiness, thievery, science, memory, creativity, the mind, occult power, gymnastics, wrestling, business transactions, the
   wisdom of rebirth, all things requiring skill and dexterity
**BODY:** governs lungs, tongue, hands, thighs, cognition, epilepsy,
   insanity, depression

---

[9] Janet and Stewart Farrar, *The Witches' Bible*, p. 88.

PLANT: almond, ash, butterbur, caraway, carrot, cascara sagrada, celery, cinquefoil, cow parsnip, devil's bit scabious, dill, elecampane, fennel, fenugreek, ferns, garlic mustard, germander, hazel, honeysuckle, horehound, hound's tongue, Jacob's ladder, lavender, lavender cotton, licorice, lily of the valley, mace, mandrake, maidenhair fern, marjoram, mulberry tree, myrtle, parsley, pellitory, pomegranate, southernwood, woody nightshade, valerian

INVOCATIONS: trickster god/desses

Goddesses:
Athena, Car, Carmenta, Carya, Ino, Ma'at, Maia, Medusa, Metis, Minerva, Phorcis, Plastene, Pombagira

Gods:
Anansi, Angra Mainyu, Anubis, Arawn, Buddha, Car, Coyote, Devil, Elegua, Ganesha, Hermes, Herne, High John the Conquerer, Loki, Lugh, Maui of the Thousand Tricks, Mercury, Michael, Nabu, Odin, Palamedes, Prometheus, Psychopompus, Qat, Q're, Raven, Satan Serapis, Tezcatlipoca, Thor, Thoth, Trickster, Ulysses

## Table 3.

MAGIC SQUARE OF MERCURY[10] (adds up to 260 in every direction).

| 8 | 58 | 59 | 5 | 4 | 62 | 63 | 1 |
|---|----|----|---|---|----|----|---|
| 49 | 15 | 14 | 52 | 53 | 11 | 10 | 56 |
| 41 | 23 | 22 | 44 | 45 | 19 | 18 | 48 |
| 32 | 34 | 35 | 29 | 28 | 38 | 39 | 25 |
| 40 | 26 | 27 | 37 | 36 | 30 | 31 | 33 |
| 17 | 47 | 46 | 20 | 21 | 43 | 42 | 24 |
| 9 | 55 | 54 | 12 | 13 | 51 | 50 | 16 |
| 64 | 2 | 3 | 61 | 60 | 6 | 7 | 57 |

[10] Janet and Stewart Farrar, *The Witches' Bible*, p. 89.

# MOON

The Moon is the most important heavenly body for witches. We draw on her power for lunar magic; we cast our spells in accordance with her cycles; we commune with the Goddess through her. She inspires and illuminates us. There are Moon gods, but the Moon has always been perceived mainly as female. The Moon is cyclical, like women. We menstruate with her. She mirrors the stages of our lives: maiden, mother, and crone. She is Changing Woman, as are we.

One way to honor the Moon is with a Full Moon dinner. Set the table with white, silver, and gold. Dress formally, in the same colors. Put night-blooming flowers in a vase, or wear their perfume. Serve Moon food: pale creamy dishes and crisp green salads, with a good white wine. A Full Moon dinner is an excellent prelude to lunar magic or for replenishing after rituals.

## SUPERSTITIONS

Mushrooms were thought to grow as the Moon waned. Werewolves were believed to take their wolf form when the Moon was full. In Britian it was considered unlucky to view the Moon through glass.

## MOON PHASES

Directions for spells often say they should be cast during the waning or waxing Moon. New witches are always asking me what this means. The simplest explanation is that the Moon wanes (grows smaller) after Full Moon, begins to wax (grow larger) again after New Moon. The easiest way to keep track of this is to be sure every year to get a calendar that has the Moon's phases on it. Many ordinary calendars have this, so it shouldn't be hard to find one.

You can consider the Full Moon as lasting three days, the one marked on the calendar, as well as the day before and the day after. This gives you more than one night every month for Full Moon magic. If a spell should be cast during the dark of the Moon, that means on the days just before New Moon, when it is hard to see the Moon in the sky.

## CORRESPONDENCES

ACTION: fertilizes, intuits, enchants
DAY: Monday (Moon Day)
TIME: night

ELEMENT: water
METAL: silver
ZODIAC: Cancer
NUMBER: 3, 6, 7, 8, 9, 13, 14, 50, 369
ASTRAL: etheric plane
JEWEL: moonstone, mother-of-pearl, pearl, quartz, rock crystal, selenite, sea-green beryl, turquoise
SYMBOL: spear, hunting horn, cow horns
INCENSE: coconut, ginseng, jasmine, lotus, sandalwood
ANIMAL: white bull, cat, dog, ibis, hare, horse, elephant, crab, stag, vixen, wolf, rabbit, swine, dolphin, seal, serpent, sparrow, wryneck
RULES: women, birth, death, time, rain, tides, the sea, dew, the waters, semen, fluids, menstruation, cold, moisture, shadow, cycles, intuition, inspiration, poetry, generation, fertility, maternity, femininity, the womb, childbirth, moods, personality, creativity, emotions, psychic powers, growth, sympathy, envy, changability, enchantment, dreams, secrets, lunacy, merchandise, theft, sloth, evil thoughts, the subconscious, the Goddess aspect, all things of a watery nature, travel (especially by water), the mysteries of time, the inner eye of wisdom, the negative, the feminine, the yin
BODY: governs head, brain, belly, left side of men, right side of women, fits, palsy, writhing, mental illness, nervous diseases, female genitals, obstruction of sinews, infirmities caused by cold moisture
PLANT: acanthus, adder's tongue, agave, banana, burnet saxifrage, cabbage, chamomile, chickweed, cuckoo flower, cucumber, fluellen, fungi, sea holly, iris, lettuce, loosestrife, lotus, madonna lily, melons, moly, moonwort, mushrooms, myrtle, night-blooming plants, opium poppy, wild pear, poppy, pumpkin, purslane, dog rose, white rose, wild rose, clary sage, St. John's flower, seaweed, soma, stonecrop, leafy vegetables, wallflower, watercress, water lily, willow, wintergreen, yucca
INVOCATIONS: Ashima
Goddesses:
Aa, Aine of Knockaine, Alcmene, Alphito, Artemis, Belili, Bendis, Britomartis, Cerridwen, Changing Woman, Ch'ang-O (Queen of the Moon), Circe, Danu, Diana, Dictynna, Eurynome, Hecate (Goddess of the Dark of the Moon), Hecate Selene (the Far-Shooting Moon), Helene (Bright Moon), Hina the Watchwoman, Inanna (Queen Moon), Io, Iole, Ishtar, Isis, Ix

Chel, Juno Luna, Levanah, Libya, Linda, Lucina, Luna, Luonno-tar, Mama Quilla (Mother Moon), Mardoll (Shining One Over the Sea), Ngame, Pasiphaë (She Who Shines for All), Phoebe (Moonlight), Phoenissa, Selene (the Radiant, the Bright-Dressed Queen), the White Goddess

Gods:

Ashimbabbar, Candra, Car, El, Gabriel, Ge, Helenus, Khonsu (the Wanderer, He Who Traverses the Sky), Nanna-Sin, Nyami-abe (Nocturnal Sun), Osiris, Pah, Phorcys, Porphyrion (the Dark Blue Moon Man), Poseidon, Sîn (Lord of the Calendar), Shiva Somantha (Lord of the Moon), Soma, Thoth, Yarikh

### )●( *New Moon* (white raiser):

COLOR: white, silver
RULES: birth, initiation, virginity, beginnings, the hunt
INVOCATIONS:

Goddesses:

Aerope, Artemis, Brighid, Caenis, Chrysaor, Clotho, Elate, Elektra, Isis, the Kotharat, Linda, Maiden, Mary, Nimuë, Prosymna, the White Goddess of Birth and Growth

Gods:

An, As-im-Babbar, Hillel

### )●( *Crescent Moon:*

Goddesses:

Stella Maris, Tiamat, Yemaya

Gods:

Aglibol, Hillel, horned gods, Nanna, Sîn, Suen, Yarisk (Lord of the Sickle)

### )●( *Waxing Moon:*

COLOR: black
RULES: birth, growth, love, beginnings, attraction, ideas, positive change
INVOCATIONS:

Goddesses:

Artemis, Diana, Epona, Maiden, Neith, Ri

### )●( *Full Moon* (zenith, red reaper):

Witches' sabbats (esbats) were traditionally held at Full Moon. This was also when sacred kings were traditionally killed.
COLOR: red, green
RULES: light, fertility, illumination, growth, transformation, nurturing, fulfillment, sexuality, maturation, love, power, maximum psychic ability

INVOCATIONS:

Goddesses:

Artemis Mounykhia, Astarte, Calliope (the Beauteous Face), Cameira, Diana, Eur-ope (She of the Broad Face), Iphigenia, Isis, Juno, Larchesis, Mari, Mariamne, Mary Magdalene, Mother, Nemesis, Nymph, Phoebe (Bright Moon), the Red Goddess of Love and Battle, Rhode, Selene, Olymene, Pasiphaë, Praxithea

Gods:

Father Nanna

)●( **Waning Moon** (dark winnower of grain):

RULES: wisdom, endings, release, banishment, intuition, prophecy, death and resurrection, divination, old age, deep secrets, reversal of fortune, postmenopausal women, the power of healing

INVOCATIONS:

Goddesses:

Anna, Annis, Astarte, Atropos, Bentheslcyme, the Black Goddess of Death and Divination, Chrysothemis, Crone, Ebule, Eur-ope, Hecate, the Hesperides, Ialysa, Levanah

## Table 4.

MAGIC SQUARE of the MOON[11] (totals 369 in every direction).

| 37 | 78 | 29 | 70 | 21 | 62 | 13 | 54 | 5 |
|----|----|----|----|----|----|----|----|----|
| 6 | 38 | 79 | 30 | 71 | 22 | 63 | 14 | 46 |
| 47 | 7 | 39 | 80 | 31 | 72 | 23 | 55 | 15 |
| 16 | 48 | 8 | 40 | 81 | 32 | 64 | 24 | 56 |
| 57 | 17 | 49 | 9 | 41 | 73 | 33 | 65 | 25 |
| 26 | 58 | 18 | 50 | 1 | 42 | 74 | 34 | 66 |
| 67 | 27 | 59 | 10 | 51 | 2 | 43 | 75 | 35 |
| 36 | 68 | 19 | 60 | 11 | 52 | 3 | 44 | 76 |
| 77 | 28 | 69 | 20 | 61 | 12 | 53 | 4 | 45 |

---

[11] Janet and Stewart Farrar, *The Witches' Bible*, p. 90.

# NEPTUNE

ACTION: fascinates
ELEMENT: water
ZODIAC: Pisces
JEWEL: amethyst, aquamarine, celestite, coral, fluorite, jade, lapis lazuli, sapphire
SYMBOL: trident
ANIMAL: marine life
RULES: glamor, scandal, protection, vision, subtlety, the elusive and intangible, altered states, poetic vision, intense emotional states, spiritual power and guidance
INVOCATIONS: sea god/desses
Goddesses:
Amphitrite, Asherah, Daeira, Doris, Eurynome, Ishtar, Leucothea, Marina, Oshun, Pasiphaë, Rahab, Salacia, Sarah, Sedna, Scotia, Tethys, Thetis, Tiamat, Yemaya
Gods:
Aegir, Dylan, Glaucus, Llyr, Make Make, Melicertes, Melkarth, Neptune, Nereus, Njoerd, Oceanus, Ogir, Olokun, Pontus, Poseidon, Proteus, Shiva, Tethra, Triton, Typhon, Yamm

# PLUTO

ACTION: transforms
ZODIAC: Scorpio
METAL: uranium, plutonium
JEWEL: amethyst, garnet, jet, obsidian, sodalite
PLANT: male fern, silverweed
RULES: transformation, rebirth, regeneration, wealth, the underworld, nuclear power
INVOCATIONS: psychopomps, underworld god/desses
Goddesses:
Allat (Queen of the Underworld), Baba Yaga, Banbha, Ereshkigal (the Great Below, Mistress of Death, Queen of the Underworld), the Erinnyes (the Solemn Ones), Gula Bau, Hathor, Hecate, Hela, Hera, Kali, Meretseger, the Morrigan, Persephone, Sheol, Styx, Sulis, Velu Mate (Queen of the Dead)
Gods:
Adonis, Angra Mainyu, Anubis (Lord of the Necropolis, the Dweller in the Mummy Chamber), Arawn (King of Annwfn), Attis, Azrael, Baal Haddad, Cernunnos (Lord of the Under-

world), Cronos, Dagon, the Dagda, Damuzi (Son of the Abyss), Devil, Dionysus, Hades (the Unseen, the Inexorable), Hercules, Hermes Psychopompos, Herne, Jesus, Mot, Nergal, Osiris (Lord of Eternity), Pluto, Pwyll Pen Annwn, Rhadamanthys, Satan, Tammuz, Taranis, Tartarus, dying-and-rising vegetation gods, Zeus Katachthonios (Zeus of the Underworld)

# SATURN

ACTION: binds, limits, restricts, obstructs

DAY: Saturday (Saturn-day)

TIME: day

ELEMENT: water, earth

DIRECTION: Center (China)

ZODIAC: Capricorn (female aspect), Aquarius (male aspect)

NUMBER: 2, 3, 7, 15

LETTER: F, S

ASTRAL: 4th plane, lower mental

METAL: lead

JEWEL: azurite, carnelian, hematite, ironstone, onyx, pearl, ruby, star sapphire

COLOR: black, blue, dark blue, indigo

SYMBOL: sickle, crutch

INCENSE: fumitory, myrrh, patchouli

ANIMAL: crow, raven, wren

RULES: knowledge, time, cold, peace, darkness, discipline, stability, social order, limitation, caution, death, building, history, solitude, sloth, tears, structures, mutation, agriculture, doctrine, temperance, binding, obstruction, old age, concrete mind, strength through persistence and endurance, working out karma through evolution

PLANT: aconite, adder, alder, beech, red beet, barley, bistort, cannabis, cornflower, comfrey, cypress tree, daffodil, dodder, dogwood, elm, royal fern, hellebore, black hellebore, hemlock, henbane, holly, horsetail, gladwin iris, ironwood, ivy, knapweed, knotgrass, love lies bleeding, mandrake, medlar, moss, mullein, nightshade, opium poppy, pansy, pomegranate tree, poplar, quince tree, rowan, rupturewort, shepherd's purse, Solomon's seal, spleenwort, tamarisk, thyme, birdsfoot trefoil, wall fern (polypody), weeping willow, wintergreen, woad, yew

INVOCATIONS: Ki'njen
Goddesses:
Aditi, Allat, Amba, Anahita, Ariadne, Ceres, Cybele Magna Mater, Demeter, Durga, the Great Goddess, Hathor, Hecate, Hera, Isis, Juno, Kali (Black Time, Mighty Time), Ops, Pandora, Pistis Sophia, Rhea, Satis, Shakti, Ushas (Mistress of Time)
Gods:
Ahura Mazda, Allah, Amun (Lord of Time), Baal Shamim, Bran, Buddha, Cronos, the Dagda, El (Master of Time), Father Time, Jehovah, John Barleycorn, Kumarbi, Khensu, Khonsu, Krishna, Mahakala (Great Time), Methuselah, Moloch, Ninib, Osiris (Lord of Eternity), Saturn, Shiva Mahakala, Thor, Thoth, Vishnu, Yahweh, Yu-Huang-Shang-Ti (Father Heaven, the August Supreme Emperor of Jade), Zurvan (Boundless Time)

**Table 5.**
MAGIC SQUARE OF SATURN[12] (adds up to 15 in every direction).

| 4 | 9 | 2 |
|---|---|---|
| 3 | 5 | 7 |
| 8 | 1 | 6 |

# SUN

ACTION: governs, promotes, illuminates, creates, achieves
DAY: Sunday (Sun-day)
TIME: noon
ELEMENT: fire
ZODIAC: Leo
NUMBER: 1, 6, 7, 8, 21, 111
LETTER: B, S
ASTRAL: 7th plane, upper spiritual
METAL: gold
JEWEL: amber, blood-red carbuncle, yellow diamond, ruby, topaz
COLOR: yellow, gold
SYMBOL: scepter, wheel, child
INCENSE: cinnamon, clove, frankincense, olibanum

---

[12] Janet and Stewart Farrar, *The Witches' Bible*, p. 88.

**ANIMAL:** lion, eagle, white horse, beetle, scarab beetle, rooster, egg, falcon, ram, sphinx

**RULES:** kingship, pride, hope, fortune, will, light, action, heat, dryness, leadership, creation, joy, lucre, success, rebirth, achievement, justice, greed, friendship, growth, healing, consciousness, heritage, illumination, inheritance, sheer light, natural power, awakened understanding, the brilliance of the intellect, eternal unchanging laws, the power urge, the god aspect, the life force, pure abstract spirit, the masculine, the positive, the yang

**BODY:** Discharges from the eyes and hot, dry, non-choleric diseases are in the Sun's domain. It governs brain, heart, marrow, sinews, the right eye of a man, the left eye of a woman.

**PLANT:** honey, acacia tree, angelica, ash, birch, bistort, broom, burnet, butterbur, celandine, centaury, chamomile, cinnamon, citrus, everlasting, eyebright, Helen's flower, heliotrope, hibiscus, hollyhock, juniper, laurel, lotus, lovage, marigold, marsh mallow, mistletoe, peony, rosemary, rue, saffron, St. John's Wort, sundew, sunflower, tormentil, vine, viper's bugloss, walnut

**AMULET:** Egyptians defined eternity as the length of time the Sun exists. Their Shen Amulet, the hieroglyph of eternity, embodies this concept. The cartouche, the symbol that surrounded hieroglyphic names, can be seen as an elongated shen. It was meant to make a name live forever.

**INVOCATIONS:**

Goddesses:

Aditi, Amaterasu Omikami (the Heaven-Radiant Great Divinity), Bastet, Brighid, Circe (Daughter of the Sun), Greine (House of the Sun), Hathor of the Horizon, the Heliades (Daughters of the Sun), Saule, Sekhmet (the Powerful One), Shams, Shapshu (Torch of the Gods), Sphinx, Sunna (Mistress Sun)

Gods:

Abraxas, Ammon Ra, Apollo, Atum, Babbar, Helios, Herakles Ogmius, Hercules Melkarth, Horus (the High One, Lord of Heaven), Horus of the Horizon, Hyperion, Indra, Inti, Khepera, Krishna, Lucifer (Son of Morning), Marduk, Mithras (Lord of Day), Ogma Sunface, Phaëthon, Phoebus, Ra (the Lord of Heaven, the King, Life, Strength, and Health), Rama, Raphael, Samson, Shamash, Sol, Surya, Uttu, Vishnu

Sun gods are often also gods of justice, who see everything under the Sun.

○ **Rising Sun** (dawn god/desses):
*Direction:* East
*Animal:* rooster
*Goddesses:* Amaterasu, Eos, Isis, Salmaone, Waka-Hiru-Me
*Gods:* Horus, Khepera, Osiris, Ptah (Opener), Salim, Salma, Savitar, Shachar

○ **Morning Sun:**
*Gods:* Kushi-Dama-Nigi-Haya-Hi (the Morning Sun)

○ **Noonday Sun:**
*Gods:* Ra

○ **Evening Sun:**
*Gods:* Hammon

○ **Setting Sun:**
*Direction:* West
*Goddesses:* the Hesperides
*Gods:* Atum, Baal Qarnaim, Osiris, Savitar, Shalim, Tayau Sakaimoka

○ **Night Sun:**
*Gods:* Atemu (the Closer), Seker (He Who Is Shut In)

○ **Solar Eclipse:**
*Gods:* Ah Ciliz

## Table 6.

MAGIC SQUARE OF THE SUN[13] (adds up to 111 in every direction).

| 6  | 32 | 3  | 34 | 35 | 1  |
|----|----|----|----|----|----|
| 7  | 11 | 27 | 28 | 8  | 30 |
| 19 | 14 | 16 | 15 | 23 | 24 |
| 18 | 20 | 22 | 21 | 17 | 13 |
| 25 | 29 | 10 | 9  | 26 | 12 |
| 36 | 5  | 33 | 4  | 2  | 31 |

---

[13] Janet and Stewart Farrar, *The Witches' Bible*, p. 89.

# URANUS

**ACTION:** overthrows, replaces
**ZODIAC:** Aquarius
**JEWEL:** aventurine, diamond, quartz, blue topaz
**PLANT:** Tree of Heaven
**RULES:** brilliance, restlessness, technology, extremes, innovation, illumination, novelty, overthrow, excitement, social awareness, sudden change, intuitive knowledge, the urge for freedom, destruction of the old to make room for the new
**INVOCATIONS:**
Goddesses:
Allat, Anath (Queen of Heaven), Aphrodite Urania, Asterie, Inanna (Queen of the Universe), Ishtar (Lady of Heaven), Isis (Queen of the Universe), Mary (Queen of Heaven), Tin Hau (Queen of Heaven), Urania (the Heavenly One, Queen of Heaven), Venus Urania
Gods:
Alalus (King of Heaven), An, Anshar, Anu, Astar, Obatala, Uranus (Father Heaven), Zeus

# VENUS

Through retrograde motions on her Earth orbit, Venus traces a five-pointed path (the pentacle) in the heavens. It takes eight Venus years, or five Earth years, for her to return to her starting point. In some ancient cultures, the death of the sacred king occurred as Venus completed her orbit.
**ACTION:** leads on, seduces, pleasures
**DAY:** Friday
**TIME:** midnight
**ELEMENT:** earth, water, metal (China)
**DIRECTION:** West (China)
**ZODIAC:** Taurus (feminine aspect), Libra (masculine aspect)
**NUMBER:** 4, 5, 6, 7, 72, 175
**LETTER:** F, Q
**ASTRAL:** 3rd plane, upper astral
**METAL:** copper
**JEWEL:** amber, emerald, jade, lapis lazuli, malachite, pearl, rose quartz, sodalite, turquoise, coral, aventurine
**COLOR:** green, emerald green, indigo, rose
**SYMBOL:** hand mirror, pentacle, pod or bud, conch shell
**INCENSE:** benzoin, jasmine, rose, violet

**ANIMAL:** dove, lynx, swan

**RULES:** love, the power of love, lust, society, desire, harmony, attraction, friendship, pleasure, beauty, sexuality, receptivity, fellowship, pilgrimage, abstract emotions, the Way, the lover, the stranger, physical passion, the yin, the yoni, the feminine,

**BODY:** The thumb is sacred to Venus. Cold and moist diseases are her domain. She rules kidneys, loins, buttocks, belly, flanks, womb, liver, heart, stomach, female genitals.

**PLANT:** Gardens are under the protection of Venus.

acacia flowers, alder, black alder, alkanet, almond oil, aloe, ambrosia, apple, artichoke, beans, birch, bishop's weed, bramble (blackberry), bugle, burdock, cape gooseberry (winter cherry), catnip, catsfoot, lesser celandine, cherry, coltsfoot, columbine, cowslip, daffodil, daisy, dropwort, elder, feverfew, fig, figwort, foxglove, geranium, goldenrod, gooseberry, groundsel, Herb Robert, jasmine, kidneywort, ladies' bedstraw, lady's mantle, mallow, meadowsweet, mint, moneywort, motherwort, mugwort, myrtle, olive oil, peach tree, pear, pennyroyal, periwinkle, plantain (herb), plum (blackthorn), quince, ragwort, raspberry, rose, damask rose, sanicle, sea holly, self-heal, silverweed, soapwort, sorrel, spearmint, strawberry, sycamore, tansy, thyme, wild thyme, Venus flytrap, Venus's looking glass, verbena, vervain, violet, wheat, willow

**Invocations:** god/desses of the morning and evening stars, love god/desses

Goddesses:

Aegea, Al Huzzah (the Venus of Mecca), Anahita, Anaitis, Anath, Aphrodite, Arsinöe, Asherah, Ashtoreth, Astarte, Atargatis, Baalith, Belili, Fatimah, Freya, Frigg, Hathor, Hesper (the Evening Star), Inanna, Ishtar, Kadesh, Lakshmi, Maeve, Mary Magdalene, Nana, Ninlil, Oshun, Rhea, Syria Dea, Tethys, Turan, Venus, Zaria

Gods:

Anael (Angel of the Star of Love), Attar, Azizos (the Morning Star), Bel, Cupid, Dionysus, Eros, Evening Star, Gendenwith (the Morning Star), Haniel, Lucifer (Son of Morning), Morning Star, Oceanus, Robin Hood, Pan, Phaëthon, Phosphoros, Salim (the Evening Star), Xolotl (Lord of the Evening Star)

## Table 7.

MAGIC SQUARE OF VENUS[14] (adds up to 175 in every direction).

| 22 | 47 | 16 | 41 | 10 | 35 | 4 |
|----|----|----|----|----|----|----|
| 5 | 23 | 48 | 17 | 42 | 11 | 29 |
| 30 | 6 | 24 | 49 | 18 | 36 | 12 |
| 13 | 31 | 7 | 25 | 43 | 19 | 37 |
| 38 | 14 | 32 | 1 | 26 | 44 | 20 |
| 21 | 39 | 8 | 33 | 2 | 27 | 45 |
| 46 | 15 | 40 | 9 | 34 | 3 | 28 |

---

[14] Janet and Stewart Farrar, *A Witches' Bible*, p. 89.

# ANIMAL KINGDOM

Animal powers can be called upon for spells, protection, divination, and battle. Witches love animals. We never harm or kill them in our rites or spells. Blood sacrifice of any sort is against our law. That "eye of newt and toe of frog" stuff is nonsense. It is hard to reconcile the gibbering witches of *MacBeth* with the proud Pagan priestesses of Egypt, Babylon, Knossos, and Ireland, or with ethical modern Wiccans. Those were the Burning Times, when magic and the craft itself became degraded under constant persecution.

Magical knowledge was once so closely guarded that code words were often used for spell ingredients in ancient recipe books. For example, blood of a goose actually meant sap from a mulberry tree and a pig's tail meant the herb leopard's bane. Patchouli leaves are still sold as graveyard dust by some occult suppliers. Some old spells that call for animal parts are included here as curiosities. I certainly do not mean for you to use them as written! These spells are mostly of use to thieves and jealous guys anyway. Rather let them amuse you, dismay you, or inspire you in image magic. Remember that the animal parts called for may just be code words for herbs, stones, or other ingredients.

The only part of an animal that it is lawful for a witch to use is one the animal gives freely when it no longer has use for it—sharks teeth, cat fur, peacock feathers, sea shells, and snake skin, for example. We otherwise use image magic instead of animal parts, or call upon deities that correspond to animals.

Meditate on the awesome prehistoric cave paintings of Europe and Africa, on how they reveal the religious importance of animals to humans. When you dream of an animal, try to speak with it. This is the way to gain knowledge. Animals often come to witches as they do to shamans, as spirit guides who help, teach, reveal secrets, bestow wisdom, and support magical workings.

An animal totem is one that symbolizes a person or group. I consider the mole to be my spirit guide and the industrious beaver my totem animal. Discovering your animal totem and spirit guide can be a part of your inner work, a way to find your path.

NOTE: Some mythical animals (such as Pegasus and Ladon) are mixed together with gods and goddesses in these invocation lists.

# CORRESPONDENCES

**MAMMALS**

Artemis is Lady of the Wild Things, also called Potnia Theron, Mistress of Animals, in this aspect. Mammals are sacred to Age, the Benin god of animals, to Diana, to the chief Navajo god, Hastseyalti, and to Merlin. "Lord of Animals" is a title for the Celtic god Cernunnos, the Siberian hunting god Hinkin, and Pasupati, the Hindu god of animals. Wild animals are sacred to Artemis, Aruru, Bêlit-ili, Diana, Dingirmah, Hannahhannas Mama, Ninhursag, Ninmenna, and Ursel.

*Land Mammals:*

*ANTELOPE:* The antelope is sacred to Dedoun, Saraddevi, and Vayu. The oryx is sacred to Set and Oya. Oryx horns were once sold as unicorn horns.

*APES:* Apes are sacred to the Devil, Isis, Mahakapi the Great Ape, Mbotumbo, Nephthys, Osiris, and Thoth. Baboons are sacred to Amaunet, Amu, Babi, Hapy, Hauhet, Heh, He Zur, Kauket, Khonsu, Naunet, Nun, and Thoth.

The monkey is a Chinese zodiac animal, symbol of cleverness and curiosity. It is sacred to Hanuman, the Lares, Sugriva, Sun Hou-Shi, and Sun Wu Kong.

*BADGER:* Badgers' feet and eyes are supposed to confer invincibility. Putting powdered badger's foot or eye in someone's food was supposed to make them love you. (Yuck!)

*BAT:* Bat is the guardian of night, associated with Halloween. Bats are considered good luck in China, where they symbolize happiness. They are sacred to Alcithoe, Arsippe, Camazotz, Fu-hsing, and Shang Kuo-Lao. Vampire bats are sacred to Ikal Ahau.

*BEAR:* The bear is both a Celtic and Native American totem beast. Its direction is West, in the Zuni tradition. Bears symbolize kingship, power, mother-cunning, and gentle strength. The bear paw (or its image, for Wiccans) is used magically for power, direction, and connection to the creator.

Bears are sacred to Andarta, Arcas, Artemis Brauronia, Arthgen, King Arthur, Artio, Artogenus and Callisto (Queen of Bears), corn spirits, Mary of the Bears, Mercury Artaios, Rhpisunt (the Bear Mother), and Ursula (Little Bear).

She-bears are sacred to Artemis, Artemis Callisto, Callisto (the She-bear), the Great Goddess, and Ursel (She-Bear). Black bears are sacred to Wachabe. The grizzly bear symbolizes motherhood.

*BEAVER:* The beaver is a Native American totem animal. It symbolizes construction, building, and the work ethic. Beavers are sacred to Castor, Great Beaver, and Wishpoosh. Taurus is their zodiac sign.

*BISON:* Bison correspond to both the planet and the element of earth.

*BUFFALO:* The buffalo is a sacred Native American totem animal, the builder of life, provider of sustenance, and bestower of curing powers. It symbolizes prayer, sacredness, plenty, and a harmonious relationship with Earth. Buffalo are sacred to Mahish, Oya, and Yama.

White Buffalo Woman, or Ptesan-wi, is a Plains Indian Earthmysteries goddess who taught the seven ceremonies and introduced the sacred pipe to the people.

*CAMEL:* Camels are sacred to the Arabian gods Arsu and Azizos.

*CAT:* Cats are the animals that most often become witches' familiars. They correspond to the Moon, can see spirits, and can walk through magic circles without breaking them. All cats were held sacred in ancient Egypt, where the great cat goddess Bast was also worshiped as Ubastet, Little Cat.

Cats are sacred to Artemis, Cat Annis, Cerridwen, Demeter, Diana, Irusan, Mafdet, the Moon Goddess, Neith, Pasht, Ra as Great Cat of Heliopolis, Sekhmet (the Great Cat), Tefnut, and Tjilpa. They are sacred to corn spirits as Corn Cat, Le Chat de Peau de Balle, and Tom Cat. Male cats are sacred to Mau, Ra, and Shu. Gray cats are sacred to Freyja, civet cats to Lady Civet Cat.

*CATTLE:* Cattle god/desses include Geus Tasan and Geus Urvani (Persian gods), Sakkan (Mesopotamian god), Vitsa-Kuva, Cattleyard Lady (Russian), and Ynakhsyt (Siberian goddess). Cattle are also sacred to Ajyst (Siberian goddess), Apedemak (Sudanese god), corn spirits, Shumuqan (Mesopotamian god), the Slavic gods Veles and Volos, and Vohu Manah (Zoroastrian god).

Cattle are sacred to the Moon deities Aine of Knockaine (Irish goddess) and the Mesopotamian gods Nannar and Sin.

The bull is a Celtic totem beast, used magically for fertility and virility. Bulls correspond to Earth, the Moon, and the element earth. Their astrological sign is Taurus. In mythology, bull gods are both consort of the Divine Cow and Bull Calf of the Mother. New Year is their station on the Wheel of the Year.

Bull's blood, regarded as having potent magical powers in ancient times, was used for divination and to feed the ghosts of heroes. Druids were wrapped in the hide of a freshly killed bull for their seership ritual.

Bulls are sacred to Adad, An (the Bull of Heaven), Anu, Astarte, Asterius (the Minotaur), Atum, Baal, Damuzi, Dionysus, El, the Goddess, the Great Goddess, Indra, Ishkur, Jupiter, Marduk (Bull-calf of the Sun), Mars, Mithras, Nanna, Osiris (Bull of the Underworld), Perun, Poseidon, Prisni, Ptah, Ra, Rudra, Serapis, Shiva, Sin, Soma, Suen, Tammuz, Teshub, Vishnu, and Zagreus. Wild bulls are sacred to Damuzi, Dionysus, Hercules, and Mithras.

White bulls, which correspond to the Moon, were particularly used for sacrifices in ancient times. Initiates into the cult of Mithras were placed under a grating over which a white bull was sacrificed, drenching them in his blood. White bulls are sacred to Baal Zephon, Menu, Min, Mithras, and Mnevis.

Calves are sacred to Atabryius, Atik (Calf of El), and Sharruma (Calf of Teshub). They are sacred to corn spirits as Corn Calf and Muhkalbchen.

The cow is the sacred animal of Hinduism. It corresponds to fertility, the planet Earth, and the element earth. Cows have symbolized the sky since ancient times, so sky goddesses can be considered cosmic cows. *The Egyptian Book of the Dead* mentions the Seven Holy Cows: Het-Kau Nebtertcher, Akertkhentetasts, Khebitetsahneter, Urmertusteshertshenti, Khnemtemankhanuit, Sekhmetrensemabats, Shenatpetuthestneter, and their bull, Kathaihemt.

Cows are sacred to Aditi, Al Uzzah, Anath, Antum, Ashtaroth Karnaim, Astarte, Banba (Woman of the Cows), Bata, Brighid, Cerridwen, Damona (Divine Cow), Diana, Gauri, Hathor, Hera, Inanna, Indra (Lord of Cows), Io, Juno, Krishna, Ninhursag, Ninsûna, Nut, Prisni, Rhea, Tellus Mater, Ushas (Mother of Cows), and Vacca. They are sacred to corn spirits as Barley Cow, Oats Cow, and Thresher Cow. Wild cows are sacred to Ninsûna (Lady of the Wild Cows).

*COUGAR:* The cougar symbolizes power, balance, speed, courage, and leadership.

*COYOTE:* The coyote is a trickster, and corresponds to the planet Mercury. Coyotes symbolize duality, humor, insight, sarcasm, playfulness, and the ability to see both sides of an issue. They are sacred to Coyote, Italapas, Mahih-Nah-Tlehey (Changing Coyote), Olle, all trickster gods, and Ueuecoyotl.

*DEER:* Deer symbolize love, gentleness, sensitivity, kindness, gracefulness, purity of purpose, and walking in the light. Deer horn symbolizes potency in China. Deer are sacred to Artemis, corn spirits, Diana Nemorensis (Diana of the Grove), Harinaigameshin, Nemesis, Tate Kyewimoka, and Tekkeitserktock. White-tailed deer are sacred to Mara Kwari and Tatosi.

Doe are sacred to Taygete, bucks to Sudrem. Powdered hart's horn was considered an aphrodisiac in ancient Europe. It was used with cow's gall as a charm for infertile women. A white hart symbolizes the soul. Roebuck are sacred to Apollo. They correspond to the number 7 and their poetic meaning is "hide the secret" (the secret name of the god).

The stag is a Celtic totem beast that corresponds to the planet and the element earth. Stags are sacred to Apollo and his sister Artemis, Cernunnos, the Great Goddess, Hercules, Herne the Hunter, Learchus, Lÿ-hsing, Merlin, Red Robin Hood, and Silvanus.

*DOG:* The dog is a Chinese zodiac animal whose planet is the Moon and whose star is Sirius. Dogs correspond to healing. They symbolize loyalty and the future. Their poetic meaning is "guard the secret." It was believed that dogs howled before a death because they could see the Angel of Death at work. Carrying a dog's heart on your left side was supposed to prevent dogs from barking at you. Dogs are sacred to Asclepias, Anubis (Guardian of the Dogs), Ares, Cuchulainn (Hound of Ulster), Dharma, Garm (Hell-Hound), Ishat (Bitch of the Gods), Mars, Sarama (Heavenly Bitch), Sucellos, Wepwawet, and Xolotl.

Romans sacrificed red puppies to the corn spirits, to whom dogs are sacred as Peas Pug, Potato Dog, Rye Dog, and Wheat Dog. White dogs with red ears are considered especially sacred and magical. It was believed in Britain that the sound of unseen geese passing overhead in the night was made by the Hounds of Hell, the white dogs with red ears who conducted the souls of the damned and unbaptized babies to an icy northern underworld. The Hounds of Hell were also called Yell Hounds, Yeth Hounds, Wish Hounds, Gabriel Hounds, Gabriel Ratchets, and, in Wales, *Cwm Annwm*.

White dogs and bitches represent corn spirits. A shaggy black dog may be the Barguest, a hideous spirit in disguise. Barguest leads a procession of howling dogs through the street when someone prominent dies.

Greyhounds are sacred to Beba, Herisepef, and Mates.

*DONKEY:* The donkey is sacred to Dionysus and Lisina, the ass to corn spirits, Cronus, Jyestha, Pan, Seth, Shang Kuo-Lao, and Silenus. Asses were considered impure by Orphics. They are connected with holly, Saturnalia, and the Christmas Fool. The wild ass is sacred to Dionysus and the ass-eared Egyptian god Set/Seth/Typhon. It was the sacred animal of the Egyptian Saturnalia.

Mules symbolize infertility. They are sacred to Mullo, Sipe Gialmo, and Vasantadevi.

*ELEPHANT:* Elephants correspond to the Moon. They symbolize greatness, wisdom, power, strength, life span, patience, and memory. Buddhists hold elephants sacred, Hindus consider them to be rain charms. Elephants are sacred to Airavata, Bera-Pennu, Dadimunda, Devata Bandara, Gajana, Ganapati, Ganesh, Lakshmi, Mahaganapati, Parvati, and Tarri-Pennu. A white elephant with six tusks symbolizes the power of wisdom to overcome obstructions. The African elephant is sacred to Apedemak and Mombo Wa Ndhlopfu.

*ELK:* The elk symbolizes strength, power, nobility, freedom, and agility.

*FOX:* The fox is a prophetic animal that corresponds to the planet Mercury. It symbolizes cunning, intelligence, twilight, and female magic. The hu hsien, Chinese fox spirits, are powerful shape-shifting air, water, and earth elementals who can pass through solid matter. The fox is regarded as a supernatural animal in Japan. Foxes are sacred to corn spirits, Demeter, and Reynard the Fox. Vixens correspond to the Moon.

*GAZELLE:* Gazelles are sacred to Anuket, Anukis, Mrgasirag, and Reshep.

*GOAT:* "The lust of the goat is the bounty of God," according to William Blake.[15] Capricorn is the goat's astrological house, summer and the waning year its seasons. Goats correspond to sex magic and sexual virility. Rubbing his genitals with the tallow of a male goat before having sex with his wife was a charm for a man to regain her love and keep her from other men. Feta cheese can be used for goat magic. The Orphic cup, drunk at dawn, contained honey and goat's milk.

Goats are able to see winds. They are sacred to Aj, Amalthea, Aphrodite of the Goats, Artemis, Athene, Azazel, Baal-Gad, Blodeuwedd, Chimaerus, Dionysus, fauns, Faunus, Freyja, the Goddess, Holda, Juno Caprotina (Juno of the Goats), Nabu, Olwen, Goat Pan, satyrs, and Silvanus. They are sacred to corn spirits as Corn Goat, Harvest Goat, Horned Goat, Oats Goat, Rye Goat, Straw Goat, and Wheat Goat. In some Afro-Caribbean magical traditions, it is believed that burning a goat's horn in alcohol averts evil, enemies, and negativity of all kinds.

Wild goats are sacred to Disani, kids to Dionysus Eriphos. The goat stag was the Greek counterpart of the Druid's immortal white hart or hind. It symbolizes resurrection and the hope of immortality.

*HARE:* The hare is associated with witchcraft in Celtic religion. A hare was the totem animal of Boadicca, red-haired warrior-queen of the Celts. Hares were held taboo in ancient Britain, where the taboo on hunting them was suspended on May Eve. Autumn is the hare's station on the Wheel of the Year.

Hares are sacred to Great Hare, Manibozho (Great Hare), Michabo (Great Hare), and Ostara.

The brown hare was believed to confer invincibility. It was held taboo by ancient Hebrews.

*HEDGEHOG:* Pixies sometimes take the form of hedgehogs.

*HIPPOPOTAMUS:* Hippos are sacred to Hathor, Ipet, Reret, Set, Ta-Weret, and Thoueris.

*HORSE:* The horse is a Chinese zodiac animal that corresponds to the Moon. When their hooves strike sparks, horses correspond to the element of fire. They symbolize stamina, strength, power,

---

[15] William Blake, *The Marriage of Heaven and Hell,* p. 32.

love, devotion, loyalty, and sacred kingship. Call upon the horse for fertility and coping under difficult circumstances.

The horse was a Celtic totem beast, symbol of energy, power, and fertility. Horses were held sacred by the Trojans, and were the clan totem of the Centaurs of Magnesia. Horsehair has magical properties.

Horses are sacred to many Celtic goddesses: Badb Catha, Epona, Eriu, Etain, Macha, Maeve, Medb, Modrun, Nemain, Rhiannon, and Rigantona. They are also sacred to Artemis, Astarte, Athene Hippia, Belenus, Bellerophon, centaurs, Chrysippos (Golden Horse), Danais, Demeter, Freyr, the Great Goddess, Hippodameia (Horse-tamer), Hippolyte (Queen of the Amazons), Minerva, Neptune (patron of horse races), Pegasus, and Poseidon Hippios (Lord of Horses). They are sacred to corn spirits as Corn Foal and Corn Horse.

The bay horse is sacred to Xanthus and the piebald horse to Balius. White horses are sacred to Rhiannon and correspond to the Sun. Mares are sacred to Agnaippe (the Mare Who Destroys Mercifully), Demeter, Epona, Melanippe (Black Mare), Nicippe (Victorious Mare), and Rhiannon. Red mares are sacred to Aine of Knockaine. A mare's tooth placed on the head was a charm against frenzied madness. White mares are sacred to Leucippe (White Mare), Rhiannon, and Rigantona.

Foals are sacred to Hippasus, ponies to Epona. Stallions are sacred to Varuna and steeds to Dadhikravan.

*HYRAX:* The hyrax is sacred to the Triple Goddess.

*JACKAL:* Jackals correspond to the planet Mercury. They are sacred to Anubis, Duamutef, Shmashana-Kali, and Wepwawet.

*JAGUAR:* The jaguar's element is earth and it is used for power. It is sacred to Ai Apaec, the Balam, Jaguar, Oka, Sinaa, and Tepeyollotl.

*LEOPARD:* Leopards are sacred to Aphrodite.

*LION:* The lion is the prime solar beast. Its planet is the Sun, its element is fire, and Leo is its astrological house. Spring and summer are the seasons of the lion. It symbolizes royalty, eternal solar light, and the present.

Lions are called upon for power, courage, boldness, protection, invincibility, and strength. Lions' eyes were believed to confer invincibility.

Lion was the fourth level of initiation into the cult of Mithras. Ancient Egyptians decorated their beds with lions to guard them while they slept. The lions of the Eastern and Western Horizons enabled them to sleep and rise again as the Sun did.

Lions are sacred to Anaitis, Anatha, Artemis (A Lion Unto Women), Atum, Cybele, David, Durga, the Goddess, Hathor, Hebat, Helios, Hera, Hercules, Inanna, Ishhara, Ishkur, Ishtar, Khnemu (Governor of Lions), Llew Llaw Gyffes (the Lion with the Steady Hand), Narasimba, Ninhursaga, Parvati, Samson, Sekhmet, Smyrna, Tefnut, Ti-Jean Pietro, Urana, and Vishnu.

The lioness is sacred to Al Uzzah, Astarte, Mekhit, Mut, Nyavirezi, Pakhet (She Who Scratches), and Shesmetet. Mountain lions are sacred to Rhea. They were a clan totem of the Centaurs of Magnesia.

*LYNX:* Venus is the lynx's planet, autumn its season. The lynx is sacred to love goddesses Lug, Mafdet, and Toa'lalit.

*MOLE:* According to Pliny, the Magi looked upon the mole with more awe than any other living creature. Moles correspond to the planet Earth, and can be called upon for Earth magic.

*MONGOOSE:* The mongoose is sacred to Atum and Ningilin. The ichneumon mongoose was called the pharaoh's cat in ancient Egypt, where it was venerated because it destroyed crocodile eggs.

*MOOSE:* Moose symbolize integrity, value, and being headstrong.

*MOUSE:* Mice symbolize pestilence and are sometimes associated with fairies. They were held sacred in ancient Philistis, Knossos, and Phocis. Mice are sacred to corn spirits and Apollo Smintheus. White mice were kept in the temples of Apollo as charms against plague and rats.

*OPOSSUM:* The opossum is sacred to Tatevali, Our Grandfather.

*OTTER:* Otters, which are sacred to the Native American goddess Otter Woman, symbolize laughter, grace, empathy, curiosity, mischievousness, and female power.

*OX:* The ox is a Chinese zodiac animal. Its season is winter; it symbolizes strength and reliability. Oxen are sacred to Artemis,

Athene, the Divine Husbandman, Epona, Gozutenno, Osiris, and Minerva. Young oxen are sacred to corn spirits. Oxen were one of the propitiatory offerings made to Osiris.

Red oxen are sacred to Seth (the Red God). Wild oxen are sacred to Buana and Rimn.

*PANTHER:* Panthers are sacred to Agassou, Dionysus, Dus-Shara, Mafdet, Muso Koroni, Set, and Sharruma.

*PORCUPINE:* Porcupine quills are charms against the evil eye.

*PUMA:* Pumas are sacred to Cit Chac Coh, Tatevali, and Tepeyollotl.

*RABBIT:* The rabbit is a Chinese zodiac animal that corresponds to the Moon. It symbolizes alertness, procreation, and nervousness. Rabbits are sensitive to the evil eye and are sometimes associated with fairies. They are sacred to corn spirits, Inaba, Kaltesh, Master Rabbit, Mexith, Rabbit, and Wenet. Rabbits' movements were once used as a means of divination. White rabbits are sacred to the Chinese goddess Chang-O, Queen of the Moon.

*RAT:* The rat is a Chinese zodiac animal that symbolizes impending wealth. Rats and bandicoots are sacred to Ganesha.

*REINDEER:* Reindeer are sacred to the Siberian god Picvu'cin, who guards them.

*SHEEP:* Sheep are a Chinese zodiac animal and a male symbol. They are sacred to corn spirits, Pan, and the Mesopotamian sheep goddess Sirtur. Bighorn sheep are sacred to Ganaskidi.

Ewes are sacred to Arne, Duttur, Khebieso, and Seret. Imbolc, for Celts, was a feast that marked the lactation of ewes. Lambs are sacred to Amnisian nymphs, Jesus (the Lamb of God), and Mariamne (the Sea Lamb).

The ram is a Celtic totem beast whose planet is the Sun. Spring and the waxing year are its seasons, Aries its astrological house. Rams are sacred to Agni, Ammon, Ba, Baal-Hammon, Benadad, Beneb-Djedet, Jupiter, Kherty, Khnum, Lugh, Mendes, Nirnali, Osiris, Poseidon, Shango, Sore-Gus, Surya, Varuna, Xewioso, and Zeus.

*SQUIRREL:* Squirrels are sacred to Ratatösk.

*SWINE:* Swine are psychopomps, connected with death and the underworld. The Moon is their planet. They are sacred to the Romano-Celtic god Moccus and to the Egyptian god Set.

Pigs are a Chinese zodiac animal that symbolize death, destiny, fertility, the underworld, immortality, and transforming powers. Pigs are able to see winds. Arkan Sonney, also called Lucky Piggies, are Manx fairy pigs who bring good luck if caught.

Pigs were held taboo in ancient Britain. Eating pork was taboo in ancient Egypt, except at the closest Full Moon to Winter Solstice, when pigs were sacrificed to Isis and Osiris. Egyptians only ate pork during the midwinter mysteries. Canaanites broke their taboo on eating pork for the midwinter Boar's Head Feast. Pork is still taboo to Jews and Muslims.

Pigs are sacred to Adoni, Alphito, Attis, Banba, Bladud, Cerdo, Cerridwen, corn spirits, death goddesses, Demeter, the Goddess, the Goddess of life and death and healing, Hades, love and death goddesses, Marica, Moccus, the Moon Goddess, Nangalha, the Old White One, Orcus, Osiris, Persephone, Phorcys, Prosperine, and Set.

The boar is a beast of death, a warrior that symbolizes wealth, courage, and warrior strength. To Celts, the boar was a totem beast and magical animal whose flesh they considered potent magic. Boars are associated with Yule. Their bristles are charms for strength and power.

Boars are sacred to Arduinna, Ares, Camulos, Freyja, Freyr, the Goddess, Nut, Orcus, Phorcys, Rudra (Ruddy Divine Boar), Twrch Trwyth, Varaha the Boar, and Vishnu. Rye Boar is sacred to corn spirits. Wild boars are sacred to Ares and Set, black boars to Set.

Sows are sacred to Cerridwen the Sow, Choere, Demeter, the Morrigan, the Goddess in her crone aspect, Marpessa, Phorcis, Sukarasya, Syr, and Vajra Varahi, the Diamond Sow. They are sacred to corn spirits as Barley Sow, Corn Sow, and Rye Sow. Hogs are sacred to Kamapua.

*TIGER:* The tiger is a Chinese zodiac animal that symbolizes yang, the feminine principle. The Chinese, who believe that tigers provide protection, assign them the following correspondences:

*Color:* white
*Direction:* West
*Season:* autumn
*Element:* water, metal

*Body:* lungs
*Planet:* Earth

The use of tiger parts in Chinese medicine is contributing to the animals extinction. Tigers are sacred to the Hindu goddess Durga. White tigers are a female symbol.

*WEASEL:* The weasel is a prophetic animal, sacred to Galanthis and to Demeter in her prophetic aspect. Thessalonian witches are said to have disguised themselves as weasels.

*WOLF:* The wolf is both a Celtic and a Native American totem beast. Wolf is Teacher and Pathfinder in Native American religion and was associated with the oak cult in Europe. Wolves correspond to the Moon and to the star Sirius. East is their direction in the Zuni tradition. The wolf symbolizes stability, thought, loyalty, success, perseverance, and the past. Wolf prints symbolize tracking and movement. Wolf has the power to remove lechery.

Wolves are sacred to Acca Laurentia, Apollo Lykeios, Artemis, Cerridwen, Fabula, Faula, Fenrir, Garm, Harpalyce, Lupa (the She-Wolf), Lupercus, Lycomedes, Lycus, Malsum, Mars, the Moon Goddess, the Triple Goddess, and Wepwawet. They are sacred to corn spirits as Barley Wolf, Corn Wolf, Oats Wolf, Pea Wolf, Potato Wolf, Rye Wolf, and Wheat Wolf.

### Sea Mammals:
Sea mammals are sacred to Dagon, Pallas, Rahab, Salacia, and Tiamat. Water is their element.

*DOLPHIN:* Native Americans regard dolphins as bringers of teachings from water, a bridge between humans and the ocean. They are ruled by the Moon. The New Year is their station on the Wheel of the Year. The Child of Promise often rode in on a dolphin

Dolphins symbolize communication, joy, kindness, playfulness, breath control, and the breath of life. They are sacred to Aphrodite, Apollo, Atargatis, Delphinus, Hat-Mehit (the First of the Fish), and Poseidon.

*PORPOISE:* The porpoise was one of the three royal fish of ancient Britain. Porpoises were held taboo by Hebrews, whose ark of the covenant is said to have been covered with porpoise skin. Porpoise confers invincibility and is sacred to Apollo and Poseidon.

*SEAL:* Seals correspond to the Moon and are sacred to Nuli'rahak (the Big Woman), Phoceus (the Seal King), Poseidon, Proteus, and Thetis. They were held taboo by ancient Hebrews. Selkies are Scottish seal fairies, found near Orkney and Shetland. Female selkies sometimes take human husbands. Male selkies raise storms and overturn boats in revenge for seal hunting.

*WHALE:* Whales are record keepers. The whale was one of the three royal fish of ancient Britain. Orcas (killer whales) are sacred to Masset San and Sga'na.

The narwhal is also called the sea unicorn. Its horn represents the spiral of immortality.

## MARINE LIFE

All marine life corresponds to the element of water. It is sacred to Djila'qon, Glaucus, Ka'cak, Kere'tkun, Neptune, Nereus, Peruten, Phorcys, Proteus, Sedna, Tinirau, and Yemaya.

*CONCH:* Conchs are sacred to Gandha Tara, Krishna, Tecciztecatl (the Conch Shell Lord), and the Tritons. Conch shells normally twist leftward, so shells that twist to the right have occult value. Conch shells are sacred to Aphrodite. A conch shell is an attribute of Vishnu; a conch called Panchajanya is one of Krishna's attributes. In India, the conch shell is a symbol of victory in battle.

*COWRIE:* Cowries are sacred to the West African vegetation god Soului and are a symbol of the Afro-Caribbean/Brazilian goddess Yemoja/Yamaya.

*CRAB:* Crabs symbolize the dreamworld. Cancer is their astrological house. They are sacred to Nzambi and Toko'yoto.

*EEL:* Eels are sacred to Riiki, the Suijin, and Te Tuna (Phallus). They were held taboo by ancient Hebrews. Reef eels are sacred to Pusiraura.

*FISH:* Fish symbolize knowledge, freedom, and death. They are talismans against drowning. Pisces is their astrological house, winter their season. Pairs of fish are a good omen, symbolizing life, birth, fertility, fecundity, and prosperity.

Fish are sacred to ocean gods like Dylan, Poseidon, Tethra (Lord of the Sea Cattle), the Tritons, and to the love goddesses

Aphrodite the Fish, Atargatis/Derceto, Dea Syria, and Venus. They are also sacred to Ea, Enki, Dagon, Hatmehyt (She Who Leads the Fishes), Hermes, Jesus, Varuna, Vatea, and Vishnu.

Cuttlefish are sacred to Aphrodite and Fe'e, the Polynesian death god. Perch are sacred to the Egyptian goddess Neith. Salmon symbolize knowledge, instinct, determination, and persistence. A salmon in a pool symbolizes philosophical retirement. Salmon are sacred to Anaulikutsaix, who oversees the salmon runs, to Fintan, and to Tsa'qamae, god of the salmon migration.

Sharks symbolize survival and adaptability. They are sacred to Chac Uayab Xoc (the Great Demon Shark), Matuka Tago Tago, and Tumu-I-Te-Are-Toka (the Great Shark). Sturgeon (one of the three royal fish of ancient Britain), were considered an aphrodisiac in ancient Greece along with tunny and periwinkles. All three fish are sacred to Aphrodite.

Jellyfish are sacred to Medusa, who was transformed into a Gorgon with snakes for hair as punishment for making love with Poseidon in Athene's temple. The octopus is sacred to the Cretan goddess. Scallops were considered an aphrodisiac in ancient Greece. They are sacred to Aphrodite and Margarito (Lady of the Pearls). Seahorses can be called upon for confidence. Sea urchins are sacred to Aphrodite. Squid are sacred to Hydra and the Goddess.

## REPTILES

Reptiles are sacred to the Chiccan, Maya rain gods of the four quarters, and to the Hawaiian reptile god Mo'o.

*ALLIGATOR:* Alligators symbolize aggression, survival, and adaptability. They are sacred to Cipactli, the Aztec Earth Mother.

*CHAMELEON:* Chameleons are sacred to the Central African god Leza.

*CROCODILE:* Water is the crocodile's element. Crocodiles are sacred to Hao, Itzam Na, Khentekhai, Nuga, Nyakaya, Osiris, Set, and Sobek (the Rager). The left eyetooth of a crocodile was a charm against fever.

*FROG:* Frogs symbolize transformation, rebirth, and teeming life. They correspond to the element of water. The frog was a symbol of resurrection for both Christians and ancient Egyptians. A frog amulet is used to invoke the power of the frog-headed Egyptian Goddess, Heket. Frogs are sacred to the Ah Hayaob (Great Frog), Heket, Herst, Nun, and Tlatecuhtli.

A dove's heart and a frog's head, dried, powdered, and sprinkled on the breast of a sleeping woman was believed to make her confess all her actions. The powder had to be removed once she woke to prevent delirium. A frog, fed to a dog in meat, was a charm to silence it.

*IGUANA:* Iguanas are sacred to Chibirias and Itzam Na (Iguana House).

*LIZARD:* The night goddess Evaki stole sleep from the eyes of lizards and gave it to all living creatures. Lizards symbolize agility and conservation. They can be called upon for dreams and are sacred to Abas, Atum, Itzamna (Lizard House), Re Atum, Saurus, and Tate Rapawiyema. Monitor lizards are sacred to Sir Monitor Lizard, spotted lizards to Ascalabus.

*SALAMANDER:* Salamanders correspond to the elements of fire and water.

*SNAKE/SERPENT:* Serpents are phallic totems, the totem beast of fire from within Earth. Snakes are Chinese zodiac animals that correspond to the Moon. They are sexual emblems and Celtic totem beasts. Water-dwelling snakes correspond to the element water; land-dwelling snakes correspond to earth; serpents in general correspond to fire. Autumn and winter are their seasons.

Serpents symbolize transformation, sexuality, renewal, change, fertility, temptation, lunar mystery, and the ceaseless lunar tides of time. Two entwined snakes symbolize healing. Snakes symbolize jealousy in Shintoism, rain and fertility to Pueblo Indians. The shed skin of a snake symbolizes rebirth and is a charm for easy childbirth. The snake's act of shedding its skin represents life, death, and rebirth. Associated with magical power by many cultures ancient and modern, serpents can be called upon for life, health, lust, and fertility.

Bio-energy (called prana, ch'i, or kundalini), is sometimes represented as a coiled snake that rests in the root chakra. Sacred to Shakti, kundalini is serpent power, the cosmic energy of the universe that rests at the base of the spine. A snake's tooth, plucked while the snake is still alive, is a charm against malaria. The sight of a snake was once believed to cause miscarriage or induce labor.

Celts held snakes sacred to Brighid, Danu, and Sucellos; Greco-Romans held them sacred to Asclepius, Athene, Delphine, Demeter, Hades, Hercules, Lamia, Medusa, Ophion, and Persephone. Hindus hold them sacred to Ananta (the World Serpent), Devi, Kundalini, Mahanaga, Nagaraja, and Shesha-Naga. Egyptians held them sacred to Amun, Apep, Atum, Hathor, Isis, Meretseger, Neith, Set, Tefnut, and Uatchit.

Snakes are also sacred to Agathos Daimon, Al Uzzah, Angitia, Angru Mainyu, Coatlicue (Serpent Lady), Dan Pietro, the Devil, Eve, Great Rainbow Snake, Kukulcan (Feathered Serpent), Libya, Mari, Nabu, Ningizzida, and Quetzalcoatl. Twin serpents are sacred to Mercury.

In *The Papyrus of Ani,* the scribe Ani takes the part of the serpent Seta for this spell:

**I am the serpent Seta, whose years are many. I lie down and I am born day by day. I am the serpent Seta, which dwelleth in the limits of the earth. I lie down, I am born, I renew myself, I grow young day by day.**[16]

The Egyptian amulet of the serpent's head, made of red stone or paste, was used to invoke the power of Isis as great Snake Goddess to repel serpents. This spell was used to empower the amulet:

**O Serpent! I am the flame which shineth upon the Opener of hundreds of thousands of years, and the standard of young plants and flowers. Depart ye from me, for I am the divine Lynx.**[17]

The adder is sacred to Nidhogge. Binding its skin to a woman's ankle is a charm to induce labor. Asps are sacred to Anatha, the Canaanite goddess of war. The cobra is the Eye of Ra. It symbolized royalty and sovereignty in ancient Egypt, where Cleopatra is more likely to have used a cobra than an asp to commit suicide. Cobras are sacred to Buto/Uadjit, Edjo, Hermouthis, Hetepes, Meretseger, Renenutet, and Sekhus.

---

[16] E. A. Wallis Budge, *The Egyptian Book of the Dead: The Papyrus of Ani,* p. 337.
[17] E. A. Wallis Budge, *Egyptian Magic,* p. 59.

Pythons are sacred to Ningizzida, Python, and the Pythian priestess of Apollo at Delphi. Rattlesnakes are sacred to Coyolxuahqui, the Aztec star goddess. Vipers are sacred to Echidne, the serpent woman of Greek mythology.

*TOAD:* The toad has been regarded as a magical creature since very ancient times. Modern science has only recently come to appreciate possible applications for the chemicals, toxic and otherwise, secreted by toads through their skin. Ash of burnt toad worn in a mojo bag around the neck is said to cure bed-wetting. Toads are sacred to the Aztec goddess Tlaltecuhtli.

*TORTOISE:* The tortoise carries the world on his back. He also rules over northern China. His season is winter and he is sacred to the Ah Hayaob, Hsi Wang, Kurma, and Lugh.

*TURTLE:* Native Americans called America Turtle Island. They considered the turtle a source of creativity. Turtles symbolize Mother Earth and self-containment.

## INSECTS

Insects correspond to the element of air.

*ANT:* Ants symbolize teamwork and self-discipline. They are sacred to Ahriman, the Persian god of darkness.

*BEE:* Bees are sacred to the Ah Muzencab, Callisto (Queen Bee), Cybele (the Queen Bee), Mellonia, Neith, and Usins. Honeybees are sacred to Melissa.

*BEETLE:* Beetles are ruled by the Sun and sacred to Ra. Scarab beetles symbolized life, creative power, and the perpetual renewal of life in ancient Egypt. Wear a scarab as a protective amulet, or for manliness or creative power. They are sacred to Atum, Iusaas, and Khepera. Egyptians wrapped scarab amulets in mummies' bandages as charms for resurrection and potential life. The amulets were usually made of green basalt, limestone, green granite, marble, blue paste or glass, or purple, blue, or green porcelain.

*The Ceremony of the Beetle:* This ceremony was used to make the Ring of Horus, a green stone scarab set in gold. Perform it on day 7, 9, 10, 12, 14, 16, 21, 24, or 25 of the lunar cycle.

- Burn myrrh incense. Fill a stone vessel with ointment of myrrh, lilies, or cinnamon. (Try steeping cinnamon sticks in unscented hand cream or petroleum jelly for a week or so.) Offer incense, then leave the ring in the ointment for 3 days.
- Decorate the altar with bread and seasonal fruits. Offer the ring on grapevines, if possible. (Try a florist or craft shop.)
- Early in the morning on the third day, take the ring out and anoint yourself with the ointment. Face east and recite this spell:

*I am Thoth, the inventor and founder of medicine*
 *and letters;*
*Come to me, thou that are under the earth,*
*Rise up to me, thou great spirit.*[18]

- Wear the ring.

*BUTTERFLY:* The butterfly symbolizes rebirth and transformation. It symbolized perfection to the Aztecs. Butterflies are sacred to Great Butterfly and Itzpapalotl (Obsidian Butterfly).

*CENTIPEDE:* Centipedes are sacred to Sepa.

*DRAGONFLY:* The dragonfly symbolizes swiftness, immortality, whirlwinds, and a carefree life. Zunis considered them shamanic creatures with supernatural powers. Dragonflies are sacred to Kangalogba and Toro.

*FLY:* Flies are sacred to Beelzebub (Lord of the Flies), to Baal-Zebul (Lord of Zebulon), and to Deus Moscarum. *Musca Magica*, the Magic Fly, was a charm the ancients made to keep flies away. According to Virgil, the charm involved making a gold or bronze fly the size of a frog while the second aspect of Aquarius was ascendant, and invoking Muiagros (Fly Catcher), the fly god Deus Moscarum, Zeus Apomious, and Apomious (Averter of Flies). Hung at the top of a post near the city gate, this charm was said to keep entire communities from being annoyed by flies.

The may-fly is sacred to the Irish hero Cuchulainn.

---

[18] E. A. Wallis Budge, *Egyptian Magic,* p. 43.

*LOCUST:* Locusts symbolize destruction. They are sacred to Apollo. Pharaoh's daughter seduced King Solomon with magic using three locusts and a scarlet thread.

*MOSQUITO:* Mosquitos are sacred to Nunusómikeeqoném.

*PRAYING MANTIS:* The praying mantis is sacred to I Kaggen.

*SCORPION:* Scorpions are sacred to Ahriman, Ishara, Nehebu-Kau, Scorpion Man, Selket, Seth, and Ti Bitjet. Scorpio is their astrological house. Babylonians believed that scorpion-people guarded the seven gates of the underworld, which was located in a mountain. The seven scorpions of Isis were called Tefen, Befen, Mestet, Mestetef, Petet, Thetet, and Matet.

*SPIDER:* Spiders connect the past with the future. They symbolize creativity, the pattern of life, and the Web. Spiders are sacred to Anansi, Arachne, Ariadne, Macardit, Marawa, Mulungu, Great Spider, Nareau (the Old Spider), Spider Woman, Thinking Woman, Tule, and Uttu.

*WORM:* Worms are sacred to the Polynesian creator gods Te-Aka-Ia-Roe, Te-Manaka-Roa, and Te-Tanga-Eugae.

## BIRDS

Birds correspond to the element of air and the planet Mercury. Spring is their season. Birds are sacred to the ancient Hindu Sun god Garuda, the Celtic goddess Rhiannon, and the Hindu god Vishnu.

Pairs of birds symbolize the power of life, spirituality, and the immortality of the soul. Omens were read in bird calls and the flight of birds in ancient times. Birds can be the message or the messenger, omens of bloodshed or prophetic knowledge.

*BLACKBIRD:* Feathers from the right wing of a blackbird, suspended by a red thread from the middle of a house that has never been occupied, were said to make it impossible for anyone to sleep in the house until they were taken away.

*BLUEJAY:* Bluejay is a trickster and Mercury is his planet.

*BUZZARD:* Buzzards are sacred to Chinigchinich. They were worshiped by Native Americans at San Juan Capistrano.

*CARDINAL:* The cardinal is sacred to Tatevali, Our Grandfather.

*CHICKEN:* The rooster is a Chinese zodiac animal and the Orphic bird of resurrection. It corresponds to the Sun. Roosters are sacred to Aesculapius, Karttikey, Kenken-Ur (Great Cackler), Lugh, Velchanos, and Zeus Velchanos. They are sacred to corn spirits as Corn Cock, Harvest Cock, Red Cock, and Stubble Cock. *The Egyptian Book of the Dead* contains the following invocation:

**I watch and guard the Egg of the Great Cackler. I grow, and it groweth; it groweth, and I grow; I live, and it liveth.**[19]

Hens are sacred to Cerridwen/Hen Wen. Their station on the Wheel of the Year is August 6 to September 2. Hens are sacred to corn spirits as Clucking Hen and Harvest Hen. Black hens are sacred to the death goddess.

Eggs symbolize initiation. They correspond to the Sun, are sacred to Helius and Vulcan. Use eggs and onions, which are both absorbatives, to purify the house on the 30th of each month, then leave them for Hecate at a place where three roads meet.

*COCKEREL:* Cockerels are sacred to the Irish fire goddess Brighid and the Hindu war god Skanda.

*CORMORANT/SEA CROW:* Cormorants are sacred to the Celtic gods Bran and Morvran (Sea Crow). Spring Equinox is their station on the Wheel of the Year. Calypso's island had oracular sea crows.

*CRANE:* Cranes can be called upon for wisdom. They symbolize solitude, longevity, independence, and literary and poetic secrets. A pair of cranes symbolizes good fortune and elegant literary style. Cranes are sacred birds, a Taoist symbol of wisdom and immortality. Alphabetic secrets were once drawn from the flight of cranes. They are associated with willow trees. August 6 to September 2 is their station on the Wheel of the Year.

---

[19] E. A. Wallis Budge, *The Egyptian Book of the Dead: The Papyrus of Ani*, p. 311.

The crane is sacred to Apollo and his sister Artemis, and to Athene, Badb, Esu, Hermes, Kali, the Morrigan, Nan-ji-Hsian Weng, Palamedes, Shou Lao, and Theseus. It is also sacred to the Triple Goddess because its mating dance has nine steps. White cranes symbolize longevity and are sacred to Hsi Wang Mu.

*CROW:* The crow is a Celtic totem beast, an oracular bird that augers battle and bloodshed. Saturn is its planet, November 25 to December 22 its station on the Wheel of the Year. Crows symbolized long life in Greece and Italy. They are sacred to Asclepias, Apollo, Athene, Bran, Coronis, Cronus, Jehovah, Saturn, Tulugusaq Yangwu (Sun Crow), and to the Celtic goddesses Badb (Crow of Battle), Eriu, Etain Echraide, Macha, Maeve, Medb, the Morrigan, Nemain, and Rhiannon. White crows are sacred to Branwen. The night crow's station on the Wheel of the Year is May 14 to June 10.

*CUCKOO:* Hebrews held the cuckoo taboo. It is sacred to Athene, Hera, and Juno.

*DIVING BIRDS:* Diving birds are sacred to Athene and Hera. They are associated with the death of the sacred king by drowning

*DOVE:* Doves symbolize long life and forgiveness. They symbolized love in China, the renewal of life to the Greeks, and deliverance to the Hebrews. A pair of doves symbolizes wedded bliss. Venus is their planet. They can be called upon for sex magic, love spells, peace, fertility, and prosperity. Irish legend has it that the souls of the blessed become doves and swans.

Doves are sacred to Aphrodite, Atargatis, the Great Goddess, the Holy Spirit, love goddesses, Lupa, Maia, Rachel, Rhea, Semiramis (Sublime Dove), Turan, and Venus. A flock of doves is sacred to the Pleiades, the Sailing Ones. The rock dove is sacred to Hercules.

Turtledoves symbolize conjugal love, fidelity, and passion. Carrying a turtledove's heart in a wolf's skin was supposed to cause you to lose your appetite forever. Hanging a turtledove's feet from a tree was believed to prevent the tree from ever bearing fruit again.

*DUCK:* Ducks symbolize happy marriage in Egypt. January 22 to February 18 is their station on the Wheel of the Year. Ducks are sacred to Penelope and Sequana.

*EAGLE:* The eagle symbolizes success, fearlessness, prosperity, clear vision, soaring spirit, and power in battle. Eagles are associated with shamans and ruled by the Sun. Summer is their season, December 22 their station on the Wheel of the Year. Native Americans consider the eagle a divine spirit and the Sun's primary servant. To Aztecs, the eagle was a symbol of heavenly power and the rising Sun. Ancient Hebrews held them taboo.

Eagles are sacred to Agni, Bel, Dushara, Ehagabal, Fintan, Ganymede, Heliogabalos, Hirgab (the Father of the Eagles), Istem, Jupiter, Sumul (Mother of the Eagles), Tate Velike Vimali, Tonatiuh (Soaring Eagle), and Zeus.

Winter Solstice is the eaglet's station. Golden eagles symbolize peace. They were held sacred in ancient times, but considered unclean by the Hebrews. The swan eagle is sacred to Niobe. Bald eagles symbolize clear vision. Royal eagles are sacred to Tatevali.

*FALCON:* Falcons correspond to the Sun and can be called upon for omens. They are sacred to Anty (He with the Talons), Calypso, Circe (She-falcon), Freya, Frigg, Horakhty (Horus of the Horizon), Horus (the High One), Khonsu, Mentu, Ra Sokar, Sopedu, Wek-wek, and Yah.

*GANNET:* Gannets are sacred to Ceyx.

*GOOSE:* The goose's station on the Wheel of the Year is October 29 to November 25. Geese are sacred to Amun, Aphrodite, Brahma, Brahmani, Gae, Geb (the Great Cackler), Gengen Wer, Hansa, Isis, Kaltesh, Ra, and Seb. Geese were offered to Osiris in propitiation. They are sacred to corn spirits as Inning Goose and Harvest Goose.

Ganders are sacred to corn spirits. Autumn Equinox is the wild goose's station. The Nile goose is sacred to Amun. Hebrews held the barnacle goose taboo.

*HAWK:* Air is the hawk's element, April 16 to May 13 its station on the Wheel of the Year. Hawks symbolize observation and messages. They represented heaven in predynastic Egypt and are considered sky messengers by Native Americans. Hawks are sacred to Ash, Circe, Fintan, Gwalchmai, Hawk Maiden, Horus, Inca, Isis, Nephthys, Qebhseneut, Sheps, and Sokar (Lord of the Mysterious Region).

Chickenhawks are sacred to Kallin Kallin, eaglehawks to Warana and Yalungur. Native Americans call the kite Clairvoyant Woman. Kites were held taboo by ancient Hebrews. They are sacred to Boreas, Isis, and Nephthys. Carrying a kite's head near your breast was supposed to grant you the love and favor of all men and women. Anointing a cock's comb with a kite's blood was believed to stop the cock from crowing again.

*The Egyptian Book of the Dead* contains the following prayer:

> **May I rise, may I gather myself together as the beautiful golden hawk which hath the head of a bennu bird. May I enter into the presence of Ra daily to hear his words, and may I sit amongst the mighty gods of Nut. May a homestead be made ready for me, and mighty offerings of food and drink be put before me therein. May I eat therein; may I become a shining one therein; may I be filled therein to my heart's fullest desire . . .[20]**

*HERON:* A heron flying out of sunlight symbolized joy and hope in ancient Egypt, where herons were sacred to Atum. Hebrews held them taboo.

*HOOPOE:* The hoopoe is an oracular bird that was said to have told King Solomon prophetic secrets. It confers invincibility and is sacred to Tereus.

*HUMMINGBIRD:* Hummingbirds symbolize optimism, sweetness, and joy. Native Americans considered the hummingbird a messenger. They charged it with the power to stop time, because of its ability to hover in the air. Hummingbirds are sacred to Ah Kin Xoc, Huitzilopochtli, and P'izlimtec.

*IBIS:* The ibis corresponds to the Moon. It is sacred to Hermes, Mercury, Rubanga, and the Egyptian Moon gods Thoth and Yah. Hebrews held the ibis taboo.

*KINGFISHER/HALCYON:* Kingfishers have the magical power to allay storms. They are sacred to Alcyone and Ceyx. Winter Solstice is their station on the Wheel of the Year.

---

[20] E. A. Wallis Budge, *The Egyptian Book of the Dead: The Papyrus of Ani*, p. 332.

The dried body of a kingfisher was a talisman against lightning. Pliny recommended dried, powdered halcyon nests as a cure for leprosy.

*LAPWING/BLACK PLOVER:* The lapwing's poetic meaning is "disguise the secret." Winter Solstice is its station on the Wheel of the Year. Lapwing eyes are supposed to confer invincibility.

Lapwings were used for augury by the Etruscans, and were held taboo by ancient Hebrews. When depicted with pinioned wings in Old Kingdom Egyptian art, they symbolized the people under the pharaoh's rule and Upper Egypt's rule of Lower Egypt. In New Kingdom art, lapwings symbolized Egypt's enemies. A lapwing with upraised human arms, in a basket with a star, means "all the people give praise." The Greek proverb "more deceitful than a lapwing" was used to describe artful beggars.

*LARK:* Summer Solstice is the lark's station on the Wheel of the Year.

*MACAW:* Macaws are sacred to Tatevali, Our Grandfather.

*MAGPIE:* The magpie is a prophetic bird of the Goddess of Death-in-Life and Life-in-Death.

*NIGHTINGALE:* The nightingale can be called upon for eloquence. It is sacred to Aedon and Philomela.

*OSTRICH:* An ostrich plume was the Egyptian hieroglyph for both the goddess Ma'at and the word *truth*. It was the Feather of Truth against which Osiris weighed the hearts of the dead on his balance.

*OWL:* Owls symbolize the collective unconscious and the wisdom of the dreamworld. They can be called upon for wisdom, truth, enlightenment, patience, and astral travel. Witches of the left-hand path sent the fetch, an owl, via astral projection to summon souls to the Sabbat.

The owl is the bird of death, death's dread messenger. Romans called owls funeral birds and believed they foretold death. In old England, it was believed that a member of the family would die if an owl perched on a castle. Anglo-Saxons called both owls and witches hags. Native Americans consider owls the totem animal of seers and mystics. Early Christians associated owls with demonic possession. Hebrews held them taboo.

Owls are the messengers of Athene, Hecate, Lilith, and Persephone. They are associated with Halloween and sacred to Annis the Blue Hag, Artemis, Asclepias, Athena, Blodeuwedd (the Owl), Gwy, Hecate, Lilith, Medusa, Minerva, Nyctimene, and Persephone.

The barn owl is the Death Owl. Placing a barn owl's heart and right foot on a sleeping man was supposed to make him answer any question asked of him. Placing this charm in your armpit was said to prevent dogs from barking at you. Hanging it up in a tree with an owl's wing was said to cause birds to assemble there.

The horned owl is sacred to Calypso. Pliny said that, according to the Magi, placing a horned owl's heart on a sleeping woman would make her tell all her secrets. Shakespeare described the screech owls power thus:

*Whilst the screech-owl, screeching loud,*
*Puts the wretch that lies in woe*
*In remembrance of a shroud.*[21]

Screech owls are sacred to Annis and Lilith. The goddess Ana was demonized by Christians into Annis the Blue Hag, who turned into a screech owl at night to suck the blood of children. Spotted owls are associated with witchcraft.

*PARROT:* Parrots can be called upon for creativity and fertility.

*PARTRIDGE:* The partridge is an erotic symbol. It is sacred to Aphrodite, the Great Goddess, all love goddesses, Perdix, and Talus.

*PEACOCK:* A spread peacock tail represents the stars in the sky. According to William Blake, "The pride of the peacock is the glory of God."[22] Peacock feathers can be used in love spells. Peacock fans figured in the rites of Juno. Peacocks are sacred to Bera-Pennu, Hera, Iris, Juno, Karttikeya, Kaumari, Mahamayuri (Great Daughter of the Peacock), Skanda, Tarri-Pennu, and the peacock angels Iblis and Taus.

---

[21] *A Midsummer Night's Dream*, v, i, 377–379, from *The Complete Works of William Shakespeare* (New York: Dorset Press, 1983), p. 193.
[22] William Blake, *The Marriage of Heaven and Hell*, p. 32.

*PELICAN:* Pelicans symbolize maternal piety. They were held taboo by ancient Hebrews.

*PHEASANT:* Pheasants were held sacred in ancient Greece. December 24 to January 21 is their station on the Wheel of the Year.

*PIGEON:* Pigeons are sacred to Nyongu, rock pigeons to Wodoi.

*PLOVER:* The white plover is sacred to Yamato-dake.

*QUAIL:* The quail is an erotic symbol, sacred to Artemis, Asteria, Delian Apollo, Hercules Melkarth, and Melkarth.

*RAVEN:* Ravens are oracular birds of death and prophecy that auger battle and bloodshed. Saturn is their planet, November 25 to December 22 their station on the Wheel of the Year. Call upon the raven for shapeshifting, shamanic power, and changes in consciousness. Native Americans considered the raven a teacher and trickster. According to Irish legend, lost souls become ravens. Ancient Hebrews considered them unclean. Raven was the first level of initiation into the cult of Mithras.

Ravens are sacred to Asclepias, Apollo, Athene, Bran, Coronis, Cronos, Fodla, Freya, Morvran, Natosuelta, Odin, Big Raven, Saturn, and to the Celtic goddesses Badb (Raven of Battle), Danu, Eriu, Etain, Macha, Maeve, Medb, the Morrigan, Nemain, and Rhiannon. The Norse god Odin was accompanied by two ravens called Huginn (Thought) and Muninn (Memory). Sea ravens are sacred to Morvran and Odin.

*ROBIN:* Robins symbolize the New Year and are sacred to the Celtic god Belin.

*ROOK:* November 26 to December 22 is the rook's station on the Wheel of the Year.

*SEA BIRDS:* All sea birds are sacred to Aphrodite and correspond to the element of water. Seagulls are also sacred to the minor Greek sea goddess Leucothea. March 19 to April 15 is their station on the Wheel of the Year. Seamews are sacred to Aphrodite, Ceyx, and Leucothea. Sea swallows are sacred to the Polynesian sea god Make Make.

*SNIPE:* February 19 to March 18 is the snipe's station on the Wheel of the Year.

*SPARROW:* Sparrows correspond to the Moon and are used in sex magic. They are sacred to Aphrodite, Venus, and Xuthus.

*STARLING:* The starling's station on the Wheel of the Year is July 9 to August 5.

*STORK:* Storks are sacred to corn spirits. Ancient Hebrews held them taboo. Stork Day is celebrated in Denmark in May.

*SWALLOW:* The swallow corresponds to those stars near the North Star that never set. It is used in magic for love charms and spells, especially those relating to new love. Swallows, which rode in the prow of Ra's solar boat, symbolized the imperishable souls of the dead in Egypt. They are sacred to Isis and Procne. *The Egyptian Book of the Dead* gives the following invocation:

> **I am the swallow. I am the swallow. I am the scorpion, the daughter of Ra. Hail, ye gods whose scent is sweet; hail, ye gods whose scent is sweet! Hail, thou Flame, which comest forth from the horizon! Hail, thou who art in the city . . . O stretch out up unto me thine hands that I may be able to pass my days in the Island of Flame. I have fared forth with my warrant. I have come with the power thereof. Let the doors be opened unto me.**[23]

*SWAN:* Swans are sacred birds, death birds, associated with poets and alphabetical secrets. They symbolize grace, balance, and innocence. Venus is their planet, Autumn Equinox their station on the Wheel of the Year. The swan represents perfection and spiritual transcendence in Hinduism and was held taboo by the Hebrews.

Swans are sacred to Aed mac Lir, Angus, Aphrodite, Brahma, Brigit, Caer, Conn, corn spirits, Cycnus, Etain, Fiachra, Fionnula, the Goddess, Midhir, Nemesis, Sarasvati, Tea, Turan, and Venus. White swans are sacred to Brigid and Sarasvati. Whistling swans correspond to Autumn Equinox. The mute swan's station on the Wheel of the Year is October 1 to October 29.

---

[23] E. A. Wallis Budge, *The Egyptian Book of the Dead: The Papyrus of Ani*, p. 331.

*THRUSH:* April 16 to May 13 is the thrush's station on the Wheel of the Year.

*TITMOUSE:* The titmouse's station on the Wheel of the Year is September 2 to September 30.

*TURKEY:* Turkeys are sensitive to the evil eye and likely to sicken or die if their farm is hexed.

*VULTURE:* Vultures are sacred to Hathor, Isis, Mars, Mut, and Nekhebet. Wear a vulture-goddess crown for spiritual develop-ment, to expand the brain, to open the third eye, or to merge with the goddess of life and death. The vulture symbolized Upper Egypt, heaven, and the female principle in ancient Egypt. When shown with the cobra of Lower Egypt, it symbolized the unity of the country. The Egyptian amulet of the vulture, a golden vulture with outstretched wings holding ankhs in its talons, invoked the protective power of Isis as Divine Mother. The amulet was em-powered with these words:

> **Isis cometh and hovereth over the city, and she goeth about seeking the secret habitations of Horus as he emergeth from his papyrus swamps, and she raiseth up his shoulder which is in evil case. He is made one of the company in the divine boat, and the sovereignty of the whole world is decreed for him. He hath warred mightily, and he maketh his deeds to be remembered; he hath made the fear of him to exist and awe of him to have its being. His mother, the Mighty Lady, protecteth him, and she hath transferred her power unto him.[24]**

Griffin vultures are sacred to Jehovah, Ma'at, and Osiris. They were held taboo by ancient Hebrews.

*WOODPECKER:* The woodpecker is a prophetic bird, the bird of the oak. Mars is its planet. It is sacred to Celeus, Dryope, Mars, Pi-cus, and Zeus Picus.

*WREN:* The wren is a prophetic bird, Drui-en, the oracular bird of the Celts. June 11 to July 8 is its station on the Wheel of the

---

[24] E. A. Wallis Budge, *Egyptian Magic*, p. 48.

Year. Wrens are sacred to Bran, Cronos, and Saturn. Bran's sparrow is another name for the wren. Wrens were associated with oak and lightning in England and substituted for the woodpecker in Ireland. European peoples considered it unlucky to kill a wren or disturb its nest. Scots called it Our Lady of Heaven's Hen:

> *Malisons, malisons, mair than ten*
> *That harry the Ladye of Heaven's Hen.*[25]

The misfortunes that could befall such a person included lightning, skin disease, broken bones, maimed hands, and cows giving bloody milk. Despite this, the wren was hunted at solstice in France and Britain, a custom that survived from pre-agricultural times.

> *We hunted the wren for Robin the Bobbin,*
> *We hunted the wren for Jack of the Can.*
> *We hunted the wren for Robin the Bobbin,*
> *We hunted the wren for everyone.*[26]

The feathers of solstice wrens were charms against shipwreck. The gold-crest wren is sacred to Cronos and Saturn. It was hunted when the Wheel of the Year turned a complete circuit.

*WRYNECK/CUCKOO'S MATE/SNAKEBIRD:* The wryneck is a magical bird, the prime orgiastic bird of the Goddess. It corresponds to the Moon. The wryneck was considered a sacred bird in Egypt and Assyria and held sacred to the Moon Goddess in northern Thessaly. It was the clan totem of the Centaurs of Magnesia and is sacred to Dionyus Ixngies, the Goddess, Io, Iynx, and Philyra.

Wrynecks were used in charms for love and rain. A live wryneck spread-eagled to a fire wheel was the love charm Aphrodite used to sustain Medea's passion for Jason. Greek witches tied wrynecks to small wheels as love charms, making a spell as the bird turned the wheel.

---

[25] Sir James G. Frazer, *The Golden Bough: A Study in Magic and Religion* (New York: The MacMillan Company, 1953), p. 621.
[26] Sir James G. Frazer, *The Golden Bough: A Study in Magic and Religion*, p. 623.

# FANTASTIC BEASTS

*BEHEMOTH:* The behemoth was a great marauding male land beast, sometimes equated with the hippopotamus. It is sacred to Bahamut, a huge fish on whom the giant bull, Kujara, stands. According to Islamic myth, this bull carries a rock of ruby on his back, and on this rock stands the angel who supports Earth on his shoulders.

*CHIMAERA:* The Chimaera (She-goat), had a lion's head, a goat's body, and a serpent's tail.

*DRAGON:* Dragons can be positive or negative. In the East, they are considered portents of prosperity and enlighteners of darkness, but in Celtic tradition, dragons bring chaos, infertility, waste, and ruin. A dragon corresponds to the element of air if it flies, the element of fire if it breathes fire, and the element of earth if it dwells in a cave. Sea dragons correspond to the element of water. Use dragons for Earth energy and serpent power. Dragons are sacred to Dahaka, Godi, Goru, Fafnir, Illuyankas (the Dragon), Irnini, Ishhara, Ishtar, Medea (Dragon Queen), Nidhogge, Ryujin (Dragon King), and Vritra. The green dragon is a male symbol. Sea dragons are sacred to Hung Sheng (the Holy Ona), who protects fishing vessels.

The dragon is a Chinese zodiac animal, believed to produce rain. It symbolizes yang, the male principle, in Tao. The Chinese assign dragons the following correspondence:

color: green season: spring
direction: East part of the body: liver
element: fire; wood

There are five kinds of Chinese dragons.

Imperial dragons, with five claws (all others have four claws);
Celestial dragons, who guard the heavenly abode of deities;
Dragon spirits, who rule wind and rain and cause floods;
Earth dragons, who clear rivers and deepen oceans;
Treasure-guarding dragons.

*GRIFFIN/GRYPHON:* A griffin is a composite beast, half eagle and half lion. It is sacred to Nemesis and can be called upon for wisdom, vengeance, and alertness to danger.

*LEVIATHAN:* The leviathan is a female sea beast, sometimes equated with the whale. It is sacred to the Mesopotamian goddess Tiamat, Dragonness of Chaos.

*PHOENIX:* The phoenix is a calendar beast, the legendary bird that is reborn from its own ashes. Egyptians used an eagle with painted wings to represent the phoenix in rituals. It is a male symbol in China. The red phoenix symbolizes longevity. It is sacred to Hsi Wang Mu, the Chinese goddess of longevity.

*SPHINX:* The sphinx is a composite beast with a woman's face and eagle's wings on a lion's body. It corresponds to the Sun and to the elements of earth and air. Call upon the sphinx for sex magic, amorousness, and riddles. It is sacred to Ashtaroth, Astarte, Athene, Horus, Osiris, and Urania. Sphinx (the Throttler) is an Assyrian calendar goddess who devours men when they fail to correctly answer her riddles.

Scientists now suspect that the Sphinx at Giza is actually at least 10,000 years old. This would make it the oldest surviving human construct, created by an unknown civilization. Sands of Time are collected from between the paws of the Sphinx. Use them for eternal spells, or add them to any spell to increase its longevity.

*UNICORN:* The unicorn corresponds to the element of spirit. Only a virgin was said to be able to capture a unicorn. A unicorn horn symbolizes power, zenith, obelisk, the upper pole, and the spiral of immortality. The Japanese unicorn is called Kirin; the Chinese unicorn is called Kilin.

# COLORS

Knowledge of colors is used for candle magic, color magic, spells, potions, powders, rituals, psychic work, worship, invocations, and altar decoration. There is a lot of color lore, but trust yourself in this, as in everything else. If every source you can find recommends blue for your spell, but you feel you should use red, use red.

## BLACK

Black symbolized resurrection and eternal life in ancient Egypt and was a symbol of wisdom to the Aztecs. It is the death color in Western countries, as it was in ancient Greece.

Saturn is black's planet, North its direction, and water its element. Black is also the color of the waning Moon. It is sacred to Babalu-Aye, Crone, Demeter, Elegba, Exu, the Great Goddess, Kali (the Black One), Maman Brigitte, Moon goddesses, Ogun, Osiris, Oya, and Yansa.

Use black for binding, banishing, mourning, divination, crone magic, uncrossing, exorcism, indrinking spells, setting limits, restricting someone or something, and reaching the deepest levels of meditation. Black is also used for hexing, retribution, and power over others.

## GRAY

Gray is sacred to the Grey Goddess, the Gray One, and to the Graiae (the Gray Ones), three Greek crone goddesses who guard their sisters, the Gorgons. Use gray for loneliness, sorrow, neutrality, and neutralizing negativity.

*silver:* Silver is the color of the New Moon, sacred to all Moon goddesses. It symbolizes life in death. Use silver for lunar magic, psychic development, and every kind of psychic work, money spells, stability, banishing negativity, and working with the Mother.

## WHITE

White corresponds to the New Moon, the direction West, and the element of air. It symbolizes death in China. William Blake referred to the "white light of reason." A white candle can be substituted for one of any other color in candle magic. A white candle turned upside down represents a black candle.

White is sacred to Aphrodite, Batala, Cerridwen (White Lady of Inspiration), Chango, Elegba, Gauri (Brilliant White), the Great Goddess, Moon goddesses, Obatala (Chief of the White Cloth), the Triple Goddess, the White Goddess, White Tara, and Yemaya.

Use white for uncrossing, indrinking, purification, protection, spirituality, healing, truth, meditation, reason, creativity, enlightenment, cleansing, clairvoyance, fallow periods, calm, love, innocence, lunar magic, spiritual strength, ecstasy, omnipotence, cosmic consciousness, male energy, rain spells, angel magic, working with the spirit world, work for small children, unbiased judgment, and making sacred space. Wear white for creation, re-creation, or Isis power.

*clear:* Clear symbolizes the spirit world and corresponds to the element of air. Use it for clarity.

## BLUE

Saturn and Jupiter are blue's planets, water is its element. Blue is a heavenly color, sacred to Aphrodite, Mary, Oshosi, rain god/desses, sky goddesses, the Triple Goddess, Yemaya, and Zeus. It is a symbol of the female, magnetic principle.

Use blue for peace, truth, sleep, serenity, communication, hope, organization, administration, tranquility, spirituality, harmony, inner light, guidance, psychic dreams, healing image spells, removing bad vibrations, making a safe space, blessing a new home, and getting in touch with your inner child.

*bright blue:* Use bright blue for protection and averting the evil eye. Vivid shades like ultramarine and electric blue are the best colors for justice spells.

*light blue:* Use light blue for spirituality, peace, tranquility, beauty, angel magic, and meditation.

*dark blue:* Jupiter and Saturn are dark blue's planets. It symbolizes infinity and is sacred to Anu, the Triple Goddess, and Vishnu. Use dark blue for justice and fertility.

*indigo:* Indigo corresponds to the planets Saturn and Venus and is sacred to the goddess Venus. Use indigo for reaching deep meditative states, or to stop someone or something dead in its tracks.

*royal blue:* Jupiter is royal blue's planet. Use it for loyalty and joviality.

*sky blue:* Sky blue is sacred to Isis.

## PURPLE

As Alice Walker pointed out in her wonderful novel, it certainly must annoy the god/dess if you walk past a field and fail to notice the color purple.[27] Purple symbolizes royalty and corresponds to the planet Jupiter. It is sacred to Babalu-Aye, Maman Brigitte, Oya, and Yansa. Use purple for wisdom, prophecy, divination, power, ambition, success, independence, magical power, astral projection, spiritual contact, and psychic work.

*magenta:* Use magenta for spiritual healing and magical workings that require a lot of energy.

*violet:* Violet symbolizes the astral plane and the Akashic Principle. Mercury is its planet. Violet is sacred to the Chinese goddess Tzu-Ku-Shen, the Violet Lady. Use violet for spirituality, intuition, insight, clarity, gay love spells, and gay sex magic.

*wine/maroon:* Dark brownish purple is sacred to the orishas Maman Brigitte, Oya, and Yansa.

## GREEN

Green symbolized youth, new life, and vegetation in ancient Egypt. It is a fairy color and a jester color and is considered a male symbol in China. Green symbolizes death-in-life and is the sacred color of Islam. Earth and Venus are green's planets, water is its element, and East is its direction. Green is sacred to Agayu, Allah, Al-Khidr (the Green One), Al-Uzzah, Aphrodite, Demeter, the Green Man, Isis (the Green One), Green Tara, Ogun, Orunmila, Osiris (the Green One), vegetation gods, and Green Zeus.

Use green for growth, harmony, prosperity, success, luck, healing, beauty, fertility, courage, renewal, love, youth, acceptance, money spells, faith, instinct, intuition, envy, garden magic, green witchcraft, fairy magic, finding a job, working with Mother Nature, making a safe space, and working with your inner child.

*emerald green:* Emerald green corresponds to the planet Venus. Use it for attraction, fertility, and any working that is social in nature.

*dark green:* Use dark green to counter ambition, greed, and jealousy.

---

[27] Alice Walker, *The Color Purple* (New York: Harcourt Brace Jovanovich, 1982).

*aqua:* Aqua is sacred to Olokun, Afro-Caribbean god of the unconscious and the ocean depths. Use it for sea spells.

## PINK

Pink is an angelic color, according to William Blake. It is sacred to Aphrodite and Venus. Use pink for happiness, youth, beauty, romance, friendship, service, fidelity, love spells, angel magic, female energy, attracting new love, drawing affection, and all emotional workings.

*rose:* Use rose for youth and love spells.

## RED

Red symbolized wisdom to the Aztecs, the Otherworld to Celts, fire and rage to the Egyptians, and sacrificial blood to the Hebrews. Red animals and red-haired strangers were sacrificed as fertility charms for grain in ancient Egypt. Red was the color of death in ancient Greece and Bronze Age Britain, where red ocher was used in burials. It was taboo for commoners to eat red foods such as lobster, bacon, or red berries, fruit, or mushrooms, except at feasts to honor the dead. Red toadstools, apples, and rowan berries were all considered foods of the gods. Sacred kings had their faces stained red, often with alder dye.

Red corresponds to the direction South, the element fire, the Full Moon, and Mars, the Red Planet. Aries and Scorpio are its astrological houses. It symbolizes the male, electric principle.

Red is sacred to Adamu, Agayu, Ares, Astarte, Chango, Elegba, Exu, Isis, Mars, the Great Goddess, Moon goddesses, Ogun, Pyrrha (the Red One), Red Tezcatlipoca, Set (the Red God), and the Triple Goddess. Hathor, Set/Seth/Typhon, the Morrigan, and Odysseus/Ulysses all had red hair. Some consider red hair a witches' mark.

Use red for lust, passion, romance, willpower, exorcism, healing, strength, health, courage, vitality, mercy, anger, brazenness, power, protection, energy, magnetism, female power, sex magic, finding love, keeping love, organic healing, and sexual energy. Wear red to combat evil.

*scarlet:* Scarlet is sacred to Aphrodite.

## BROWN

Brown corresponds to both the planet Earth and the element earth. It is sacred to Earth god/desses and corn mothers, as well as to the orishas Agayu, Babalu-Aye, Oya, Maman Brigitte, and Yansa.

Use brown for grounding, balance, level-headedness, decisiveness, telepathy, Earth energy, material increase, Earth magic, finding lost items, and working with animals.

## YELLOW

Yellow corresponds to the Sun. Center is its direction. Yellow symbolizes the creative, feminine power. It is a jester color that also symbolizes bile, in the sense that Baudelaire used the word *spleen.* Yellow was the death color to Mayans, and was associated with Judas and with the Spanish Inquisition. Convicted murderers once wore yellow gowns for execution. Yellow is sacred to Orunmila, Oshoshi, Oshun, Shakti, and to all Sun gods.

Use yellow for attraction, centering, power, happiness, confidence, jealousy, joy, creativity, divination, unity, a new home, personal charm, solar magic, astral projection, the power of concentration, the power of persuasion, finding your center, making a safe space, and to activate any magical working.

*saffron yellow:* Saffron yellow is sacred to the Egyptian Sun god Amon.

*gold:* Gold corresponds to the Sun and fire is its element. Gold has god energy and is sacred to Oshun and to all Sun gods. Use the color gold for attraction, solar magic, money spells, influencing cosmic forces and the astral planes.

## ORANGE

Mercury is orange's planet, fire its element. Use orange for success, energy, creativity, travel, strength, balance, communication, intellectual pursuits, and attracting love or romance.

*copper:* Copper is sacred to the Native American goddess Copper Woman. Use the color copper in money spells.

## PASTELS

All pastel colors correspond to the element of air.

# METALS

The Four Ages of Man were the Gold, Silver, Bronze, and Iron Ages. The pulling of the sword from the stone in Arthurian legend may be read as an allegory for the art of metallurgy. Alchemy usually refers to the transmutation of base metals into precious ores. Western alchemy was concerned with the quest for the Philosopher's Stone, which was supposed to turn whatever it touched into gold. Immortality, on the other hand, was the goal of Chinese/Taoist alchemy. The word *alchemy* comes from Arabic, *al khemia,* which is, in turn, derived from the ancient Egyptian word *qemt.* According to J. G. Frazer, in the *Golden Bough,* "Alchemy leads up to chemistry."[28]

## ALLOYS

Ancient Egyptians thought that alloys possessed magical powers. They correspond to the planet Mercury. Pisces is their astrological house.

## BRASS

Brass corresponds to the astrological house Taurus.

## BRONZE (alloy of copper, tin, and zinc)

Taurus is bronze's astrological house. Use bronze for matriarchal power.

## COPPER

Copper was one of the seven noble metals of antiquity. Venus is its planet. The ancients actually called copper Venus because of its easy union with other metals. It corresponds to the letter I and the jewel amethyst. Taurus and Libra are its astrological houses. Copper is sacred to Copper Woman, the Goddess, and Oya.

---

[28] Sir James G. Frazer, *The Golden Bough: A Study in Magic and Religion* (New York: MacMillan, 1953), p. 106.

Use copper in money spells. It is reputed to strengthen the generative function in men and women and ward off bacterial infection. A copper disk placed in contact with the abdomen is said to prevent cholera during outbreaks.

**ELECTRUM** (alloy of silver and gold)

Electrum was one of the seven noble metals of the ancients.

## GOLD

Gold was one of the seven noble metals of the ancients, used by alchemists to make Tincture of the Sun. Gold was once thought to be the congealed breath of white dragons. It is ruled by the Sun and its nature is male. Leo is gold's astrological house. It represented East to the Mayans. Gold corresponds to diamonds, the heart, and the letter E. It increases the power of gems that are set in it.

Gold is sacred to Califia, the Goddess, and Hathor (Gold of the Gods). Sheeps' fleece was once used to collect telluric gold that was washed downstream from its source. The myth of Jason and the Argonauts may represent the "fleecing" of King Colchis by poaching gold from his rivers and streams.

Bacchus granted a boon to the Phrygian king, Midas. Although he was already rich, Midas asked that whatever he touched be turned to gold. He ended by having to take a ritual bath in a river to remove this gift or else starve to death.

The Saxons thought gold taught honesty and integrity. It symbolizes success, greed, power, authority, wealth, status, simplicity, and perfection. Use it for wisdom, common sense, longevity, comfort, and money spells. Gold amulets are charms for depression, infirmities, comforting and strengthening the heart. Carry gold balls in the palms of your hands to increase vitality.

Red gold symbolizes Jannath el-Firdaus, 8th stage of the Islamic paradise.

## IRON

Iron is the warriors' metal, one of the seven noble metals of the ancients. It corresponds to the planet Mars and the jewel emerald. Aries and Scorpio are its astrological houses. Iron is a charm against ghosts and spirits, to whom it is obnoxious. It is sacred to Jarn Saxa (Iron Dirk), Mars, Ogun, and Touia Fatuna (Iron Stone Goddess).

## LEAD

Lead was one of the seven noble metals of the ancients. Silver and lead were extracted from the same mixed ore in medieval alchemy. Greeks used lead plates for binding and cursing, engraving them with the person's name and then burying them.

Saturn is lead's planet, Capricorn and Aquarius its astrological houses. It is sacred to the Goddess. Lead corresponds to the spleen, the letter U, and the jewel turquoise. It is said to quicken lust.

## PLATINUM

Platinum has female energy. Virgo and Pisces are its astrological houses. Wearing platinum jewelry is said to be helpful for constipation.

## PLUTONIUM

Pluto is plutonium's planet, Scorpio its astrological house. Don't even think about using it, because of its radioactivity.

## QUICKSILVER/MERCURY

Mercury is quicksilver's planet, the lodestone its jewel, Gemini and Virgo its astrological houses. Quicksilver symbolizes living and the female principle. Use it for transformation, shapeshifting, and the power of becoming fluid.

NOTE: Although the ancients used it in alchemy and it is still used in some folk magic traditions, mercury is poisonous and should never be ingested or kept long in contact with the skin.

## SILVER

Silver, called luna by astrologers and alchemists, is one of the seven noble metals of the ancients. It corresponds to the Moon, to crystals, and to the letter A. Cancer is its astrological house. Use silver for protection, lunar magic, and to comfort animal spirits.

Silver also corresponds to the brain, so wearing silver jewelry is said to help neuralgia, epilepsy, and brain diseases. Carry silver balls in the palms of your hands to clear your head. Silver is sacred to Arianrhod (the Silver Wheel), Califia, the Goddess, and the Celtic hero Nuadha Argetlam (Nudd of the Silver Arm).

White silver corresponds to Jannatu el-Na'im in, Dar el-Jannah (the Gardens of Delight), 6th stage of the Islamic paradise.

## STEEL

Mars is steel's planet, Aries and Scorpio its astrological houses.

## TIN

Tin was one of the seven noble metals of the ancients. It is sacred to the Goddess and symbolizes gentle striving in relation to a secret hope. Tin corresponds to Jupiter, the letter O, and the jewel carnelian. Sagittarius and Pisces are its astrological houses.

## URANIUM

Pluto is uranium's planet, Aquarius its astrological house. It has too much radioactivity to be used magically.

# ROCKS AND GEMSTONES

I have been in love with rocks since I was 18. They're tactile, sexy, beautiful . . . the very Goddess herself. My first rock was a small, ocean-rounded stone that I picked up on the beach in Tangiers. I wanted a piece of Africa to carry away with me, so I put it in my pocket. I have it still, when so much else has not remained.

Some of the occult claims made for stones are patently ridiculous—especially the medical ones. Nevertheless, rocks do have definite metaphysical properties. Bedouins wear gemstone necklaces for healing and protection. There is much lore associated with stones, and New Age mysticism is expanding this occult repertoire.

Angels were once believed to reside in precious stones. The seraph Azazel is said to have taught humans the nature and uses of stones. Treating a precious stone with affection, as if it were a sentient being, is said to improve its color and luster.

## GODDESS ROCKS

All rocks are sacred to the Goddess, but some stones are particularly suited to her worship or invocation. These can be of any size, but must be naturally occurring formations:

rocks with female form;
circular stones with holes through them;
spiral or cylindrical rocks;
yoni rocks that have clefts, holes, or depressions.

Particular goddesses may be invoked with the type of rock sacred to each—white granite for Allat, turquoise for Hathor, and so on.

The most precious rock I ever had was a goddess rock from Egypt that I called the Sekhmet Stone. It was about 2 inches long, light and medium brown, an "Inundation rock," found inland but smoothed by who knows how many centuries in the Nile. It looked like a small figure of Sekhmet with her hands clasped before her, her face worn off but her crown still in place. It was a natural thing, not crafted, but formed of earth and water. I loved that rock at first sight—the way it looked, how it felt in my hand, its symbolism, and its potency.

I made that rock an object of devotion, prayed to it as a religious icon, kept it on my altar, used it in spells and rituals. I poured magic into the Sekhmet Stone until it became an object of great power. It was very precious to me. I held it tightly through two days of labor, confident in its power to protect my baby and myself. I kept removing the fetal monitor because I knew my son was fine. I refused to allow my arms to be tied down, so that I could hold the stone during the C-section. I was still holding it when my son came fist-first into this world.

Doctors pump drugs into you once a baby is born, when the real work of sewing you back together begins. Things got hazy after that. I'm sure I had the Sekhmet Stone in the recovery room, but I lost it somewhere between there and the maternity ward. My husband searched for it, but we never found it. I was distraught over its loss, until my sister pointed out that it had done its job for me and had moved on to help someone else.

I had another goddess rock from Egypt, one that sat in a bowl of pearl barley on my desk. After several millennia in the Nile, it looked like the Venus of Willendorf. I used it to worship the Great Mother, but somehow it just wasn't the same.

The Sekhmet Stone is out there, somewhere, full of power and magic. Cherish it if it comes to you.

# CORRESPONDENCES

When you have a stone that feels magical to you but you aren't sure exactly what kind of rock it is, use color correspondences to determine its use: pink stones for love spells, brown rocks for grounding, red stones for sex magic, green ones for money spells, and so forth.

**AGATE** (variety of quartz; crystallized silica that has bands or clouds of colors)

Earth is agate's planet and element. May and June are its months, Gemini and Virgo its astrological houses. Occultists consider the agate malignant. Orpheus is supposed to have said that wearing an agate ring makes the immortal gods pleased with you. It was said that binding an agate to your arm or to the oxen's horns while plowing would cause Ceres to descend, bestowing fruitfulness.

Use agates for balance, grounding, eloquence, prudence, garden magic, and a better personality. They are charms against thunder, sorcery, venom, poison, and fiendish possession. Drinking vessels were once carved from agate, because it was believed to be hostile to poison. Persian magi burned agates to avert storms.

Agates have been used to treat alcoholism and skin eruptions. There is an old belief that they can staunch blood from wounds. Agates with serpents engraved on them are sacred to Asclepias, supposed to cure snake bites and scorpion stings. Use green agates for health and red agates for strength, courage, peace, longevity, healing, love spells, garden magic, and protection. They are a charm against mosquitos. The banded red agate corresponds to the letter C and was held sacred to Ephraim by the Hebrews. August 5 is its station on the Wheel of the Year. Use it to strike your enemies with fear.

Blue-lace agate is a charm against stress and family quarrels. Brown agates are for battle and money spells. Taurus is the moss agate's astrological house. Also called tree agate, it is helpful with garden magic and good for inner work. It is also used for happiness, longevity, and money spells. Use black agate for courage and success in competitions. Black agates with white veins give help in adversity, protect against physical danger, overcome peril and terrible things, strengthen the heart, and make men strong, pleasant, and attractive.

**ALABASTER** (soft, translucent variety of gypsum that has a fine grain and is usually white)

Alabaster was used for making ointment boxes and sarcophagi in ancient times. Ointment of alabaster was used to prepare the dead for burial. Use alabaster for victory and friendship.

**AMBER** (hard, translucent, yellow substance that is the fossilized resin of coniferous trees)

Humans have been using amber to make jewelry for at least 10,000 years. It was gathered in Europe by ancient goddess-worshipping peoples. The Greeks called it electron. Pliny complained that amber charms cost more than slaves in ancient Rome.

Mercury and Venus are amber's planets, Leo and Aquarius its astrological houses. November is its month and December 23 its station on the Wheel of the Year. Amber symbolizes life, divinity, and the Sun. It is sacred to Amberella, Apollo, Benjamin, Electra, the Electrides, and Oshun. Amberella, worshiped in the Baltic as a sea goddess, left chunks of amber on the shore as farewell gifts for her family when she went to dwell underwater with the prince of the sea. The Electrides wept so much when their brother, Phaëton, died that they were metamorphosed into poplar trees, and their tears into amber.

Use amber for spirituality, memory, history, courage, healing, luck, strength, beauty, love spells, positive energy, and balancing yin and yang. Amber's nature is electric, as is jet's. Amber beads are alternated with jet to make witches' necklaces. Amber necklaces are charms against sore throats, and to protect children from witchcraft and sorcery. Washing amber is said to make a woman urinate if she is not a virgin.

Amber has been used to treat asthma, toothache, water retention, sore throats, swollen glands, the head and womb, and to relieve stress and tension. It supposedly works against contagion, drives off adders, and causes weight gain.

**AMAZONITE** (variety of feldspar, usually greenish blue)

Amazonite corresponds to the heart chakra. Virgo is its astrological house. Use amazonite for balance, self-confidence, sending love, calming the nerves, and dispelling fear and worry. Gem essence of amazonite is said to embody universal love.

**AMETHYST** (purple or violet crystallized quartz)

Bacchus loved a nymph, but she spurned him because of her Dianic vow of chastity and was transmogrified into an amethyst. Once called the Violet Ray of Alchemy, amethyst corresponds to the planets Jupiter and Pluto, to the element of fire, and the letter M. Thursday is amethyst's day, February its month, and September 2 its station on the Wheel of the Year. Sagittarius, Aquarius, and Pisces are its astrological houses. Amethyst is sacred to Alahah, Issachar, and Manasseh. Those with a rosy hue are sacred to Venus. Christians hold amethyst sacred to St. Matthew.

Use amethysts for calm, balance, peace, happiness, protection, meditation, spirituality, transformation, inspiration, healing, fertility, temperance, chastity, sobriety, sleep, vigilance, hunting, courage, purity, psychic dreams, divine love, vision quests, psychological healing, stilling the mind, victory over enemies, the gift of tongues, and understanding things that are felt. Amethysts can be used to treat addictions, compulsive behaviors, blood clots, some cancers, and low self-esteem. Potions of amethyst were used for fertility and to expel poisons.

Amethysts are said to clear the mind, sharpen the wit, make you expert in business, subdue passion, protect soldiers, banish the desire for alcohol, cause antipathy to wine and drunkenness, and turn away evil thoughts. It was once thought to be impossible to get drunk if you drank from an amethyst vessel.

### AQUAMARINE (greenish-blue beryl)

Neptune is the aquamarine's planet; October is its month. Gemini, Virgo, and Scorpio are its astrological houses. Aquamarine is sacred to all sea goddesses. Use aquamarine for peace, tranquility, compassion, protection, scrying, health, sea spells, psychic work, and soothing the heart. It can be used to treat grief, pain, and difficult situations.

### ASBESTOS (fibrous silicate, no longer used in magic because of its carcinogenic properties)

Asbestos was once used to kindle eternal flame and make garments that could not be burned.

### AVENTURINE (green or sometimes bluish quartz)

Venus and Uranus are the aventurine's planets. Use aventurine for tranquility, meditation, clarity, balance, creativity, joy, healing, good luck, money spells, developing mental powers, and energizing the nervous system. It can be used to treat the eyesight.

### AZURITE (blue, semiprecious stone of copper silicate)

The azurite's planet is Saturn. Use azurite for intuition, understanding, and increasing your psychic abilities.

### BERYL (precious and semiprecious stones of various colors)

The beryl makes happy marriages, reconciles married couples, and banishes idleness and stupidity. Use it for scrying, healing, eternal friendship, rain spells, and sending energy. Beryls have been used to treat jaundice and liver complaints. Christians hold them sacred to St. Thomas. Beryls engraved with a crow that has a crab beneath its feet were once used for joy, lasciviousness, exultation, acquisition, union, and conjugal love.

Emeralds are bright-green beryls, aquamarines greenish-blue ones. A beryl that varies in color from pink to peach is called morganite.

Sea-green beryls are sea jewels that correspond to the Moon. They are believed to work by lunar magnetism and can be used for scrying while the Moon waxes. They are said to work best if you are in a purified state, fasting and abstaining from sex. February 18 is the sea-green beryl's station on the Wheel of the Year, N is its letter. It symbolizes the sea voyage of Hercules. Hebrews held sea-green beryls sacred to Zebulon (He Who is Among the Ships).

Green beryls symbolize male and female and are mediums for magical visions. Use green beryls for fame, renown, constancy, longevity, understanding, wedded love, a good marriage, and reconciling differences between friends. They are said to preserve bodily health, drive away poisonous air, and repress luxury. Carrying a green beryl is supposed to overcome debate and drive away enemies and make them weak.

Yellow beryl is known as the stone heliotrope. Heliotropes were used with juice of sunflower or the plant called heliotrope for invisibility:

*To many a gift divine this Stone lays claim;*
*Surpassing which the power that makes its fame*
*Is,—when conjoined with Herb of title quaint*
*Same as its own; whilst, spoken by a saint*
*Are incantations, holy and a spell*
*Invoked,—with words the pious tongue can tell,*
*Of gem, and Plant combined, the wearer that*
*Becomes invisible to eyes of men.*[29]

## BLOODSTONE/GEMMA BABYLONICA (dark-green chalcedony, a variety of quartz that is streaked with red)

Bloodstone is a very powerful stone that works like jasper. It corresponds to both the planet Earth and the element earth. March is its month, Aries and Scorpio its astrological houses. Bloodstones were used with heliotrope by Babylonian magi to confer invisibility. They were said to turn water red. A bloodstone anointed with heliotrope juice and placed in water was said to make the Sun seem bloody, as if in eclipse, and to make a cloud arise from which dew would fall like rain. Pliny recommended bloodstones for viewing solar eclipses.

---

[29] William T. Fernie, *Precious Stones: For Curative Wear, Other Remedial Uses and Likewise the Nobler Metals* (Kila, MT: Kessinger Publishing, 1942), p. 183.

Ancient warriors carried bloodstone amulets because bloodstone was believed to staunch blood flowing from wounds. To stop bleeding, hold a heart-shaped bloodstone in your right hand and wet it with cold water from time to time. The Isis Knot, the ancient Egyptian amulet of protection that some say represents her menstrual pad, was made of bloodstone.

Use bloodstones for longevity, mental balance, money spells, opening doors, physical healing, overcoming enemies, breaking free of restrictions, increasing business, aligning energy along the spinal column, a good reputation, and a fiery, ardent disposition. They can be used with crystals, especially rose quartz, to treat obsessions, aggression, and overindulgence.

Bloodstones are said to remove toxins from the blood. Wearing a bloodstone ring was a treatment for hemorrhoids.

**CARNELIAN** (pale-red semitransparent stone, a variety of chalcedony)

Earth and Saturn are carnelian's planets, July and August its months. Aries, Taurus, and Virgo are its astrological houses. Carnelian is sacred to Isis. Egyptians believed that a heart amulet made of carnelian brought the protection of Ra and Osiris.

Use carnelian for protection, courage, wisdom, health, longevity, peace, harmony, cheerfulness, healing, concentration, mental balance, creative balance, inner work, good fortune, sexual energy, preventing or destroying fascination, and accessing past-life information. Carnelian is a charm against illness, plague, poison, and skin diseases. It has been used to treat anger, depression, lethargy, and the bloodstream.

White carnelian corresponds to the letter D. June 10 is its station on the Wheel of the Year. In Hebrew mythology, it is sacred to Asher and Yahalem. Christians hold red carnelian sacred to St. Bartholomew.

**CELESTITE** (strontium sulfate, frequently pale blue)

Celestite is a heavenly stone that corresponds to the planet Neptune. Use it for detachment, perspective, angel magic, divine inspiration, and access to angelic realms. Keep it by the bed to aid lucid dreaming.

**CHALCEDONY** (variety of quartz, a semiprecious stone that is usually bluish gray)

Chalcedony's astrological house is Cancer. It is specific against phantasms and illusions and banishes fears, sadness, and nightmares. Use it for protection, physical strength, and a peaceful disposition. Perforated and suspended, it makes the one who possesses it fortunate at law. Chalcedony is supposed to increase lactation and quicken the powers of the body.

Black chalcedony prevents hoarseness and heals the voice. Wear brown chalcedony on a necklace to win lawsuits, ward off fantastic illusions, and preserve the body against adversaries. Christians hold white chalcedony sacred to St. James.

*chalcedonyx/chalcedon/chalcedonite:* A banded variety of chalcedony used as a gemstone, a microcrystalline quartz with black, white, red, or brownish opaque and translucent bands. Use chalcedonyx for strength.

*chrysoprase:* An apple-green variety of chalcedony. June is the chrysoprase's month. Christians hold it sacred to St. Thaddeus. Use chrysoprase for serenity, trust, good luck, and eloquence.

*sard:* A yellow or orange-red gemstone, a variety of chalcedony. Sard was believed to cure tumors, protect against snakebite, and heal wounds not caused by iron. Its qualities are binding and blood staunching. Sard has been used to treat bleeding and eye injuries. Pinkish stones are the best for minor bleeding. Sard rings were worn to stop nosebleeds.

Red sard corresponds to the letter B. Aries is its astrological house, December 24 and New Year are its stations on the Wheel of the Year. Hebrews held red sard sacred to Adam (the Red Man) and Reuben (the first born).

## CHRYSOLITE (yellow, olivine, or olive-green stones, some which are of gem quality)

Chrysolite corresponds to the planet Jupiter. September is its month, Leo and Libra its astrological houses. Christians hold it sacred to St. Matthias. Use chrysolite for prudence and to protect from folly and allay rage. It is said to prevent fevers and treat delirium.

Yellow chrysolite is the golden cup of Hercules. L is its letter, January 21 its station on the Wheel of the Year. Yellow chrysolite was held sacred by the Hebrews, for whom it corresponded to the Month of Repose. It is said to prevent fevers and madness, and to dispose toward repentance. Set in gold, yellow chrysolite protects against night terrors. Green chrysolite symbolizes Daru el-Qarar, the Dwelling Which Abideth, 3rd stage of Islamic paradise.

*olivine/peridot:* A deep olive-green chrysolite, peridot symbolizes the thunderbolt. Mercury is its planet, Leo and Virgo
its astrological houses. Use peridot for health, healing, attracting, sleep, unblocking, purification, money spells, feeling protected, stimulating the mind, balancing mind and body, and
allowing the heart to open. A pale-green olivine set in gold ex-
pels fantasies and drives away foolishness.

*chrysoprase:* An apple-green chrysolite, this gemstone improves eyesight, and makes you joyful and liberal.

## CINNABAR (bright-red mineral, mercuric sulfide)

Cinnabar was used in Taoist alchemy to make potions of immortality.

## CORAL (stony white or reddish substance, the skeletons of ma-rine invertebrates)

Neptune and Venus are coral's planets, water is its element, Libra and Pisces its astrological houses. Coral is sacred to all sea
goddesses and the orishas Olokun, Oshun, and Yemaya. It is associated with Medea. The blood from her severed head dripped
onto seaweed and turned it into coral. According to another
myth, the blood itself solidified and was placed in the ocean by
sea nymphs, whereupon it became coral. Paryata is a mythical
coral tree of India.

Pieces of coral with silver bells attached were once given to
children as charms to frighten away evil spirits. Romans gave children coral amulets for healing and protection. Gauls adorned their
weapons and helmets with coral. Coral charms shaped like hands
or horns avert the evil eye. Magus made coral amulets that "suspended even by a thread . . . prevent all harm and accidents of violence, from fire, or water, and help them to withstand all their
diseases."[30]

Use coral for love, harmony, wisdom, healing, personal transformation, and going over floods. Coral protects against incantations, demons, tempests, depression, fear, robbers, fascination,
poison, and thunder. It is said to banish foolishness, pacify tempests, baffle witchcraft, and counteract poison. Powdered and
mixed with seed, coral protects crops from blight, thunderstorms,
caterpillars, and locusts.

---

[30] William T. Fernie, *Precious Stones: For Curative Wear, Other Remedial Uses and
Likewise the Nobler Metals*, p. 294.

The color of coral is said to deepen when it is worn by a man, and pale when it is worn by a woman. It is also said to change according to the health of its wearer, growing pale with illness. Coral was believed to be a brain tonic and to regulate menstruation. It was said to dry, cool, bind, and staunch blood. It has been used to treat teething, epilepsy, convulsions, and whooping cough.

Green or yellow coral symbolizes Jannatu el-Khuld, the Garden of Eternity, first stage of Islamic paradise. Pink coral corresponds to Tuesday. Aquarius is white coral's astrological house, Tuesday is its day. A necklace of white coral is a charm against stomach problems. Black coral causes melancholy. Red coral *(Corallium rubrum)* is held sacred in India, and has occult and medical properties. It is said to cure indigestion if continually worn close to the body.

## DIAMOND (crystallized carbon)

Diamonds turn spells and enchantments back upon their makers. Uranus is the diamond's planet, April its month, Friday and Saturday its days, Aries its astrological house. The most powerful diamond is one received as a gift, not purchased or coveted. The power of a diamond is multiplied by being paired with a lodestone. Diamonds are said to lose their power according to the sins of their owners. It was once believed that diamonds could only be broken by goats' blood.

Diamonds symbolize truth, innocence, justice, faith, and the impassivity of fate. Use them for courage, love, clarity, invisibility, strength, joy, peace, hardness, purity, protection, manliness, healing, spiritual centering, and spiritual ecstasy. Diamonds avert panic, pestilence, enchantment, ghosts, nightmares, calamities, strife, riots, sorrows, enchantments, sleepwalking, and invasion by fantasies or illusions of wicked spirits. They have been used to treat indigestion, mental illness, and demonic possession. Diamond powder is a charm against lightning.

Wearing a diamond is said to make you magnanimous, bold and daring in transactions, strong and firm against enemies, and to grant you victory in court or in war if your cause is just. Diamonds, impel you toward good. Wear them on your left arm for victory, or to overcome enemies, madness, or brawling. Diamonds were believed to tame wild beasts, keep the limbs whole, sweat in the presence of venom or poison, and to be antidotes to poison when worn in rings.

**DIORITE** (granular crystallized rock composed of feldspar and horneblend)

Ullikummi, the Diorite Man, was a stone giant in Hittite/Hurrian mythology. He drove the goddess Hebat from her temple, but all the gods joined together to defeat him.

**EMERALD** (bright-green precious stone, a variety of beryl)

The emerald is a heart stone with magical, talismanic, and medical properties. It corresponds to the planet Venus, the element earth, and the months of May and June. Wednesday is its day, Taurus, Cancer, and Libra its astrological houses. Emeralds are sacred to Mercury, Sudurjaya, Venus, and Vishnu. Christians hold them sacred to St. John. According to some myths, demons and wicked spirits guard emerald mines. The Holy Grail was reputed to be a chalice carved from a single emerald.

Use emeralds for love, harmony, protection, prophecy, balance, healing, money spells, improved memory, emotional recovery, success in love affairs, and increased understanding. They can be used to treat anger, folly, lust, and foolish fears. An emerald ring strengthens the memory and prevents giddiness. An emerald necklace is a charm against fear and epilepsy.

It is an ill omen when an emerald falls from its setting. Wear emeralds on Fridays for good luck. They are said to change their appearance when a lover is faithless or someone bears false witness. Emeralds strengthen friendship, eyesight, and constancy of mind. They augment riches; they comfort and save. Emeralds are charms against nightmares, nocturnal emissions, eye problems, stupidity, and disturbances.

Emeralds supposedly cure plague, stop bleeding and dysentery, preserve against decay, improve liver function, restore sight and memory, aid in childbirth, and heal the bites of venomous creatures. They were once believed to send evil spirits howling into space and to preserve the chastity of women. They were said to shatter in the presence of the unchaste, to blind serpents that looked upon them, and to break apart in despair if they were unable to render metaphysical assistance.

**FLUORITE** (crystallized calcium fluoride that can be colorless, or colored by impurities)

Neptune is fluorite's planet. Use it for grounding energy and opening yourself to the influence of other stones. Green fluorites balance the hormones and are helpful after childbirth and during puberty and menopause. Purple fluorite is for manifesting changes in your life.

## FOSSIL AMONITE

Wear a fossil amonite on your left arm to overcome enemies.

## GARNET (hard, brittle, crystalline stone whose red variety is used as a gem)

Garnet is the stone of love. Mars and Pluto are garnet's planets; January is its month. Aries, Scorpio, Capricorn, and Aquarius are its astrological houses. Use garnets for imagination, joy, protection, compassion, purification, healing, love spells, and good luck. They strengthen auras, enhance strength in magical workings, make one faithful and true, give constancy in love, and help channel kundalini energy. Garnets have been used to treat depression and heart palpitations. They are said to preserve health, aid circulation, and stop the spitting up of blood.

Fire garnets correspond to the letter F and the element of fire. March 18 is their station on the Wheel of the Year. Hebrews held them sacred to Judah. Fire garnets are said to promote both joy and discord between lovers, to preserve health, resist depression, and quiet heart palpitations.

*carbuncles:* Cabochon-cut garnets have occult properties similar to the ruby. They have been used to treat depression, plague, and heart palpitations. Bright stones are male, duller ones female. They are said to enable one to see in the dark when worn as a necklace. Noah supposedly hung up a carbuncle to light the ark.

Blood-red carbuncles were considered malignant by occultists. They correspond to the Sun and the letter S. April 15 is their station on the Wheel of the Year. Hebrews held blood-red carbuncles sacred to Gad and assigned them Kadkod, the month of the raiding party.

## GLASS

Glass was once believed to be solidified dragon's breath. Glass rings were called adder stones in ancient Britain, where they were used by Druids as charms against disease.

**GNEISS** (metamorphic rock, recrystallized granite with dark and light bands)

Greenish-yellow gneiss from Iona, Scotland, is a charm against drowning.

**GRANITE** (crystalline igneous rock used in building)

White granite is sacred to the Arabian goddess Allat.

**HEMATITE** (iron ore that may take several forms: lustrous black crystals, stones in shades of steel gray to reddish black with a metallic sheen, or even red ocher, a powder)

Hematite corresponds to the planet Saturn. Use it for grounding, healing, focus, self-discipline, and removing negativity. It is said to stop bleeding. Hold a hematite in your hand when you are looking for answers. Egyptians made the amulet of the two fingers of Horus from obsidian or hematite. The hematite amulet of the pillow, placed with a mummy to protect its head, can be used for healing:

**Thou art lifted up, O sick one that liest prostrate. They lift up thy head to the horizon, thou art raised up, and dost triumph by reason of that which hath been done for thee. Ptah has overthrown thine enemies, which was ordered to be done for thee.**[31]

**IRONSTONE** (iron ore colored by silica impurities)

Yellow ironstone corresponds to the planet Saturn.

**JADE** (compact variety of horneblende that may be white or green)

Jade is the stone of perfection. It was held sacred in China as the Jewel of Heaven, the essence of heaven and Earth. Chinese considered it a male symbol and believed it conferred nine virtues: benevolence, knowledge, righteousness, virtuous action, purity, endurance, ingenuousness, moral conduct, and music.

Venus and Neptune are jade's planets, water is its element, and Taurus its astrological house. Jade is sacred to the Aztec goddess Chalchiuhtlicue (Her Skirt is of Jade). It is a happy omen, a good luck charm, and a diviner of judgments. Use jade for wisdom, healing, immortality, charity, love, longevity, garden magic,

---

[31] E. A. Wallis Budge, *Egyptian Magic*, p. 47.

weather magic, protection against accidents, and balancing yin and yang. Wear a jade necklace to expel urinary gravel and break up kidney and bladder stones.

Virgo is green jade's astrological house. Dark olive-green jade brings luck.

**JASPER** (brown, green, yellow, or reddish quartz stone; green stones with red flecks are the most valuable)

March is jasper's month. Hebrews held it sacred to Benjamin, Christians to St. Peter. It was a Christian belief that jasper was transformed into bloodstone when the blood of Jesus fell upon it from the cross. Egyptians made an eye of Horus amulet from jasper and empowered it by reciting chapter 140 of The Book of the Dead over it. Laid upon a mummy, this amulet made the deceased a god and guaranteed him a seat in Ra's boat.

Use jasper for eloquence, courage, good fortune, counter-charms, healing, financial success, magical visions, and protecting your beauty. It is a charm against phantasms, nightmares, and witchcraft. Wear jasper for a fiery, ardent personality.

Jasper is a charm against epilepsy, fevers, and water retention. It is said to relieve pain and strengthen the brain. Wear a jasper necklace to strengthen the stomach. You can make a charm against kidney stones by engraving a scorpion on a jasper while the Sun is in Scorpio.

Green jasper is for healing and empathy. Clear green jasper corresponds to the letter sound *NG*. October 28 is its station on the Wheel of the Year. The Hebrews held clear green jasper sacred to Dinah. Use red jasper for rain spells, protection, inner strength, and turning a hex back upon its maker. It can be used to treat fear and mourning.

Use brown jasper for grounding and centering. Mottled or leopardskin jasper is a charm against drowning. It will bring you what you need. Carving a cross upon it is said to make it into a charm of protection against all the elements.

**JET** (hard, shiny, intensely black carbon stone formed of fossilized wood)

Pluto is jet's planet, earth its element, and Capricorn its astrological house. Jet is sacred to Pan and can be worn to invoke Cybele. Also called black amber, jet beads are alternated with amber ones to make witches' necklaces. Because both stones are electric in nature, the necklaces are helpful in raising power and directing energy. It was an occult belief that jet absorbs part of your soul if you wear it.

Jet can be used for health, healing, divination, sorcery, and confronting your dark side. Wear it to prevent nightmares. Smoke from burning jet is said to drive away serpents, bring women out of trances, diagnose epilepsy, and confirm virginity. Washing jet is supposed to make a woman urinate if she is not a virgin. Jet was boiled in wine for toothache and also used to treat diarrhea and water retention.

**LAPIS LAZULI** (deep-blue semiprecious stone)

Lapis lazuli is the stone of teachers. It was used to decorate Uruk, Babylon, and other ancient Mesopotamian cities. Silver, gold, and lapis lazuli were used in Egyptian, Sumerian, and Canaanite architectural design. Egyptians used it to make the amulet of the heart. Lapis corresponds to the planets Neptune and Venus, to the throat chakra, and the letter H. Libra and Sagittarius its astrological houses, May 13 is its station on the Wheel of the Year. Lapis lazuli symbolizes summer, the dark-blue sky, and the color of the throne of the Judeo-Christian god. It is sacred to Isis, Levi, and Sin, the Babylonian Moon god.

Use lapis for clarity, vision, love, joy, fidelity, understanding, gentleness, psychic work, higher wisdom, cosmic connectedness, and the ability to see into the future. It acts like sapphire when worn as a jewel. A lapis necklace drives fright away from children. Wear it over the heart to connect heart and mind.

Lapis lazuli has been used to treat depression, mental illness, melancholy, recurrent fever, boils, sores, epilepsy, apoplexy, and the spleen. Lapis strengthens eyesight and the heart and prevents fainting and miscarriage. Wear it in the 3rd trimester of pregnancy as a charm to bring the baby to full term.

**LODESTONE** (magnetic iron ore that is used in compasses)

Lodestone is a guiding stone, the leading star, and a Heraclean stone. Its quality is binding, astringence, and magnetism. Lodestones are traditionally stored in a dry place, wrapped in a scarlet cloth. Use them for love potions, protection, restful sleep, getting a husband to forgive infidelity, and reconciliation, especially of married couples.

Lodestones are used in hoodoo (African-American folk magic) to draw money, power, love, luck, gifts, favors, blessings, success, a job, and so on. In this tradition, lodestones are carried in mojo bags, dressed with oil, "fed" with iron filings called magnetic sand, and used in pairs for love spells and sex magic. They are also steeped in oil with other ingredients to make attraction oils for spells and rituals.

Lodestones make men gracious and elegant, and persuasive conversationalists. A talisman of diamond, sapphire, and lodestone is said to give near-invisibility. Garlic is supposed to counteract lodestone's virtues, goat's blood to restore them. Powdered and scattered surreptitiously over coals, lodestone is said to make everyone leave the house in a panic. Wear it to treat gout, cramps, swellings, pain, rheumatism, and neuralgia. Lodestone is believed to cause depression and stop bleeding.

Placed under the head of a sleeping women, blue lodestone is supposed to make her embrace her husband if she is faithful, to fall out of bed if she is unfaithful. Powdered, scattered on coals, and put into the four corners of a house, blue lodestone is supposed to make everyone who is sleeping there get up and flee the house, leaving everything behind.

**MALACHITE** (bright-green stone of copper ore with black markings)

Malachite corresponds to the planet Venus, the letter R, and the month of December. November 25 is its station on the Wheel of the Year. Use malachite for success, harmony, love spells, emotional balance, reducing stress, and strengthening the mind, body, and inner eye. In the body, malachite corresponds to the solar plexus and the heart chakra. It is a charm against cholera and colic. Dark-green malachite preserves an infant's cradle from spells.

**MOONSTONE** (pearly, opalescent feldspar stone, usually bluish or silvery, used as a gem)

The moonstone is held sacred in India, but considered ominous and malignant in some traditions. It corresponds to the Moon and to Monday. Cancer is its astrological house. Moonstone's luster is believed to mirror the lunar cycle. It is sacred to Aphrodite, Diana, the Goddess, Selene, and all Moon goddesses.

Use moonstones for passion, serenity, reunion, good fortune, emotional balance, improving selfishness, protection away from home, strengthening psychic abilities, enhancing the feminine, and increasing sensitivity to natural cycles. It is a good luck charm when given by a groom to his bride. Moonstone balances hormones and treats obesity.

Gray moonstones are used for unblocking, white moonstones for balancing male and female energies.

**MOTHER-OF-PEARL** (hard, iridescent material from the inside of certain sea shells)

Mother-of-pearl is ruled by the Moon and corresponds to the elements of water and spirit. It contains the essence of Great Rainbow Snake. Ho Hsien-Ku became the Immortal Maiden Ho by eating powdered mother-of-pearl.

Use mother-of-pearl for protection, maternal love, and to treat weak men. Hold it under your tongue on the first or 10th day of the Moon to gain knowledge of things to come; on the first and 29th days of the Moon to forejudge and prophesy. Mother-of-pearl is said to heal tuberculosis and to predict the viability of a business. It is supposed to stick close to the heart if a business is viable, but cause the heart to jump away from it if the business will not be successful.

**OBSIDIAN** (volcanic glass, dark glassy lava, usually black, used as a gemstone)

Obsidian is extremely powerful, an agent for the transformation of energy and emotions. Pluto is its planet, Capricorn its astrological house. Obsidian is sacred to the Aztec god/desses Itzcoliuhqui (the Twisted Obsidian One, God of the Curved Obsidian Blade), Itzpapalotl (Obsidian Butterfly), and Itzapapalotl-Itzcueye (Possessor of the Obsidian Skirt).

Use obsidian for grounding, scrying, binding, and transformation. Aztec magicians used obsidian mirrors for scrying. John Dee used a polished obsidian disk to receive angelic messages. Obsidian is one of my favorite stones with which to work. I add it to mojo bags for people who are struggling with making changes in themselves or in their lives.

Black obsidian is the most powerful, sacred to the Aztec god Tezcatlipoca. Use it for insight, grounding, binding, and scrying.

**ONYX** (variety of chalcedony with layers of various colors)

Cupid used his arrow to cut Venus's nails while she slept. The clippings fell into the Indus River, where they sank and were metamorphosed into onyxes. Saturn is onyx's planet, July its month, Leo and Capricorn its astrological houses. Use onyx for protection, sincerity, balance, defensive magic, and emotional balance. It is a powerful stone for self-control, gives help in adversity, and is said to prevent epileptic seizures when worn at the neck.

Onyx has a bad reputation. It is said to incite quarrels and contention and cause depression and strange dreams. Wearing an onyx supposedly invites ugly visions and assault by demons at night, lawsuits and quarrels during the day. An onyx with white veins provokes sorrow, debate, fear, and terrible fantasies. All these negative effects are neutralized by also wearing a sard.

Black onyx mirrors all aspects, positive and negative, of the self. It works like jasper, and is used for grounding, stability, personal transformation, and overcoming bad habits. Black onyx is said to cause bad dreams, strengthen bone marrow, and increase saliva in boys. Hold it to the eye to remove impurities. Blue onyx corresponds to the throat chakra and is used for higher inspiration.

*sardonyx:* A variety of onyx with layers of white chalcedony and brown or reddish sard, this gemstone corresponds to the month of August. Leo is its astrological house. Christians hold it sacred to St. Phillip. Sardonyx averts depression and makes you cheerful. It has been used to treat tumors.

**OPAL** (quartz gemstone of various colors that is usually milky and iridescent; Harlequin opals are rainbow-tinted; wood opal is opalized wood)

An opal contains the virtue of every stone whose color it contains. Mercury is the opal's planet, October its month. Taurus, Cancer, Virgo, and Libra are its astrological houses. Opals have been linked to misfortune. They are considered bewitching, mysterious, unlucky, and the embodiment of the evil eye. Carrying an opal wrapped in a bay leaf was said to confer invisibility and blind nearby persons.

The opal is the stone of Hercules. It allows you to see. Use opals for inspiration, hope, unblocking, invisibility, confidence, emotional balance, astral projection, past-life work, inner beauty, good luck, victory against adversaries, linking the physical to higher planes, and gaining access to cosmic consciousness. Opals have been used to improve eyesight and treat sadness and eye diseases.

Black opals allow you to see yourself. They can be used for inner work and raising power. Fire is the element of the fire opal (also called girasol). It is good for money spells.

## PEARL

Pearls fall to Earth when celestial dragons battle one another. Ti-Tsang Wang, the Chinese god of mercy, was a smiling monk who wandered the caverns of hell, his path illuminated by a shining pearl. Venus is the pearl's planet, water its element. Gemini, Cancer, and Aquarius are the pearl's astrological houses. Pearls are sacred to Marian, Muttalamman (the Pearl Mother), and Yemaya (Holy Queen Sea). Wear a pearl when asking blessings of Isis. Hindu deities are often depicted adorned with pearls.

Pearls symbolize tears and feminine virtue. Use them for purity, good luck, chastity, emotional clarity, sea power, love spells, money spells, and restoring the spirit. They have been used to treat indigestion and infections and are worn for their tonic influence on the health.

White pearls symbolize Dar el-Jannah, Dwelling of Peace, the second stage of Islamic paradise. Large pearls symbolize Jannatu el-'And, the Garden of Perpetual Abode, the 4th stage of Islamic paradise. Use freshwater pearls to learn to love yourself and accept love.

## PYRITE (iron disulfide, also called firestone and fool's gold)

Mars is pyrite's planet, fire its element. Use it for vitality and to strengthen the will. Pyrite is said to improve circulation in the body.

## QUARTZ (common stone, silicon dioxide, with hexagonal crystals; quartz occurs in large formations, may be colored, colorless, translucent or opaque)

Quartz is particularly useful to witches. Solar magic can be worked by standing in sunlight with a piece of quartz in the palm of each hand, over the chakras, to channel solar power. I use four small pieces of quartz—clear, rose, purple, and pale green—for many things. Sometimes I place them on my altar, at the quarters, while I work a spell. I also use them to empower things, such as powders and amulets. Holding a rock crystal to your forehead is helpful in psychic operations like calling, far-sensing, and far-seeing.

My quartzes "live" in the black velvet bag where I keep my tarot cards, along with what is now my most precious rock. A bedouin, an old man in tattered robes, approached me while I was at the Step Pyramid in Zaqqara and tried to give me something. I shied away, assuming he wanted to sell me some tourist goods. I couldn't speak Arabic then, so I didn't understand what he was saying until someone translated. He wanted to give me a white rock, one he said was from the original covering of the pyramid. He refused to take money for it, insisted that he must give it to me as a gift because it was meant for me. He went away as soon as I accepted it.

The rock is a piece of what I assume to be limestone that sparkles in sunlight. It has a terracotta-colored patch on the back, as if it were once indeed attached to something. There are temple complexes at Zaqqara as well as the Step Pyramid, so there is no way of knowing with certainty the origin of this stone. One of the myths about pyramids is that they were originally covered in white limestone and that this limestone acted as a radio receiver, making the structures into communication devices. This theory has always sounded farfetched to me, but who knows. I keep the Zaqqara rock with my quartzes to "tune" them, and I must say that my tarot cards give amazingly accurate readings.

Quartz corresponds to the planet Uranus. Cancer is its astrological house, spirit its element. Every quartz contains the essence of Great Rainbow Snake. Use quartzes for purification, protection, spiritual awakening, banishing negativity, and amplifying psychic energy. Sorcerers manipulate quartzes in sympathetic magic.

Rose quartz is a stone of love, ruled by the planet Venus. It treats sadness, stress, and tension. Use rose quartz for friendship, love spells, emotional balance, ending loneliness, success in court cases, and learning to love yourself. Mercury rules the smoky quartz. Earth is its element. Use smoky quartz for balance and grounding.

*crystal/rock crystal:* Clear, colorless quartz crystals that absorb and amplify energy. They can be put in a place that has bad vibes, left there for a while to absorb them, then taken away and washed. This will improve the energy of the place. The Moon rules rock crystal, which was once thought to be the spittle of purple dragons. Earth, water, and spirit are its elements, Gemini and Aquarius its astrological houses. Crystals are sacred to the orishas Olokun and Yemaya.

Use crystals for clarity, strength, vitality, psychic work, and mental stimulation. Placing a large crystal over your third eye amplifies your psychic powers. Crystal balls, made from rock crystal, can be used with the Sun to kindle sacred fire. This can be done by laying one on wood chips, in the Sun. Rock crystal was used to kindle sacred fire for the Eleusinian

Mysteries. Romans used crystal balls to cauterize wounds. Crystal prisms make rainbows appear.

Rock crystal's nature is astringent. It has been used to treat colic, diarrhea, gout, stones, and water retention. Steeped in honey, it is said to increase lactation.

*cairngorm:* Semiprecious stone of yellow or brownish quartz, yellow cairngorm corresponds to the letter T. July 8 is its station on the Wheel of the Year.

*geode:* Hollow nodule of stone lined with crystals, geodes can be of any size. Large or small, an unopened geode is an exciting thing, because you never know just what it might contain. You can saw one open with a special saw, but it is a lot more fun to make a ritual out of it—a Rite of Opening the Geode. Their natural way of opening is in a tumble down a mountain, so if you can safely drop yours from a height without injuring anyone or anything, try it.

Geodes are said to treat epilepsy, prevent premature birth, mitigate the dangers of childbirth, and make poisoned meat harmless. Wear a small one on your left shoulder for conjugal love.

**RUBY** (red corundum)

The ruby is an occult stone that has a psychic, magnetic influence on sensitive persons who wear it. Rubies correspond to Mars and the Sun. July is their month and Sunday their day. Aries, Cancer, Scorpio, and Capricorn are their astrological houses. Rubies correspond to the heart chakra. Hebrews held them sacred to Reuben. A ruby is said to become dark red and cloudy when evil is about to befall its wearer, and to turn dark when peril threatens either its wearer or the one who gave it as a gift.

Wear rubies for happiness. Use them for leadership, invulnerability, prudence, compassion, health, protection, energy, wealth, power, joy, love spells, opening hearts, overcoming fears, and healing your relationship with your father. Rubies avert nightmares, danger, sadness, sin, vice, wicked spirits, and foolish or evil thoughts. Touch all four corners of a house, garden, or vineyard with a ruby to preserve it from lightning, tempests, and worms.

Rubies are said to make you cheerful, restrain lust, strengthen your immune system, disperse infections, keep your body safe, ward off plague and pestilence, and protect against poison.

*spinel/balas ruby:* Lighter than a true ruby, spinels are used for protection against lightning and to restrain passion and fiery wrath.

## SALT

Salt and water have always been used to perform magic. Salt's element is earth. It is sacred to Aphrodite, the Goddess, Huixtoxihuatl, sea goddesses, and Sulis. Use salt for purification, consecration, and removing bad vibes from objects. Sea salt is sacred to ocean deities. Its element is water. Use it for purification, sea spells, and in merfolk rituals.

## SAPPHIRE (blue corundum)

Sapphires are associated with sacred things. Buddhists believe they have sacred magical powers and reconcile man to god. The high priest of Egypt wore a sapphire called Truth on his shoulder. Sapphires were worn by those questioning the oracle of Apollo at Delphi. Star sapphires are more powerful than ordinary ones.

Neptune is the sapphire's planet, April and September its months. Its days are Wednesday and Saturday. Taurus, Virgo, Sagittarius, and Pisces are its astrological houses. The sapphire's quality is cold, dry, and astringent. It is sacred to Apollo and Prometheus. Christians hold it sacred to St. Andrew. Pale-blue stones have male energy, dark-blue stones female energy.

Sapphires open the third eye. Use them for psychic work, meditation, peace, clarity, healing, power, truth, prosperity, luck, chastity, love spells, money spells, defensive magic, pacifying enemies, spiritual understanding, developing psychic abilities, making animal spirits flow, and procuring favor with princes. Sapphires have powers against fear, enchantment, enemies, sorcery, captivity, negative thoughts, and the blues. They are said to make people safe, peaceful, friendly, devout, and to impel them toward goodness and confirm the soul in good works. Sapphires are also supposed to sharpen the intellect, assuage the wrath of the Judeo-Christian god, invigorate body and soul, kill noxious and venomous creatures, and prevent their bites.

Sapphires have been used to treat depression, sores, fevers, bleeding, vision problems, and sore throats. They were believed to strengthen and refresh the heart and to maintain power and manly vigor in the body. They were applied to the forehead to stop nosebleeds and to inflammations to reduce them.

## SELENITE (transparent, crystallized variety of gypsum)

The Moon rules selenite. It soothes and nurtures and is used for inspiration, lunar magic, and protection from negative energy.

**SERPENTINE** (mottled stone, usually dark green)

Use serpentine for protection, especially from venomous creatures. Yellow serpentine corresponds to the letter G. September 30 is its station on the Wheel of the Year. In Hebrew mythology, it is sacred to Dan.

**SCHIST** (crystalline metamorphic rock that splits easily into layers)

Aboriginal Egyptian amulets, the earliest discovered to date, were carved of green schist in animal and other shapes. They were found laid on the breasts of the dead. These amulets were replaced in dynastic times by rectangular plaques of green schist with words of power engraved on them.

**SODALITE** (transparent or translucent mineral, usually blue, found in lava rock)

Venus is sodalite's planet. It is used for energy and to treat depression. Blue-speckled sodalite corresponds to the planets Pluto and Venus. Use it for transformation, physical healing, and to open the throat chakra.

**TIGER'S EYE/CAT'S EYE/CHATOYANT** (chrysoberyl, semiprecious quartz stone that usually varies in color from golden-yellow to brown)

Tiger's eye corresponds to the planets Mercury and Mars, the element earth, and the months of August and November. Thursday is its day, Gemini and Leo its astrological houses. Tiger's eye is sacred to Bast and Sekhmet. Arabs believed that djinn dwelt in it. Roman soldiers wore engraved stones as protective talismans.

Use tiger's eye for good luck, protection, courage, beauty, warmth, energy, wealth, healing, divination, gambling, and money spells. It also gives pleasure, averts the evil eye, and helps to distinguish between need and desire. Tiger's eye has been used to treat depression. Placing it under the tongue was said to confer prophecy and wise judgment.

**TOPAZ** (corundum, gemstone that may be white, clear, pink, wine, pale blue, pale green, brown, or yellow [the most precious])

The power of a topaz is believed to increase and decrease with the Moon. Its inner radiance dispels darkness; its energy is affected by heat, pressure, and friction. Topaz is said to lose its color in the presence of poison. Its planets are Uranus and Mercury. Air is its element and November its month. Gemini, Leo, Sagittarius, and Scorpio are its astrological houses. Topaz is sacred to Ra. Christians hold it sacred to James the Less.

Use topaz for protection and to attract love. Topaz treats grief, anger, covetousness, cowardice, nightmares, sleepwalking, lunatic passion, and sexual excess. It obtains the favor of princes and links higher and lower consciousness. Set in gold and worn as a necklace (or as a bracelet on the left arm), it brightens the wit and acts as a charm against sorcery and magic.

The topaz has been recommended for arthritis, rheumatism, inflammations, digestive problems, and mental illness. Some bind it to wounds in the belief that it will stop bleeding. Some apply it to the nose for nosebleeds.

Blue topaz corresponds to the planet Uranus. Use it for inspiration, focus, clarity, dispelling darkness, and the assimilation of abstract knowledge.

**TOURMALINE/TURMALINE** (crystallized silicate that polarizes light; it comes in many colors, including red [rubeolite] and blue [indiolite]; some varieties are of gemstone quality)

Tourmaline's quality is electric. Libra is its astrological house. Occultists considered tourmaline unlucky and malignant. It was used with topaz for healthy teeth and bones and to treat varicose veins and baldness.

Blue tourmaline relieves stress and can be used to induce peace and sleep. Black tourmaline is for protection and deflecting negativity, green tourmaline for creativity, protection, money spells, business success, and balancing male energies. Use it for refining, strengthening, and directing the will as well. Pink tourmaline is for protection, devotion, sacrifice, love spells, and balancing female energies. Red tourmaline is for courage and energy. Watermelon tourmaline corrects imbalances, eases guilt, attracts love and friendship, and strengthens empathy.

**TURQUOISE** (opaque bluish-green or sky-blue precious stone)

Turquoise symbolizes the sky. It is a sacred stone to many Native American nations, used in medicine bags. Muslims engrave turquoise with Koranic verses as amulets. Turquoise corresponds to Venus and the Moon. December is its month, Sagittarius its astrological house. It is sacred to Hathor (Lady of the Turquoise) and Sopedu (patron of turquoise mines).

Use turquoise for success, friendship, money, love, healing, courage, protection, good fortune, cheering the soul, and manifesting spiritual qualities on the physical plane. It prevents accidents, especially while horseback riding. Suspended within an empty glass, a turquoise is said to tell time by the number of times it strikes the side of the glass. A turquoise brings happiness and good fortune when given with love. Turquoises were given as love tokens in Germany, where their color was believed to last as long as the love did.

Remove a turquoise at once if it turns green, because it will bring misfortune. They are said to change color according to their owners' health and mood, growing pale with illness or sorrow, losing their color at death, but gradually regaining it with a new, healthy owner:

> *As a compassionate Turquoise that doth tell*
> *By looking pale the wearer is not well.*[32]

They are also said to move when danger threatens the person wearing them, and to lose their beauty if purchased rather than given or received as gifts.

The turquoise supposedly renews mental abilities, preserves from contagion, strengthens the eyes, and improves nutrition.

**ZIRCON** (crystalline mineral of various colors, some varieties of which are used as gemstones)

Aquarius is the zircon's astrological house. Use zircons for wisdom, honor, and driving away evil spirits. They are said to relieve insomnia. Consult Part III (Colors) for information on how to use different colored zircons.

*jacinth/hyacinth:* Orange or reddish gemstone, this variety of zircon may also be yellow, brown, green, gray, or white. Jargoon is a smoky white variety.

January is the jacinth's month. Cancer, Virgo, Sagittarius, and Aquarius are its astrological houses. Use jacinths for wis-

---

[32] William T. Fernie, *Precious Stones: For Curative Wear, Other Remedial Uses and Likewise the Nobler Metals*, p. 271.

dom, honor, prudence, money spells, and improving the personality. Wear it to avert evil spirits. Wear it on a ring for riches. Holding a jacinth in the mouth is said to cheer the heart and strengthen the mind. Jacinth supposedly strengthens the heart, treats insomnia, and protects against plague, lightning, poison, pestilence, and air pollution. It was used in vinegar for cough, rupture, and melancholy.

The blue jacinth is specific for insomnia. Wearing a green jacinth on the neck or finger is said to make strangers sure and acceptable to their guests. A green jacinth with red veins set in silver has the most power.

The yellow hyacinth is used for peace, concord, cooling inward heat, and strengthening the mind toward good things. Christians hold pink hyacinths sacred to St. Simeon.

# LETTERS

Vowels are sacred to Carmenta, the Fates, the Goddess, and the White Goddess.

**A** is the birth letter. It corresponds to the metal silver.

**B** symbolizes inception. It corresponds to the Sun and the jewel red sard.

**C** is the sacrosanct letter of the swineherd magicians of the Goddess. It corresponds to the planet Mercury and the jewel banded red agate.

**D** corresponds to the planet Jupiter and the stone white carnelian.

**E** corresponds to the metal gold and the season autumn.

**F** symbolizes fire. It corresponds to the planets Saturn and Venus and to the jewel fire garnet.

**G** corresponds to the jewel yellow serpentine.

**H** symbolizes premarital chastity. It corresponds to the jewel lapis lazuli.

**I** is the death vowel. It corresponds to the season winter.

**J** is a royal consonant. It symbolizes new life and sovereignty.

**L** symbolizes regeneration. It is sacred to Hecate and corresponds to the jewel yellow chrysolite.

**M** corresponds to the Moon and to the jewel amethyst.

**N** symbolizes flood. Sea-green beryl is its jewel.

**NG** corresponds to the jewel clear green jasper.

**O** is the letter of initiation into the mysteries of love. It corresponds to the season spring and the metal tin.

**Q** corresponds to the planet Venus.

**R** symbolizes death and corresponds to the stone malachite.

**S** corresponds to the Moon, the Sun, and to Saturn. Blood red carbuncle is its jewel. S is sacred to Athene and symbolizes female enchantment.

**T** corresponds to the planet Mars, the metal copper, and the jewel yellow cairngorm.

**Th** corresponds to the planet Jupiter.

**U**  corresponds to the metal lead and the season of summer. It is the vowel of sexual passion and symbolizes consummation. U is sacred to the Death-in-Life goddess.

**W**  corresponds to the planet Mercury.

**Y**  symbolizes generation.

**Z**  symbolizes angry passion.

# NUMBERS

Pythagorus tells us that "Number is the ruler of forms and ideas, and the cause of gods and demons. All things are assimilated by numbers."[33] Pythagoreans swore their oaths on the Holy Tetractys, the Pyramid of Pythagoras.

.

. .

. . .

. . . . .

In this pyramid, each row of dots has its own symbolism: Position—Expansion—Surface—three-dimensional space. It is also a symbol of the Triple Goddess: Beginning—Prime—End.

Use the numbers 8, 6, 4, 2 on your fax machine, modem, or cell phone to summon Baduh, the spirit who speeds the transmission of messages. In metaphysics, zero equals 22.

1 corresponds to the fixed stars, Mercury, and the Sun. One is the monad, the unit, the source of all numbers. Use the number one for beginnings, individuality, achievement, inspiration, leadership, creation, ideas, invention, originality, determination, independence, drive, incentive, courage, ambition, selfishness, undue force, good fortune and that which is about to take shape.

2 corresponds to Mars and Saturn. It is the cause of increase and division. Use the number two for balance, sharing, agreement, partnership, duality, assimilation, sensitivity, vision, modesty, insight, envisioning, diplomacy, imagination, application, intuition, waiting, receptivity, imperfection, good fortune, gentle persuasion, the directed intellect, and the security of emotional commitment.

3 corresponds to Mars, Jupiter, Saturn, and the Moon. It is the number of the whole—the beginning, the middle, and the end. Three is the power of unity: mind, body, spirit. It represents the

[33] Robert Graves, *The White Goddess* (New York: Farrar, Straus & Giroux, 1966), p. 251.

cycles of a woman's life: maiden, mother, crone. Three is sacred to the Triple Goddess.

Use the number three for love, friendship, popularity, charm, diplomacy, expression, harmony, enjoyment, criticism, feelings, sharing, impulsiveness, communication, good fortune, and the dynamic flow of action and power through the word that goes forth and comes into being.

4 is the number of the four quarters of the sky and the number of the elements. It is the square, the physical world, the highest degree of perfection. Four corresponds to Earth, Jupiter, Mercury, Venus, and Mars. It was regarded as holy in ancient Egypt, but is considered unlucky in Japan.

Use four for manifestation, wholeness, formation, foundation, building, stability, planning, organization, loyalty, results, concentration, practical application, good fortune, conscious structure, hidden feelings, all-or-nothing love, high sex drive, blocks, limitations, and opposition.

5 is the Grove of the Senses, the sweet cauldron of the five trees, and of the five vowels. It is the pentacle, the stations of the Goddess—birth, initiation, consummation, repose, death. Five symbolizes the variously colored world, the material and spiritual worlds. It corresponds to the planets Jupiter, Venus, and Mars and the trees apple, elder, and willow. It is the cauldron of Cerridwen, sacred to Carmenta, the Goddess, Kali, Minerva, and the White Goddess.

Use five for sensuality, passion, freedom, love, spirituality, mystery, magnetism, attraction, wanton sexuality, travel, expansion, adventure, new opportunities, recreation, new thinking, change, the desire to know, inspiration, and optimism.

6 is the number of life, the balancing factor. It corresponds to the Sun, the Moon, and the planets Venus and Mercury. Six is sacred to the Near Eastern gods Haddad, Reshep, Rimmon, and Teshub.

Use six for love, balance, intellect, emotions, care, imagination, harmony, glory, service, comfort, adjustment, compassion, interference, social consciousness, family matters, peak experience, emotional consciousness, and the search for perfection.

7 is a sacred number, a spiritual number, the number of the heavens and the seas. It is the mystical number of Jehovah and was adored by Pythagoreans. Seven is a Moon number that corre-

sponds to the Sun and the planets Saturn and Venus. It is sacred to Athene and Yemaya. The roebuck is its animal.

Use seven for completion, knowledge, accomplishment, wisdom, intelligence, discovery, peace, health, observation, faith, meditation, holiness, light, perfection, fear, investigation, mysticism, ultimate truths, good fortune, female enchantment, passion as an end in itself, escapism, doubt, skepticism, and that which exists but cannot be seen.

**8** is both a practical and a sacred number, held sacred to the Sun in Egypt, Babylon, and Arabia. It is the mystic number of solar increase and alludes to the relationship between Earth and Venus. Seven was adored by Pythagoreans. It corresponds to Mercury, the Moon, and the Sun. Holly is its tree. Eight symbolizes Poseidon's unshakable power and is a potent symbol of Venus, emblazoned on her shield. Sacrificial barley cakes were decorated with eight-armed crosses.

Use eight for infinity, power, increase, duplication, success, enlargement, attainment, accomplishment, patience, ambition, organization, discipline, pride, commitment, fertility, recognition, spiritual fortitude, hard work, and power from within that enables.

**9** is the light bearer, the prime Moon number. It corresponds to the Moon, and to almond and hazel trees. Nine was the sacred number of orgiastic Moon priestesses. It is sacred to the Muse, to all Moon goddesses and all triple goddesses. It was Dante's mystic number and was adored by Pythagoreans.

Use nine for wisdom, lunar wisdom, completion, sacred magic, lunar magic, culmination, wholeness, the seeds of new beginning, inspiration, creativity, magnetism, good fortune, independence of mind, fulfillment, achievement, selflessness, impersonal love, idealism (cloud nine), human rights, emotional extremes, emotions that are deeply felt but not expressed, and having to let go of that which is cherished.

**10** contains the sum of the four prime numbers. It denotes all systems of the world and comprehends all musical and arithmetic proportions. Use ten for perfection and cyclical beginnings.

**11** is a spiritual number that corresponds to the plant ivy. Use eleven for insight, intuition, unconventionality, inspiration and joy.

**12** is the number of a complete cycle of manifestation. It corresponds to guelder rose and oak. Use twelve for established power.

**13** is a sacred number, the end and the beginning, the number of moons in a year. Held unlucky in the West, where buildings are numbered without a thirteenth floor, the number thirteen invokes no fear in witches. Thirteen corresponds to the elder tree and is sacred to the White Moon Goddess. Use it for lunar magic and witchcraft.

**14** is a Moon number, the number of days in the unlucky first half of a lunar month.

**15** corresponds to the planet Saturn, is sacred to Inanna, Irnini, Ishara, and Ishtar. It was a number of prime importance in the Feast of the Tabernacles at Jerusalem. Use fifteen for completeness (3 x 5).

**16** is the number of increase. It corresponds to the planet Mars.

**19** is a golden number, the number of the Great Year. It reconciles solar and lunar time and is the number of years of a sacred king's reign.

**20** is sacred to Shamash/Babbar/Utu, the Mesopotamian Sun god.

**21** is the number of the rays in Akhenaton's Sun. It corresponds to the Sun.

**22** is the god force, a mystical number of Jehovah. It represented the value of pi, which was once a religious secret. Use 22 for perfection, completion, control, and vision.

**30** is sacred to the Mesopotamian Moon gods Nanna and Sin.

**34** corresponds to the planet Jupiter.

**40** is sacred to the Mesopotamian gods Ea, Enki, and Nudimmud.

**42** is light, glory, and peace multiplied by life, a mystical number of Jehovah.

**45** is the pentad of the Goddess of the Year.

**50** corresponds to the Moon.

**60** is sacred to Anu, the Babylonian creator god.

**65** corresponds to the planet Mars.

**72** is a grand solar number and the sacred number of Stonehenge. It corresponds to the planet Venus.

**111** corresponds to the Sun.

**175** corresponds to the planet Venus.

**260** corresponds to the planet Mercury.

**369** corresponds to the Moon.

**432** symbolizes the renewal of an aeon.

**25, 800,** or **25,920** all represent the period of a Great Year, the entire cycle of the zodiac.

# GLOSSARY

These words and terms may be difficult to find in regular dictionaries. Different traditions sometimes use the same word in different ways, so I have given more than one definition for some entries.

**Akashic Records:** astral record of everything that has ever happened

**amulet:** something that is worn for protection, usually jewelry

**ankh:** ancient Egyptian symbol of life; it looks like a cross with a loop at the top

**astral projection (AP):** an altered state, often achieved via trance, in which the consciousness is freed from the physical body

**athame:** ceremonial knife used in magic and rituals; in classical Wicca, an athame is only used ritually and must have a black handle

**aura:** bio-energy field of a living creature

**banishing:** a magical working performed to remove evil, threats, darkness, negativity, or people embodying those qualities

**Book of Shadows:** a witch's handwritten book of spells, rituals, and magical information

**botanica:** a Santerian shop that sells herbs, charms, candles, religious statues, and so on.

**bruja/brujo:** Spanish for witch. (j is pronounced like h)

**Burning Times:** historical period in Europe when Christians persecuted and tortured witches and alleged witches; thousands were put to death, usually by hanging or burning at the stake

**chakra:** any of the seven energy nodes of the human body

**chalice:** a ceremonial goblet that represents the element of water

**charm:** a magical object, action, or incantation that effects magic, or averts evil or danger

**Circle:** a group, less formal than a coven, of witches who practice, worship, celebrate, or study together

**clairvoyance:** psychic ability to know things beyond your immediate knowledge (also called ESP and second sight)

**coming out of the broom closet:** living openly as a witch

**consecration:** a ceremony that dedicates a thing or place for sacred use

**corn spirit:** spirit of a grain crop, embodied in an entity, person, or animal

**coven:** organized group of witches who practice, worship, and/or celebrate together; covens traditionally consist of no more then thirteen members, and are led by a high priestess and a high priest

**Covenstead:** place where a coven of witches usually meets, often the home of the high priest/ess

**Craft:** witchcraft

**croning:** ceremony held to mark a woman's transition from mother to crone, the final phase of a woman's life

**crystallomancy:** divination by crystals, usually a crystal ball

**dedicant:** a new witch in the period of study and apprenticeship before initiation (traditionally a year and a day)

**deosil:** clockwise

**divination:** any practice that reveals the future or unknown things, often involving tarot cards, runes, and crystal balls

**eclectic:** a witch who works with deities from or worships within more than one culture or mythological system

**elder:** witch who has attained a position of respect in the craft; coven member who has attained an advanced degree of initiation

**Esbat:** coven meetings held at the Full Moon; incorrect designation used by some witches for the Lesser Sabbats

**evocation:** calling upon spirits, elementals, or other entities

**faery:** alternative spelling for fairy, to distinguish it as a belief system

**familiar:** animal, usually a cat, with whom a witch establishes a special psychic/magical relationship; familiars offer help, companionship, protection, and usually unconditional love as well

**Fivefold Bond:** ritual tie that links wrists, neck, and ankles

**Fivefold Kiss:** ritual greeting of eight kisses between witches of opposite genders in classical Wicca, on the feet, knees, pelvis, breast, and lips

**flying ointment:** paste, usually containing herbs, that is applied to the skin to aid in astral projection

**folk magic:** a culture's traditional magical practices

**Gardnerian:** of or relating to Gerald Gardner, who is credited with reviving Wicca in modern times; any formal Wiccan tradition that follows Gerald Gardner's system

**granny woman:** a female shaman, usually of the Appalachian Mountain region of the United States

**grimoire:** Book of Shadows, a handwritten book of spells and magical information

**gris gris:** French patois word for a charm

**hex:** n. a spell, usually negative; the evil eye, a curse; v. to cast such a spell

**hedgewitch:** a walker-between-worlds, a non-Wiccan witch with a shamanistic path

**hidden children:** witches who must keep their religion secret, the hidden children of the Goddess

**high priest/ess:** witch who has attained a tradition's highest degree of initiation and leads a coven

**hoodoo:** African-American folk magic tradition

**HP/HPS:** high priest/high priestess

**I Ching, The Book of Changes:** Chinese system of divination that uses yarrow stalks or coins inscribed with hexagrams

**incubus (pl. incubi):** malevolent male entity that takes sexual possession of sleeping women

**invocation:** calling upon a god/dess for help or to empower a spell

**juju:** West African word for magic

**karma:** that which accrues and is carried over from one lifetime to the next, can be positive or negative, according to the lives you have led

**kitchen witch:** witch who uses mainly practical magic centering on the home, hearth, and family

**kundalini:** dormant bio-energy resident in the base of the human spine, in the root chakra, released through yoga and other practices for enlightenment, intelligence, and spiritual insights

**libation:** liquid offering to a god/dess, such as wine or milk, usually poured out upon the earth, but may be poured into a fire or offered in another way

**mage, magus (pl. magi):** someone who is adept at magic but not a witch; in some Wiccan traditions, a male witch who has attained more than the first level of initiation

**magick:** ceremonial or ritual magic, high magick; alternative spelling for magic used by some witches and other practitioners to distinguish it from the illusions and prestidigitation of stage magicians

**maiden:** stage of a woman's life between menarche and motherhood or mentoring; assistant high priestess in a traditional coven

**Matrix:** word used to describe the universe as the Goddess-web-of-life

**medicine bag:** Native American shaman's pouch, usually containing herbs, stones, feathers, and so on

**medium:** person who is able to channel spirits or other entities

**mojo:** Afro-American word for magic

**mojo bag:** small bag, usually containing charms or talismans, worn around the neck for power, protection, and so on

**necromancy:** divination via spirits of the dead

**novice:** someone who has just begun studying the craft

**OBE:** out-of-body experience, astral projection, lucid dreaming

**Ogham:** any ancient Celtic magical alphabet

**Old Soul:** person who has been reincarnated several times

**omen:** anything that may be interpreted as a sign, positive or negative, from the universe

**oracle:** place or method for divination by means of deities, as interpreted by a priest/ess, including the flight of birds, the sound of splashing water or rustling leaves (the most famous oracle of the ancient world was that of Apollo at Delphi)

**orisha:** any deity in the Santerian religion

**Ouija board:** board printed with letters and simple words that is used for communicating with spirits and operated by two or more people touching a paten that moves around the board pointing to letters or words

**pentacle:** five-pointed star, usually inside a circle; one of the suits of a tarot deck

**pentagram:** pentacle that is written, printed, or drawn; five-pointed star inside a circle

**postulant, neophyte:** new member of a coven, someone who has not yet been initiated

**praña:** Hindu word for bio-energy, the vital force shared by every living creature

**poppet:** humanoid figure that is used to represent someone for a spell or other magical working

**psychometry:** drawing psychic impressions from objects while handling them

**psychopomp:** god/dess who guides souls to the underworld or afterlife

**reincarnation:** transmigration of the soul, metempsychosis, rebirth in another body after death

**runes:** ancient Nordic alphabet, marked on stones or sticks and used for divination; magical chants or songs; any magical alphabet or the stones, cards, or sticks on which it is printed

**Sabbats:** eight annual Wiccan festivals (see Part I, About Wicca)

**Sands of Time:** sand taken from between the paws of the Great Sphinx in Egypt, used to make spells and charms permanent

**Santeria:** Afro-Caribbean Earth religion that joins Yoruban god/desses with Catholic saints

**scrying:** divination by means of gazing, for instance into water, a dark mirror, a crystal ball, or a bowl of black ink

**séance:** gathering of people, usually seated around a table, for the purpose of communicating with spirits

**shaman:** priest and medicine man, usually of Native American or Siberian peoples; shamanic practice includes magic, healing, shapeshifting, communication with ancestral spirits, and divination

**shamanka, shamaness:** words sometimes used for female shamans

**shapeshifting/skinwalking:** shamanic practice, often aided by drugs, drumming, and/or dance, of mentally assuming animal form

**sheikh/sheikha:** modern Egyptian Arabic words for magical adepts

**sigil:** occult or mystical sign, a paper talisman

**skyclad:** ritual nudity, insisted on in some Wiccan traditions

**solitary/solitaire:** witch who practices alone, without a coven

**sorcerer/sorceress:** traditionally a person who practices black magic, usually by aid of malevolent spirits; modern term used by some magic-users to differentiate themselves from witches

**succubus (pl. succubi):** malevolent female entity that takes sexual possession of sleeping men

**Strega:** Italian magical tradition

**Summerlands:** place where we rest after death, between incarnations

**synchronicity:** meaningful coincidence

**talisman:** magical object, usually made or carved at an astrological moment suitable to its purpose

**Tantra:** Hindu path based in kundalini yoga and sex magic as a way to enlightenment

**the tarot:** ancient system of cards used for divination

**telekinesis:** ability to move objects with your mind (also called psychokinesis, PK; telekinesis is a very rare gift that usually manifests accidentally when a person is angry or upset and is most often seen in adolescents and fades with age)

**third eye:** chakra in the middle of the forehead

**totem animal:** animal that represents a person, tribe, or other group

**warlock:** old term for a male witch that no one uses anymore; men who pretended to be witches in order to penetrate covens and betray witches during the Burning Terms

**Wheel of the Year:** annual cycle of the Sun, the Moon, the seasons, and the zodiac

**white witch:** witch on a right-hand path

**widdershins:** counterclockwise

**witch doctor:** African shaman

**witch's ball, witch ball:** mass of dried entwined herbs blown about by the wind, any small tumbleweed; glass ball with a mottled surface hung in a window to thwart witches and trap their spells; fancy-dress party attended by witches

**witch's bottle:** sealed bottle placed in the house or buried on the property for protection. There are many ways to make a witch's bottle. Some witches use the detritus of the year—broken pottery, rusted nails, junk mail, and so on. Witches sometimes add something personal—hair, nail clippings, urine, a bloody bandage or tampon. This sort of bottle is always buried, usually at Samhain (for the new year). Another type is a bottle filled with salt and sugar, and/or herbs for blessings like protection, happiness, prosperity, and charms to avert specific threats. This type of bottle is secreted somewhere in the home.

**witch's ladder:** type of knot magic in which charms are knotted or braided, with specific magical intention, into cords, to make a powerful talisman; cord with 40 knots in it, or a string of 40 beads, used as a meditation device or aid to concentration

**Witch Queen:** high priestess whose coven has hived off two or more new covens

**wizard:** someone who practices magic, but is not a witch

**wort, wortcraft:** herb, herbalism

**yin/yang:** opposite but balancing male and female principles—yin is female (Moon) energy, negative and passive; yang is male (Sun) energy, positive and active

**Yoni:** female genitalia as a sacred symbol of life, creation, fertility, sexuality, the Goddess, and so on

# BIBLIOGRAPHY

*Al Ahram Weekly.* Cairo: Al Ahram Publishing, 1993-1994.

Anand, Margo. *The Art of Sexual Magic.* New York: G. P. Putnam's Sons, 1995.

Aristotle (attributed to). *Secretum Secretorum,* Sami Salman al-A'War, trans. Beirut: Dar al-'Arabiyah lil-Tibaàh, 1995.

Barrett, Francis. *The Magus.* London: Lackinghan, Allen, and Co., 1801: Reprinted York Beach ME: Samuel Weiser, 2000.

Best, Michael R. and Frank H. Brightman. *The Book of Secrets of Albertus Magnus of the Virtues of Herbs, Stones and Certain Beasts.* York Beach, ME: Samuel Weiser, 1999.

Blake, William. *The Marriage of Heaven and Hell.* New York: Dover Publications, 1994.

Budge, Sir E. A. Wallis. *Egyptian Magic.* New York: Dover Publications, 1971.

————. *Gods of the Egyptians.* New York: Dover Publications, 1969.

————. *Egyptian Book of the Dead: The Papyrus of Ani.* New York: Dover Publications, 1967.

Bulfinch, Thomas. *Bulfinch's Mythology.* New York: Modern Library, 1988.

Campbell, Joseph. *The Masks of God* (4 volumes). New York: Viking Press, 1975.

Cott, Jonathan. *The Search for Om Sety: A Story of Eternal Love.* Garden City, NY: Doubleday, 1987.

Cotterell, Arthur. *The Encyclopedia of Mythology.* New York: Smithmark, 1996.

————. *A Dictionary of World Mythology.* New York: Oxford University Press, 1990.

Crosse, Joanna. *The Element Illustrated Encyclopedia of Mind, Body, Spirit and Earth.* Boston: Element Children's Books, 1998.

Culpepper Nicholas. *Culpepper's Complete Herbal and English Physician.* Glenwood, IL: Meyerbooks, 1990.

Cunningham, Scott. *Cunningham's Encyclopedia of Magical Herbs.* St. Paul, MN: Llewellyn Publications, 1999.

Durdin-Robertson, Lawrence. *The Year of the Goddess: A Perpetual Calendar of Festivals.* London: Aquarian, 1990.

Dunwich, Gerina. *The Concise Lexicon of the Occult.* New York: Citadel Press, 1990.

Elaine, Loretta. *Gems for Friends.* http://www.gems4friends.com.

Eyiogbe, Baba. *The Way of the Orishas.* http://www.seanet.com/Users/efunmoyiwa/ocha.html.

Farrar, Janet and Stewart. *A Witches' Bible.* Custer, WA: Phoenix Publishing, 1996.

Fernie, William T., M.D. *Precious Stones: For Curative Wear, Other Remedial Uses and Likewise the Nobler Metals.* Kila, MT: Kessinger Publications, LLC.

Fischer-Schreiber, Ingrid et al. *The Encyclopedia of Eastern Philosophy and Religion.* Boston: Shambhala, 1994.

Fortune, Dion. *Psychic Self-Defense.* York Beach, ME: Samuel Weiser, 1992.

————. *The Sea Priestess.* York Beach, ME: Samuel Weiser, 1991.

Frazer, Sir James G. *The Golden Bough: A Study in Magic and Religion.* New York: MacMillan Company, 1953.

Garen, Nancy. *Tarot Made Easy.* New York: Fireside, 1989.

Goodrich, Norma Lorre. *Ancient Myths.* New York: Meridian Books, 1994.

Grant, Michael and John Hazel. *Who's Who—Classical Mythology.* Routledge Who's Who Series. London: Routledge, 1995.

Graves, Robert. *The White Goddess.* New York: Farrar, Straus & Giroux, 1996.

————. *The Greek Myths, Volumes I and II.* Baltimore: Penguin Books, 1955.

Grigson, Geoffrey. *The Goddess of Love: The Birth, Triumph, Death and Rebirth of Aphrodite.* London: Constable, 1976.

Hamilton, Edith. *Mythology.* Boston: Little, Brown and Company, 1942.

Hart, George. *A Dictionary of Egyptian Gods and Goddesses.* Boston: Routledge, Kegan & Paul, 1986.

Ions, Veronica. *Egyptian Mythology.* New York: Peter Bedrick, 1983.

Jacobsen, Thorkild. *The Treasures of Darkness: A History of Mesopotamian Religion.* New Haven and London: Yale University Press, 1976.

Jordan, Michael. *Encyclopedia of Gods.* New York: Facts On File, 1993.

Lewis, James R. and Evelyn Dorothy Oliver. *Angels A to Z.* New York: Gale Research, 1996.

Kinsley, Davis. *Hindu Goddesses: Visions of the Divine Feminine in the Hindu Religious Tradition.* Berkeley: University of California Press, 1998.

Lestat. *Of Gods and Men: The A-Z of Mythology and Legends.* http://www.clubie.ie/lestat/godsmen.html.

Lindemans, M. F. *Encyclopedia Mythica.* http://www.pantheon. org/mythica/.

MacLennan, Bruce. *Biblioteca Arcana.* http://www.cs.utk.edu/ ~mclennan/OM/BA/.

Matthews, Caitlin and John. *Encyclopedia of Celtic Wisdom.* Boston: Element, 1994.

Meadows, Kenneth. *Earth Medicine: A Shamanic Path to Self-Mastery.* Boston: Element, 1997.

————. *The Medicine Way: Revealing Hidden Teachings of the Native American Medicine Wheel.* Boston: Element, 1996.

Monaghan, Patricia. *The Book of Goddesses and Heroines.* New York: E. P. Dutton, 1981.

Noble, Vicki. *Motherpeace: A Way to the Goddess Through Myth, Art and Tarot.* St. Paul: Llewellyn Publications, 1997.

Osborn, Harold. *South American Mythology.* New York: Peter Bedrick Books, 1986.

Owen, D. W. *A Small Dictionary of Pagan Gods and Goddesses.* http://www.waningmoon.com/guide/library/lib00019q. html.

Parker, Derek and Julia. *The Power of Magic.* New York: Simon & Schuster, 1992.

Prime, Lynda June. *Gemology.* http://www.dirt-dog.com/kynna/ gemology.htm.

Rosenberg, Donna. *World Mythology: An Anthology of the Great Myths and Epics.* Lincolnwood, IL: NTC Publishing Group, 1993.

Said, Dr. Rushdie. *The River Nile, Geology, Hydrology and Utilization.* New York: Pergamon Press, 1993.

Sajdi, Rami. *Desert Land.* http://www.corp.arabia.com/Desert-Land/.

Shakespeare, William. *The Complete Works of William Shakespeare,* edited by John Dover Wilson. New York: Dorset Press, 1983.

Shakir, M. H. (trans). *Holy Qur'an.* Elmhurst, NY: Tahrike Tarsile Qur'an, 1985.

Shearer, Alastair. *The Hindu Vision: Forms of the Formless.* New York: Thames & Hudson, 1993.

Siren, Christopher. *Assyro-Babylonian Mythology FAQ*. http://
pubpages.unh.edu/~cbsiren/assyrbabyl-faq.html.
————. *Canaanite/Ugaritic Mythology FAQ, ver. 1.2*. http://
pubpages.unh.edu/~cbsiren/canaanite-faq.html.
————. *Hittite/Hurrian Mythology REF 1.2*. http://pubpages.u
nh.edu/~cbsiren/hittite-ref.html.
————. *Sumerian Mythology FAQ*. http://pubpages.unh.edu/
~cbsiren/sumer-faq.html.

Spence, Lewis. *The History and Origins of Druidism*. N. Holly-
wood, CA: Newcastle Publishing Co., 1995.
————. *An Encyclopaedia of Occultism*. Secaucus, NJ: Citadel
Press, 1993.

Starhawk (Miriam Simos). *The Spiral Dance: A Rebirth of the Ancient Religion of the Great Goddess*. San Francisco: HarperSanFrancisco, 1989.

Stewart, R. J. *Celtic Gods, Celtic Goddesses*. London: Blandford,
1996.

Sykes, Egerton. *Who's Who: Non-Classical Mythology*. New York:
Oxford University Press, 1993.

Valiente, Doreen. *Witchcraft for Tomarrow*. Custer, WA: Phoenix Publishing, Inc. 1978.

Waldherr, Kris. *The Book of Goddesses*. Hillsboro, OR: Beyond
Words Publishing, 1995.

Watterson, Barbara: *The Gods of Ancient Egypt*. London: B. T.
Batsford, 1984.

# INDEX OF SPELLS

Use these spells "as is" or adapt them to suit the circumstances that bring you to needing such a spell.

## ANCIENT EGYPTIAN SPELLS FOR EMPOWERING AMULETS

# INDEX

Eileen Holland is a solitary eclectic witch, a Wiccan priestess, and a poet. She calls her path Goddess Wicca. As webmaster for Open, Sesame, one of the Internet's most popular sites for Wicca, witchcraft, and pagan spirituality-racking up 46,000 hits per month-she has helped many seekers along their paths. She lives in New York City and is currently writing a book about mythology.